"See this?" Th[...]ly managing the lift of a question. "See it?"

Wanda looked at the small, limp thing. Red curls, sewn smile, floppy beanbag limbs. A stuffed doll.

"This is you," he said. It seemed important to him that she understand. He repeated the words, enunciating clearly. "This is you."

"Me," she agreed. The young prostitute had no strength to argue.

"You," he said, nodding, smiling, pleased to find her such a quick study. He gripped the doll's head with both hands and squeezed, wrenching it halfway off. The doll's eyes stared wide and lidless, the fixed smile was grotesque.

"This is you," he said again, holding up the doll's remnant like some small animal's hide.

She wasn't the first, she wouldn't be the last. . . .

SHATTER

SHATTER
by
Brian Harper

A SIGNET BOOK

SIGNET
Published by the Penguin Group
Penguin Books USA Inc., 375 Hudson Street,
New York, New York 10014, U.S.A.
Penguin Books Ltd, 27 Wrights Lane,
London W8 5TZ, England
Penguin Books Australia Ltd, Ringwood,
Victoria, Australia
Penguin Books Canada Ltd, 10 Alcorn Avenue,
Toronto, Ontario, Canada M4V 3B2
Penguin Books (N.Z.) Ltd, 182-190 Wairau Road,
Auckland 10, New Zealand

Penguin Books Ltd, Registered Offices:
Harmondsworth, Middlesex, England

First published by Signet,
an imprint of Dutton Signet,
a division of Penguin Books USA Inc.

First Printing, January, 1995
10 9 8 7 6 5 4 3 2 1

Copyright © Douglas Borton, 1995
All rights reserved

 REGISTERED TRADEMARK—MARCA REGISTRADA

Printed in the United States of America

PUBLISHER'S NOTE
This is a work of fiction. Names, characters, places, and incidents either
are the product of the author's imagination or are used fictitiously,
and any resemblance to actual persons, living or dead, events, or locales
is entirely coincidental.

Author's Note

I'd like to offer my sincere thanks to all those who assisted me with this project, including:

Kevin Mulroy and Joseph Pittman, who each contributed valuable editorial insights that made *Shatter* a much better book than it otherwise could have been;

Jane Dystel, my agent, whose courtesy and professionalism make working with her a pleasure;

and Spencer Marks of the Los Angeles Police Department, who graciously took the time to read the book in manuscript form. As always, he caught and corrected many more mistakes than I'll publicly admit to. Of course, any remaining errors are mine alone.

Prologue

At the end, Donna Wildman had to be there.

She sat in the last row of the spectators' seats, in a crowded courtroom in Superior Court. The reporters sitting up front hadn't seen her, and she was grateful for that.

Slight agitation in the closer seats, a ripple of turning heads, and two marshals led Wayne Allen Stanton inside.

Stanton walked slowly, dragging his feet, staring down at his manacled hands. He seemed unconscious of his surroundings, oblivious to stares and pointing fingers. Occasionally he would shake his head and mumble some unintelligible parody of speech.

In the two months since his arrest, he had undergone a variety of treatments, all of which had proved useless. He was too far gone for Thorazine, Depizol, Clopixol, or any of the other standard antipsychotic drugs.

It was just as well. Were he ever restored to sanity, he would have to stand trial for the murders of Karen Holcoft, Patricia Coster, and Beverly Ann Silks. And the victims' families would be forced to relive the horror, unbury their dead.

Donna watched as Stanton was eased into a chair at his attorneys' table. His head nodded, shoulders slumping; in the wrinkled yellow jumpsuit, reminiscent of pajamas, he gave the impression of a man asleep.

"Hello, Donna."

She glanced up, mildly startled, and saw Sebastián Delgado taking a seat beside her. "Seb. What are you doing here?"

"As your former boss—I might even say, your mentor—I intend to share your moment of triumph." He spoke, as always, with clipped precision, his words flavored with the Guadalajara barrio of his youth.

"Triumph?" Her own speech, spiced by nothing more exotic than New Jersey, invariably struck her as coarse and uncultured in his presence. "I don't know if that's the word for what I'm feeling right now."

He studied her, his gray eyes softening with concern. "You look tired."

She waved a hand at Stanton. "It's this. The case."

"The case has been closed for two months."

"Not for me, it hasn't." She forced a smile. "It took a lot out of me. You know . . . the pressure."

"Donna Wildman knows how to deal with pressure."

"Maybe not as well as you think."

"I saw how you performed on the Gryphon task force. You handled yourself fine. If you hadn't, I never would have sponsored your application to NCAVC."

Her smile this time was genuine. "I appreciate that, Seb. But the Slasher case—it was different. I wasn't just one more cop on a task force. I had all the responsibility. Every day that went by without an arrest . . ."

"I know how it is," Delgado said. "It takes over your life."

She nodded. *Takes it over*, she thought bitterly. *And wipes it out.*

She'd had a life before all this started, before a random maniac had launched his destructive career. Now she had nothing. She was alone.

And the worst of it was that the fault—the guilt—was hers. If guilt was the applicable concept here. She wasn't sure. She supposed it was. Most people would say so.

But then, most people hadn't been inside the San Fernando Valley homes where the Slasher had done his work. Hadn't smelled the copper-penny stink of blood. Hadn't seen Karen Holcroft, torn up in her kitchen like a butchered carcass. Patricia Coster, drowned in a toilet, her hands outstretched in a final plea for mercy. Beverly Ann Silks, dead in her parked car, the windshield coated in red.

Donna shuddered, half closing her eyes.

Her problem was that she felt it too much—identified with each victim on a personal level—and so became a victim herself. If she could learn detachment, indifference . . .

But she couldn't. And so to save other lives, she wrecked her own. Senseless, pointless, but there it was.

"If you're not here to celebrate," Delgado said softly, "what made you come?"

She shrugged. "I just . . . wanted to see it end. Wanted to write a finish to it. If that makes any sense."

"Perfect sense. My wife did something quite similar once."

"Your wife?"

"After the Gryphon case, she drove up to Idaho, alone, simply to see Franklin Rood's grave. It was her way of convincing herself that the ordeal was finally over." He frowned. "It was an ordeal for you—this investigation."

"Yes."

"Was it worth it?"

She looked at Wayne Allen Stanton, seated between his two attorneys, his head drooping. So quiet now, so calm. Yet she knew the raging violence he had unleashed, the furious punishment he would inflict again, if ever he got the chance.

A monster. A nightmare. That was what she had hunted down and locked securely in a cage.

No more slaughtered women. No more kids who would return from school to find the kitchen floor slick with their mother's blood.

"Yes," Donna said firmly. "It was worth it."

Delgado squeezed her arm. "Good."

The judge entered, and the disposition of the prisoner commenced.

The procedure was a pure formality and took less than ten minutes. Early in the case, the D.A. had expressed his intention to contest an insanity plea on the part of the defense. His resolution had wavered and finally dissolved after a team of psychiatrists unanimously concluded that the defendant was incompetent to stand trial. The resulting deal between the defense and the government had eliminated the need for even a sanity hearing. All that remained was the *pro forma* business of disposing of Wayne Allen Stanton's life.

Donna approved of the decision. Stanton was the rarer type of serial killer, the disorganized asocial, a paranoid schizophrenic with no conception of the moral implications of his acts. There was no point in trying him. He was a broken thing, a misprogrammed machine, hopelessly out of contact with reality; he could not be held responsible for the misery he'd caused.

She watched as Stanton's attorney prodded him to his feet. The prisoner stood before the bench.

The judge was a round-faced, middle-aged woman,

ordinarily affable, but stern now, in the presence of so much death.

She spoke slowly, apprising the prisoner of the charges against him and the conclusions of the psychiatrists' reports, but the only words that mattered were the last ones she uttered.

"It is the order of the court that you be remanded to the custody of St. Mary's Hospital and Health Center in Sherman Oaks, for purposes of further evaluation and treatment. A written progress report shall be submitted to the court by St. Mary's within ninety days of your commitment, and a review of your case shall be undertaken, if necessary, at that time.

"That will be all. Court stands in recess."

Stanton showed no reaction to the words. For all practical purposes, he was not in the room.

Delgado touched Donna's hand. "I'd advise you to get out before you're spotted by the fourth estate."

"Good plan."

They left quickly, escaping even before Stanton had been led away.

Striding down the corridor at Delgado's side, Donna tried to identify what she was feeling. Relief? Or only emptiness?

"It's done," Delgado said simply.

"Done," she agreed.

"What's next for you?"

"Oh, they keep me busy over at Headquarters Bureau. I've got a full caseload."

"But nothing like this."

"At the moment—no. There will be, though. Always more of them out there. Sometimes I just can't believe how many there are."

Delgado pursed his lips, hearing the bitter weariness in her tone. "How are things otherwise?"

"You know me. Wildman the workaholic. There's never much going on with me . . . otherwise."

"I seem to recall that you were seeing someone."

"Not anymore," she said too sharply. "Look, I'd better get going. Say hello to Wendy for me."

"I'll do that. And congratulations on a job very well done."

"Thanks, Seb. Thanks."

Donna walked away, not looking back. She wished she didn't envy Wendy and Sebastián Delgado quite so much.

They'd made a life together. Neither of them had to lie alone at night in the friendless dark.

You didn't have to be alone, a heartless inner voice chided. *Wouldn't be, if you hadn't messed up.*

Or maybe it was the Slasher who had messed her up. Or maybe . . .

Hell. It didn't matter. Too late to do anything about it now.

Too late—such ugly words. *Too late.* The most painful words she knew. *Too late.*

Too late for everything, except regret. Never too late for that.

Head down, eyes burning, Donna hurried through the courthouse doors into a dismal January rain falling like tears.

1

Something was wrong with the guy. She wasn't sure what. His come-on was smooth enough, his grin friendly and unthreatening, but there was a hint of strangeness about him, an aura of not-quite-right.

Maybe it was his eyes. They burned with an intensity that was more than carnal, a hot febrile glow.

"I said, what kind of party did you have in mind?"

She realized he was asking the question for the second time. *Come on, Wanda, pay attention. This is business.*

"Whatever you're up for, baby," she answered sweetly. "You party with me, you're getting the best."

The words were a formula learned on the street. She was smart enough to despise the charade of romance she offered, along with the men who believed in it. Real romance was a beautiful thing, she was sure, but so far she had encountered it only in thrift-shop books.

Traffic blurred past on Corona Beach Boulevard, a river of headlights and taillights throwing the john into shadowy relief against the dark mass of his parked car. He leaned forward into the streetlight's glow. A brief, tight smile split his face.

"I like it when a girl goes down on me. My wife used to do that sometimes. She did it extremely well. How about you, darling? Can you do me like that?"

He was squinting hard, his irises squeezed into slits. The rest of his face was okay, but those eyes still made her nervous.

She almost told him to get lost. She was broke, though, and he was the first action she'd seen all night. *Go for it.*

"Mister," she said with a practiced wink, "I swear I can make you feel real good."

The wink was meant to be sultry, but her round face made it merely childish. She looked like a girl flirting at a school dance. Ten weeks on the street had not aged her very much. Some tricks still asked if she was a virgin before she showed what she could do.

"How good?" he pressed.

"I'll put you in heaven. In heaven with the rest of the angels."

He barked a sound that might have been laughter. His breath brushed her face and she smelled alcohol.

Drunk. That explained the shine in his eyes.

She relaxed a little. She had no problem dealing with drunks. They could get violent, but she knew how to handle herself. Attached to her fingernails were razor tips; she could slash and stab like a wildcat if a trick turned mean.

"So what's the price of admission to heaven these days?" he asked.

"For a hose job? Forty bucks. In advance."

"Twenty."

"Come on, don't waste my time."

"Thirty, then. Final offer."

"Hell . . . okay."

Thirty was pretty good money, actually. She would have done it for less.

He took out a wallet and removed a twenty and a ten. She stuffed the bills in the pocket of her blouse.

"You want I should do you in the car?" she asked him.

"No. Not in the car."

"Okay, there's a motel down the block. We can get a room for a half hour, but you gotta pay—"

"We're not going to a motel."

"Right. No motel, no car. So where *are* we going?"

"Police station." He flipped open the wallet to display a gold badge. "You're under arrest."

"Shit." The guy was a cop. A cop with liquor on his breath. That was a new one.

"Turn around," he ordered. "Hands behind your back."

She obeyed. He snapped on a pair of cuffs.

"In the car."

"Aren't you gonna read me my rights?"

"Later."

"Look, maybe we could work something out—"

"Just get in the car, sweetcakes."

She climbed into the backseat. He slid behind the wheel. The engine turned over and the sedan snaked into the ribbon of traffic.

Rows of darkened storefronts passed by. A bum lay curled on a bus-stop bench under a drift of ratty blankets. Kids in Raiders jackets loitered in a cone of glareless sodium-vapor light.

Corona Beach was a crummy town, she decided. Almost as bad as L.A. Worse, maybe. The L.A. cops didn't breathe kerosene in your face when they busted you. Didn't slap cuffs on a working girl either, unless she got wild.

But she'd known she would be hassled by the law no matter where she went. At least here she wouldn't have to worry about Jay Cee.

Jay Cee was a Hollywood pimp, a wiry black dude with straightened hair, and he'd been out to make Wanda his girl. "If you workin' my territory, pretty

thing, you workin' for me," he'd said to her in his
mushmouth drawl. "Anyways, you be needin' a man
to keep you safe on these streets."

Keep her hooked on junk, was what he meant. She
knew the routine. Make the mistake of being alone
with him just once, and he would find a way to get
the needle in your arm. One fix, and you couldn't
live without the brown sugar. Then you were Jay
Cee's slave, and he would be pimping you hard, taking your money, doling out skin pops till you were
scrawny and blotchy and half-dead. When you were
no good to him anymore, he'd kick you loose and
you'd die in an alley.

Wanda had seen it happen, had seen the results.
Cinderella and Sugar used to whore for Jay Cee, and
look at them now. Burnouts, only a few years older
than she was and already limping like wounded animals toward death. The only way they could make
any money was by pimping some younger, fresher
girl, the way they'd pimped Wanda when she was
new in town.

Well, not anymore. She was through working for
Cindy and Sugar, and she wasn't going to work for
Jay Cee or anyone else.

I'm an independent contractor, she thought.

She liked that term: independent contractor. She'd
heard it once on some TV show, and it had stuck
with her, as her idea of a good thing to be.

To preserve her independence, she had fled Hollywood, taking an RTD bus, getting off a mile south
of the airport in this seaside town wedged between
El Segundo and Manhattan Beach.

There was no particular reason why she'd chosen
to stop here, except that the town had looked tacky
enough to provide her with business opportunities,
yet small enough not to ruin her prospects with
undue competition. She'd had high hopes about the

tricks she could turn, the money she could pull in, the new freedom that would be hers.

And now, on only her second night, she'd been busted. Fantastic.

As the car continued north, the scenery improved. No more boarded-up windows; sheets of plate glass glowed like giant picture tubes, showing frozen images of the luxury on display inside. Pool halls and cheap motels gave way to boutiques and beauty parlors. Couples sipped drinks at outdoor cafés. A crowd of young people in stonewashed jeans milled around outside the entrance to a movie theater under a rippling banner of marquee lights.

The town was nicer than she'd realized. She hadn't seen this section before. Hadn't had any reason to see it. This neighborhood was too upscale for her. But just wait. Someday she would have money. A rich john would marry her, or she would open her own escort service—and, count on it, she would treat her girls better than Cindy and Sugar had treated her.

Anyway, something would happen, something good. She was still young, only seventeen. She had time to work out the details.

A complex of one-story white brick buildings, bracketed by windmill palms, slid into view. In front was a lighted sign: CORONA BEACH CIVIC CENTER. As the car drove past, she saw a glass-walled lobby, a uniformed cop at a desk. The police station.

Slowly the station receded, passing out of sight.

"Think you missed your stop," she said politely. Her mom had raised her to be courteous, and the lesson had stuck.

The cop didn't answer, just kept driving.

Jeez, he must really be tanked. But maybe that was okay. If he was obviously drunk, he couldn't charge her with soliciting, could he?

Of course he could. Cops could do anything. Cops were like God.

The car hooked west, coasted downhill a few blocks, and turned onto a two-lane road that ran along a high bluff overlooking the sea.

A cookout fire burned on the beach. Glittery screams of laughter rose over the crash and drag of the surf. In the distance a carousel flashed like a diamond on the long finger of the Corona Beach Pier, extending into the black waters of the bay.

Wanda watched the pier through the rear window till a bend in the road swept it from sight. Then there was nothing but the dark sea and the empty road and the moonless sky, and as the car rolled on, engine humming tunelessly, she began to be afraid.

"Hey, mister . . . you *are* a cop, right?"

"Sure I am."

There was an edge of malicious humor in his voice, and she wasn't sure if his answer was serious or not.

Now that she thought about it, she hadn't gotten much of a look at that badge. Could have been a fake. You could buy one in a novelty store for five dollars.

"You running me out of town?" she asked, almost hoping the answer would be yes. "It's okay with me if you are. Just drop me off at a bus station." Actually she would have to go back to her hotel for her things, but she wasn't about to admit that. "Really. Get me on a bus, and I'm gone."

"Yeah." His soft chuckle frightened her. "You're gone all right."

"I . . . I wasn't looking for any trouble."

"Maybe I was, though. Ever think of that?"

A beating rhythm filled her head. It took her a moment to realize that she was hearing the sound of her heart in her ears.

She tried to figure out what this guy was after. If

he wanted a freebie, all he had to do was ask. He could park on any side street and she would show him a good time right here in the backseat.

No, that couldn't be it. There was no need to drive this far from the center of town for that kind of action. Unless he had something else in mind. Something she might not want to go along with.

With her hands manacled behind her, she couldn't use her nails. Couldn't do anything.

She tugged at the handcuffs. The cold metal rings chewed her wrists like hungry mouths.

In Hollywood she'd heard stories of girls picked up on the street to be found, later, feeding flies in a Dumpster or an abandoned car. Working outcall had been safer, but there'd been no money in it. Cindy and Sugar had taken everything, including her cut.

The money seemed meaningless now. She wondered why it had ever been a consideration.

She thought there was a good chance this man meant to rape and kill her. The rape part wouldn't be so bad, not much worse than what she did on the job every damn night, but the dying would be tough. She wasn't ready for that.

If she died, if the police found her body, they would have to call her mom. How much would they tell her? Would they say she'd been a whore?

Her mom still thought Wanda had a regular job. If she found out the truth, she might slash her wrists again, and this time Wanda wouldn't be there to call 9-1-1, wouldn't be there to save her from bleeding to death on the kitchen floor.

She hoped the cops had enough sense to lie, to say she'd been hit by a bus or something.

A spin of the steering wheel, a hiss of brakes. The car pulled onto a dark side road and slowed to a crawl.

She stared out the side windows, drawing quick

shallow breaths. Dark humps of hills crowded the left side of the narrow road. On the right stretched an unfenced field. The dim outline of a building, large and featureless and functional, hovered in the far distance, blurred by mist.

Nobody around. No people, no traffic.

She pulled harder at the cuffs, knowing it was useless to try working her hands free, trying anyway.

Now the car was easing off the road onto a dirt shoulder edged by a gray waste of weeds. Motion stopped. The engine died. In the abrupt stillness she heard a faraway hum, a faint, steady throb, like an echo of her speeding pulse. It came from the building, a power-plant sound.

The driver's-side door creaked open. Crush of footsteps on dirt. Squeal of hinges, sigh of shocks: the rear door swinging wide.

The man leaned in, his face half-lit by the yellow ceiling bulb. She saw his eyes. They were glazed and dead now. No personality registered in their glassy emptiness. It was as if a switch had been flipped, shutting off the person he had been, leaving only a programmed machine.

A psycho—Christ, he's not just drunk, he's some kind of nut . . .

Cold rippled over her. Buzzing panic thrummed in her brain.

She shrank from him. His hand closed over her arm. Roughly he hauled her out of the car, threw her down on her knees. A jolt of pain slammed through her, and she heard herself whimper.

"Please, mister, please don't hurt me. Cut me a break, okay?"

No reply.

He popped the trunk lid, lifted out a duffel bag. Rummaged in it, found a pair of black leather gloves, pulled them on. His actions unnaturally deliberate, the expressionless pantomime of a sleepwalker.

"Come on, talk to me. I don't like you being so quiet all of a sudden. Say something, will you, say something to me."

The trunk lid slammed shut. A bang like a gunshot.

She watched him, wishing she knew what to say.

He shrugged the duffel bag over his shoulders, then leaned down, reaching for her. She spun onto her back and kicked. He caught hold of her flailing feet and held on as she twisted and screamed.

She shook loose one foot, pistoned a kick at his midsection. He grunted, doubling over. She kicked again; he sidestepped the attack. Her shoe spun off and spiraled into the tall weeds beyond the car.

He spoke one word. *"Bitch."*

Red heat flushed his face. His nostrils dilated; he blew a snort of air. Clutching his stomach, he circled her, his mouth chewing soundless curses.

Two quick steps closed the distance between them. His foot went up, smashed down, stomping on her collarbone. A hard, solid thud of impact, a wet snap, a sunburst of pain.

Static rose in her ears, and she went away.

Her next awareness was of a series of bumps and jolts and a cloud of choking dust. He was dragging her off the road into the field. Thorns and brambles caught at her clothes, sliced her skin.

He pulled her into a muddy ditch strewn with burst trash bags. Somebody had been dumping garbage here. Glass shards and rusted cans spilled through rents in the green plastic.

He let go of her, then lifted the duffel bag off his back and began pawing through it again.

She lay stunned, winded, waves of pain broadcast in widening circles from her collarbone. It occurred to her that she would never be rich now. Never be anything.

"All wrong," she murmured as her eyelashes fluttered against a burning rush of tears. "Turned out all wrong."

She might as well have stayed in L.A., gone to work for Jay Cee, stuck the needle in her arm. Might as well have ended up like Cinderella, like Sugar, wearing makeup to cover the lines in her young-old face, aimlessly prowling the boulevards, a gaunt apparition in cast-off clothes.

From the bag the man removed a small limp thing. He thrust it at her face.

"See this?" His voice was flat, barely managing the lilt of a question. "See it?"

Red curls, sewn smile, floppy beanbag limbs. A Raggedy Ann doll.

She thought of her favorite stuffed animal, Penny the Penguin, the friend from her childhood who had made the great trip west with her, the trip ending tonight.

"This is you," he said. It seemed important to him that she understand. He repeated the words, enunciating clearly. "This is you."

"Me," she agreed. She had no strength to argue.

"You," he said, nodding, smiling, pleased to find her a quick study, and then he gripped the doll's head with both hands and wrenched it halfway off, a rush of cottony fibers spilling out, the doll's eyes staring wide and lidless, the fixed smile abruptly grotesque like the gape of a corpse.

He tore off the head and savaged the doll, stripping it of arms and legs, pouring out clumps of stuffing, until only flaps of ripped fabric remained.

"You," he said again, holding up the remnant of the doll like a scrap of some small animal's hide.

Tears watered her world like a hard downpour.

Wanda shut her eyes and went home, back to the two-bedroom apartment where she had lived with her mom for the first sixteen years of her life. She found her mother in one of her good moods, not blue, not crazy, and hugged her tight, so glad to see her again. She didn't let go even when the pain started, even when she felt the excruciating pops of broken bones in her face and chest.

There were screams but she didn't hear them. No one heard them but the man with the badge and, at the Phaethon Waste Disposal Facility a quarter-mile away, a security guard who paused to listen to the faint, shrill cries, then shrugged.

Wind must have shifted, he decided. You could hear some drunken kids carrying on down at the beach.

The thought reminded him of a girls' volleyball game he'd watched in Manhattan Beach last weekend. As he patrolled the incinerator complex, restlessly fingering his utility belt, he remembered the players' olive legs, their oiled backs, their buttocks so tight and firm.

When he listened again, a short while later, he heard no sound but the dull, pulsing roar of the furnaces, ceaselessly disposing of the city's vast waste.

2

Mark Logan was pulled out of sleep by the shrilling of the telephone. He fumbled the handset off the cradle, blinking at spears of light thrown by the lamp across the room.

"Logan."

"Detective, this is Walters." Commanding officer of the midnight-to-eight watch. "We've got a homicide."

Logan twisted into a sitting position. The room swanboated and his head swam.

"Where?"

"Body was found on Bay Street and Third. Dumped, Kurtz says." Sergeant Kurtz was the supervisor of patrol units on the morning watch.

"Kurtz is there already?"

"He found her."

"A woman?"

"Girl. Teenager."

"Local girl? Someone we know?"

"Kurtz doesn't recognize her. There's another unit at the scene; they can't make a visual I.D. either."

"All right. Call Barnes. And Anderson. And the coroner."

"Kurtz already requested a morgue wagon. I'll get the other two. And, Detective—the sarge says this is a bad one."

"Okay, Jim. Thanks."

Logan hung up. Stood. Another lurch of nausea. His knees jellied. He gripped the nightstand till the feeling passed.

The sky beyond the curtained windows was coal dark. His desk lamp, left on when he removed his soiled jacket and pants and collapsed into bed two hours ago, burned with a feverish yellow heat. The bulb glared out from under a crooked shade, casting his huge disfigured shadow on the bare walls.

He tried to concentrate on the immediate situation. He was a detective, there had been a homicide, he had a job to do.

All right. What was his first move? What action would he normally take?

His head pounded. It was hard to think.

Log in the call. Yes.

He checked the clock, found a new steno pad and a pen. On the first page he wrote: *14 June. 0145 hrs. Lt. Walters. Homicide. Bay & 3rd.*

He had to follow procedure, do everything right. No mistakes. Not on this one.

On this one he could not afford mistakes.

He asked himself if he had time for a shower, decided he did not. It wouldn't look good if he took long arriving.

He washed his face, toweled off, ran a comb through his brown hair. Took a swig of mouthwash and sloshed it around in his mouth till his tongue was numb and his gums were stinging. Spit it into the sink and breathed against his open hand, testing for the smell of liquor. There was none he could detect.

He dressed quickly, putting on fresh clothes. His shoes were muddied; he brushed them clean.

Before leaving, he inspected himself in the bathroom mirror. The crescents underscoring his eyes were darker than usual. Other than that, he looked all right.

He drove his personal car to the scene, the warm air of a June night blowing through the open window. Chief Mueller had denied his request to home-garage a department vehicle. Logan had enjoyed the privilege until last year, and most other CBPD detectives continued to do so. Denial of the permit was a bad sign.

"The proverbial thread," Barnes had told him, smiling but stern. "That's what you're hanging by, my friend."

The town was dark and still, the only sound a jet's distant thunder. Logan headed north along elm-lined streets, past rows of Craftsman bungalows. The homes were expensive, three hundred grand and up, occupied by retired couples and young two-income families.

Though a suburb of L.A., with a population of eighteen thousand, Corona Beach had not yet developed a city's gritty ambience. Much of it still had the feel of a small midwestern town dropped improbably at the lip of Santa Monica Bay. Softball on summer nights, moths beating at porch lamps, kids on bicycles trailing thin cries as they chased the fading twilight.

The south end was different. It was a puzzle of narrow streets and cheap hotels, and it kept the police in business.

Logan hooked east for a few blocks, then turned onto Corona Beach Boulevard, the north-south thoroughfare bisecting town. As more young professionals moved in, the older, homier shops and lunch counters were closing, replaced by upscale boutiques and cafés. Parts of the boulevard already resembled Melrose Avenue in West Hollywood, consciously trendy, aggressively hip.

Static buzzed on his rover radio. It lay on the passenger seat, turned to Dispatch 1, the public-safety frequency shared by the South Bay cities of Corona Beach, Manhattan Beach, and El Segundo. He heard a second patrol unit call in a 10–23 at Bay and Third, heard Kurtz tell the dispatcher that no further assistance was required, heard the dispatcher put out a Code Four on the incident.

Logan smiled briefly. All four blue-and-whites on patrol must have been hoping to crash the party. Everybody wanted to be in on this one.

Everybody but him.

The intersection of Third and Bay was a mist of flickering dome lights. Logan parked behind Sergeant Kurtz's cruiser and got out. As he approached the line of yellow evidence tape strung between a patrol-car bumper and a fire hydrant, he popped a breath freshener in his mouth. Mouthwash wasn't always enough.

Joe Kurtz was talking to two young patrol officers who looked excited and jumpy. The girl lay a few yards away in the middle of the street, her skin washed pale by a corner light.

Logan barely glanced at the body. Time for that later. He stopped before Kurtz and nodded hello.

Kurtz returned the nod. "Detective."

At thirty-eight, Joe Kurtz was three years older than Logan, but he looked like a much younger man. Mineral water and health foods kept him lean and fit. He worked out for two hours or more in the station-house gym every day after completing his shift.

Standing beside him, Logan felt the contrast between Kurtz's ostentatious vitality and his own puffy eyes and aching head. The sergeant, studying him with cool eyes, seemed to reach a similar point in his own thoughts.

"Guess they got you out of bed," Kurtz said mildly, with a polite smile.

"It was no loss. I was sleeping alone."

"I know how *that* is."

Logan didn't want to hear it, didn't want to commiserate about loneliness with Kurtz or anyone else. His pain was a private, furtive thing; he would not hoist it into the light.

Kurtz was staring at the body. "Look at her. Christ, she was young."

Logan did not look, not yet. "When did you find her?"

"One-thirty-five. Right before that, I helped out on a four-fifteen over on Primrose—couple of drunks." Logan wondered if that detail had been inserted for his benefit. "I was cruising, and then she was right there in my headlights like roadkill. Sorry. Shouldn't have said that."

"Think she's been here long?"

"Can't tell. It's a dump job, I'm pretty sure. You couldn't do a thing like this right here in town."

Logan looked around. The brick mass of a warehouse towered over one side of the street, facing a row of older one-story shops, dark and closed.

"This district is deserted at night," Logan said. "If the killing was quick, somebody might get away with it, even out in the open."

"It wasn't quick. Bastard took his time with her. Look for yourself."

"In a minute." Logan wouldn't be rushed. He would be staring into her face soon enough. "How much traffic comes down this street at night, you think?"

"None. Or hardly any. No reason to come this way."

Logan nodded. "Bay Street dead-ends a block west of Third. So you can't even use it as a shortcut."

"Nobody takes shortcuts in this town at one A.M. Even the main drag isn't crowded after midnight."

"So she could have been here awhile. An hour or more."

"She could." Kurtz pressed his palms together in an isometric exercise, a habit of his. "I'll check with Alvarez and see if anybody patrolled this street during his watch." Lieutenant Alvarez commanded the night watch, four to midnight. "That would give us a time frame. You know, say she wasn't here at eleven-fifteen; then we know she was dumped sometime after."

"Right," Logan said. "Do that."

Headlights splashed the asphalt. An unmarked Chevy parked alongside Logan's Buick Skylark sedan. A tall, stoop-shouldered, sad-eyed man emerged from behind the wheel, grunting as he straightened up. A second man, thirty years younger and thirty pounds lighter around the waist, climbed out on the passenger side, lugging a forensic kit and a camera bag.

Logan lifted his hand in a wave. The older man nodded back and trotted toward him. "Picked up Timmy on the way over," he explained unnecessarily, with a nod at his companion.

Tim Anderson's mouth puckered. He didn't like being called Timmy. But he put up with it, because nobody argued with Lieutenant Ed Barnes. At fifty-five, Barnes was a thirty-three-year veteran of police work, the most experienced man in the CBPD other than Chief Mueller himself.

A UCLA graduate with a bachelor's degree in biochemistry, Barnes had enlisted in the LAPD in 1961, put in three years on the patrol side, then moved over to Scientific Investigation Division, eventually serving as commanding officer of Criminalistics Section. Five years ago he'd retired on a full pension. The Corona Beach P.D. had lured him back into active service as a crime-scene investigator. He ran the department's crime lab, assisted by Anderson and another civilian. He was a gentle, polite authoritarian, and he knew his stuff.

Logan worked with Barnes on most cases. He didn't like to think of Barnes as his best friend; such an acknowledgment only highlighted the aridity of his social life. Anyway, they had the kind of friendship best left unstated, an affinity of companionable silences and the precise interlocking of mental gears.

Lately their former closeness, if that was what it should be called, had become strained. Barnes was growing more cordial and less friendly. Unvoiced reproval glimmered in his eyes whenever Logan was hung over, which was increasingly often.

Kurtz filled in Barnes on the details. "Did you touch her?" Barnes asked.

"Only her neck. I was checking for a pulse. I had to be sure."

"Nothing else? Okay. Timmy, why don't you get started? Don't be stingy with film; department's paying for it." Barnes always said that; his little joke. "Joe, we're going to need better illumination to properly check out the body. There's a couple of arc lights in storage, and a portable generator."

Kurtz got on the radio to the watch commander, relaying the request. Anderson screwed the flash attachment onto his Canon AE-1 and exposed a thirty-six-shot roll in a series of clicks and shutter flashes. Light and dark alternated like a procession of days and nights in a super-accelerated filmstrip. The girl's body seemed to waver in the white strobe light.

While they waited for the equipment, Logan and Barnes went around to the four beat cops, asking if they had seen the victim before. None had. Logan took down each unit's identification number and time of arrival. Barnes kept asking, "Touch anything?"

In ten minutes Lieutenant Walters arrived with the two lamps and a Craftsman 750-watt generator. Anderson began setting up the equipment. Walters and Kurtz took a look at the body. Walters returned, shaking his head.

"Kurtz didn't exaggerate. It's a bad one. Jeez."

For him, this was a crude expletive. Jim Walters never swore.

"Mueller coming?" Barnes asked.

"No. I phoned him at home after I called you. He asks if there's any press here. I say no, not yet. I doubt anybody's awake at the *Guardian*, and the L.A. papers aren't going to cover this; too small-time for them. So he says, okay, he'll be in early in the A.M. to plot strategy."

"Plot strategy?" Logan was amused.

"That's what he said." Walters sounded defensive. "He can do it. He's still sharp, you know."

Logan didn't answer, just walked away. Contempt was readable in the turning of his back.

"They used to get along fine," Barnes said in a low voice, "him and Mueller."

"Yeah. Till he started boozing." Walters leaned closer. "You know what else the chief said? Quote: It looks like Logan's got his hands full of something other than a bottle for a change."

Barnes said nothing to that. He took off his glasses, put them on again. Bifocals, brand new. Still hadn't gotten used to the damn things.

"You smell his breath?" Walters asked, not letting it go. His bald head was shiny against the dark.

"Nothing to smell."

"Listerine."

"That a crime? I knew a lot of guys at Parker Center who could've benefited from better dental hygiene."

"Yeah," Walters said, smirking. "Right."

Anderson was ready by then. The two lights were in place, plugged into yellow extension cords that ran to the generator. He started the motor, then flipped a toggle switch on each lamp. The street was painted in white glare and long shadows.

Barnes found Logan standing alone. "Let's go."

They approached the body single-file. Bending down, Barnes grunted. It was the same noise he'd made getting out of the car.

"You feel okay?" Logan asked.

Barnes touched his stomach. "Indigestion."

They crouched beside the girl. She lay on her back, legs twisted, arms splayed. Automatically Logan translated the human reality before him into an impersonal list of characteristics. White female, mid to late teens, brown hair, brown eyes, five-two or -three, about one hundred pounds. The reductionist inventory made her an object, not a person. She was easier for him to look at that way.

He took a breath, then focused his gaze on her face. Bruises tattooed her skin. Her delicate features had been beaten in. Her nose was pulp; streams of dried blood curved from the nostrils. Between split lips, swollen and slightly parted, Logan could see chipped teeth and bloodied gums. Her eyes were open, staring out of purple hollows.

Slowly Logan clenched his fists. After a long moment he let his hands curl open again.

He thought he should say something. "Poor kid," he managed.

Barnes was unshaken. "I'd estimate her age at sixteen."

"About that."

"Hooker."

"Think so?"

"The outfit says whore."

She wore a low-cut, short-sleeve red blouse, a purple mini, and a single high-heeled shoe. The clothes were ripped, the shoe crusted with black crumbly soil.

"She's pretty clean for a working girl," Logan said. "No track marks on her arms. Clothes of good quality too."

"Escort service, maybe," Barnes conceded. "Or she might just have been new. The new ones, they're not so burned out yet. They dress up, take a shower sometimes, stay away from the junk."

"Could be." Logan checked her hands. "Blood under the fingernails. She's wearing razor tips."

"Definitely a pro." Barnes removed two paper bags from the forensic kit. "Killer could be a john who got out of control."

"There are deep cuts in her palms. She might have been clenching her fists so tight the razor tips punched right into the meat of her hands."

"Hope not. That would mean it's her blood under the nails. And it would mean she was conscious when the guy did this to her."

"She had to be. Her eyes are open."

"Unless he opened them after death. They do that sometimes. I'll try to pull prints off the eyelids at the morgue. You never know, we might get lucky."

Barnes bagged her hands, preserving the nails for scrapings and the fingertips and palms for prints. He bagged her shoeless foot too; plantar prints could be checked against hospital records of babies' feet.

Logan took out a pocket flashlight, lifted the girl's skirt, and aimed the beam between her legs. Black lace panties. Torn.

"Looks like she was raped."

He replaced the skirt and raised his head. Barnes was examining the girl's upper body.

"Bruises all over the exposed parts of her torso," Barnes said. "He must have beaten her in the stomach and chest. Probably broke some ribs. Maybe fractured her collarbone too." He pulled on white cotton gloves and searched the girl's pockets. "No money, no keys, no I.D. And if she had a purse, it's gone."

Logan checked the underside of her blouse collar. "Here's something. Clothing-store label. Hollywood Hot is the name of the place."

"Good, we'll get LAPD to check it out. Maybe some sales clerk will remember her." Barnes studied her dress. "Dirt and grass stains on her clothes. She was killed out in the open, someplace muddy."

He carefully lifted one arm, encountering the gentle resistance characteristic of the initial onset of rigor.

"Look at the lividity pattern. The killer left her lying on her side at first."

Logan saw the purple discoloration along the side of her arm. The blood had settled there immediately after death.

"Kurtz was right," Logan said. "She was dumped here."

"After being beaten to death in a yard or field." Barnes gazed thoughtfully at the bloody riddle sprawled at his knees. "And raped, probably. Or maybe the guy waited till she was dead before he did that part of it."

"Either way"—Logan kept his voice even—"we are dealing with one crazy son of a bitch."

Barnes nodded. "Crazy enough to do it again, maybe."

"A repeater? Think so?"

"In my experience, a crime this violent and irrational suggests a compulsion to kill. Especially if it's a stranger homicide, which I'm betting this one was. I wouldn't be surprised if he's done it before, someplace else—and if he does it again. Possibly in some other town. Or possibly here."

"Jack the Ripper in Corona Beach. Great."

"There's one major difference between our man and old Red Jack," Barnes said quietly. "Jack was never caught. This guy will be."

Logan heard a strange note of excitement in the older cop's normally phlegmatic voice. "You've wanted one like this for a long time, haven't you?" he asked with a slight smile.

Barnes drew back slightly, shoulders hunching. His eyes locked on Logan's. "I never wanted anything like this. What do you think, I'm happy this girl is dead?"

"Of course not."

"So what the hell are you trying to say?"

"I only meant, it's a challenge going up against somebody like this."

"I don't need that kind of challenge. All right?"

Barnes kept staring at him, his eyes focused in a frank, unwavering gaze.

"Yeah, all right, all right," Logan said. "Forget I said anything."

Barnes nodded and resumed his work. Logan watched him. He asked himself how many suspects he had interrogated in his career. Hundreds.

People telling the truth, he had observed, rarely met your eyes for long. Only liars did that.

He wondered why Ed Barnes had felt the need to lie.

Dawn was blooming in the window shades of the Corona Beach P.D. administrative office. Mark Logan, bone-tired, hurting everywhere, typed up his notes on a borrowed typewriter at a secretary's desk.

Above the desk hung a snapshot of the softball team fielded by the police department in last year's charity game. The fire department had beaten them 6 to 2, and still wouldn't let them forget it.

Losing had been all right. Logan had fielded several grounders at first base and smacked a run-scoring double in the sixth inning. A boisterous female voice had cheered him from the stands.

The day seemed very bright in memory, so bright the radiance of it made his eyes sting with held-back tears.

That chain of thoughts sidetracked him. It took him half an hour to finish his report. He put a copy in Chief Mueller's in-basket.

As he was leaving, he ran into Barnes in the hall. "Nothing in the Dumpsters, nothing in the alleys," Barnes reported, brushing dirt off his pants.

"Surprise," Logan said mildly.

Barnes looked him over in the hallway's fluorescent chill. "You really look like shit, you know."

Logan smiled. "Thanks for the ego boost."

"Been drinking?"

Logan thought about denying it. No point, not with Barnes. "A few pulls on the bottle."

"You'd be better off pulling on your dick." He took off his bifocals, frowned at them, and replaced them on the bridge of his nose. "You know, Mark," he added in a softer tone, "you've got to forget about her."

Logan flinched. Fatigue made him cruel: "Have you forgotten Marjorie?"

Barnes's hand moved to his stomach again. "No," he said. "So I guess I shouldn't talk."

Already Logan regretted the words, quick and thoughtless as a trigger pull. Barnes's wife had died last February, by suicide. The trauma of discovering her body, unmoving in the brackish water of the bathtub, had aged him ten years.

"Sorry, Ed," Logan said quietly.

Barnes massaged his belly. "It's all right. Forgetting—it's tough to do, I guess." His mouth squirmed into a grimace.

"Now *you* don't look so hot."

"Indigestion, like I said before. Too much Mexican food."

"It'll kill you."

Barnes's cool gray eyes regarded him from over the frames of his bifocals. "So will booze."

3

A desk fan buzzed in the hot office, turning in jerky half circles. Each time the focused breeze passed over Mark Logan's typed one-page report, a corner of the paper flapped wildly like the wing of a trapped bird. The rest of the sheet was anchored under a chrome ashtray, already dark with ash. Though it was barely nine, Hugo Mueller had started his third cigarette.

Snakes of smoke wound their coils around the three men facing Mueller's desk. Joe Kurtz squirmed irritably, hating to inhale carcinogens. Jim Walters and Ed Barnes breathed with easy stoicism. Walters, a devout Christian, had no fear of cancer. God would call him when it was his time to go. Barnes had lost all concern for his health after Marjorie died.

" 'Morning, gentlemen," Mueller rasped. He was a large, solid man, thick-necked and square-jawed. His gray hair was trimmed in the Marine crew cut he had worn since joining the CBPD forty-five years earlier. "I know you're busy. Won't keep you long. This isn't a strategy session exactly—we'll save that till this afternoon and corral all the relevant parties."

His head turned in slow semicircles like the fan, his gaze surveying the room. "Ed, you look all in. Better go home and grab some sleep after we're finished."

"Wish I could," Barnes said. "I've got to run up

to the morgue and print the deceased. Autopsy's at noon."

"Logan attending?"

"He'll be there. He's getting some rest now."

"I'm sure he is." Mueller tapped the fluttering page with a fat forefinger. "I read his report a little while ago. You all saw him at the scene?"

Nods and noises of assent.

"How did he look?"

Silence stretched in the room. Finally Barnes spoke up. "He looked okay."

Mueller squinted, studying him. "You're trying to snooker me."

"All right, maybe he'd had a few."

"More than a few, I'll wager. Joe, you talk to him?"

"Yeah, Chief. He appeared fatigued, but alert. As far as I could tell, he followed procedure."

"You don't know the procedure for a homicide dick."

"I took the detective's exam," Kurtz said, offended. "Passed it too—oral and written. I might be investigating homicides right now, except Annie didn't want me to take the pay cut." Detectives earned five percent less than sergeants. His wife hadn't liked that. Ex-wife now. "I know what to look for."

"Sure, sure, I hear you." Mueller's tone implied that exams were one thing, field work another. "Jim, how about you?"

Walters was torn between two Christian duties, truthfulness and loyalty. "Detective Logan was visibly tired, like Joe said," he answered after a brief moral struggle. "Of course, it was the middle of the night."

"I know what time it was." Mueller stamped the cigarette into the ashtray with an angry jerk of his hand. "Okay, let's cut the BS, shall we? Logan's no good anymore. We all know that. I knew it before I

called you in here. Sure, he's still capable of participating in the investigation in some capacity. But we
can't count on him to clear this case. Not by himself."

"We can assign Hill and Reynolds to assist," Walters suggested. The two detectives made up the department's entire Narcotics-Vice section.

"I was planning to do that anyway." Mueller
reached for another cigarette, then withdrew his
hand in a rare gesture of self-restraint. "Assuming
the girl was a whore, we'll need them to work the
street. But that's not a sufficient solution."

He leaned forward, his swivel chair creaking.

"This is a big one, my friends. Nastiest crime our
town has seen in years. A hooker gets killed—nobody cares. But a hooker gets beaten to death like
this girl did, gets her pretty face hammered inside-
out—all of sudden people care. You know why? Because a crime like this says *psycho*. And who knows
with a psycho? He did it once, he might do it again.
Your daughter could be next, or your wife, or you.
There's going to be a furor about it, and I don't mean
Adolph. Which is why I'm bringing in outside help."

"Outside?" Kurtz frowned.

Mueller nodded. "Just got off the phone with Commander Adams of LAPD Personnel and Training. I
requested the services of a detective trained in behavioral analysis, to work up a psychological profile of
this loon. Adams has got to clear it with the Director
of Operations, but I'm pretty sure the request will be
approved—probably by this afternoon."

"You put much faith in profiles?" Walters asked
skeptically.

"Me, I'm an agnostic on the subject. Maybe they
work, maybe they're just mumbo-jumbo. But it sure
looks good to say you've called in an expert, FBI-
trained, with a track record. It should take some of
the heat off us, for a while at least."

Barnes ran a hand through his thinning hair. *FBI-trained*, he was thinking. "Wait a minute. There's only one profiler in the LAPD who went through the NCAVC program."

"That's who I asked for."

Walters and Kurtz caught on. "Oh, Christ, Chief," Kurtz groaned, then looked guiltily at Walters for having taken the Lord's name in vain.

"What is this?" Barnes's voice was thick. "Some kind of game you're playing?"

Mueller felt a warm flush of anger at the back of his neck. "The only game I play, Lieutenant, is called cops and bad guys, and I've been playing it since Maggie Truman was banging out 'Chopsticks' in the White House."

He sucked a shallow breath to calm himself. No good promoting conflict. He needed everybody with him on this.

"Listen," he said more reasonably. "This is a small department. Our Homicide-Major Crimes section consists of a single detective. And he's turned into a lush. Now we've got a high-publicity murder on our hands and nobody competent to investigate it. So what am I supposed to do? Let him screw up so we all get shitcanned? At least this way we spread the blame around. And who knows, maybe this profiling works."

"Guess you're right," Walters ventured. Kurtz echoed him: "Right."

Only Barnes kept quiet.

"Anyway," Mueller added brusquely, "the decision's made. I just wanted you to be informed. Now get out of here. I've got work to do."

Alone in his office, the chief lit another cigarette and asked himself if he had done what was right. He didn't know. But he had done what was necessary.

The murder would start to generate public pressure very soon. Al Klein, editor of the Corona Beach *Guardian,* had already called for details; this week's edition would be out later today. By afternoon the story would be all over town.

Frightened people were desperate people. They needed reassurance. Failing that, a scapegoat.

A third of the city council had been pushing for Mueller's retirement since he turned sixty-five two years ago. His allies had held them off. If he didn't make rapid progress on this case, or at least give the appearance of taking bold steps and decisive action, those against him would become a majority. He would lose the mayor's support. He would have to go.

Mueller closed his eyes and pictured a future without work. CNN chattering on the tube to bring voices into his lonely bungalow. A trip to the drugstore as the highlight of his morning. A nap in the afternoon, longer each day. Maybe he would wear slippers around the house. He could hear the scuffing of plastic soles on short-nap carpet, on linoleum tiles.

"Should have married Virginia." He surprised himself by expressing the thought aloud. "Her—or somebody."

Too late now. All he had was his job. Lose that, and he might as well swim out into the bay and not stop till exhaustion dragged him to the silty bottom.

So he would fight to hold on as long as he could. Besides, he rationalized, an obsession was like any other illogical thought process; it had to be dealt with directly.

Mueller had once known a man with a neurotic terror of driving the freeways. One day he'd gone out boldly to face his fear. Panic had killed him on the 405; the CHP had pulled his body from the folded wreckage. But others had faced the object of their anxieties and had come away victorious, renewed.

"Kill or cure." Mueller nodded grimly, liking the words. He said them again: "Kill or cure."

A spasm of coughing bent him double at his desk.

Kurtz cornered Walters in an alcove near the chief's office.

"Jim, I need to talk to you."

Walters nodded slowly. "I think I can guess why."

Kurtz looked away. "I know you can." He struggled to suppress a shiver, and failed. "Hell, this has got me all rattled. I could hardly sit still in there."

"Keeping secrets isn't healthy, Joe," Walters said in a tone of mingled sternness and compassion. "In fact, it isn't even possible."

Kurtz paled. "You don't mean you'd . . . tell?"

Walters laid a comforting hand on his shoulder. "Of course not. I'm no Judas. You put your trust in me; I won't betray it." His hand pulled free, and his voice turned colder. "What I meant was, there's someone who always knows all our secrets—even the ugliest ones."

"I'm not sure I believe that."

"You don't want to believe." The compassion was gone from Walters's voice. His words were a crisp pronouncement of pitiless judgment. "Because you're afraid."

Kurtz looked at him, at the mouth drawn in a bloodless line, the eyes narrowed and cold, the gleaming hairless dome of his head, as smooth and curvilinear as a round-nose bullet. He wished he had Jim Walters's strength.

Joe Kurtz was strong in some ways—physically fit, robust and muscular, a man who lifted weights and hunted deer and traded locker-room stories with easy, raucous humor. But inside he was weak, and he knew it. Weak and easily hurt, afraid of the dark, fearful of solitude. He longed for the certainty of the hard, unchanging absolutes Jim Walters had built his life around.

If he hadn't been so weak, he would not have yielded to temptation, would not carry the burden of this secret guilt that only Walters had been allowed to see.

"I guess you're right," he whispered. "I'm afraid. Afraid of what I got myself into." He studied the lieutenant's eyes for a glimmer of empathy, found none. "This whole mess—I just want to make some sense out of it and . . . and put it behind me."

"Doesn't look like you'll be able to do that for a while."

"No. Not for a while."

Walters stepped closer, his gaze curiously intense. "Did you enjoy it—having her that way?"

Kurtz licked his lips. "Sure I did. What do you think?"

"Because it was forbidden, was it better?"

"Maybe."

"Did you feel guilty afterward?"

"I don't know what I felt—or what I'm feeling now."

"Was that little bit of pleasure worth all this pain?"

Joe thought it over. Thought for a long time.

"Yes," he said finally. "It was."

Walters turned away. "You're not ready to be saved."

"I guess I'm not."

"Then there's nothing I can do for you."

"You can be my friend."

Abruptly, Walters smiled—a rare kind of smile for him, spontaneous and warm, appealingly human.

"Yeah," he said. "I can do that." He clapped Kurtz fondly on the back. "Don't worry, Joe. You'll get through this. And meanwhile your secret is safe with me."

He walked off, down the hall. Kurtz stared after him, wishing that, for just one day of his life, he could be what he thought Jim Walters was.

4

The gun in both hands, sights lined up, silhouette target at ten yards, and she was thinking of the apartment as she fired—two quick shots—the cracks of sound muffled by her ear protectors, the ejector flipping the empties out of the gun, then two more shots—the apartment again—she was following Delgado into that dark place, obsessively tidy, the air misted with disinfectant spray. Scope out the living room, then fast into the kitchen, pivoting in the doorway—point and shoot—another two rounds, her ears ringing now despite the earmuffs. Then do it again—bathroom, bedroom, closet—the apartment bobbing behind her gun sights, an ambush possible at every corner.

Donna pumped her fifteenth and sixteenth rounds, emptying the clip. A motorized pulley brought the target forward into the glare of the ceiling lights. She tipped her goggles up onto her forehead and inspected her work. Fourteen hits, eight in the X-ring.

"You're dead, Franklin," she said with a smile.

She hadn't had to use her gun when she and Delgado and Tom Gardner broke into Franklin Rood's apartment in West L.A. Rood hadn't even been home. But that was something none of them had known going in.

Reliving the incident helped focus her mind and

improve her accuracy. Besides, it was a kick to imagine blowing that evil son of a bitch away.

She sent the target back to fifteen yards and popped in a fresh clip. She was using low-powered loads, plastic bullets suitable for practice shooting. The pistol was her department-issue Beretta 92SB, a good gun kept in perfect condition, the checkered black walnut grips rubbed with linseed oil, the five-inch barrel shining blue-black like an albacore's dorsal fin.

Before resuming practice, she tucked the gun in the armpit holster under her suit jacket, then drew it several times, testing to make sure the low post of the front sight didn't snag.

Satisfied, she took aim again, entered the apartment again, fired at Franklin Rood, murderer of women, again. Again. Again.

With her ears screaming and the outside world muffled, it took her a moment to hear the complaint of the beeper hitched to her belt.

The phone number on the liquid-crystal display didn't mean anything to her, though the prefix implied Parker Center as a point of origin. She found a phone in the hall.

A secretary answered. "Personnel and Training, Commander Adams's office."

Adams. What the hell? "This is Detective Wildman. Got a message to call the commander."

After a brief pause she was connected with Adams.

"Detective, the Director of Operations just approved a request for your temporary reassignment, on an outside-agency loan, to the Corona Beach P.D. They've got a one-eighty-seven that could be up your alley—"

Eyes shut, she felt the hallway lurch, the floor shiver. No earthquake, only the trembling of her body.

"Where did you say I'm going?" she interrupted.

"Corona Beach." He heard the discomfort in her voice. "There a problem with that?"

She straightened her back, gripped the phone tighter. "No. No problem. Except ... I'm knee-deep in a nasty two-sixty-one, trying to work up the suspect's profile, and next week I'll be testifying in the Caravazzo trial—you know, that freak with the scissors—and there's a seminar coming up on June twentieth that I'm supposed to run ..."

She was fumbling for an excuse and being pretty obvious about it.

"Captain Lewis said you were keeping busy," Adams commented mildly, "but he felt the Corona Beach case should take priority over most of your other duties. It should be only a one- or two-day assignment. You'll be done in plenty of time to prepare your court testimony."

"Yes, sir." No point arguing; the decision had been made. "What *is* the Corona Beach case, exactly?"

"Sex killing of a prostitute. They're worried they may have a repeater on their hands."

"When do they want me?"

"Right away."

"I'm on lunch, getting in some work at a private range. Can I finish up?"

"Sure, take another twenty minutes. I didn't expect the authorization to come down this soon anyway. When you're done with target practice, you'll have to confer with Captain Lewis about temporarily transferring your caseload. And I know you'll want to tie up any loose ends with the other detectives at Homicide DHD. Just get over to the Corona Beach P.D. by midafternoon and nobody will squawk."

"Right, Commander." She was about to hang up when another question occurred to her. "Did Chief Mueller make the request personally?"

"Matter of fact, he did. You know him?"

"Slightly. I, uh, know a few people in the CBPD."
She was smiling when she said it, and she felt proud
of herself for being able to smile.

"So this is nice, then. A little reunion for you."

"Oh, yeah." The sound she made was close to
laughter. "We're one big happy family."

She returned to the shooting gallery. Mueller was
awfully damn insensitive to bring her in. That fat
chain-smoking bastard. Damn him to hell. Him and
the whole fat, spoiled city of Corona Beach.

She finished her second clip, squeezing off rounds
so fast the heat of the action scorched her fingertips.

Then she switched to her backup weapon, a snub-
nose airweight Smith. It was light enough to serve
as a good ankle gun, an option she rarely exercised
but liked to have available.

She loaded the revolver with range ammo, .38 Special rounds composed of sintered iron, manufactured
to disintegrate on impact, eliminating the danger of
ricochets. The cylinder held five rounds, and she
fired them all in rapid sequence, her feet planted in
the Weaver stance, both arms forward, muzzle
flashes reflecting on the polarized lenses of her goggles like distant lightning.

Donna did not think of Rood's apartment. She did
not think of anything. A humming heat filled her
mind. It could have been anger or fear.

Examining the target, she found that she'd scored
three hits, only one in the kill zone.

A poor performance—but then, her hands had
been shaking.

5

They rolled her out on a gurney and transferred her to a stainless-steel table in the autopsy room. She lay there naked, her slight body limp. Rigor had come on rapidly, as it often does in cases of violent death, and had passed with equal speed.

Around her drifted a cloud of murmurs, the voices of pathologists and their assistants working on other bodies at other tables. The air was tainted with evil smells. Logan drew slow breaths through his mouth, trying not to catch the scent of incipient decay.

The trip to the Forensic Science Center of the L.A. County Coroner's Department had left him unsettled and edgy. When he left Corona Beach at eleven, having snatched only four hours' sleep after completing his report, the morning fog typical of June had not yet completely burned off. He drove through a shimmering ground cover of mist, passing under the wheeling shadows of gulls. The drive had the magical quality of a dream, and briefly he felt refreshed and young, as if last night had never happened.

Then a blur of freeways rocketed him into downtown L.A., where the streets were narrow canyons walled in by looming high-rises, where trash swam in the gutters and derelicts lined the sidewalks. The filth and stink of the city slapped him out of his dreaming mood. He passed into reality like a baby pushed along the birth canal, ripped from tranquillity, thrust rudely into glare and noise and pain.

Now here he was among the dead, looking at the beaten girl without a name. He felt tired. There was a cold, greasy, sick feeling in his stomach, and he wished he could lie down.

Logan watched Martin Teeter turn on the tape recorder and adjust the microphone suspended over the girl. The pathologist was small, birdlike, and a whistler. Word was that his childhood nickname had been Tweeter; his colleagues used the name behind his back.

Teeter described the subject's physical characteristics in his brisk, chirpy voice. Race: Caucasian. Sex: female. Age: fifteen to seventeen. Weight: 102 pounds. Height: sixty-two inches. A transcription of his remarks would become part of the autopsy report.

X-rays were taken. They showed multiple skull and sinus fractures, a broken clavicle, a cracked rib, and a hairline fracture of the radius of the right arm.

Then Teeter examined her body, describing her external injuries one by one.

Bruises mottled her torso, arms, and blood-crusted face. Her left side was darkly livid, settled blood discoloring her skin like a port-wine stain.

A small hole in her abdomen, circled in ink, marked an incision made by the coroner's investigator at the crime scene. The cut had permitted the insertion of a thermometer in the upper quadrant of the liver; the temperature reading had been 92.4. Body temperature typically drops one degree per hour after death, but for a thin victim, scantily clad, left exposed to cool night air, a faster rate of cooling is possible.

Taking rigor, livor, and lividity into account, the

investigator had estimated the time of death as between nine and midnight.

Ink smudged the girl's fingertips and palms and the soles of her feet; Barnes had printed her earlier that day. The inked prints had come out fine, but the search for latents on her body had proved frustrating. Barnes had swabbed her skin with a solution of alcohol, benzidine, and hydrogen peroxide, then brushed it with powder. Her eyelids had yielded nothing; the same was true of her buttocks and back. On her left breast he had found three smooth, featureless partials.

"Gloves," Barnes had reported to Logan by phone before heading home. "Loverboy wore gloves. Gave her tit a squeeze after he finished pounding."

Now gloved hands were again moving over her body. Teeter's hands, measuring, probing.

"Oblong antemortem contusion ten centimeters in length on the right forearm above the elbow. Rectangular antemortem contusion seven centimeters in length on the posterior aspect of the right shoulder . . ."

"Blunt instrument do the damage?" Logan asked.

"Yes. Something long and probably cylindrical—a baseball bat or tire iron, probably."

The pathologist took note of various scrapes and minor cuts on the girl's arms and thighs. "It appears she was dragged on her back or her side, over rough ground, possibly through brambles or sharp debris."

Logan nodded. "Her clothes were smeared with dirt, and our forensics expert found grass stains on the back of her blouse." Barnes, assisted by a morgue attendant, had stripped the body and taken the skirt and torn blouse as evidence.

"It fits," Teeter said. "The murder scene was probably a park, a vacant lot, something like that."

He turned his attention to her delicate hands, peering at them through a magnifying lens. The dark red crescents of fingernail marks on her palms were evident. Barnes had scraped and clipped her nails before printing her.

"Antemortem abrasions on both capri. Indications of histaminic reaction." Teeter looked at Logan. "Her wrists were bound."

"With rope?"

"I don't think so. Rope causes more of a friction burn. And when rope is used, the hands are usually tied together in such a way that the skin is chafed only in certain areas. For instance, you'll see abrasions on the back of each wrist, but not the front—or vice versa. Here the abrasions go all the way around each carpus, three-hundred-sixty degrees. Her hands were moving independently of each other, and she was turning them every which way."

"Cuffs," Logan said.

"Yes, that's what I was thinking. Better check your colleagues, make sure no one's missing a pair, ha ha."

Logan didn't laugh.

Teeter snapped close-ups of the abrasions, then drew blood and, with tweezers, plucked a few pubic hairs. While an attendant labeled the samples, the pathologist spread the girl's labia and beamed a miniature flashlight between her legs.

"Vagina is badly bruised. Clear indication of penile penetration."

"Was she alive when he raped her?"

"Can't tell by looking. Serotonin tests on the bruises ought to give us a better idea."

Teeter took vaginal, anal, and oral swabs. He scraped dried blood from her nostrils, then sketched her injuries onto an outline diagram. His pencil scratched busily.

Logan studied the corpse. He lowered his head to smell the dead girl's hair. Picked up the magnifying glass and stared closely at the spaces between her toes.

"She wasn't homeless," he said. "She had shelter, with access to a bath or shower. Her hair is clean, and it still carries the scent of shampoo. She'd been on the beach recently, subsequent to the last time she bathed; there's sand between her toes."

"Not dirt, like on her clothes?"

"No, this is sand. Look for yourself."

Teeter examined her feet. "You're right. Of course, she might have lived on the beach and used the public showers."

"Her skin is too pale. No suntan. A hotel near the beach is more probable."

"Okay, I'm convinced. Now, can I open her up?"

Logan didn't even flinch when Teeter made the coronal mastoid incision, bisecting the scalp. The skin of the girl's face loosened, and Teeter gently pulled it down, exposing the pink shock of her skull. Her face was a wrinkled skin flap, a discarded rubber mask.

Logan thought about masks. Everybody wore one. The closed, unreadable expression that concealed his churning thoughts—it was a mask, and if he were to pull it down now, what would the pathologist see and how would he describe it to the whirring tape recorder?

The girl's nasal cavities were sealed with bone splinters and plugs of dried blood. There were zigzag cracks in the maxilla, the right zygomatic arch, the nasal bone, the left and right sphenoids, and the frontal bone.

"He beat her unconscious," Teeter said to Logan after recording his more technical remarks. "Then he beat her to death. Then he went on beating her after she was dead—probably for several minutes." Disgust choked his voice. "She couldn't even feel anything by that point, but he kept on trying to torture her."

"That's how rage is." Logan's own voice was calm, thoughtful. "You get so furious you have to keep hurting and hurting—even when you're not hurting anybody anymore, except yourself."

Teeter cocked his head at a quizzical angle, a jay on a windowsill. "You know all about that kind of rage, don't you, Detective?"

"I've had a few bad nights," Logan said evenly.

Teeter nodded and looked away. "Well, whoever did this was having a bad night too."

He sawed off the top of the skull and cut loose the brain. The left temporal lobe was swollen and dark with extravasated blood. "Here's what killed her. Subdural hematoma, intracerebral hemorrhage."

The chest cut followed. The smell of hydrogen sulfide rose from the thoracic cavity.

"Fragment of the fifth rib punctured the left lung and the left ventricle of the heart." Teeter drew liquid from the lung, cut open the pleural membrane. "Not much blood inside," he told Logan. "Her heart was barely pumping by then."

Organs came out, were drained of fluid samples, sectioned, placed in jars. The left kidney was badly bruised, as was the right adrenal gland.

"Food in her stomach," Teeter reported.

"Then her last meal couldn't have been more than three or four hours prior to death."

"Probably closer to one or two hours. The stomach contents are only partially disgested."

"Can you identify what she ate?"

"Bread, cheese, something red with chunks in it— spaghetti sauce, I guess—and, uh, mushrooms . . ."

"Pizza," Logan said. "Mushroom pizza."

"Must be. I think I see sausage too."

Teeter finished the internal examination, summarized his findings, and closed up the body. The attendant took it away, the scuffing of his rubber-soled antistatic shoes competing with the squeak of gurney wheels.

"I don't usually let the job get to me," Teeter said wearily, "but this was an ugly one. Christ Almighty, what kind of guy are we dealing with here?"

Logan thought that was a good question. He had wondered about it too. Driving to the autopsy in the bright June sunshine, he had searched for the answer by peering into the darkest parts of himself.

"Someone who doesn't give a damn anymore," he said quietly. "Someone who's just had enough."

6

"You're late."

Logan shut the conference-room door. He gave Mueller a hard stare.

"Autopsy ran long," he answered, his tone empty of apology.

Mueller caught the stare and the tone. He mashed out his cigarette. "Let's get started."

The chief was seated at the head of a long mahogany table, flanked by six men and two women. To his right were the deputy chief, the patrol commander, the public information officer, and the city attorney. Opposite them were the department's two Narcotics-Vice detectives, one Juvenile detective, and Ed Barnes.

Logan took the seat next to Barnes. He was the odd man out; the chair facing him was empty.

Barnes greeted him with a curt but not unfriendly nod and a momentary flicker of expression in his eyes. Logan could not interpret what he read there. Wariness? Sympathy? A silent warning?

Then Mueller was speaking again. "Since you attended the postmortem, Detective Logan, perhaps you'd care to fill us in."

Perhaps you'd care to kiss my ass, Logan thought edgily.

He and Mueller had been friendly once, had even socialized now and then at backyard barbecues. Now they were in a state of hostility just short of open warfare. The chief was angry at Logan for letting himself go—angry and also grieved, his face reflecting the stern sorrow of a parent disappointed by a favorite child. And Logan was angry at Mueller for not understanding, for expecting him to bear up manfully under his load of suffering, for demanding more of him than anyone had a right to ask.

He knew Mueller had stopped respecting him months ago and saw him now as a bad cop, a stumblebum, an alkie. Logan in turn viewed Mueller as old and befuddled and out of touch, a figurehead holding on to his job through sheer inertia and a few well-massaged political connections. Neither man worked very hard to conceal his contempt for the other.

Flipping open his steno pad, Logan summarized Teeter's findings.

"Anything else?" Mueller asked when Logan looked up from his notes.

Logan considered mentioning his beach-hotel hypothesis, decided against it. He could check it out on his own.

"Only that I sent Ronni to the morgue to work up a facial-reconstruction sketch," he said. Veronica Broderick was a forensic artist in Barnes's lab. "She'll fax it to us as soon as she's done."

"Why not just use a retouched photo?" That was Linda Wells, who handled PR.

"You haven't seen the girl," Mike Garfield, the city attorney, told her gently. Garfield had arrived at the crime scene shortly after the coroner's investigator. "She doesn't look much like herself anymore."

"Make copies of the fax for Reynolds and Hill," Mueller said. "They'll distribute them on the street."

Logan nodded. "I'll fax it to the LAPD too. There was a store label on her blouse marked Hollywood

Hot. According to L.A. Information, there's a store by that name on Santa Monica Boulevard near Western. Somebody from the Hollywood division has to run over there and see if the sketch rings a bell."

"Sounds good, do it," Mueller said brusquely.

He knew Logan would do it even without authorization. In principle, Mueller supervised the nine-person detective division, playing the role of a detective captain in a larger department. In practice, most of the detectives followed their own leads. The hands-off approach worked most of the time, when the caseload was light, the crimes relatively minor. But with this one . . .

"I'll run a search on her prints," Barnes was saying. "If she'd been a working girl for long, she'll probably show up in the JDS." The Justice Data System, created by the Sheriff's Department, maintained records of all adults and juveniles arrested in the country. "If that doesn't pan out, I can ask Santa Monica to run a statewide search on CAL I.D."

"Or we can try the FBI," Jodi Carlyle, the Juvenile officer, suggested. "The Identification Division has a print file for missing persons. Of course that'll work only if she's a runaway and has been printed. And if anybody ever bothered to report her as missing." Lots of times nobody did.

"All right, one of those approaches ought to get us the victim's I.D." Mueller chewed a thumbnail, an unconscious habit when he didn't have a cigarette in his mouth. "How about the killer? Any ideas?"

The deputy chief, a thin, whippet-faced man named Hardy, spoke up. "CCAP."

Mueller scowled. "Refresh my memory on that particular acronym."

"Career Criminal Apprehension Project. It's an LAPD database of paroled felons; they use it for MO runs."

The chief nodded approval of the idea, and Hardy looked pleased.

"We've got to call the other departments in the area too," Reynolds of Narcotics-Vice said. "I know they haven't got anything this bad or we would have heard about it, but they may have an unsolved rape or assault with some similarities."

"Who's available for that detail?" Mueller asked.

"Give it to Grange," Hill, the other Narcotics-Vice man, suggested. "He's good on the phone. Used to be a telemarketer."

"No shit?" Reynolds was surprised.

"Yeah, down in San Diego. Hawked gold coins to investors back in '81. Then the precious-metals market tanked, and he wound up being a cop."

"This is all very interesting," Mueller observed with a nice note of sarcasm, "but shut up about Grange already." He turned to Captain Osmond, commander of the thirty-two-officer patrol division. "John, I want your people out there tonight rounding up every known sex-crime offender in town."

Osmond pursed his lips. "You mean Gavins, Wilcox, Bobby Allen? Losers like that?"

"Right. All the usual assholes. Pull 'em in, and we'll grill 'em hard."

"None of them did it," Logan said calmly.

Mueller regarded him with irritation. "No? Why the hell not?"

"Whoever killed this girl was smart enough to wear gloves and move the body. He left no prints and gave us no murder site to examine, which means almost no physical evidence to work with. The excons you're talking about are all idiots. They invariably leave witnesses or living victims or obvious clues. Take Bobby Allen. He rapes his girlfriend and beats the hell out of her, then goes home for a hot shower. He's surprised when the cops show up. It's never occurred to him that his girlfriend would have him arrested."

"So maybe he wised up while he did his time in Chino," Hardy said, puppy-eager to defend the chief's plan.

"Not this much."

"Haul them in anyway," Mueller ordered Osmond. "We're covering all the bases. Speaking of which, there's a chance the guy will return to the dump site. I want a patrol unit cruising the area at regular intervals—every fifteen minutes at least."

"I'll pass the word to the watch commanders," Osmond said.

Logan shrugged. "Another waste of time. He won't go back. If he wants to relive the killing, he'll go to the scene of the murder. And we don't know where that is."

Mueller glared at him. "Maybe he'll revisit both places."

"No. He'll play it cautious and smart. He'll stay clear of Third and Bay."

"How can you be sure?" the chief demanded.

Logan flashed a chilly smile. "Because that's what I'd do."

"We need to put out a statement," Linda Wells said after a brief, crackling silence. "Klein is driving me crazy with calls."

Mueller considered the problem. "List the victim's descriptors, but be vague on the condition of the body."

"Can I say she was beaten?"

"With a blunt instrument, uh-huh. And tell them she was sexually molested. Include Ronni's sketch, if you get it in time, and a request for assistance." Mueller glanced at Osmond. "Have we narrowed the time frame?"

"Somewhat. A unit patrolled Bay Street at approximately twenty-three hundred hours and saw nothing unusual."

"So she was dumped between roughly eleven and one-thirty A.M." Mueller returned his attention to Wells. "Ask anyone who was near the location during that time period to contact us. Give out the switchboard number."

"Klein's been asking if we think he could strike again."

"No comment on that. The killer's future actions are pure speculation. For all we know, he's a drifter who's already crossed the Arizona border. Or maybe he's swinging from a ceiling beam right now. These fruitcakes terminate themselves pretty often."

"Not often enough," Reynolds groused.

"No speculation," Mueller repeated to Wells. "No gory details. No scare-mongering."

"Gotcha," Wells said.

"And show me the statement before you release it."

"Chief, you're not going to rewrite me again?"

"I'm a frustrated editor. Sue me." Mueller's gaze ticked toward Logan, then slid away. "Now there's one other . . . um . . . sensitive matter that I need to bring up. Owing to the sensational nature of this case, and in consideration of our limited departmental resources, I've felt the need to go outside the usual channels. . . ."

Logan wondered what the hell he was talking about. Outside the usual channels? He hadn't called in a psychic, had he? If so, it was proof the old man was sliding into senility like a mammoth into a tar pit.

"Admittedly the circumstances may create something of a personal strain, but we're all adults here." Mueller lit another cigarette. "The bottom line—"

A knock on the door.

Mueller looked at Logan again. Hesitated.

"Come in," he called.

The door swung open. Logan turned in his chair, and suddenly there was a noise in his head, the conch-shell roar of rushing blood.

"Sorry to interrupt," Donna Wildman said. "I just arrived, and the desk sergeant told me to barge right in."

"That's perfectly all right, Detective," Mueller said from far away. "I think you know most of these people."

Logan put his hands in his lap, out of sight, and made them fists.

She surveyed the table. "Sure do. John, Linda, how are you? Hi, Jodi, Frank. Ed ..." Her gaze stopped on Logan. "Hello, Mark."

"Donna." The word scraped his throat raw.

"I don't believe we've met." Garfield offered his hand. "Michael Garfield, city attorney."

"Donna Wildman. LAPD Headquarters Bureau, Homicide Special Section." Her attaché case popped open with two brisk snaps. "I don't know if Chief Mueller has explained why I'm here."

"I was just getting to it," Mueller said.

"Well"—she took the chair opposite Logan—"I'm on an outside-agency loan for the purpose of preparing a personality profile of your killer."

"Detective Wildman is a graduate of the NCAVC Police Fellowship program," Mueller said. "She's had experience tracking sexually motivated murderers."

Garfield blinked recognition. "Oh, right. You were on the Gryphon task force, weren't you?"

"That was before I went through the training program. Actually, the Gryphon case was what got me interested in profiling. The FBI's behavioral analysis dovetailed pretty closely with Franklin Rood's personality."

"Didn't help Delgado catch him, though," Logan said. His mouth was tight.

She met his eyes. "Different cases break different ways. Sometimes it's physical evidence. Sometimes profiling. Other times, who knows? Luck, intuition, serendipity . . ."

"Things just work out."

"Yes."

"Or they don't."

"That's right."

"And either way, it's no one's fault. Is that it?"

"Hold on a minute." Garfield was irritated. "I'd like to think we can all work together on this case. Finding fault isn't going to get us anywhere—"

"We weren't discussing the case, Mr. Garfield," Wildman said quietly.

The attorney blinked, then understood. His voice was very small. "Oh."

"Mike moved here a few months ago from Orange County," Barnes told Wildman. "We hired him to replace Paul Stewart. Paul died, you know. Heart attack."

"I heard."

"Anyway, he's new to Peyton Place. Hasn't had time to catch up on all the plot threads."

Garfield spread his hands, embarrassed. "I wish somebody had told me."

"Yeah," Logan said. "Wish they'd told me too."

He got up abruptly. His head pounded. Red haze misted the room.

"But I guess it was a lot more entertaining this way."

The door slammed hard on his way out. He heard it rattling in its frame as he walked blindly down the hall.

7

The feel of her skin against his. The rounded softness of her breasts and the hard stops of her nipples. The wiry strength in her legs, straddling him. The tendons of her neck drawing taut as she threw her head back with a hiss of violent pleasure.

Logan wanted to think about something else—anything else—as he drove aimlessly through town, but memories of Donna Wildman, of her body, kept boring into him like an auger's ruthless bit.

Donna bending over the nightstand brushing her hair, clothed in one of his Arrow shirts and nothing else, her white buttocks exposed and, in the crease of her legs, the fuzzed shadow of her sex.

Donna rolling with him on the bed, her hands in his hair, her breath on his neck, her soft laughter playing in airy counterpoint to the complaints of the mattress springs.

Donna taking him into her mouth while he gazed down at her, hypnotized by the sleek lines of her shoulders, the lean, flexing muscles of her back, the smoke-and-chestnut tangle of her hair.

For a long time he circled Corona Beach, trying to shake free of the hurtful past. Somewhere he stopped to buy a pint of brandy. He took a few swigs and let the slow burn in his throat travel through his body and calm his mind.

After a while desire faded, overtaken by hate.

It was always this way. First he would remember how good she had been for him, how much he had needed her. Then he would remember her grotesque violation of his trust.

Her betrayal wouldn't have hurt as much as it had, wouldn't have kicked the props out from under him and dropped him to his knees, if he hadn't been so vulnerable. But Donna was the second woman he had lost.

First came Sharon.

Sharon . . . and little Mark.

No.

Don't think of them.

Damn it, don't.

He couldn't stop himself. Some cold finger turned to that page of his life and prodded him to look.

He remembered the summer night, three years ago, when he went for a solitary walk on a stretch of beach beyond the pier. Ropes of heavy cumulus, silvered with moonlight, were strung across the vast pinwheels of the constellations. The surf beat at the shore, doing its grim work, wearing down the land.

His son would be born in ten weeks. He marveled at that fact. His hands made unconscious fondling gestures as he walked, as if the infant boy were already squirming before him, gurgling at his touch.

He tried to imagine how many fathers throughout history had pondered the gift of a child. Turning, he looked at the line of footprints that marked his paces, ink-spot wells standing out like moon craters against the bleached sand, and he thought of the unbroken line of generations behind him, each one a separate step along a continuing journey.

Fathers and sons, the seed endlessly passed on, humanity forever renewed. In that sequence of giving and receiving life, he thought he saw a clue to the meaning of existence. He reached for words to name it, straining, failing, like a child standing on tiptoe to touch the sky.

When he returned home, Sharon smiled and said he looked stoned. "Haven't been smoking any illegal substances, have you?" she teased.

He only kissed her and kissed her and lay his head on her round belly, listening to the life within. After a long time she heard him weeping without sobs, and she made no more jokes, just held him and rocked him in her arms.

A week later she was dead, her beautiful face crushed like paper, the baby a stillborn obscenity.

The first report reached him over Dispatch 1, on a Tuesday afternoon, while he was working. An auto accident on Corona Beach Boulevard. One fatality: female Caucasian, mid-twenties. The radio chatter included no mention of the miscarriage, and he didn't make the connection with Sharon until the RTO recited the license number.

He drove to the accident scene in a groggy haze. Mueller tried to keep him away from the wreckage, tried to stop him from seeing her—folded between the driver's seat and the dashboard, her face a flattened mask, flies droning while the useless paramedics tried to brush them away. Logan insisted on seeing for himself. The bloody thing between her legs made him sick and dizzy.

Witnesses explained what had happened. Crossing the intersection of Corona Beach Boulevard and Pier Avenue, Sharon's car had been blindsided by a second vehicle, a rusted-out Firebird that had run the stoplight. The driver, Cory MacMillan, was a kid of high-school age. He and his three passengers, none over eighteen, had received only minor injuries.

Logan met Cory MacMillan the next day, when the boy was arraigned on charges of reckless driving and vehicular manslaughter. He was blond and tan, proud of his good looks, quick with a smile of practiced cockiness. His companions in the car had already told police that Cory had been showing off, driving too fast, ignoring stop signs, laughing at their terror. "Ride of death!" he kept shouting as the summer air lashed at his long uncombed hair through the open windows. "You're on the fucking ride of death!"

In the courtroom, Cory apologized to Logan for having killed his wife and unborn child. "Sorry, man," he said with a little shrug and a helpless open-palmed gesture, as if it were just one of those things. Logan turned away without speaking, his mouth a white line.

The trial began three months later and lasted only two days, ending in verdicts of guilty on both counts. In handing down sentence, the judge showed leniency in consideration of the defendant's age, his previously clean record, and his carefully rehearsed remorse. Cory MacMillan was sentenced to four years in a correctional institution. Good behavior secured his release on parole within fourteen months.

For two years Logan didn't date at all. Going through Sharon's things, he found a journal she had kept intermittently since college. He spent long nights reading the entries, learning her secrets, discovering hidden corners of her that he had never known in life. The journals kept Sharon alive for him, held him back from thoughts of suicide. While he read it, he was with her, as intimately as when they had lain together.

There were days when he drove to the nearby cemetery where she and little Mark were buried. In solitude he communed with them, wishing he believed they could hear his whispered prayers.

Finally he put the journal away, stopped visiting the graves. Time to get on with life. Not long afterward he met Donna, braved a new start. He dared to fall in love again.

And she betrayed him, humiliated him, exploited his trust, squandered his love.

Bitch.

Cheating, faithless bitch.

Their affair lasted seven months. Its termination was as quick and final as the slam of a door.

He refused to discuss things with her, to hear her explanations, to listen to more lies. He only wanted it to be over, so that he could be alone with his pain and never have to see her again.

But now, goddamn it, she was back.

8

Images of the dead girl flickered in her thoughts as Donna Wildman drove to the Corona Beach Pier.

She had looked over the crime-scene photos while Barnes briefed her on the case. Ed had said nothing personal to her, had not even acknowledged their former friendship. His curt professionalism signaled resentment and dislike. Loyalty to Mark had always made him unsympathetic to her side of the story.

She hadn't seen Ed since Marjorie's funeral in March. His deterioration shocked her. At fifty-five, he was tired and bitter and old. Energy entered him only when he spoke about the investigation. He still loved a challenge, apparently, and a stranger homicide was the most difficult crime to solve.

After the briefing, she'd asked where she could find Mark.

"How would I know?"

"Come on, Ed. He's your friend."

"The pier," he'd answered finally, cleaning his bifocals so he wouldn't have to look at her. "He goes there sometimes."

She parked at the curb, then walked onto the pier, her shoes clacking on the boards. Past the rusted railings lay the wide, smooth beach, speckled with towels and folding chairs and people who had no work to go to on a weekday afternoon. To the north and south, the coastal mountains cupping the bay rose up like walls of gray smoke, tremulous with distance, blurred by ripples of heat. The blue-green water was an expanse of winking spangles and soft shadows, massaged by currents, pulsing gently like a vast heart.

She found Logan at the far end of the pier. He was seated on a bench, looking toward the white haze of the horizon, a bottle in his hand.

"Mind if I join you?"

He didn't answer, just tipped the bottle to his mouth. She had thought he was drinking beer, but up close she saw that it was brandy.

She sat on the bench also. For a few minutes there was silence between them, tense and painful.

She found herself studying his face. It was the same face she remembered, all sharp angles and hard edges. His brown hair was longer now, testing departmental limits; it rippled in the salted wind. There was a squint in his eyes that hadn't been there before, and a tightness to his mouth that spoke of pain. Stubble dusted his cheeks; his jacket and pants were rumpled, his tie spotted with coffee. He had let himself go.

She turned her head, staring at the scalloped surface of the bay. A gull dipped and rose, dipped and rose. riding the chancy air currents like a kite.

"Relaxing here," she said.

"That's not why I come."

She was glad he'd spoken. "Why, then?"

"To be alone."

She cast a careless hand at some kids eating hot dogs at a lunch stand, fishermen with lines in the water, a couple posing for a photo snapped by a helpful stranger. "Plenty of people around."

"Nobody who knows me."

"In that case, you're still alone. Because I don't know you, Mark. I'm not sure I ever have."

He snorted in dismissal. "Mueller send you to find me?"

"I came on my own. We've got to work together."

"So let's work. What do you need?"

"Details of the crime scene, the body."

"Barnes can give you that."

"He already did. But I want it from you."

"All the details are in my report. And my notes." He pulled a steno pad from his jacket and tossed it in her lap. *"Adios."*

She didn't pick up the pad. "That's not what I meant. I want to hear your impressions."

"I do a pretty good Jack Nicholson."

"So I noticed."

That almost made him smile. "Quick. Pretty damn quick, Wildman."

She had always liked it when he called her by her last name. In bed sometimes it had been *Miss* Wildman, tender and teasing, or *Detective* Wildman, a blunt command. At other times, just Donna, over and over, his fingers in her hair, his breath on her neck, "Donna, Donna, Donna . . ."

"All right." He stood up. "Ask me some questions and I'll tell you what I know."

Without waiting for a reply, he sauntered away. She followed, angry at him for the contempt he projected, angry at herself for letting him get to her.

"Let's begin with the victim," she said, her voice brisk, professional. "I understand you think she was a prostitute."

"That's our working hypothesis." The last word came out slightly slurred. "Nobody on the force recognizes her, but her style of dress suggests a street-walker or a call girl."

"Which do you think she was?"

"Street whore."

"Why?"

"She had razor tips. Call girls generally don't need those. They deal with a higher quality clientele: vacationing businessmen, bored suburbanites. Not violent types."

They passed a ragged man strumming a guitar and singing about hard times. Coins and crumpled bills littered his open guitar case.

"Okay, I'll buy that," Donna said. "Still, we can't be certain she was killed by a john. Suppose it was her pimp."

"A pimp wouldn't leave the body in the street. He'd hide it, bury it, cut it up and put the pieces in garbage bags."

"Because he'd figure he's the obvious suspect. But what if he's trying to throw us off by making it look like a random homicide?"

"Too complicated. These guys don't think that way."

Logan leaned on the railing under a salt-silvered sign: NO OVERHAND CASTING. Waves slopped against the pilings, the creaming surf flecked with kelp.

"Besides," he added, "if a pimp did kill her, all he'd have to do is dispose of the body secretly, and her disappearance would never even be reported. Nobody keeps track of hookers."

"Point taken. So we can assume the suspect approached her as a customer. Brought along handcuffs and gloves. The handcuffs might be part of some S-and-M ritual, but the gloves indicate premeditation; nobody wears gloves in L.A. this time of year."

A fisherman reeled in his line with a whirring chatter of gears. Logan moved on, Donna with him.

"If he approached her as a john," she added, "he must have at least rudimentary social skills."

"Which are generally characteristic of the organized nonsocial type. Most disorganized asocials are schizophrenics, incapable of verbal manipulation. Correct?"

Donna smiled. "You heard that at the seminar."

"Where else?"

"I'm surprised you remember it."

"I remember everything about that day, Donna. Every detail."

They had met a year ago at a daylong seminar in criminal profiling offered by the LAPD to detectives from neighboring departments. Donna had hosted the conference, a duty expected of officers who'd completed the NCAVC Police Fellowship program.

Afterward she and Mark had gone to a café and talked for hours. Two nights later, on their third date, they had made love for the first time. Briefly Donna's mind wandered; she smiled at memories of intimacy.

The smell of fish, pungent and close, reached her through the doorway of a seafood restaurant and pulled her back.

"He cleaned out her pockets also," she said. "And dumped the body. An organized killer would do those things; the disorganized individual would flee the murder site in a panic."

Criminal profiling distinguished between organized and disorganized killers on the basis of MO. Those who killed on impulse, in a frenzy, were the disorganized asocials. The organized nonsocial, a rarer type, was methodical and cautious, and for those reasons even more difficult to apprehend.

"So we've accomplished step one," Logan said. "We can classify him."

Donna hesitated. "Well . . . almost."

Logan waited, knowing she had more to say.

"What bothers me is the beating the girl took. So . . . excessive. Crazed." Donna gazed up at the spoked silhouette of the Ferris wheel, inactive now, waiting for night and crowds. "The classic organized type can be savage with the body, but it's an orderly, controlled brand of savagery. Not like this. This man ... he was out of control. For some period of time, he lost his grip. Pounded her and pounded and pounded ..."

She shook her head to free herself from the lurid images chasing the thoughts in her mind.

"That type of frenzied violence doesn't fit the pattern," she added softly.

"He's a mixed type, then. Features elements of both. That's possible, isn't it?"

"Oh, yes. Profiling isn't an exact science. An offender with mixed characteristics is relatively rare, at least based on what we know—but certainly possible." She shrugged. "It will complicate the profile, that's all."

"Well, you don't shrink from challenges."

The pleasure she took in the offhand compliment surprised her.

"There's another aspect of the case that may be significant," she said as they walked on. "He left the girl at Third and Bay. Pretty good place to dump a body at night. No witnesses likely to be around. Dead-end street; no traffic. Sort of an out-of-the-way spot—"

"He's a local," Logan cut in, anticipating her conclusion. "Knows the town."

It was satisfying to share a thought with him again. "Right. Even so, you'd think he would have left her in a vacant lot or under the pier. Someplace where she might not be found for days."

"But he didn't. He left her out in public."

"Which means?"

He cocked an eyebrow. "You're the goddamn profiler." But he answered the question anyway: "He's smart, but nervy. He knew he had to transport the body from the murder site to minimize the physical evidence, but he didn't want to cover up his handi-work for long, much less let it rot in a ditch."

Logan drained his bottle and flipped it into a trash can. For a man who had consumed a pint of brandy, he was disturbingly lucid. Donna knew he'd been drinking too much since the end of their affair; on several nights he'd called her, incoherent and abusive. But she hadn't thought he'd been drinking every night. Now she wondered.

"He wanted publicity, news coverage," she said. "Is that what you're suggesting?"

"The organized killer usually seeks notoriety. He keeps scrapbooks of newspaper clippings about himself—or videotapes of TV news reports, as in the case of your friend Rood."

She smiled. "You really are knowledgeable on this subject."

When he turned to her, there was sadness in his glance, and pain. "I learned it all from you," he said simply.

"Thanks." She looked away, feeling heat in her face; she hadn't expected kindness from him, and it was hard to take.

"Now," he said more sharply, "let's cut the text-book theorizing. Give me *your* impressions."

An airliner took flight out of LAX a mile north, the thunder of its engines painful like an earache. Donna waited for it to roar past, its outline ghosting into a band of high cirrus.

"I understand he raped her?" she asked thoughtfully.

"Yes."

"While she was alive, or . . . ?"

"We don't know yet."

"Either way, it shows he wasn't feeling rushed or panicky. He took the time to do what he wanted once he had her under control. That suggests a mature individual, not a kid. Possibly a man in his thirties or early forties."

"What else?"

"He killed her at night, after nine. Could be a night owl. Has a night job or hangs out at bars, something like that. He may be married or living with a partner, but given his hatred of women, I'd say it's more likely he's had a failed relationship and lives alone."

"Get inside his head."

"He's fantasized the crime, rehearsed it mentally, for a long time—months or years. The way he beat her, obliterating her face, suggests he personalized his victim. Perhaps he saw her as a particular woman from his past. Do you think she was attractive?"

"Hard to tell. I'd guess so."

"Tall?"

"Only five-two."

"My height," Donna said. "Brown hair and eyes too. Like me . . ."

"Hey, look what we have here."

Logan pointed to a circular pavilion near the entrance to the amusement arcade. Broad windows framed a double procession of motionless horses, multicolored like gum balls, blurred by old glass.

"The carousel." Donna smiled. On July Fourth last year, they had ridden those horses like carefree children while fireworks whizzed and bloomed in the night sky. "Too bad it's not open."

"It's only in use on weekends and holidays. I think I know a way inside, though. Around back."

The rear door was unlocked. Logan ushered her into the cavernous dimness. Their footsteps cracked hollowly on lustrous hardwood. They circled the carousel, the pale glow of the windows limning their figures, long shadows fanning out before them. In the shifting light, the carved stallions seemed to caper and prance.

"Didn't mean to interrupt your analysis," Logan said. There was no emotion in his voice. If being here revived good memories, he wouldn't show it. "Go on."

She had lost track of her thoughts. It took her a moment to refocus on the case.

"Okay, let's see. Since he transported the body, we know he had access to a vehicle. The fact that he emptied her pockets may suggest he took some personal items as souvenirs. He probably comes from a broken home or an abusive family; most organized nonsocials do. He's of above-average intelligence, may hold a skilled job, probably has a high birth-order status—first- or second-born son."

The horses watched her, their huge heads grotesque in the uncertain light.

"You're still going by the book, Detective," Logan said. "What does your intuition say?"

"Feminine intuition?"

"Cop's intuition."

She did have one idea, wasn't sure she wanted to share it. Oh, what the hell. "I think he was posing as a cop."

Logan put his hand on a wooden saddle, gripped it tight. He stared at her. "What?"

"It would be the easiest way to get her into cuffs."

"There are lots of ways for a trick to handcuff a whore. You must have more to go on that that."

"Just little things. Like the way he dumped her body in plain sight—to get press coverage, you said. I'm not so sure. If you want media attention, you drop the body outside KABC or hang it from the HOLLYWOOD sign. Or you go after middle-class victims the way Rood did. Killing a hooker and leaving her on a dead-end street in Corona Beach won't get anyone interested except the local papers."

"So what *was* the purpose of dumping her there?"

"To involve the police as soon as possible. The Corona Beach police."

"He wants to follow the investigation up close?"

She nodded. "He's interested in the police. Maybe has fantasies of being a cop. Hell, he might have applied for a job. I'd like to go through your personnel files, see if any rejected applicants fit the profile."

"Sounds like a long shot."

"Probably is. Still, I wonder ... Were her hands cuffed behind her or in front?"

"Does it matter?"

"If she was cuffed behind her back, she would've had fewer options. Couldn't have used her razor tips. A would-be cop is likely to know that."

Logan opened the cuff case on his belt and removed a pair of handcuffs. "Hold out your hands."

"You arresting me?"

"I'm trying to answer your question."

She extended her hands in front of her. Logan snapped on the cuffs.

"Hope you've got the key to those things," she said.

"I do. Twist and tug like you're panicky and trying to get loose." Logan watched her. "Okay, you're chafing the back and sides of each wrist, but not the front."

"That's because it's awkward to hold your hands in the palms-out position and try to pull them apart. It's an unnatural motion."

"Right." He unlocked one cuff. "Turn around, put your hands behind your back." The cuff clicked shut. She fought to free herself again. "In that position, you tend to rotate your wrists more. Can you feel that?"

"Yes. I can pull every which way. So I'm abrading every part of the wrist, front and back."

"That's the pattern we saw at the autopsy. The

abrasions were evenly distributed around each carpus."

"So he did secure her hands behind her back. That supports what I'm saying. Now uncuff me, will you?"

A tick of silence. "I don't know if I should. I like seeing you helpless. It's a new experience for me."

She turned to face him, manacled hands squirming. His gray eyes glinted with mockery or malice. The smell of brandy was strong on his breath.

Abruptly she became aware that she was alone with him. They had entered via the rear door; nobody had seen them come in. He was hostile toward her, and he'd had too much to drink.

"Hey," she said nervously, "quit weirding me out. Get these goddamn things off me."

He smiled. "Scared of me, Donna?"

She thought of her Beretta, snugged in its pancake holster under her left arm. Useless now.

"I said, are you scared?"

She wasn't sure how to answer. Deny it, and risk making him angry? Admit it, and encourage him to string out whatever sick joke he was playing?

She gambled on the truth. "Sure I am. You're being bizarre, Mark. And my wrists are starting to hurt."

He absorbed her answer with no change of expression. "Turn around."

She hesitated, then showed her back to him. Tensed her body for quick defensive moves if he got rough. Waited, heart pounding hard at her temples.

Then the turn of a key—click—again—and her hands were free.

She massaged her sore wrists. "What the hell was that about?"

"I wanted to see you sweat."

"You hate me that much?"

He put the cuffs back in their case. "I hate you as much as I used to love you. That's a lot, Donna."

She watched him walk away. At the door he stopped.

"You still carrying, even when you're off duty?"

She touched her armpit holster. "Sure."

"Keep doing that." He turned to go.

"Why the advice?"

His voice bounced echoes off the curved walls. "If this nut is as interested in police work as you say, he'll know what profiling means. And you can bet he'll find out you're working the case before long. Mueller's certain to publicize it. Bringing you in was probably a PR stunt anyway."

She let the insult pass. "So?"

"So the guy may not like the idea of you climbing inside his skull and dissecting what's in there." He gave her a hard stare. "I wouldn't."

The door boomed shut behind him. Donna lowered her head, studying her red wrists. Her body trembled with aftershocks of nervous tension.

She wondered if Mark could be right about the prospect of danger, or if that was only wishful thinking on his part.

Would he like to see me become a target? Even see me killed? Is he hoping for that? Does his hate run that deep?

The question frightened her, because she had no answers.

9

Logan was angry at himself for the rest of the day. What he'd done with Donna had been stupid.

He lay on the couch watching shadows stretch across his living room. There was beer in the refrigerator, Scotch and rum in the kitchen cabinet; he drank nothing. He knew what Chief Mueller and most of the other cops thought, but it wasn't true; he was not an alcoholic. Though he could easily become one, he had not yet crossed the line.

Of course drunks were always in denial. Maybe he had crossed the line without knowing it. He was sure Donna thought so. He'd read pity and disdain in her face when she sat beside him on the pier.

He wondered if she was thinking of him right now. Feeling sorry for him. Sorry—and guilty.

He wanted her to feel guilt. He wanted her to lie awake in the haunted night, tears hot in her eyes.

She had cried on the night he confronted her, the night he threw his knowledge of her betrayal in her face. Shoulders jerking in small spastic pops, she paced the living room, plucking tissues from a dispenser and shredding them into a rain of ragged bits like flower petals, while with terrible sincerity she justified herself and finally pushed the blame on him. On *him*.

Logan hadn't hated her until then. Even his discovery of her secret liaison had not been enough to breed hatred in him. But when she said it was his fault, his guilt—in that moment their relationship was over.

He had lived with guilt after Sharon's death. Irrational guilt at not having been in the car with her, not having died in her place. Guilt at drawing breath while she and the baby moldered underground.

For two years his guilt hung on like a stubborn house guest, until he met Donna and expelled it at last. He would not invite it back into his life. He would not accept any responsibility for the actions she had taken. He had punished himself enough.

Yet he supposed he was punishing himself anyway. Since the crackup of their affair, he had been drinking too much and working too little. His career and his health were slipping away.

And Donna had gone on doing her job and clearing cases, making a name in the LAPD, the only FBI-trained profiler in the department, the expert, the glamour girl, the ambitious detective on a fast track to D-3 status. Probably screwing some lieutenant or some fashion-plate TV reporter who gave her multiple orgasms every night.

God damn her to hell.

At seven, Logan stood under a steaming shower spray to clear his head. The brandy had percolated through his system, and he was conscious of a slight hangover and the beginnings of hunger.

The drive to the civic center was short, the traffic thin at 7:45. On the ocean's horizon the sun lay flattened, a smeared yolk running red.

In Cotter Park, the big arc lights were on. A bat clipped a softball past third base, and an outfielder sprinted for it in a haze of white candescence. From the bleachers a lone woman yelled encouragement. Logan thought of Donna cheering him at last year's charity game, the memory clear and sharp like broken glass.

Storefront windows glowed softly in the downtown strip. A teenage boy and girl, hands linked, were briefly silhouetted in the doorway of a frozen-yogurt parlor. Then they were inside, pointing at the menu of flavors. Logan had gone there with Donna and, since then, a few times alone. It was a place made for friends and lovers, where a solitary individual felt unwanted and exposed.

He stopped at a red signal and watched a troop of small children scurry past on the crosswalk. The sight of kids always squeezed his throat shut.

Not long after he had moved in with her, Donna had raised the subject of a family, speaking tentatively, aware that he still thrashed in the night sometimes with nightmares of the life in Sharon's belly, the life that ended as a red excrescence between her legs. He's surprised her by saying he would like a child—just one—a little boy, he hoped. He had not forgotten that line of footprints in the sand.

Of course everything had come apart before they could even discuss marriage, let alone plan a pregnancy. For the second time he'd been cheated of a child.

Just as well, he thought bitterly. *If she'd had a baby, how would I know it was mine?*

The driver behind him tapped his horn, and Logan realized the stoplight had cycled to green.

He drove to the civic center just down the street, parked in the rear lot, and slammed the car door hard. But he couldn't slam the door on the remembrances continually surfacing in his mind. They were still with him as he crossed the spread of asphalt in the fresh-fallen dark.

Barnes was leaning over a microscope when Logan entered the lab. The forensics staff was gone. They worked normal hours. They had lives. Ed had been like them until Marjorie opened her wrists last March, leaving a note that said only, "Feed the cat."

Now he spent nearly all of his time here, amid the specimen slides and fingerprint cards. At home he had nothing, not even the cat. It had run away.

The door hissed shut. The snick of the latch made Barnes look up. Something like embarrassment registered in his eyes.

"Mark. Good to see you."

"You knew about Donna coming here." No need to pose it as a question.

Barnes nodded. "Mueller briefed me and Walters and Kurtz. I don't know who else he told."

"Not me. But I wouldn't expect him to tell me. He doesn't respect me anymore, thinks I'm a bad cop. He's probably right. Good cops don't drink on duty. They don't show up at a crime scene hung over. Like I was, last night."

"You were okay last night. You handled it."

"Whatever. The point is, I don't expect anything from Mueller."

"But I'm not Mueller," Barnes said, understanding. "We talked on the phone when you were still at the morgue. Did you know then?"

"I knew. But I didn't want to break it to you that way. I thought I'd tell you in person before the meeting." He spread his hands. "You got there late."

Silence ticked in the room. Logan considered the answer.

"Okay," he said finally.

"I wouldn't blame you for thinking I let you down."

"I don't think that. It's all right. Forget about it."

For a moment neither man said anything. Logan let his gaze drift around the lab. It was a large windowless room, hidden at the rear of the station. Five years ago its resources had been modest; fingerprint card files, a Folmer-Graflex fingerprint camera, a comparison microscope, an X-ray machine, a basic chemistry lab, and collections of cigarette butts, tire treads, and ammunition.

Then Barnes had taken over. He had pushed for a modern facility, well-equipped, adequately staffed. He'd made his case before the city council. Corona Beach, population eighteen thousand, had higher per-capita crime rates than Albuquerque or Dallas. Proximity to L.A. was one reason; the town's run-down south side was another. It was expensive to farm out work to private labs, time-consuming to route everything through the county. The drain on money and time reduced the department's effectiveness. Criminals were getting away.

Remarkably the council had allowed itself to be persuaded. Additional funds had been earmarked for the lab. Over time, Barnes had acquired iodine- and cyanoacrylate-fuming cabinets, polarized-light and fluorescence microscopes, a fiber database, a paint-sample file, and a ballistics tank.

Now he was lobbying for a mass spectrometer and gas chromatograph. With that equipment he could analyze solid or liquid samples personally, rather than relying on an outside lab to do the work.

Barnes broke the brief silence with a question. "Donna find you?"

"We talked."

"Can you work together? She'll probably be on this detail just a couple of days."

"We'll manage." Logan changed the subject. "What's the story on the print run?"

"Sheriff's Technical hasn't done it yet. JDS computer is down. I sent a soil sample from the girl's shoe to BioServe for a complete chemical analysis; the lab's backlogged, may not have results for forty-eight hours. Same old story: delays, delays. But I did find something interesting when I brushed off her clothes." He nodded at the microscope. "Take a look."

Logan squinted through the eyepiece at a gray thread magnified sixteen times. "Synthetic fiber?"

"Polyester. Coarse texture. Lobbed cross-sectional shape."

"Carpet."

Barnes nodded. "I got three of them off her skirt and one off her blouse. All like this."

"Can you do anything with them?"

"Sure. I can convict the guy once you catch him. Get me carpet fabric samples from his house; if there's a match, I'll be the prosecution's star witness."

"I was hoping for more immediate help."

"I'll go through our files and see if I can narrow down the fiber type or even determine the manufacturer. It's doubtful; there are thousands of polyester weaves. And if I do strike gold, it won't help you find him unless there's something unique about this carpet. For instance, say it was used only in a certain model of mobile home. Don't get your hopes up."

"Find anything else on her?"

"A few hairs—her own. Normally you can't be completely sure, but these hairs display shouldering, same as hers, and that's such a rare trait it's enough to prove a match. The blood and skin under her nails were hers also. She's O positive, by the way. Pathology called with the results of the swabs. No semen in any of her holes. Rectum wasn't bruised, so I think we can rule out anal intercourse. Vagina shows clear signs of penile penetration; when the guy raped her, either he didn't ejaculate or he used a condom. One good thing: the vaginal swab yielded saliva. He's a secretor, and they typed him from it. Type A."

"The A antigen is most common among whites," Logan said thoughtfully.

"People of European extraction, right. But we can't specify his racial identity from his blood group. There are too many exceptions."

"Still, as a general rule . . ."

"Most Type A's are Caucasians, and most Caucasians are Type A's," Barnes said, finishing Logan's thought. "Including me."

"And me."

"Well, let's hope neither of us did it."

Logan only smiled. "We can use the blood type to eliminate some of the knowns Mueller wants to round up."

"I told him that, but he wants them pulled in anyway. Claims maybe they'll know who did it even if they're not personally responsible. Like there's a sex-pervert grapevine or something."

"Brilliant."

"It's all for show. You know that. He's doing everything possible to *look* busy."

"That's why he brought in Donna."

"Maybe. She's sharp, though. And sometimes profiling can crack a case." Barnes caught the coldness in Logan's eyes and added hastily, "Have you seen the sketch?"

Ronni Broderick's pad lay on a shelf next to a plaster cast of a shoe print. Visible through the thin paper, beneath the front- and side-view portraits, were schematics of the skull from two angles, marked with reference points.

Logan picked up the pad. The dead girl stared at him, and he stared back.

She had looked like Donna—not a lot, but enough.

"She was pretty," he said after a silent moment. The words seemed pointless, a compliment paid to the dead.

"Uh-huh. No wonder she got the guy's attention."

"You make copies of this?"

"There's a hundred on your desk. Another two hundred went to Reynolds and Hill. They'll pass 'em out on the street."

"How about the LAPD?"

"I faxed it to Hollywood Division, along with info on the clothing store."

"Thanks, Ed. I should have been here to do that."

"You had other things on your mind."

10

On his way out, Logan stopped in the detective squad room to pick up the photocopies. He found Donna alone, eating a McDonald's cheeseburger and studying the case file.

He thought about apologizing for this afternoon. Pride vetoed the idea.

"Barnes tell you the results of the vaginal swab?" he asked as he bundled the Xeroxed sheets.

She nodded. "Saliva. The killer was intimate with her."

"If you can call it that."

"That's how *he* would think of it."

He wanted to go. Something made him approach her instead. She was seated at Grange's desk, her brown hair loose, longer than it had been when they lived together, spilling prettily over her thin nervous shoulders.

"Wrists still sore?" he heard himself ask, his voice clean of sarcasm this time.

She looked up. The fluorescent light was unkind, rendering her face wan and faintly greenish, a faded Polaroid. He noticed the dusting of small freckles on her cheeks and remembered kissing her there.

"No," she answered, "they're all right now."

She watched him, not trusting his politeness. Her eyes were chestnut brown, matching her hair, and very alert. He liked their glittering perceptiveness, their cool and level scrutiny.

"I shouldn't have played that game with you," he said, surprising himself with the statement. "Especially not in the carousel house. That's a memory we ought to keep unspoiled."

"You didn't spoil it."

"Good."

She dropped her gaze to the desk. The half-eaten burger lay on the blotter, nesting in its crumpled wrapper. Her voice was low: "On the pier you said you hated me. Know what I think?"

His gut tightened. He waited.

"I think you hate yourself."

"Don't start talking like a psychologist, Donna." The anger was back, his old friend, his drinking partner, pulsing hot and strong. "Ten months at Quantico didn't make you a Ph.D."

"I think at first you blamed yourself for what went wrong between us," she told him calmly. "That kind of blame is hard to take, so you projected it onto me."

There she went again: blame. Always blame, always guilt.

"You can't convince me it's my fault," he said as the muscles of his back bunched up with sudden tension. "I didn't make you jump into bed with another guy."

"Maybe you did." She spoke in the dispassionate, analytical tone of a therapist, conspicuously avoiding judgment, maintaining the careful distance necessary for objectivity. "It was hard to be close to you, Mark. It's not as if I didn't try reaching out. You kept pushing me away."

"So I'm a shit in two different ways." He saw her flinch a little at the words and the contempt packed in them. "I made you feel abandoned, then I blamed you for seeking affection somewhere else. Is that where your psych training gets you?"

"I'm not saying you're a . . . a bad person." Cracks appeared in the glaze of her composure. Her lip trembled. Wetness sparkled on her lashes. He had rattled her, and he was glad. "It's just that, ever since you lost Sharon and . . . and the baby, you've been afraid. I'm not even sure if you know how afraid you are, afraid all the time, and angry. Do you?"

"Don't analyze me. I'm not one of your pet sociopaths."

A muscle in her cheek fluttered. Her voice thickened. "You're afraid, so you won't commit too deeply. Won't trust another person to be there for you."

"With goddamn good reason, in your case." He felt a familiar tension in his arms, the urge to pummel.

She dragged an unsteady hand across her eyes. "You can't even hear what I'm saying."

His fault again. Naturally.

"I hear you," he said, his voice dangerously soft. "I just think screwing around on the side is a funny way to develop this mutual trust you're all of a sudden so big on." He leaned closer, fury banging a drumbeat in his head. "Who was he, anyway?"

She drew back. "I said I'd never tell you that."

"Enough time has passed. I've got a right to know."

"No."

"Was it somebody in town? A friend of mine? Another cop?"

She turned away, shaking. "For Christ's sake, can't you just let it go?"

The question struck him as funny. Savage hilarity roared in him.

Let it go? Pretend it never happened? Is that what you

want, Donna? Sure, I can do that. And while I'm at it,
I'll let Sharon go too. Let my whole life go. You bitch.
You smug, superior little bitch.

It took an effort to squeeze his rage into mere
words. "Fuck yourself," he said, his mouth twisting
in the shape of a snarl.

Her retort snapped at his heels as he walked away.
"Hey, fuck you too, Logan. *Fuck you too!*"

There was a little bit of Jersey in her voice when
she got mad. He remembered it from their last, pointless fights, the verbal battles concluded only by sun-
rise and exhaustion. Even at the end, he had liked
hearing her talk like that, tough and streetwise, the
lady cop who'd shared his bed.

Crossing the motor-pool lot, Logan decided he still
liked it. He wondered why, and what he was supposed to do about it now.

11

South of the pier, Corona Beach turned mean. Paint started to peel. Lawns became plots of weeds. Cars lost their wheels and found cinder blocks to sit on. Gang signatures crawled up stucco walls like spindly black salamanders.

Until thirty years ago there had been no bad part of town in Corona Beach. The crime rate in those days was laughably low. People kept their doors unlocked, their windows open at night to let in the sea air. In yellowed editions of the *Guardian* on file in the newspaper's morgue, the police blotters listed few offenses more serious than jaywalking, loitering, and expectorating in public.

In the 1960s, things began to change. Dropouts from UCLA and USC discovered the town, flocked here. Many of the older houses on the south end, poorly maintained and undesirable, were rented out to communal groupings of unemployed young people subsisting on care packages from home.

They brought in drugs, their symbol of freedom from authority, and the drugs attracted other kids, less interested in political and social statements.

Eventually the rebels gave up on whatever unfocused message of protest they had dreamed of delivering. They left Corona Beach, returned to college. But the drugs and the kids who had learned to profit from them remained.

With the drugs came the culture of immediacy, of thoughtless hedonism and brutalizing self-abuse, common to every underworld. When everything was for sale, nothing could be of value. In the seamy south-side streets, one could purchase any item or service: a gram of coke, a hurried sex act, a gun, a stolen car, a contract on a life.

Logan parked the unmarked Chevy on a side street off Seaview Avenue, the road that ran along the bluff above the beach. He stuffed forty folded sketches in his jacket pocket.

There were half a dozen food stands that sold pizza in this neighborhood. If the girl had stayed at a beach hotel, she had probably eaten her last meal at one of them.

He knew no better way to track her. No formal crime network operated here, only a loose interlacing of ethnic gangs and independent hustlers. A newcomer, a runaway, would not know where to go or whom to see. She would have kept to herself, feeling her way, wary of her environment.

Logan pictured her staying in a hotel, perhaps walking alone on the beach in the evening—he remembered the sand between her toes—then going out at night to ply her trade without a pimp.

It was doubtful anyone had really known her. But someone might have seen her. That would be a start.

The night air cooled his face as he walked. His anger had retreated. He was calm and controlled again.

Miguel's Burger N' Taco served pizza slices. Logan knew Miguel. He knew most of the neighborhood people who stayed in close contact with the street. Twenty-eight of the thirty-four homicides he'd investigated in the past ten years, as well as most of the major assaults and other violent crimes in his caseload, had taken place in the south end of town. Locals who watched shadows and heard whispers were his best resource.

Miguel studied the sketch with his one real eye. The other eye was glass. It was of poor quality and looked like a marble. He enjoyed taking it out and rolling it between his fingers while the empty socket gaped.

"Never see her," he said finally. "She the dead girl left in the street?"

"How'd you hear about that?"

"The paper." Miguel held up this week's *Guardian*, which had come out in midmorning. "They say the chief brings in the FBI."

"Not the FBI, just a cop who was trained by them. Was that in the paper too?"

"Sure."

"Let me see."

The third paragraph of AL Klein's bylined article contained a reference to an unnamed FBI-trained expert personally called in by Mueller. The chief had leaked the news to Klein even before Donna's arrival. Politics. He was trying to keep the city council off his back.

"You're being used, Donna," he muttered. "How do you like the feeling?"

"Excuse me?" Miguel's eye was looking at him with bright interest. "You say something?"

Logan shook his head and handed back the paper. He accepted a free chicken taco and a Coke before moving on.

No luck at the next three places. Logan left copies of the sketch with the proprietors and their customers. "Show it to your friends, ask if anybody's seen her. Poor girl's folks are sick about this." The line won sympathetic nods.

At Pier Pizza, inaccurately named considering that the pier was a half-mile north, he got results.

"Yeah, I seen her. She was in last night. Dressed real cheap, and she had makeup on her zits."

The counterwoman, Sheila, wore no makeup herself. She was large, sullen, and mannish, and she had hair on her arms thick enough to comb. She treated her body like a sack of garbage she had to drag around.

"What time was she here?"

"Shit, I dunno."

"Try to remember."

Sheila sighed, fatigued by the request. "I guess it was right after I took my break. My eight o'clock break. So maybe, like eight-fifteen."

Logan probed her memory for details. There were few. The girl had entered and left alone. She had ordered two slices of pizza and a soda. Conversed with no one. Left no tip. Sheila had never seen her before.

"She in trouble?" Sheila asked indifferently.

"She's dead."

"Huh." Her shoulders lifted, sagged. "Then I guess she's outta trouble for good."

Logan had been hoping the girl had eaten dinner with a friend, preferably a male friend with Type A blood. It would have given him an angle to pursue, a way to keep busy and maybe find someone who could be seen as a likely suspect.

Well, there was still the question of where she had been holed up. In her room there might be items that would establish her I.D. That was something anyway.

He spent an hour walking from one hotel to the next along Seaview and its side streets, past snoring scarecrows on bus-stop benches and trash-can fires in pocket parks. A shambling female figure coughed

a demand for money and pitched obscenities at him
when he turned away. He left her standing in a
wedge of sodium-vapor light, her body canted at a
crazy angle, screaming.

My night to get cursed out by women, he thought.

In musty lobbies with soiled carpets and garage-
sale furnishings, clerks looked at the sketch and
shook their heads. Logan knew none of them. Hotel
jobs had a high turnover, and it had been a while
since he'd worked the street.

The Corona Beach Arms was less elegant than its
name. It stood at the corner of Seaview and Bennett,
four stories of white-painted brick, pale in the misty
night. The lobby door groaned open under Logan's
hand. He smelled mildew and ashes.

Jungle noises twittered and croaked from the
black-and-white TV behind the desk. A British narrator explained the ecosystems of rain forests.

"May I help you?" the clerk asked. He was young
and serious. His courtesy seemed unnatural in this
part of town, a jarring false note, like a wristwatch
glimpsed on the arm of a movie gladiator.

"I'm a police officer." Logan badged him, pushed
a copy of the sketch across the desk. "Have you seen
this girl?"

"Her? Yeah. Checked in night before last."

As a boy, Logan had played chess for relaxation
and escape. The cool pleasure he had taken in captur-
ing an opponent's queen was the same order of joy
he felt now, as he contemplated the successful out-
come of a secret strategy.

"She a runaway?" the clerk asked.

"What makes you say that?"

"She looked sort of young to me, and she only had
but one suitcase. And, I don't know, she seemed
lost."

"Any idea where she came from?"

"We didn't talk much. Hey, is she okay?"

"She was murdered."

"Here in town? Oh, man."

"Can you show me her room?"

"Yeah, sure. Come on."

The narrator was discoursing on endangered species as Logan and the clerk started up the stairs to the second floor.

"I can't believe she got killed," the clerk said over the tramp of their shoes on the uncarpeted treads. "I've never met anybody who got killed before. Murdered, I mean. I knew a guy in college who committed suicide. Went out in the woods and hanged himself from a tree. But that was different."

Hanged himself, he had said. Not *hung* himself. And he'd gone to college and he watched documentaries on PBS.

"What are you doing in this job?" Logan asked. "You could do better."

"Well, the thing is, I need to work nights so as to be available during the day. For casting calls."

Logan nodded sympathetically. "Any luck?'

"I've only been out here a few months." He tried to keep it casual, holding pain and disappointment tight inside him. Logan knew how that was.

They went down a creaking hall. It occurred to Logan that the clerk fit the profile reasonably well. Intelligent, articulate, nocturnal. Too young, though. Donna had put the killer in his thirties.

Still, he would have to be checked out. If he had no alibi, he would be asked to provide a blood sample. A formality, of course. Logan knew this kid wasn't guilty.

The girl had stayed in Room 217. It was a narrow cell, sparsely furnished. The bed had been made. A soiled suitcase lay on a bureau.

In the bathroom Logan found a toothbrush, a half-

squeezed tube of Crest, a bottle of nail polish, a hair-
brush, eyeliner, lip gloss. The bathroom mirror must
have held her reflection a little more than twenty-
four hours ago as she made herself pretty. He studied
the silvered glass if looking for an afterimage of
her face.

"Sad, isn't it?" the clerk said when Logan stepped
back into the main room.

"What is?"

"That this is where she wound up. This is the last
place she got to. You think she expected better?"

"We all expect better," Logan answered.

"Yeah. I guess we do. And most of us end up in
a bad place too, huh?"

Logan said nothing to that.

There was no phone in the room. Silently Logan
and the clerk returned to the lobby. The clerk
thought of those months of casting calls and all the
head shots and doctored résumés he'd sent out to no
response. Logan thought of Sharon, of Donna, of the
empty bottles in his wastebasket.

Most of us end up in a bad place. Yes.

He wanted a drink. The desire scared him because
it felt too much like need.

In the lobby he called the station and spoke briefly
with the night-watch commander. Then he left the
clerk at the desk, climbed the stairs alone, and went
back into Room 217.

For a moment he just stood there. He wanted to
feel the room around him and the night beyond the
room, as an unborn child may sense its mother
through the womb.

The window was shut, traffic sounds muffled. The
thump of a pop-music beat bled through the wall
from the room next door. Somebody had a radio in
there, the volume dialed high. Logan wondered if
some noise like that had kept the girl awake as she

lay on the bowed mattress in the dark. Well, she slept soundly now in the morgue.

He jerked a pair of white cotton gloves out of his jacket pocket, pulled them on, and got to work.

The suitcase was unlocked. Inside was a meager wardrobe, haphazardly packed. A paperback romance novel. A sewing kit. A package of condoms. One poignant item: a stuffed penguin shiny with wear. Clipped to its wings was a name tag filled out by a child's careful hand. "Penny," it said. Penny the Penguin.

In a zippered pouch he found a small spiral notebook with a folded paper in it. The paper was a handwritten letter, undated, with no letterhead. It began, "Dear Wanda," and was signed "Mom."

"Wanda," Logan said, testing the name. "Wanda."

He read the letter, then flipped though the notebook. Pages of poetry, Wanda's clumsy efforts at self-expression, riffled past.

He stared at the notebook for a long time. Then he refolded the letter and placed it at the bottom of the suitcase under a pair of patched jeans. The notebook he concealed in his breast pocket. Its outline did not print too badly against his jacket.

Removing evidence was a crime. He wondered what Donna would think. Perhaps she would observe that taking a personal item linked to the victim was something the organized nonsocial killer would do.

Logan continued his search of the room, the notebook of poems hidden close to his heart.

12

Donna was still at the station when the watch commander informed her of Logan's call. She ran into Barnes in the hallway, his forensic kit bumping against his hip as he walked.

"Can I ride over with you, Ed?"

He didn't look at her. "I've got to pick up Tim Anderson on the way. He's our photographer."

"I remember Tim. I don't mind a short detour."

"Okay, then."

He was silent at the wheel, his face rippling with road lights.

"Mark's drinking a lot, isn't he?" she asked. "Worse than I thought?"

"He drinks. Not when he's on duty."

"He was drinking on the pier today."

"Today was unusual."

Another stretch of silence. Conversation was the reason she'd ridden with Barnes, but he wasn't having any.

She pressed him with another question. "Is he an alcoholic?"

"Ask him."

"I'm asking you."

"I'm not a doctor. I couldn't say."

The car eased to a stop before the apartment building where Anderson lived. Barnes tapped the horn.

"Why won't you talk to me?" Donna asked. She

knew he was showing loyalty to Mark, but hell. She and Ed had been friends once. She remembered last Christmas at Arrowhead, everybody drunk, Ed smooching with her till Marjorie chided Mark into making an arrest.

"If he's drinking," Barnes said slowly, "who drove him to it?"

"That's unfair."

"He was vulnerable after Sharon. He was like a dog that's been kicked. Then you come along and kick him again."

"I'm worried about him now," she said quietly.

Barnes was unmoved. "Too late."

The lobby door banged open. Tim Anderson hurried down the steps and slid into the backseat. He noticed Donna only after the car had started moving.

"I heard we brought you in. Good to see you, Donna."

He seemed to mean it. It was nice not to be hated by somebody in Corona Beach.

Logan met them inside the doorway of Room 217. Donna assessed him as tired but sober.

"You already search the place?" Barnes asked, noting the cotton gloves Logan wore.

"Once over lightly. All her stuff is in the bathroom and the suitcase."

"Anything interesting?"

"Clothes, a book, a stuffed animal."

"How'd you track down where she stayed so quickly?"

Logan explained about the sand between her toes, the absence of a suntan, the shampoo scent in her hair.

"You're a good cop, Mark," Donna said when he was through.

A shrug was his answer.

Barnes stared down at his feet. He had stopped listening to Logan and seemed abruptly discouraged, almost sulky, his lower lip jutting out in a childish pout.

"Goddamn it," he whispered.

Donna blinked at him. "What's wrong?"

"The carpet. Look at it."

It was a gray short-nap carpet, pressed flat with wear. Logan was first to see what he meant. "This is where the fibers came from."

The older man nodded grimly, lamplight winking off the steel rims of his bifocals, and ran a hand through the sparse threads of his hair. "I'll pull a few fibers and put them under the comparison 'scope along with the ones from her body. I'm willing to bet they'll match."

"One less piece of useful evidence," Donna said. The fibers would be of value only if they came from the killer's home.

Barnes sighed. "Leaving us with zilch."

"There's the saliva sample." She tried to sound upbeat.

"All that tells us is he's Type A. And that's not enough to secure a conviction, assuming we ever catch him."

"Maybe you can DNA-type him through the saliva and convict him that way."

"No chance. I can't type him from that sample. If I could, I'd have FedExed it to Lifecodes already. It's too small and too badly degraded."

Donna could think of nothing else to suggest. She didn't remember Ed being so pessimistic, so grouchily helpless. She wondered if her presence had something to do with it, or if he'd been this way since Marjorie died.

Or had he nursed black moods all along, but only in private? Perhaps Marjorie alone had seen that part of him, had lived with it, had known it intimately for years. Perhaps her daily exposure to her husband's dark side was what had finally driven her to suicide.

Disturbing thought—but one that might be the answer to the otherwise insoluble riddle of Marge's death.

Barnes went through the suitcase. Donna inspected each item after he put it aside. Anderson snapped photos of the penguin for no particular reason.

"So what can you tell me about her?" Logan asked Donna as Barnes neared the bottom of the suitcase.

The question was a challenge. He was testing her. That was all right. Lots of men had tested her in this job.

"Her sneakers are old, badly worn, but scrubbed clean," Donna said, gathering and organizing her thoughts as she spoke. "She cared about her appearance even when she wasn't working. Cared about her health too—three condoms are missing from this package. She probably took them with her when she went out. Made her customers use them, I hope.

"Obviously she was still young in some ways. Look at this damn thing." She fingered Penny the Penguin. "Most likely something from her childhood she took with her when she left home. See that worn part of the fabric? I'll bet she slept with the doll against her cheek. Firmer than the pillows in this rat trap.

"She was sentimental; the romance novel shows us that." Donna opened the book to the inside page. "Someone's marked a price here: twenty-five cents. That's what you pay at a thrift shop or a yard sale. Her sewing kit had gotten some use; that pair of jeans has been sewed up in two places, and patched. She knew how to stretch her money, which tells me she didn't have much."

Logan considered all that. "A girl her age, as attractive as Ronni's sketch showed her to be, should have done pretty well."

Donna thought so too. "Under other circumstances I'd say she blew her earnings on drugs. But according to the case file, Toxicology found nothing in her system, not even booze. And there were no needle marks, right?" Logan nodded. "Teeter do a thorough check? Armpits, crease of the buttocks, backs of her knees?"

"He looked everywhere. She was clean."

"Ulceration of the nasal membranes?" That could indicate cocaine use.

"Her nose was crushed, but as far as Teeter could tell, there wasn't any."

"So the money didn't go to support a habit." Donna stared at a loose flap of wallpaper that hung down like a panting tongue. "She might have had a pimp who took everything she made; possibly she came here to get away from him. Or she might have been inexperienced, just starting out. Or maybe she simply wasn't any good at hustling. Some girls aren't. They're too passive, too helpless."

A frown pinched Logan's mouth. "She couldn't have been very damn helpless with those razor tips."

"Well"—Donna was tired and a little fed up—"someone who reads romances and cuddles a penguin isn't exactly a hard case." She shook her head to clear anger away. "Don't think of her as your typical hooker, all right? This wasn't some strung-out zombie doing skin pops and waiting to die. She had some brains, some tender feelings, and she wanted to survive. She cared whether she lived or died. She intended to have a life."

"That's a lot to get out of a suitcase," Logan said.

Donna showed him her shoulder. "You asked for my analysis. That's it."

A low whistle sounded. It came from Barnes.

"Now what do we have here." His voice was whisper-soft. "Hey, Mark, looks like you missed something."

At the bottom of the suitcase, under a second pair of folded jeans, he had found the letter.

It was written on plain paper in a neat, crabbed hand that became looser and less tidy toward the end. Barnes read it first, then passed it to Logan, who looked at it for a long time before handing it to Donna.

Dear Wanda,

Thank you so much for writing, it was good to hear from you and to know you're all right. I was getting so worried, I couldn't think straight. Yesterday Mr. Carson made me take the afternoon off because I kept forgetting to put the invoices in the boxes. I don't see what the big to-do was about, anyway. People know what they ordered, and if they get peonies instead of crocus bulbs, they'll have to send them back, invoice or not.

I'm happy you're working but I wish you'd tell me more about your job. It must be exciting there in the big city. Do you ever see movie stars in Hollywood? Or do they all live in Beverly Hills and out by the beach? Those California beaches must be something. I would like to see the ocean someday. Lake Michigan is nice but I'm sure it's not the same.

Summer's coming, the flowers are in bloom. I guess it's summer all the time on the west coast. This TV comic called it the "left" coast, ha ha. I think he meant because they are so liberal out

there, like that Jerry Brown. Remember he came
to town during the primaries and you took a
picture of him marching with that sign? He kept
saying he was for the working people but I
don't know.

We have to be for ourselves because nobody
else is really for us. It's a hard life, but I guess
you're finding that out.

Did you take Penny with you? I looked for her
yesterday and she was gone. I thought maybe I
could smell you in the fabric, the smell of your
hair. You're so beautiful, I don't know how such
a lovely girl ever came out of me.

Honey, I miss you so very much. I wish you
would call so I can hear your voice. Make it
collect, I don't mind. I tried getting your number
from information but the operator said you were
not listed. Do you have a phone? You can call
from a booth.

Please please call, baby. God I've got to stop
now or I'll be no good for the rest of the day.

I love you, Wanda. Come home if things
don't work out for you there. Remember
you've always got me, and Mommy loves her
special girl.

Kisses and hugs,

Mom

Donna's eyes were burning as she gave Tim the
letter. "Hell," she whispered.

Barnes stood with his head lowered, mouth drawn
tight. Only Logan revealed no reaction. His face was
closed and empty. She hated him for his remoteness.

"Almost wish I hadn't found that," Barnes said.

"It helps us, though." Donna held her voice steady.

"We can locate her mother through it. Wanda's mother." She felt the need to say the name.

"Think so?" Barnes took the letter from Anderson and studied it again. "There's no address. She obviously works in some kind of mail-order nursery, but there must be hundreds of those. Near Lake Michigan, apparently. That narrows it down somewhat, but not enough."

"Which states border Lake Michigan?" Donna asked. Geography was not her strength.

Logan answered. "Michigan, Illinois, Wisconsin, Indiana."

"A lot of territory," she conceded. "Still, there was something else. . . . The part about Jerry Brown." She took the letter and read from it. " 'Remember he came to town during the primaries and you took a picture of him marching with that sign?' "

"Brown was all over the country in '92," Barnes said. "He could have been anywhere."

"You're not listening. He was marching with a sign. Sounds to me like he was on a picket line. Which would fit in with this next line: 'He kept saying he was for the working people . . .' I say we find out how many picket lines he joined in towns near Lake Michigan. Then see if any of those towns has a mail-order nursery."

Barnes studied the idea. "Might work," he said slowly. "Of course the Sheriff's Department may come through on the print run, once their computer is back on line."

"If that doesn't pan out, I'll try this strategy tomorrow."

"Right."

Logan had watched the exchange impassively. Now he turned to her with a thoughtful smile. "You're a good cop, Donna."

She heard the deliberate echo of her words to him.

For a moment she held his gaze, trying to judge if his statement had been an honest compliment or only another jab of mockery.

Then she turned away, her heart beating hard, sudden heat in her face.

It had not been mockery. His eyes had told her that.

13

At home, in bed, Logan lay awake for more than an hour, reading Wanda's poetry. The crisp whisper of each turning page seemed loud in the stillness.

As a poet she had been talentless but eager. The stilted lines ached with desperate sincerity.

Several of the poems concerned her mother. Their triteness could not conceal genuine emotion—love and yearning, the pain of separation. She already had been a runaway when she started the notebook. It was a record of her feelings about life on the street.

The few references to prostitution were safely ambiguous. Perhaps she had been ashamed.

Donna was right. The girl had been young. The street had not toughened her much.

Logan read, his face closed like a door, secrets locked inside. If the words pained him, if they made him grieve, he did not show it, was not even consciously aware.

Ed Barnes fixed himself a peanut-butter sandwich as a bedtime snack. Peanut butter was high in fat, but with Marjorie dead, he no longer gave a damn.

The refrigerator came awake with a rattle and hum. He listened to its idiot noise as he flipped through the Corona Beach *Guardian,* delivered to his house shortly before noon.

Wanda's murder was the headline story. Barnes had read the article several times.

When he finished the sandwich, he washed it down with milk. Skim milk, a habit Marjorie had forced on him, now too long confirmed to break.

He put the plate and glass in the sink. Then he removed a pair of kitchen shears from the odds-and-ends drawer and cut out the article.

In his bedroom he kept a scrapbook. He pasted in the story with rubber cement. It made an interesting addition to his collection.

Relieving himself, he glimpsed his reflection in the bathroom mirror. The rumpled bathrobe and loose pajamas made him look old and befuddled. He was only fifty-five, but could have been mistaken for seventy.

He tried not to look at the bathtub when he left. The tub was where Marjorie had cut her wrists. Both wrists, opened vertically, with no hesitation marks. She had been serious, all right.

Coming home from work, finding her in the maroon water—the memory was blunt and shocking, still.

He wondered if the trauma of that discovery had unhinged him, made him insane.

Sometimes he thought so. Sometimes he thought he was as crazy as goddamned Logan.

Pain and loss were cripplers of sanity. A man could take only so much. Then—snap—he was a broken thing.

Look at Logan, drinking his career away.

Hell, Barnes, look at yourself.

He rarely drank, but he had different compulsions. His work. The scrapbook. Other things.

He knew the hour must be late if he was having these thoughts, these bad thoughts. He ought to sleep. Sleep without dreams.

The bed felt good when he settled into it. He left the windows open to let in the smell of the night.

Alone in darkness, he remembered Marjorie. He wanted to think tenderly of his wife. But it was hard to forgive her for what he saw as a betrayal. She had left him, abandoned him, and her last message had said nothing of thirty years of marriage, nothing of her reasons for ending her life. It had merely reminded him to feed the cat.

Anger tensed his body.

That fucking cat.

Last in his wife's thoughts. More important to her than he had been.

He released his anger with a sigh. It didn't matter now. The cat was gone. He was alone.

He rolled onto his belly, pressed his face to the pillow, kissed it, thinking of Marjorie's face, the down on her arms, the soft hills of her breasts. He felt the stirrings of an erection. Then it died as he became conscious of the acid burn of tears.

He reached out to his wife's side of the bed. His hand felt only smooth sheets and the slight depression in the mattress that marked the place where she had slept.

Joe Kurtz paced the ticking darkness of his bedroom.

He had been restless all evening. Earlier he had thought of calling Lynn, even going over to her place, but in his present mood he was afraid of what he might give away, what secret he might inadvertently confess.

Instead he had simply kept to himself, staring out the window at the roof of the night. The sky was cloudless and bright with flung handfuls of stars. Rare to see the night sky so clearly this close to L.A.

Normally you had to drive far into the desert to escape the blaze of city lights.

Watching the stars relaxed him. He took comfort in their great distance, their permanence, their slow, clockwork wheeling from horizon to horizon. The comfort lay, oddly, in seeing himself as an infinitesimally small part of the universe, of no importance, a blip of life, here for an instant, then winking out. A dust speck in a world of purely mechanistic phenomena, where there was no supreme intelligence studying and gauging his actions, a world where he was free to do as he pleased.

No guilt, in such a world. No guilt for anything, ever. Things happened, that was all.

He had almost persuaded himself of the validity of this outlook, new to him and refreshing, when he heard a memory of Jim Walters's voice, quoting Deuteronomy, the ancient book of laws: "Every man shall be put to death for his own sin."

Suddenly the vastness of the universe was of no further comfort. He felt exposed, vulnerable, a scrap of flotsam whirling through the void with nothing to cling to, nothing to cower under, no place to take cover and hide.

That was when he had started pacing. He circled and recircled his small bedroom in the dark, spurred by one thought, endlessly repeated.

If there was justice in the world, it would find him. And it would punish him for what he had done.

14

Donna's West L.A. condo was three rooms and a
patio on the ground floor of a stucco warehouse with
a Tudor facade. She'd bought the place four years
ago; for a while Mark had lived here with her, giving
up his own apartment and covering half of her mort-
gage payments.

Now that she was alone again, the condo seemed
somehow too roomy for her and too busy with memories. Still, she had held on to it. Moving was such
a hassle, she told herself. And some of the memories
were good.

Not only memories of Mark. Another man had
loved her here, in this bedroom. Mark believed that
she should feel guilty and cheap about that. Maybe
she should.

But Mark didn't understand, did he? That was the
whole problem. He had *never* understood.

The Slasher horror was a thing she'd had to face
alone. And she had found she couldn't face it.
Couldn't. She wondered how many people could.

The investigation had been the first major test of
her profiling skills. She'd completed the NCAVC
training program only six months earlier, and though
she'd handled some routine homicides as a profiler,
there had been nothing like this.

It was bad right from the start. The first victim was
a mother of two children; her boys, aged nine and

eleven, found her when they came home from school.
The older one had been shocked into muteness; the
nine-year-old could not stop screaming.

The woman had been savaged in the kitchen. The
room was a slice of chaos, a wedge of pandemonium
cut loose from hell, and in the middle of it was a
spread-eagled corpse, slashed seventy-nine times,
striped and spangled in red, a crimson harlequin.

Donna had a strong stomach, but she threw up
when she saw the body and inhaled the gagging cop-
pery stench of blood.

She began work on the profile immediately, working under the breath-stopping pressure of the knowledge that a crime so violent and senseless was almost
certain to be repeated, probably soon.

From the disorder of the murder site and the apparent spontaneity of the attack, it was clear that the
killer was a classic disorganized asocial, probably a
paranoid schizophrenic. She saw him as young, in
his mid-twenties, the age when symptoms of his illness were most likely to reach critical proportions.
He would be socially inept, sexually inexperienced,
slovenly and malnourished, either unemployed or
holding down a menial job. In all probability he had
been intermittently institutionalized since adoles-
cence. Recently, she speculated, he had been main-
streamed by a psychiatric hospital and, a week or so
before the murder, had failed to show up for a scheduled injection of Thorazine or some other antipsychotic drug.

The profile was discreetly distributed to local mental-
health facilities. Before any of the institutions responded, a second woman was killed a half-mile
from the site of the first murder, her body discovered
by her housekeeper.

Again Donna was plunged into a cave of death—
the bathroom where the victim had fled after ward-

ing off the killer's initial attack. He had kicked open
the locked door, hacked at her as she tried to squeeze
out the small casement window, then thrust her head
into the toilet and held her down while the knife
grooved deep tracks in her buttocks and thighs. She
had been left slumped over the commode, her head
underwater, legs twisted in a red puddle soaking
slowly into the rug.

The exact cause of death—drowning or heart failure—was not known until the autopsy revealed pul-
monary edema; the fluid clogging her lungs matched
a water sample drawn from the toilet.

The murder triggered Donna's first nightmare
about the case. She jerked out of sleep, deep in the
belly of the night, and blinked at the claustrophobic
darkness. Mark lay beside her. She woke him, tried
to talk about it. He wouldn't listen. He turned away.

"Just a bad dream," he said in a gruff, hard voice
that was new to her. "Forget about it."

She could not forget, because in the dream she was
the woman in the bathroom, clawing at the window
frame, shrieking for help as the blade chewed her up
and drank her blood, and then water was rising to
cover her head, and her screams became a flurry of
air bubbles gurgling around her and she couldn't
breathe, couldn't *breathe*.

She lay awake till morning, drawing shallow
scared breaths and wishing she had someone who
would hold her, soothe her.

That day, a break in the case. The administrator of
a Woodland Hills hospital called to report that the
profile correlated precisely with the case history of a
former patient, Wayne Allen Stanton.

Stanton's listed address was within a five-minute
drive of both murder sites, but he was no longer
living there. He had gone on the run. In a wastebasket in his bedroom, evidence technicians found a

knife scabrous with brown crusted blood. The blood was that of the Slasher's first victim.

For two days a task force of plainclothes and uniformed officers hunted Stanton. For two nights Donna stole what sleep she could until new nightmares visited her.

Mark showed no sympathy, no interest, even when she woke with a scream that scared them both. His eyes were chilly and remote, his face a carved mask. She began to hate him, even as she began to understand.

When the phone rang at 9:30 A.M. on the third day, Donna was sure Stanton had been found. She was wrong. The Slasher had claimed another victim.

This one had been torn up in her garage as she returned from dropping off her daughter at preschool. She must have been unbuckling her safety belt when a knife burst through the open car window like an angry bird and pecked wildly at her face. Both carotid arteries had been severed in the attack. Her head had lolled forward onto the steering wheel, sounding the horn in an endless monotone. A neighbor had called the police about the noise.

The horn had been disconnected by the time Donna got there, though the woman's body had not yet been moved. Donna didn't want to go into the garage. It was too much like walking into one of her nightmares. But she made herself do it, because she was supposed to be a tough cop, and a tough cop, especially a woman, could show no weakness.

So she went in. She told herself she had seen worse. She had seen Franklin Rood's headless women, and the things he kept in his trailer. She had seen the photographs and videotapes from the Behavioral Science Service's archives at Quantico. She could handle this.

She did. But afterward, when she was alone, in an

alley off the side street where she had parked, she fell on her knees and cradled her head in her arms and shook with helpless racking sobs for some unknown stretch of time.

That afternoon, the task force finally found Stanton, registered under his own name in a flophouse motel less than two miles from where he lived, and only a few blocks from the scene of the latest murder.

He offered no resistance to arrest. He admitted everything. Of course he had killed them. Not that he'd wanted to. He had been told to do it. By the man in the TV. The man who delivered the news on Channel 4.

It was all very simple. The Russians used to be our enemies, but now they were our friends. People were no longer afraid of nuclear war. This was a bad thing. It had upset the balance of terror.

The balance of terror, the man on TV had explained in his calm, trustworthy voice, was what kept the earth turning. If there was too little terror, the earth would shudder to a stop. The sun would bake half the world dry, while the other half, left in shadow, would freeze. In this catastrophe the human race would perish.

Wayne's mission was nothing less than to prevent Apocalypse. He could accomplish this end only by creating more terror to redress the balance. The three murders had been only the beginning. Many more people would have to die in order to ensure humanity's survival. He hoped the authorities would understand.

They understood very well. They remanded him to the temporary custody of a state psychiatric hospital, where he began undergoing the exhaustive treatment and diagnosis necessary to determine if he was competent even to stand trial.

Donna's profile had been instrumental in clearing

the case. She was briefly a media hero. Her instructors at Quantico called with congratulations. Sebastián Delgado, who had supervised the Gryphon task force, took her out to lunch. Among her superiors there was speculation about how high Donna Wildman would rise.

Everything should have been fine. It was not.

Donna sighed, surfacing from the stream of memories. No point in reliving all that. Going through it even once had been enough.

Briskly she changed into satin pajamas. The Beretta went under the bed, within easy reach should she need it.

Target practice had been good this morning, at least until her beeper had gone off. She liked punching holes in the targets, liked fighting the gun's recoil with the isometric tension in her arms.

Some half-logical connection directed her mind from the explosive violence of the range to dead Wanda. She shuddered, remembering the photos Tim had shot.

Pity for the girl was useless. Only action counted. She paced the bedroom in her slippered feet, organizing her schedule for tomorrow.

First thing to do was pursue her strategy for finding Wanda's mother if the print run came up empty.

Then review the Corona Beach P.D. personnel files for rejected applicants who might fit the profile she was developing.

Finally, write up the profile itself. Then her job would be done, and she would be free to return to her normal duties, probably the day after tomorrow.

Only one more day of this, I hope. Thank God.

Donna slipped into bed, switched off the lights. In darkness the memories rushed in on her again, and with them came the tightness in her chest, the pressing urgency of the race to find the Slasher before he killed again.

The tension and strain of the investigation were entirely understandable, of course. Everybody got that way in the heat of a major case. Even Delgado, usually so cool, had been a bundle of emotional trip wires during the hunt for the Gryphon.

Yes, all that was normal. What was unexpected, what she couldn't cope with, was that Stanton's arrest had done nothing to relieve that stress. Nightmares continued to cut short her sleep, even invading her waking life in the form of panic attacks that left her dizzy and drained. Memory flashes of savaged women razored her concentration, punched holes in her thought. Though the case was closed, it would not leave her mind; like a nagging infection, it hung on, leeching her of strength.

She tried talking to Mark, but still he wouldn't listen, refused to connect. "You'll get over it"—that was his mantra, insistently repeated past the point when it had lost all meaning.

His insensitivity was less cruel than it seemed. It was a defense mechanism, an extreme form of denial. He could not bring himself to confront what she was facing, accept it, internalize it, because her feelings were too much like those that had swamped him after Sharon's death.

Smashed and bloodied housewives, shattered families, grieving husbands—it was too close to the central tragedy of his own life. He had wrestled with torment for two years, till finally he had fallen in love again, daring a fresh start. Now the new woman in his life was stirring up all the old ugliness and hurt, pulling him back into that bad place, threatening the precarious equilibrium of his inner peace.

She understood. If she had blundered into any other thicket of pain, he could have eased her free and salved her scrapes and cuts. But not this time. In this matter he was paralyzed by his own unhealed wounds—and she was on her own.

Yet she couldn't face it alone. She needed someone to talk to. There were times when she thought she would go crazy, end up institutionalized alongside Stanton, if she didn't share her anguish.

So she had found somebody who let her share it. And then Mark found out, and their relationship, just like that, was over.

Everything was over. And she was alone.

Two weeks later, she had attended the disposition of the Slasher case. She'd watched as Wayne Allen Stanton, now formally acknowledged as unfit to stand trial, was committed to a mental hospital, in all probability for the rest of his life.

The image of Stanton's face, bloodless and hollow-eyed, had stayed with her for days afterward. She could not seem to forget it.

Even in an institution, medicated with Thorazine and securely restrained, the Slasher had managed to tear up another life.

Hers.

15

Barnes grabbed Logan in the hall on the way to an 8:00 A.M. conference.

"Just got off the phone with Sheriff's Technical Services. Computer's finally back on line. I've got good news and bad news about the cold search they ran on her prints. The good news is she had a record in the county. I pulled her rap sheet out of the Personal History Index once they gave me her name."

He showed Logan the printout. "Two arrests on solicitation charges—sixteenth of May, third of June. Both in L.A. Token fine and suspended sentence each time."

"What's the bad news?"

"She used fake I.D. The name on her driver's license was Louise Anne Shepherd. Date of birth: twenty-one February, 1974."

"That would have made her twenty years old."

"Right. But she wasn't more than seventeen."

"Maybe she just looked young."

"No, I talked to Teeter about that when he called with the results of the serotonin tests. The X-rays show that her basilar joint hadn't fused, and there's uncalcified cartilage at the juncture of the knob and shaft of both femurs. A fully grown adult doesn't display those characteristics. Teeter estimates her age at seventeen. Anyway, there's no question the I.D.

was phony. The address on the license is a con-
demned warehouse on Seward Street."

"DMV issue it?"

"Their records indicate they did. Of course a
skilled hacker can break into the system and create
false entries, but I doubt any scam artist would
bother in this case. All Wanda needed was paper to
back up the license, and I'm betting that's all she
got."

"Quality paper?"

"Looks like it. The Social Security number checks
out, so whoever sold her the I.D. must have tapped
into S.S.A. files to claim an unused number for her.
After that, it would be easy enough to produce a
facsimile of a birth certificate or a Social Security
card. Then all she had to do was walk into a DMV
office, pass the tests, and get her license the regular
way."

Logan nodded. Underground services of that kind
were increasingly common in California. Illegal im-
migrants and people with bad credit ratings were the
prime customers. New I.D. solved a lot of problems,
but it didn't come cheap; the basic name change
could run fifteen hundred dollars.

"Funny she knew enough to even find an opera-
tion like that," he said slowly. "You wouldn't think
a newcomer would be so cozy with black-market
operations."

"Wouldn't think she'd have the bucks to pay
them, either."

"Unless she had assistance from somebody more
experienced. A pimp, maybe."

"Could be. The thing I don't get is why she needed
a fake identity in the first place. She doesn't seem
like the type who'd have felony warrants out on her,
and she sure wasn't dodging creditors."

Logan knew the answer to that one. "She just

needed to be older. That way she could show her I.D. to tricks who were worried about getting nailed for statutory rape. And she avoided being tagged as a runaway juvenile by the cops."

Barnes pushed open the conference-room door. "Makes sense, I guess. She changed her name for the same reason: didn't want to be sent home."

"Home must have been pretty bad if it scared her worse than the street," Logan said, seating himself at the crowded table.

"Her mom didn't seem so awful in that letter."

"Maybe the letter didn't tell the whole story."

Chief Mueller cleared his throat. "I take it you two have something to share with the rest of the class?"

The class consisted of the same faces from yesterday's meeting, plus Grange and Estevez from Burglary, and Donna, of course. She looked tired and stressed, more fidgety than usual.

"A little something," Barnes answered. "Not much."

"Whatever it is, let's hear it." Mueller tapped a pack of Marlboros against his palm till a cigarette slid out. "We can all use some encouragement."

Barnes reported the results of the print run, concluding that her I.D. was worthless.

"Even if the age and address are bogus," Reynolds objected, "the name she used could be legitimate."

"We have no reason to think she ever went by the name Louise. Or Anne, for that matter."

"You've got no reason to think she didn't."

Obviously he hadn't heard about the letter. "Tell him, Mark."

Logan explained how he'd located the hotel room. "In her suitcase Ed found a letter to the girl from her mother. The mother addressed her as Wanda."

"No last name?" Jodi Carlyle asked. "Damn. I

could have pulled it out of the NCIC database in two seconds if her mom ever filed a report."

Mueller lit his cigarette and asked Barnes if there were any new results from the lab tests.

"Still waiting for an analysis of the soil taken from her clothes. Serotonin tests on the vaginal contusions establish that she was raped postmortem. He used her dead body, didn't take her while she was alive."

"What a sicko," Deputy Chief Hardy observed.

Mueller impaled him with a brief but lethal stare. "Think we already knew that."

Barnes had nothing else. Mueller turned to Osmond for an update on patrol activities.

"An X-car prowled the area around Third and Bay all night. No suspicious activity. My other units rounded up most of the known sex offenders in town and brought them in for questioning."

Grange and Estevez had handled the interrogations. "Most of those guys aren't Type A," Estevez said. "The others have alibis that check out. They all claim no knowledge of the crime."

"Dead end," Grange agreed. "Same story with my phone calls to other departments. They've all had some sexual battery cases, but nothing like this."

"CCAP came through with a possible MO match," Estevez said. "Paroled felon who served time for a sex crime. Beat up his girlfriend, cut his initials in her stomach. LAPD's looking for him now."

"Sounds promising," Hardy said. Using CCAP had been his idea.

Logan nettled him. "I don't think so. Lawyers and stupid criminals initial their work; our man wouldn't."

Hardy had no answer to that. Twice rebuffed, he sulked.

Reynolds and Hill had spent the night walking the south end of Corona Beach Boulevard, handing out more than a hundred sketches. "The front desk has gotten a few calls from people who think they saw her," Hill said. "Nothing solid, but the desk officer is filling out a tip sheet, and we'll follow up."

Mueller rejected that strategy. "Let Carlyle, Estevez, and Grange handle the follow-ups. I want you two to continue working the street. Try to find someone who saw the pickup."

"It probably looked like an arrest."

Everybody turned to Donna.

"Excuse me?" The cigarette in Mueller's mouth mashed his words.

"I think he was posing as a cop," she said. "He probably cuffed her as if making an arrest."

"A phony cop, Jesus." Hardy had paled.

Mueller crushed his cigarette in an ashtray. "How sure are you?"

"Can't be certain. But it's the scenario that makes the most sense."

Linda Wells spoke up. "If there's a nut out there making bogus arrests and we don't tell the public, we'll catch some major flak for it later."

"We're not publicizing Detective Wildman's speculation or anybody else's," Mueller said firmly. "Facts we'll release as necessary. Not hunches, not opinions, not . . . intuition."

Donna frowned at the word but let it pass.

The chief fixed his gaze on her. "If this guy is a would-be cop, how does that help us nab him?"

She was ready for that question. "For one thing, he may drive a car that resembles an unmarked police cruiser. I mean either a Chevy Caprice or some similar sedan, possibly outfitted with a CB radio and a big antenna plugged into its tail. Local service stations and places that install car radios may remember a vehicle like that.

"It's possible he reads magazines with true-detective themes. You can make inquiries at local newsstands. He may collect guns, handcuffs, vests, and other law-enforcement paraphernalia; again, check with local dealers—gun stores, military surplus, pawn shops.

"Probably he owns a police scanner and monitors your traffic. There are clubs for hobbyists like that. Electronics stores serve as networking centers for these people. Our man might be someone who spends a lot of time at the local Radio Shack, talking about the action he heard on the police bands last night.

"Then there's the possibility that he hangs around right outside the station. Do you ever hold an open house?"

"Occasionally," Mueller said.

"Maybe he's already taken a guided tour of your facilities. And maybe if you advertise another one, he'll come again."

"How would we recognize him if he did?"

"You wouldn't, just by looking at him. But I could go on the tour myself, posing as a civilian, and strike up conversations with likely prospects. I might shake something loose."

"It's a thought," Mueller conceded.

Linda Wells looked unhappy. "We can't be giving tours when we're supposed to be working all-out on this case. It gives the wrong impression."

Mueller sighed. "Not catching this asshole makes us look even worse. All right, Detective Wildman, I'll take the open-house idea under advisement. And we'll look into exploring some of the other avenues you suggested, if we can spare the resources." He surveyed the room. "Anybody have anything else?"

"The desk clerk at the hotel," Logan said. "Might want to check him out. If he's got no alibi, we could request a blood sample."

"What makes you suspect him?" Mike Garfield, the city attorney, asked.

"He'd met the victim, he works nights, he seems intelligent enough to avoid the obvious mistakes."

"That's pretty thin. He'll have to agree to give blood voluntarily. You've got no probable cause, no grounds for a warrant."

"Not yet," Logan said. "Let's take a look at him and see."

"If the clerk is the one"—Mueller was studying Donna—"that would blow the phony-cop theory out of the water."

She shrugged. "That's what theories are for. To be tested. But the clerk is too young; I don't think he did it. And Mark doesn't think so either."

Logan cocked an eyebrow at her. "How do you know what I think?"

"Seven months together should count for something," she said coolly.

"Not for much," he answered. But he was smiling.

Logan should have typed up his daily report last night, but at the end of his long day, operating on too little sleep, he'd said to hell with it. He did it now, tapping keys on an electronic typewriter in the detective squad room. It was one of two typewriters shared by nine officers, none of whom could type.

Across the room, the phone at his desk chirped. Grange was closest to it.

"Get that for me, will you, Joe?"

Casters squeaked as Grange rolled his swivel chair to the desk. "Detective Division, Grange." A beat, then he looked up. "LAPD. Something about the girl."

Logan crossed the room and took the phone. "Logan."

"Detective, this is Bob Sinclair, Hollywood Vice. I

ran down that lead in your homicide case—the clothing store. One of the sales clerks definitely remembers the girl shopping there. Says she came in probably six or seven weeks ago with some friends. The friends sounded like two girls I've busted a couple times. Hookers. They work the corner of Hollywood and Western."

"What are their names?" Logan found a scratch pad and uncapped a ballpoint with his thumbnail.

"Cindy Fredericks, nineteen, five-one, hundred-ten pounds, Caucasian, brown and brown, street name Cinderella. Ellen Sterrit, also nineteen, five-two, hundred-ten, Caucasian, blue eyes, blond hair, street name Sugar."

"The clerk couldn't I.D. the victim?"

"No, he saw her only that one time. Remembered her because she was pretty. A lot better looking than Cindy and Sugar, though that's not saying much. They've been on the street too long."

"These girls—they work days?"

"Not often. During the day you can find them sometimes at a diner called Big Phil's on Sunset near Normandie. Look, Detective, I wish I could pursue this further, but what with the manpower cutbacks, our own caseload's got us swamped."

"I understand. Think I'd like to look around myself, though. See if I can find those two."

"Fine by me. I'll pull their files and fax you the mug shots so you'll know who you're looking for."

"Thanks, appreciate it. Big Phil's was the place?"

"Yeah, on Sunset. If not there, maybe a bar called Midnight Blue at Santa Monica and Vermont. A lot of the girls and their pimps hang there."

"These girls whoring for a pimp?"

"Far as I know, they're freelance. Not sure a pimp would take them on now, anyway."

"That bad, huh? And both of them only nineteen?"

"Wait till you get the mugs. Believe me, these are the oldest nineteen-year-olds you'll ever see."

Faxes of the photos arrived ten minutes later. Cinderella Fredericks and Sugar Sterrit stared at the camera, hating it, hating everything. Even in the bleary photocopies, their faces were raw and hard. They looked like gangbangers, hard cases. There was nothing feminine left in them and—Sinclair had been right—nothing young.

It seemed odd to think of Wanda having this pair as friends. What had they thought of Penny the Penguin? Perhaps she had kept it a secret. Logan was beginning to believe she'd had many secrets.

He found Barnes in the crime lab.

"Want to take a run up to Hollywood?" He explained why. "I've got a feeling these two may know how Wanda got her hands on that expensive I.D."

Barnes thought so too. Besides, it was never a good idea for a cop to go alone into an unfamiliar neighborhood.

Logan was glad to have him along, and not just for companionship. There was something he'd needed to ask for a long time, something he wouldn't put off any longer.

He waited till they were out of Corona Beach, racing toward L.A. on the northbound 405. Then casually he said, "Donna looked tired this morning."

Barnes grunted. "I didn't notice."

"She was looking good, though. Still looks good."

"I'm not about to witness a triumph of hope over experience, am I?"

"No chance. I'm still nursing blisters from the last time I got burned."

"Yeah, she really fucked you over." Barnes's voice carried a heavy load of bitterness. "That bitch."

Logan wondered if the bitterness was born of loyalty to him, of memories of Marjorie, or of something else.

"History now," he said. "I won't forgive her, though."

"I wouldn't."

"The guy she did it with—that's a different story." He kept his tone light. "I don't hold a grudge against him."

"Why not?"

"Because if a woman offers what Donna's got, you're a fool not to take it. No matter who gets hurt."

Barnes said nothing. Logan wanted to know what he was thinking. Wanted it very much.

Marjorie had killed herself shortly after he and Donna split up. It had occurred to him on sleepless nights that the two events might have been connected.

If Marge had found out that her husband of thirty years had been screwing his best friend's lover, would the shock have been enough to drive her to suicide?

He pictured her settling into a warm bath, ribbons of blood unwinding from her wrists. Tried to imagine what she had been thinking as the water swirled with pink clouds, then slowly thickened to the color of burgundy.

No way to know. But Ed might have some idea.

"I never found out who it was," Logan said. Control kept his face calm and blank, but the grip of his fingers on the wheel was painful. "I figure it might have been somebody I work with."

Barnes frowned, registering—what? Surprise? Concern? Impossible to tell.

"What makes you think that?" Barnes asked.

"The way her eyes dart away whenever I ask if it was another cop."

"Huh." A noncommittal sound. The older man's

hands made small nervous hops, like rabbits, in his lap.

Logan powered past a slow pickup. Three Mexicans and a dog lounged in the truck bed. The dog looked excited and the Mexicans looked bored.

He listened to the road hum for a few moments. He thought how good it would be if his mind were like that, a humming monotone, void of curiosity, void of suspicion, forever. Then he asked the question.

"Was it you?"

Barnes turned in the passenger seat, blinking as if sun-blinded, his face bracketed by a smear of racing guardrail. "You serious?"

"I'm serious."

"Goddamn it, Mark."

"She's a very attractive woman. I remember how you two carried on at Arrowhead."

"God *damn* it."

"So it wasn't?"

"Fuck you."

"That's not an answer."

"You want an answer? It wasn't me. All right? It wasn't me."

"Okay, then."

"Yeah, right, it's okay. Everything's okay. Jesus Christ, I'm just about the only one that's stuck by you. Just about the only . . ."

"Only friend I've got? Yeah. But I had to know."

"You're an asshole." Barnes was still hot.

"Probably. But it's driving me crazy—not knowing. It's making me insane. You know how that is?"

Barnes stared tensely out the window. He wouldn't answer.

"Ed?"

He wouldn't answer.

16

Donna Wildman, walking fast through the CBPD station house, the drumbeat of her heels accenting the rhythm of her stride.

Since the print search hadn't yielded Wanda's identity, it was time to try an alternative approach. She could get to the L.A. Central Library in twenty minutes, then conduct a database search. The descriptors—

A large uniformed figure stepped out of an office without looking, and Donna came up short against his chest.

She almost snapped at him, then saw who it was. She drew a quick, shallow breath as their gazes locked.

"Donna," he said. "Hello."

She was glad Mark wasn't present to hear how he'd spoken her name, with a lover's tenderness and a poignant tinge of pain.

"Hi, Joe," she answered simply.

Sergeant Joe Kurtz looked down at her, his smile clean and white against the tanned planes of his face. He nodded, a slow, knowing nod that seemed wise.

Donna was abruptly conscious of the hard, sculptured body half-concealed beneath the blue uniform. She remembered the bunched muscles of his back, the ropy hardness of his legs and arms. The memory had a tactile immediacy that startled her. She took a step backward.

"Thought you'd be in your civies by now," she said pointlessly. It was almost nine-thirty, and the morning watch ended at eight.

"I just supervised an arrest. Had to talk to Walters about the booking charges."

He cocked a thumb at the room he'd just left. Donna looked through the doorway and saw Lieutenant Jim Walters, the morning-watch commander, sharing a pot of coffee with Lieutenant Anderson, who had taken over on the day watch. Walters caught her glance and returned it with a cool, reproving frown.

She wondered what the disapproval was about. Walters was something of a puritan—had Joe told him about their affair? It was possible; they were good friends, went camping together sometimes. Hell.

She eased clear of the doorway, out of Walters's line of sight. "What sort of incident was it?" she asked Kurtz, just for something to say.

"Residential four-five-nine on Elmwood. Three juveniles trying to jimmy open the screen door in broad daylight. Neighbor called it in."

"Young kids?"

"Oldest is fourteen."

"Damn."

"You said it."

Down the hall, a couple of patrol officers came out of the squad room in a blare of boisterous voices. Kurtz took Donna's arm—she was surprised to feel her heart kick at his touch—and led her a few paces away, into an alcove where they would be less visible.

When he looked at her in the sudden privacy they shared, there was sadness in his face. It matched the tone of voice she'd heard when he first spoke her name.

"So," he said.

She spread her arms and let them drop at her sides. "So."

"How are things going?"

Though she knew the question was personal, she answered it in safely professional terms. "Frustrating so far. We don't even know the victim's identity. No suspects, no leads."

"Sounds rough." His gaze said that she was evading the real issues between them, and that he was faintly amused by her timidity, and faintly disappointed. "My report satisfactory?"

As the first officer on the scene, he had kept a log of the night's activities. It was part of the case file.

"Extremely satisfactory," she said.

"I thought you might want to interview me yesterday. To fill in any gaps in the log."

"I assumed there were no gaps."

"Did you read Logan's report?"

"Yes."

"Any omissions?"

"No."

"But you interviewed him."

"I *conferred* with him. We have to work together."

"Of course." He seemed to find humor in her answer, or in her forced formality. "What's that like? Working together?"

"Tense." She didn't want to talk about this anymore. "How about you, Joe? How are *you* doing?"

"Well enough. Just going along." He looked away, mirth fading from his face. "You know, when Mueller called you in, I wasn't sure how I felt about it. Wasn't sure I wanted to see you again."

"I can understand that."

"Getting over you has been sort of like dealing

with a terminal illness." He was trying for a light note but not quite hitting it. "First denial, then bargaining, then anger."

"Where are you now? Depression? Or acceptance?"

"I don't know. I told you I wasn't sure how I felt."

He had not taken it well when she ended their affair, immediately after Mark found out. For a month afterward, he'd harassed her with pleading phone calls. One bad night he'd visited her condo, asking for another chance. He'd scared her then. He was—almost—scaring her now.

"I'd like to think you'd gotten past the worst of it."

Kurtz shrugged. "I'm no longer hung up over you, if that's what you're asking. At least, not in any major way." He grinned almost boyishly. "Got myself a new girlfriend and everything. I must be healing."

"That's good, Joe. I'm happy to hear that. You serious about her?"

"Semi-serious. Oh, Lynn's great. Real sweet." A tightening of his facial muscles, and his smile turned vaguely hungry, vaguely cruel. "Not as creative as you were, though. Sexually, that is."

He moved a step closer. She smelled sweat and aftershave. The mingled scents triggered a stream of associations that made her briefly dizzy.

"I never thought of myself as creative." She hoped he couldn't see her discomfort.

"Just horny, huh?"

"Lonely is more like it."

"I know that feeling. You going with anyone now?"

"I met somebody, uh-huh. Lawyer. Nice guy." That was a lie. There had been no one in her life since Mark.

"So you're not lonely anymore?"

"No," she said firmly.

"Good. I only want the best for you, Donna. You deserve someone special in your life."

The words sounded good, but his grinning sincerity troubled her; it was overdone, like a bad makeup job, highlighting what it was intended to conceal.

She lifted her head, looked into his eyes. She saw longing there, longing and the bitterness of frustrated desire. And she knew that he still wanted her, had never stopped wanting her.

Fear fluttered in her chest, moth wings beating at her heart. She took a step back, out of the alcove. "There's someplace I've got to be."

"Yeah, me too. We'd both better get going."

"Take care."

"You too, Donna."

As she moved away, his gaze lingered on her body like a groping hand.

At the end of the hall, she glanced back. Kurtz stood motionless, arms akimbo, watching her. From a distance he looked leaner and still more hard-bodied than she remembered: strong legs, narrow hips, wide shoulders.

Then she was out the rear door, under the open sky, but still thinking about Joe Kurtz, who had been there when Mark wasn't, who had given her what she needed.

The relationship had been little more than a few tender words, some shared hurt, and a month of stolen afternoons in which they had experimented with varieties of physical pleasure. It had not been the worst experience of her life, but it had grown old pretty fast.

For her, that is. But not for him.

For him, their former intimacy was still a burning need. He had not given her up.

Donna wasn't happy about that, wasn't flattered,

wasn't amused. She disliked obsessiveness. Even feared it.

Obsession was a common theme of the men she profiled. She had seen what it could do—and where it could lead.

17

"There they are."

Logan nodded at the door as two listless skeletal figures, ambiguously female, drifted in.

Barnes grunted, unsmiling. He'd had little to say during the past two hours as they waited at the counter in Big Phil's. They had watched customers pass in and out of the diner, a Hollywood mix of young professionals and street scum, both types twitchy and anxious, hooked on coke or booze, courting burnout or suicide. The parade of hopelessness would have discouraged conversation even if Barnes hadn't still been pissed off.

"Let's do it," was all he said now.

They corralled the girls into a booth, showing their badges and explaining that they only wanted to talk.

"That ain't LAPD tin." Sugar Sterrit tossed back a handful of loose, stringy hair the color of cobwebs.

"We're from Corona Beach," Logan said.

Cinderella Fredericks exhaled a jet of smoke in his face. "Where the fuck is that at?"

"Just south of L.A. Near the airport."

The town was only twelve miles away, but Logan wasn't surprised the girls hadn't heard of it. Street people were psychological prisoners of their neighborhoods. Many spent years in Hollywood without ever seeing the ocean. Some didn't know there *was* an ocean.

"We understand you knew a girl by the name of Wanda," Barnes said. He had taken off his bifocals to look less grandfatherly. His myopic squint made his face mean. "Went shopping with her at a store called Hollywood Hot maybe six weeks ago."

"Nah, we never been there," Sugar said, lying to a cop for the pure pleasure of it.

"You were seen in the store. Wanda was with you."

"Never knew no Wanda. Never knew nobody. Go on home, Mr. Policeman. You got no business here."

Sugar curled her lip. Cinderella winked at Logan and blew smoke in his face again.

Logan's gut clenched. Anger sang in his locked jaws, his gritted teeth.

He leaned forward and slapped the cigarette out of Cindy's mouth. The flat of his hand lashed her cheek like a whip.

A beat of startled silence, then both girls were squealing in an ecstasy of indignation. "Hey, what the *shit*?" "Police brutality, man. Anybody got a camera?" "Motherfucker fucking *hit* me!"

"*Shut up!*" Barnes growled, silencing them.

A biker at the next table started to rise, chivalrous fantasies crowding his head. Logan badged him and he sat down instantly with the programmed meekness of a man who'd done time.

"Now, look," Logan said. His voice was dangerous because it was so oddly flat. "We came all the way up here to talk about Wanda, and we don't intend to fuck around."

Sugar nestled in the banquette's vinyl cushions. "So what about her?"

"She was murdered," Barnes said.

Logan watched the girls for a reaction and saw a shared thrill of malice in their eyes.

"Stupid little cunt," Cinderella said slowly, letting

her tongue taste the words. "Whoever offed her did a public service."

"She was one bad baby," Sugar agreed. "Nobody's gonna miss that rat-fuck."

"What've you got against her?" Barnes asked.

"She fucked us over. Walked out on a business deal and cost us a piece of change." Sugar smiled suddenly, her yellow grin shocking like an outbreak of rash. "Hey, you gonna talk to us, you gotta feed us. We came here to eat."

Logan glanced at Barnes. It was easier to oblige them than to waste time arguing.

"Order what you want," Logan said. "We'll cover it."

"Ooh, that's more like it," Cinderella cooed. "Now you're being nice, acting like gentlemen."

"Keep this up," Sugar said, "and we could get to *like* you."

Logan ignored the come-on. "Tell us about your business arrangement," he said, using the edge of his voice.

The story came out slowly, under repeated pressure, like paste squeezed from a tube. Cindy and Sugar had met Wanda two months ago, shortly after her arrival in L.A. "She was ripe," Cindy said. "Looked like a goddamn cheerleader."

"All-fucking-American," Sugar said wistfully.

Like lampreys the two hookers had fastened themselves to Wanda, setting up a "partnership." They bought sexy clothes for her and helped her get a driver's license.

"With fake I.D. to back it up," Barnes pointed out as the girls' lunch orders arrived.

Sugar was offended. "No way, honey. We never bought no fake nothing."

Logan gave her a hard stare. She weakened.

"Well ... okay," she mumbled. "Maybe it wasn't, you know, completely on the up-and-up."

"You go to a credit repair clinic?" Barnes asked.

"Yeah. Cost us a chunk of cash, too. Seventeen hundred. Cleaned us out."

"Why'd you want to spend that much just for an I.D. card?"

This time Cindy answered. "It was, you know, an investment. We had *plans* for that bimbo."

"Big plans," Sugar added with the same wistful air.

"What was her name?" Logan asked.

Cindy shrugged. "You already know it. Wanda."

"Her *full* name."

"Shit, I don't know. Garner or Garvey, I think. Something like that."

The girl had not been much to them, not even a name.

They'd run an ad, with Wanda's photo, in a pornographic newspaper sold in vending machines. "The ad said if you wanted to get to know her, you should call our number," Cindy explained, biting into her chili-cheeseburger like a starved animal. "It was sort of an escort service. Totally legit."

It had been an outcall prostitution service, obviously. Wanda had escorted her clients no farther than their bedrooms.

Logan remembered her mother's letter: *I'm happy you're working but I wish you'd tell me more about your job.*

"She made good money," Sugar said, chewing sloppily. "But she got greedy. She wanted more, more, more."

"How big was her cut?" Barnes asked her.

The girl's eyes flickered in the prelude to another lie. "It was a good cut. Like, half, I think."

Logan smiled at that. "Half?"

"Maybe a third."

"Right," Barnes said, disgust thickening his voice. "Maybe five percent is more like it. Or maybe nothing at all."

"She got greedy," Sugar repeated with stupid stubbornness. "We were good to her, treated her right."

"We spent a lot of money on that little fuck," Cindy said petulantly. "Had to make back our investment. She didn't understand business considerations like that."

Logan knew that Wanda had probably earned back the $1700 for the I.D. after her first week on the job, but he didn't argue. "What happened after she got greedy?"

"Ran out on us," Sugar said. "Set herself up on her own."

"Street whore is what she turned into," Cindy muttered with contempt, as if being an unpaid call girl had been more respectable. "No pimp, no organization behind her, no nothing."

Barnes asked how Wanda had done on the street.

"Like shit." Sugar showed a reptilian smile. "She was no fucking good at hustling. Couldn't, like, stand up for herself, so she'd get squeezed off the good corners onto the side streets where you don't get any major action."

"And she was too, whatchacallit, selective," Cindy said. "There was lots of stuff she wouldn't do. I mean," she added quickly, "that's what we heard."

"What wouldn't she do?"

"Letting the guy go in the back door was one thing. And any kind of S and M. I mean, plenty of girls don't go for the rough stuff, but Wanda wouldn't even play tie-me-up."

"She wouldn't let a trick handcuff her?" Logan asked.

Cindy snorted a laugh. "No way."

" 'Course, if you're into that," Sugar whispered, "we can work it out. There's an alley in back. You cuff me and I'll go down on you real nice."

"For twenty bucks," Cindy put in.

"For thirty you can do us both. Slap us around too, if that's how you get off."

Logan shifted in his seat. Under his jacket, his shirt was clammy with a chill trickle of sweat.

"You like that idea," Sugar said, watching him, eyes wide and unblinking in a snake's lidless gaze. "'Don't you, Officer?"

He guided his voice along steel rails. "Do you remember any of Wanda's clients? Either from the service or the street?"

Sugar studied him a moment longer, then shrugged. "Yeah, some."

"Were there any who seemed dangerous?"

"Not *our* customers," Cindy said. "We was running an escort service like we told you—"

"Cut the crap. We know what kind of service you had going. Tell us about the tricks. The nasty ones."

Cinderella half-shut her eyes, registering a rare authentic emotion: weariness born of the daily experience of horror. "Baby, they're *all* nasty. Any trick you turn can be a freak. No way to tell up front. No way."

"There was this guy I did once," Sugar said, her tone conversational now, almost friendly. It was not often she got a chance to tell war stories. "He looked real normal, not like a wacko. He wanted to tie me up, and I let him. Then he takes out these scissors and comes at me, says he's gonna cut off my nipples, make 'em into earrings. I kick him in the nuts and start screaming, and he gets freaked and blows." She touched her breasts. "That's how come sweet Sugar's still got her titties."

"Did Wanda know that john?" Barnes asked.

"Him? Nah. I only saw him that one time. But there's plenty of crazies out there."

"Yeah," Sugar said. "Like the Rag Doll Man."

Logan ran his hand along the edge of the table, feeling the smooth chrome. He waited to let Barnes ask the question, but Barnes kept silent.

"Who's that?" Logan asked finally.

"Another psycho. Friend of ours named Billie told us about him." Cindy finished her burger with an animal gulp. "She was working the boulevard and this guy picked her up."

"When?"

"Like, a month ago. So they go to a motel and he takes off his belt and ties her to that wooden thing on the bed."

"The headboard," Logan said.

"Yeah. Then here comes the weirdness. He's got this shopping bag with him, and he pulls out this rag doll."

"Billie said it was a Raggedy Ann," Sugar commented. "I had one when I was a kid."

"He says to her, 'I'm gonna do you like I do this little raggedy bitch.' And he starts ripping up the doll. I mean, tearing it all to shit with his fucking hands. And poor old Billie's, like, apeshit with fear."

"But the guy didn't do nothing to her," Sugar said. "Just left her there, tied up."

"She report it?" Logan asked.

"Motel clerk did. He found her. But the fucking cops don't care. They never do a damn thing."

"Did Billie give them a description?"

"Man, she was so freaked out, she couldn't describe her own mama."

"If she ever met her mama," Sugar added pleasantly, and both girls laughed.

"This man didn't beat her?" Logan asked. "Rape her?"

"Nothing like that," Cindy said. "Wasted the doll, is all."

"Where's Billie now?"

"Hell if I know. I ain't seen her on the street since then. Jay Cee could probably tell you."

"Jay Cee?"

"Boy, you really ain't from around here, are you? Jay Cee's a big man in this neighborhood. Lots of girls work for him."

"We used to, ourselves," Sugar said. "Till we decided to freelance."

Till he kicked you loose, Logan thought. "Did Wanda ever work for Jay Cee?"

Cindy shook her head. "After our little misunderstanding, she wouldn't work for nobody. But Jay Cee, he kept trying to talk her into it."

"He can be *real* persuasive," Sugar said.

"So he was interested in Wanda?"

"He had the hots for her." Cindy gave Logan a sly look. "Maybe he's the one that wasted her."

"What makes you say that?"

Sugar answered with a shrug. "Had to be somebody."

The two girls glanced at each other, and Logan saw it again: that gleam of malice in their eyes. He understood the situation. They resented Jay Cee for cutting them loose, leaving them to con newcomers like Wanda or hustle the most desperate tricks, and now they saw a chance to get him in trouble, make him a suspect, take their revenge. Still, it was a tip that would have to be checked out.

Barnes came to the same conclusion. "Where can we find this gentleman?" he asked without too much sarcasm.

"He lives in the Regal," Cindy said. "It's an apartment building on, uh, Las Palmas and Fountain."

"You gonna pay him a visit?" Sugar asked eagerly.

"We might."

She smiled. "If it turns out he's the one that did Wanda, would you tell him something for us?"

"What?" Logan asked.

"Just say ... thanks."

Cinderella tittered, and Sugar Sterrit dipped her fingers in a pool of ketchup and licked her dripping hand.

18

It took Donna only ninety minutes in the L.A. Central Library to track down Wanda's mother.

At a database terminal she conducted an on-line search of general-interest periodicals, primarily newspapers. She began by punching three descriptors into the subject field: Jerry Brown, campaign, Michigan. The system selected every article in which all three terms appeared. Scanning the titles and text, she noted the dateline of every story covering the candidate's participation in a strike or march. She did the same for Illinois, Wisconsin, and Indiana, compiling a list of seventeen towns.

An almanac gave her the appropriate area codes. Using a pay phone in the lobby, charging the calls to her phone card, she dialed Information in each area and requested the number of the local chamber of commerce.

More calls. A series of frustrating responses to her inquiry: "No, nothing like that in Muskegon." "Sorry, the Battle Creek business directory shows no listing for an establishment of that kind."

She was near the end of her list when Joliet, Illinois, gave her the answer she was hoping for. "Why, sure. Garden Gifts does a big mail-order business. They send out thousands of catalogs, full-color, glossy paper, real slick."

She got the nursery's number, called the switchboard. Her breath seemed stuck at the back of her throat as she asked to speak with Mr. Carson. That was the name Wanda's mother had mentioned. Her boss or supervisor.

"One moment, please," the receptionist replied.

Carson worked there. She'd found the place. *Yes*.

"She shoots and she scores," Donna breathed.

A click, a hum, and Mr. Carson was on the line. "May I help you?"

She identified herself and explained that she was looking for a female employee. "Don't know her name, but her job is to pack shipping cartons, and she has a teenage daughter named Wanda who left home not long ago . . ."

"I know who you mean. That's Jo Ann Gardner. We used to rib her about her name, Gardner—us being Garden Gifts, you see. But she's not with us anymore."

"No?" Damn.

"Actually, I'm afraid I had to let her go within the past month. She had, uh, some personal difficulties."

"Her daughter missing, you mean."

"That made things worse, but she was bad off before that. You did say you're a police officer?"

"LAPD. Yes, sir."

"Then I guess I can tell you. Jo Ann suffers from emotional problems. She's prone to depression—I mean she gets it bad. Not all the time. Some days she's sweet as you please, but other days she's list-less, sort of shell-shocked, like a robot. She wasn't one of our more dependable employees. Toward the end she wasn't even coming to work on a regular basis. I had to terminate her, sorry to say."

"Your company doesn't have a medical plan that will cover treatment?"

"Our plan covers the basics, but not psychiatric care. That can be an expensive proposition."

Donna understood. Her dad ran a drugstore in a small New Jersey town; she knew about the profit margins of modest businesses, and how any increase in costs could kill you. Still, she wished there had been a way to get Jo Ann on an antidepressant before Wanda had run off. A daily dose of lithium or imipramine could have saved two lives.

"Do you have any idea where I can find Mrs. Gardner now?" she asked.

"Personnel must have her address on file. I can connect you."

"If you would, please."

"Uh, Detective? This is about her girl, isn't it?"

"I'd rather not say what it concerns."

"Well, I just want to say—if you've got Wanda there and you're thinking of sending her back—it was a terrible home environment. There were just the two of them, Wanda and Jo Ann, struggling on Jo Ann's paycheck, which wasn't much, and when Jo Ann got blue she'd start talking mean. She used to tell Wanda that the girl was an accident—which is probably true, since Jo Ann didn't have her till she was thirty-five. And she'd say that Wanda had been nothing but a burden, and if Jo Ann were ever to commit suicide, that'd be the reason why. It was tough on the kid, that's all I'm saying. Poor Wanda might be better off where she is."

Donna pictured a body wrapped in clear plastic in the morgue. *No*, she thought, *she's not better off. Not that way*.

All she said was, "I'll keep that in mind, Mr. Carson."

The Personnel Department gave her Jo Ann Gardner's home address and phone number.

Now that she'd found the woman, Donna almost lost her nerve. She didn't want to make the next call. *Maybe she won't be home*, she told herself like a coward as she punched in the 815 area code and seven digits. *Maybe she found another job and she's at work now.*

The phone was answered after ten rings. A flat, torpid voice muttered, "Hello."

She licked her lips, found some moisture in her mouth. "Jo Ann Gardner?"

"That's me."

"Mrs. Gardner, this is Detective Donna Wildman of the Los Angeles Police Department." She let her tone of voice be a warning, a way to prepare the woman for the shock. "I have some bad news for you."

"About Wanda?"

"Yes."

"She in some kind of trouble?"

Donna hesitated. The beat of strained silence told Jo Ann the answer.

"I see," she said. Her voice dragged lower, scraping the bottom of her throat with a raspy sound. "She's dead, isn't she?"

"Yes, Mrs. Gardner."

"Call me Jo Ann," she said absurdly.

"Okay, Jo Ann. And you call me Donna." Careful, careful. Her words like tender fingers stroking an injured bird.

"Wanda is dead. Well, what do you know."

She said it indifferently. Donna found it hard not to be angry with her for that. But remember the letter: *Mommy loves her special girl.* Jo Ann was not herself now. She had been herself when she'd written those words.

"I'm very sorry," Donna told her. The pointless formality of the statement made it somehow obscene.

Mrs. Gardner was silent for a moment. Over the crackle and hum of the long-distance connection rose the tinny whisper of a conversation between two other women: ". . . chased the car and got run over." "Oh, what a shame." "Such a good dog too. Gary cried when he heard."

They were talking about death also. A run-over dog, a runaway child—to the universe, a small distinction. Each one chasing something, each one left lying in the road.

"Jo Ann?" Donna asked tentatively.

"Doesn't matter anyway. She was never supposed to be born in the first place." The woman had fallen straight to the bottom, to that ugly place where depression turns to hate. "If her father had worn a rubber she never would've existed. Told him to wear one but he was too drunk that night. Then he scats, and I'm stuck raising her by myself."

Donna thought of the condoms Wanda carried. Perhaps it hadn't been AIDS that scared her. Perhaps it had been the fear of repeating her parents' mistake.

"How'd it happen anyway?" Jo Ann asked. "She kill herself? Wouldn't blame her if she did."

"She was murdered." It came out harsh despite the softness of her tone; some words could not be gentled.

"Murdered, huh." Jo Ann's voice conveyed no shock, no sorrow. "You catch whoever did it?"

"Not yet."

"Don't try too hard. They did her a favor. Put her out of her misery. Wish somebody would do the same for me."

Donna tried to think of something to say.

"I tried plenty of times to do myself in," Jo Ann went on lifelessly. "Pills, mostly. Once with a knife. But it's harder than you'd think. Now I'm doing it with food. Going to eat till my heart gives out. Eat myself to death. Looking forward to it. Christ, yes."

Donna became aware that Mrs. Gardner was crying. There was no sound of tears, only the too-frequent intake of breath, shaky and shallow, like the catch-and-gasp sobbing of a child.

She shut her eyes and pictured Jo Ann, a fat woman with an iguana's unblinking, heavy-lidded stare. Depression would have brought on psychomotor retardation, rendering her stuporous, inert. She might be slumped against a wall or sprawled in a chair. Probably she was in her bathrobe, having long since lost the energy to shower and dress. The room around her would be a sty, but she wouldn't notice. Her cheeks would be ribboned with shining tears, her nose running, mouth hanging open; she wouldn't notice any of that, either.

Most likely she didn't even know she was weeping, didn't realize that she had just suffered the final loss in a lifetime of losses, that grief had her now in its cold clutch and never would let go.

"Only thing there is in this world to look forward to, you know," Mrs. Gardner was saying aimlessly. "Being alive is no good, no good at all, not for a minute. We're all lost, aren't we? Lost in the dark. Nobody should ever be born. Best that way. Best for everyone."

A long time later Donna hung up. She had listened to Jo Ann ramble and cry for thirty minutes, and had offered whatever pale comfort she could find. It had not been enough.

She called Mr. Carson again. "Is there anybody at the company who's friendly with her? Who would go visit her?"

"You're afraid she'll do something serious."

"She's extremely upset."

"Did Wanda talk to her? Is that what set her off?"

"Wanda is dead."

He took that in. "Okay," he said slowly. "I think Gwen Resnick and Jo Ann are still pretty good friends. I'll let Gwen know what's happened and give her the afternoon off."

Donna thanked him. Then she stood in the lobby, her hand on the cradled phone. She felt tired. She felt like quitting her job.

19

Before leaving the diner, Logan used a pay phone to call Bob Sinclair, the Hollywood Vice detective who'd run down the clothing-store lead.

"Yeah, I know Jay Cee," Sinclair said around a mouthful of sandwich. "He's no killer. Those bitches are just blowing smoke."

"That's how we read it too. But we need to cross all our *t*'s on this one."

Sinclair provided Jay Cee's real name—Justice Christian Emory—his arrest record, and his address and apartment number, along with some advice.

"He's got this bodyguard, Kinshasa. Mean motherfucker. If he gives you any trouble, tell him Detective Sinclair will be real disappointed if you two aren't treated right."

Jay Cee lived in one of Hollywood's better neighborhoods, where grunge and neon had been held more or less at bay. Lining the streets were apartment high-rises that dated from the Depression; aspiring writers and actors had roomed here and ridden the Red Line trolleys to Paramount or MGM in search of work. It seemed like a less complicated time.

"Think this creep did it?" Barnes asked as Logan parked outside the looming apartment complex called the Regal.

"If he had, he would've disposed of her body in such a way that it would never be found."

Barnes nodded. "Probably." He was still angry, doling out his words with miserly reluctance.

The Regal was eight stories of Art Deco elegance, avant-garde once, monumental kitsch now. Rows of fluted columns bracketed paneled windows and elaborately carved reliefs depicting stylized ferns and deer. The lower walls were webbed with tagger signatures and gang graffiti, and the brass fixtures over the lobby doors had been tarnished algae-green by the span of years from the thirties to the nineties, but in most respects the building had held up remarkably well. Living in this part of town, in this landmark structure, Justice Christian Emory was doing far better than he deserved.

Logan and Barnes rode the creaking elevator to the eighth floor. The doors struggled open, exposing a long hallway dimly lit with simulated hurricane lamps.

The carpet was relatively new, still plush. It absorbed their footsteps as they approached the apartment. Logan rang the bell. He was aware of the gun under his jacket. Nothing more than that; simply aware.

A security chain rattled. A latch bolt was drawn back with the ominous ratcheting noise of a shotgun's slide handle feeding a shell into the chamber. The door jerked open, and a huge man thrust his face belligerently out.

"What do you want?"

Kinshasa, obviously. Logan looked him over with insolent indifference before responding. Though in his mid-thirties, the bodyguard wore the flat-top hairstyle favored by black teens. His copious jacket could not conceal the thick bulges of his deltoid and trapezius muscles or the subtler bulge of the magnum holstered to his ribs. In his hand was a small square bottle of something with a faint turpentine smell.

"Police," Logan said after a long moment. He flipped open his badge case. "We want to talk with Jay Cee."

"I don't know who you're fucking talking about."

"Bob Sinclair said we could find him here."

"Sinclair can take it up the ass."

"This pertains to a homicide investigation. If your employer won't cooperate, he'll just buy himself trouble."

"Bite moose." He started to shut the door.

"Kinshasa." The cool, languid voice came from inside the apartment. "Don't be chilling the Man. You tell Johnny Law to make himself at home."

With a sideways shake of his head, Kinshasa invited them in.

They entered a large sunlit room crowded with expensive furnishings in a variety of styles. The place had been decorated with an excess of money but a deficit of taste. White wicker armchairs flanked a low-slung sofa with bright yellow, red, and blue cushions. An amoeboid spread of tinted glass on stiletto legs—a coffee table—rested on a delicately textured Persian rug. Tubular accent tables and a Queen Anne bench, a stretch leather chaise and a Chippendale recliner were scattered throughout the room with the randomness of driftwood and kelp on a beach.

Most pimps in Logan's experience were scruffy street hustlers living in poverty. This one had risen higher than his competitors and clearly meant to advertise that fact. Logan doubted it was accidental that he'd taken an apartment on the top floor.

Jay Cee lounged on the sofa, insufficiently impressed with his visitors to rise. His long, lanky body was decked out in pale green chinos and a blousy shirt the texture of velour. His bare feet, propped up on one arm of the sofa, were enormous, the toes wiggling dexterously.

"What can I be doing for you gentlemen?" His smile revealed a missing upper incisor.

"I'm Detective Logan; this is Lieutenant Barnes. We're with the Corona Beach P.D."

"Corona Beach—shit, I been through there. Not much going down in that penny-pool rest stop. What's a jerk town like that even need you dicks for, anyways?"

"Things happen sometimes. Like the night before last. A girl was murdered."

"Now, ain't that a damn shame. Hold on a minute while I wipe my eyeballs dry."

"You may have known this girl."

"I do know enough of them."

"Her name was Wanda."

"Don't you say." He registered no reaction. "Pretty little brown-eyed piece of trade? That Wanda?"

Barnes removed a photocopy of Veronica Broderick's sketch from his pocket, unfolded it, and showed it to Jay Cee. The pimp still had not risen to a sitting position. His toes rippled like piano keys as he studied the photo. Several of his toenails were painted bright vermilion; the rest were untouched.

Logan glanced at Kinshasa and this time identified the bottle in his fist. Nail polish.

He had been brushing paint on Jay Cee's toenails when the bell rang. Had he been massaging those bare feet, too, and teasing them with kisses? Logan was suddenly certain that Kinshasa was more than a bodyguard.

"Yeah, I knew her," the pimp said finally. "She got cooled, you say? Real tragic. What's it got to do with me?"

Barnes answered. "We understand you wanted Wanda to work for you."

"I made the offer. Wouldn't you?"

"And she turned you down."

"She figured she was too good for honest work."

"Didn't that piss you off?"

"No dumb-fuck ho gonna piss off Jay Cee, grandpa. And no dumb-fuck East Jesus jakes, neither."

Barnes stiffened. It was the "grandpa" that got to him. Logan picked up the interrogation before it could get sidetracked.

"Did you know Wanda had left town?"

"She didn't 'xactly clear her travel schedule with me."

"Did you know?" he repeated.

"I get around. Street ain't keeping no secrets from Jay Cee."

"Then you could have tracked her down."

"Why would I?"

"To make her come back. Or teach her a lesson for running away."

"My man, I got more *important* things to do."

"Yeah," Barnes said gruffly, still peeved at the grandpa jibe, "like pimping teenage girls till they drop."

Kinshasa stirred. Jay Cee calmed him with a loose wave of his hand. His fingers were long, the nails well-manicured and painted the same shade of vermilion as his lacquered toes.

"Don't go throwing no tired old shit like that," he said mildly. "None of that there bullrag has ever been substantiated." He drew out the syllables of the last word as if drawing the last puff of flavor from a good cigar.

"Here's something maybe we *can* substantiate,"

Logan cut in. "Your whereabouts two nights ago, between nine and one."

"Don't know as I recall." Jay Cee rolled his head on the satin pillow to look directly at Logan. "How about you, Chief? You know *your* whereabouts?"

"That's not an issue here."

"Why not? How can I be sure you didn't chill this poor white working girl yourself? You're all wound up, Mister Man, and sort of guilty-seeming, if you ask me."

Though he knew the words were only cheap taunts, Logan found that his brain had stalled; no speech came.

Barnes rescued him. "Shut up, you little asshole, and answer the question."

The pimp's grin, all white teeth and a single gap, was a photonegative of a jack-o-lantern's carved smirk. "So now which of them things am I supposed to do? Shut up or answer?"

"Pretty clear you don't want to do either," Logan said. He turned to Barnes. "Bastard's got no alibi. Let's talk to Sinclair about bringing him in."

"Hey. Hold the phone."

Jay Cee was sitting up now. That had gotten his attention.

"I'm alibied for that night. Hell, for every night. I always hang in the same bottleshop. Place called Midnight Blue over on Vermont."

Logan remembered Sinclair mentioning the bar. A dive for pimps and their girls.

"How about him?" He jerked a thumb at Kinshasa.

"He was with me. Always is. He's my shadow."

"You cast a damn big one," Barnes muttered.

"That's 'cause I am a damn big man." Jay Cee thumped his chest lightly for emphasis.

Logan's chuckle was rewarded with the pimp's

pained stare. The stupid little shit really did think he'd made it big.

"We'll check out your story," Logan said. "If it doesn't hold up, we'll be back."

Jay Cee stretched out again, curling and uncurling his toes. "Always a pleasure, gentlemen."

Kinshasa trailed Logan and Barnes to the door. Logan's hand was on the knob when a scuffle of bare feet on carpet drew his gaze to the hallway just off the living room.

A girl shambled toward them, small, slender, very pale, naked except for an oversized T-shirt. She had brown hair, a smoke-and-chestnut heap of it like Donna's. Her eyes, widening as she raised her head, were brown like Donna's, also.

She stared at the two cops, her gaze ticking from one to the other, then expanding to include them both.

Her thin shoulders shook. She made a gagging sound.

"You," she whispered.

Her stare remained fixed on Logan and Barnes as she took a stumbling step backward.

"Oh, God. Oh, holy Jesus." The words moaned up from some deep well of fear at the bottom of her throat. "It's him." Still shivering all over like a wet dog. "It's him."

She was in shadow now, retreating down the hallway, her hands feeling their way along the wall. Ambient light made sparkling pinpoints of her eyes.

"The Rag Doll Man. Oh, Christ, it's him—*the Rag Doll Man!*"

20

Donna picked up a fast-food lunch on her way back to Corona Beach. At the station she told Mueller that Wanda's identity had been established, her next-of-kin informed. The chief was grumpily gratified.

"What next?" he asked, starting on his second pack of the day.

"I'd like authorization to look at the files of rejected job applicants. Our would-be cop might have tried to get himself hired."

"Sounds reasonable, I suppose. If he *is* a would-be cop." Mueller clearly had his doubts. "Lieutenant Brody will show you where he keeps those records."

Brody directed her to the appropriate file cabinets and departed, leaving her alone with his secretary, Lynn, in the administrative office. Lynn chatted noisily on the phone, making a movie date, her voice irritating as the whine of a drill. Finally she concluded the call—"Okay, Mom, see you at eight"—and left for lunch, shutting the door behind her.

In the welcome silence Donna carried a stack of rejected-applicant folders into Brody's private office and started reading. As she worked, she unwrapped and ate her roast-beef sandwich, now cold.

There had been only seventeen male applicants in the past three years; the department had not been advertising for recruits. All had taken the Minnesota Multiphasic Personality Inventory exam. Checking the scores, she found two candidates who interested her.

The first had scored above seventy on three MMPI scales: Masculinity-femininity, Paranoia, and Social Introversion. The zigzag lines on his chart drew a portrait of a morbidly suspicious social maladroit prone to gender confusion.

Had doubts about his masculinity nurtured a hatred of women? Hatred that drove him to kill a girl, rape her corpse, part her unresisting legs to lick her sex?

Licking. Saliva. "Oh, shit."

She had forgotten the results of the serological analysis: the killer had Type A blood. She checked this man's medical record—he was Type O—and ruled him out.

The other candidate, more promising, was Type A. He'd tested above the mean on several MMPI scales and spiked notably high—nearly ninety—on scale number four. That scale measured characteristics subsumed under the label Psychopathic Deviate: lack of affect, irresponsibility, disregard of others. Sociopathic tendencies, common in lust murderers. He also scored high on the K verification scale, which counted conventionally correct answers chosen by test-takers to "fake good."

A borderline sociopath attempting to pass for normal but not quite pulling it off. A possibility. She put the file aside.

One prospect out of seventeen men. It wasn't much.

Still, she continued to view this approach as faintly promising. A man with a fascination for police work might well have applied to the force, only to be turned down.

For that matter, he might have applied more than once. Hell, he might even have been accepted. . . .

She stiffened.

Until this moment it hadn't occurred to her that the killer might be a working cop, a member of the force.

Was it possible? No, of course not. This man's pathological hostility would raise a red flag on any MMPI test. He would be instantly disqualified.

But some people could beat the MMPI. And in other cases the problem developed later in life.

Okay, so maybe—just maybe—it could happen. Was there anything in the MO that indicated actual police training?

Only that he'd cuffed Wanda behind her back. And that the girl had submitted without apparent struggle; the blood under her nails was her own.

Of course the cuffs might have been introduced as an element in a bondage game. That would explain her willing cooperation. But would Wanda, childish Wanda with her paperback romance and her penguin, have played along with that kind of game?

Maybe yes, if the john had been familiar, someone she trusted. But she hadn't been in town long enough to develop regular customers here. She'd checked into the Arms the day before she was murdered.

Besides, she'd been careful to protect herself: the condoms, the razor tips. Not the type to take chances.

Most probably, then, she had allowed herself to be cuffed because she'd thought she was under arrest. A phony cop with a novelty-shop badge could have fooled her.

But a real cop, with a real badge, would be so much more convincing.

If the pickup had taken place in town, then a CBPD badge would have been less likely to raise suspicion than a badge from another municipality. And a CBPD cop would be able to follow the investigation from the inside.

Donna nodded, letting the thought reach a conclusion formed in words in her mind: *There's a chance that an officer in the Corona Beach Police Department killed that girl.*

Trembling, she stood up slowly. She returned the rejected-applicant folders to the file cabinet.

Brody and his secretary were still out. She was unobserved.

In another cabinet, a few yards from the first, were three drawers marked PERSONNEL.

She found herself staring at those drawers.

You have no authorization to look in there, she reminded herself. *Besides, they're probably locked.*

She approached the file cabinet. Tested the top drawer.

Unlocked.

No. Don't even think about it.

She ran through all the reasons why this was a bad idea. She could be on the verge of buying herself some big-time trouble. And not just disciplinary action.

If the killer really was a member of the department, and he learned she'd been reviewing the personnel files . . .

The mottled ruin of Wanda Gardner's face surfaced in her memory. Donna wondered what her own face would look like after being pounded like ground meat.

She pushed the thought aside, drew a breath of courage, and opened the drawer.

Quickly she lifted out a thick sheaf of folders—employee files A through F—and carried them into the other office. They made a dull thump when she dropped them on the desk.

All right. If she was going to do this, she would have to work fast and efficiently. And she would have to be alert for that secretary, Lynn, or for Brody himself.

Nobody hired by the department would have scored prohibitively high on any MMPI scale. What could she look for? Only an overall pattern, not pathognomonic of major psychological dysfunction, but indicative of a certain personality type. Specifically, high scores in Paranoia, Psychasthenia, possibly Masculinity-femininity, and of course Psychopathic Deviate. Okay.

The initial eliminations went quickly. Roughly a quarter of the employees were female. Of the men, half had the wrong blood type. The first Type A she found was Ed Barnes.

Ed a killer? Silly thought.

To be thorough, she flipped through his file. There was no MMPI chart. Barnes had not taken a psychological exam when he was hired. His long tenure in the LAPD had been a sufficient qualification for the job.

His LAPD Personal and Work History Summary, Form 1.6, was attached. Donna noted three references to "complaints" during his time as a beat cop shortly after he'd joined the force. All three charges had been sustained, but the summary provided no details, and she found no Complaint History form in the file.

She wondered what sort of complaints had been filed against Ed so long ago. There was no way to know without obtaining access to his Division Employee Folder in the LAPD Personnel Records Section.

Forget about it, she told herself.

Ed wasn't the man she was hunting. Of course not.

Even if he did project a good deal of hostility toward her—hostility that might not be tied exclusively to his loyalty to Mark.

The killer would resent her for trying to get inside his skull. Mark had warned her about that, and he was right.

And Ed was showing unmistakable signs of strain, wasn't he? His gloom and moodiness had even prompted her to wonder if he had made life intolerable for Marjorie, if that was why she had slit her wrists.

Suicide . . .

Could the shock of losing his wife have unhinged him? After so many years of stalking killers, had he decided to switch roles with them, to give in to the darkest part of himself?

The organized nonsocial killer's first homicide is frequently precipitated by pre-crime stresses. Words from some half-remembered monograph in the *FBI Law Enforcement Bulletin* slipped through her mind like a water moccasin through the oily shallows of a swamp. *An emotional trauma, most typically the loss of a loved one, appears to be among the most common triggers.*

Absurd. This was Ed Barnes she was thinking of. A gentle, decent man staggered by tragedy, doing his best to cope.

She did not pull his file. But she tucked away a half-formed question in some mental drawer.

In the first batch of folders, three employees with the right blood type had mildly suspicious test results. She put their records aside and took out a second heap of files, G through L.

Joe Kurtz was in that group. Type A, she noted uneasily. She did not want him on her list. Scrutiny of his past might expose their relationship.

His MMPI chart disturbed her. He scored within normal limits on most scales, but uncomfortably high on K. Had he been falsifying his answers, marking the responses he assumed to be expected of him? If so, his conventional scores in the other categories could be highly misleading.

Still, a lot of people tried to skew the test results to their advantage, particularly when taking the test in the context of a job interview. There was no solid basis for adding Joe to her list, no actual reason to distrust him at all. Except . . .

He found the body.

First rule of any homicide investigation: Whoever finds the body is a potential suspect.

Of course it was entirely plausible that Joe had come across the body by chance, while patrolling the streets, as he claimed.

But there was another scenario. Suppose he killed Wanda earlier that night and dumped her there—then became impatient when she hadn't been noticed after a couple of hours, and decided to call in the report himself.

She wouldn't even consider the idea if not for his MMPI results—and his evident obsession with her. Obsessiveness was a characteristic trait of the organized nonsocial type.

And, she added, frowning, *Wanda did look a bit like me.*

She had noticed the resemblance in the forensic sketch. Nothing uncanny about it, just a vague similarity; brown hair and eyes, and a mouth shaped something like hers. There were a million women and girls out there with those features; probably just a coincidence. Probably.

But she would have to consider Joe a possible suspect anyway.

More names, more charts, and then she was halfway through the L's, looking at a gummed sticker on a folder tab that read: LOGAN, MARK / 129.

Well, it wasn't Mark, obviously.

She nearly passed over the file without opening it. Then she froze, the folder in her hand, sudden heat in her face.

She thought of the game Mark had played with

his handcuffs in the carousel house. The smell of brandy on his breath. His brooding hostility.

And he was Type A. She knew it, without needing to check his medical record.

The sour flavor in her mouth was the residue of horseradish and sesame seeds. It only tasted like fear.

Donna opened Mark's folder and looked at his MMPI chart.

He tested slightly high on three scales. Paranoia: 68. Psychopathic Deviate: 64. Psychasthenia: 72.

The numbers implied a man overly suspicious, prone to irrational fears or obsessive-compulsive behavior, somewhat remote and alienated.

If you didn't know him, if you were going by the scores and blood type alone, would you pull the file?

Yes, she decided.

She looked at the date on the chart. He had taken the test thirteen years ago. Before he lost Sharon. Before he fell in love with an L.A. cop, then broke up with her when he learned she was unfaithful.

Both events had changed him, the collapse of their love affair perhaps even more than the death of his wife. The tendencies lightly outlined in the test results must have been strongly reinforced.

Where would he score now? As high as eighty on Psychasthenia? Ninety on Psychopathic Deviate? Higher than any rejected candidate had scored?

And Wanda looked like me. At least a little bit. Was it me he was beating, killing? The woman who'd cheated on him ... driven him to drink ... ruined his life?

No. Stop this. Stop it.

She couldn't stop it. Couldn't.

Eyes closed, palms flat on the steel desktop, Donna ran through the profile of the killer that had been taking shape in her mind, comparing it point by point with the man who had been her lover for seven months.

Thirty to forty years old. Yes.

Above-average intelligence. Yes.

Socially competent. Yes.

Skilled professional. Yes.

Night owl. Yes.

Failed relationship in his recent past. Yes.

First- or second-born. Yes; his two brothers were both younger.

Mobile; has a car. Yes.

Local resident. Yes.

Follows the investigation closely. Yes.

Police officer or wanna-be. Yes.

Emotionally repressed. Yes.

Strong need for control. Yes.

Verbal skills. Yes.

Uses handcuffs. Yes.

Unresolved hostility toward women. Well, he was hostile as hell to her.

Precipitating stress. The breakup of their relationship?

She didn't want to believe that, because then indirectly she was responsible. If she hadn't taken another man into their bed, if she'd been able to work things out, Wanda Gardner might still be alive—

No, don't think that way. Goddamn it, Wildman, you know better than that.

Anyway, it can't be Mark.

Can't be.

"Can't be," she breathed aloud.

But she wasn't sure.

21

The girl was drooling a thick rope of spittle when Logan reached her. She had slumped against the wall, staring blankly ahead, after her last scream.

He fingered her carotid artery, found a pulse. Quick and strong, but not as fast as his own heart was pounding. Her shout still clanged in his memory like an echo of nightmare.

There was a curious tilt to the floor that hadn't been there before. The apartment seemed very hot. Concentration was difficult. He squeezed his mind into focus as he studied the girl.

Though she was listing to her left, her muscles were not lax but rigid, her hands fisted as if in cadaveric spasm. The smell of ether clung like perfume to her body.

He stared into her eyes. The pupils were constricted, the eyeballs twitching laterally in nystagmic oscillations.

"Dusted," he told Barnes as the older man arrived at his side.

PCP use was less common than it had been, now that crack had invaded the streets, but there was still a ready market for phrencyclidine and the myriad designer drugs that mimicked its effects. Logan had no way of knowing which chemical clone the girl had inhaled or ingested. Most likely she herself didn't know or care. The high was all that mattered. The illusory escape.

Jay Cee approached in a languid saunter, his long, supple body gyrating loosely to unheard music. "Apologies for the outburst, Officers."

Logan channeled the residue of his fear into anger. "You don't seem particularly surprised."

"I'm used to it. The little cooz goes apeshit now and again. 'Cause of some medication she's on. Doctor's orders."

"She's on PCP or something like it."

"No way, Jack. She's taking these pills, these black mollies a doctor gave her for a nervous condition. I can show you the RX."

"Some other time." He turned to Barnes. "What is it? Some kind of seizure? Status epilepticus?"

"No, not that bad. She's just gone from excited catatonia to stuporous catatonia. That happens with a low to moderate dose of phrencyclidine. It's called the ripple effect."

"Should I call the paramedics?"

"Not much they can do that we can't. Let's get her on the couch."

They half-led, half-dragged the girl into the living room and stretched her supine on the sofa where Jay Cee had been reclining not long before. It was like handling a corpse. Her legs and arms were stiff as if with rigor mortis.

"Got any cranberry juice or orange juice on hand?" Barnes asked Jay Cee.

"Fuck, what you think this is, a restaurant?"

"She needs ascorbic acid in her system. It'll acidify her urine, flush out the PCP."

"Ain't no fucking PCP. I told you that."

"You told us bullshit," Logan interrupted. "Have you got the juice or not?"

"Some OJ in the fridge," Jay Cee admitted.

"Get it," Barnes snapped.

Jay Cee hesitated, then nodded at Kinshasa. The bodyguard moved off through a doorway onto a tiled floor. A fluorescent light flicked on.

"How about Valium?" Barnes asked. "Any of that lying around? Don't shit me this time."

"Yeah, I got some. Helps me sleep."

"She needs one pill. It'll block her adrenaline flow," he added for Logan's benefit.

Administering prescription medicine to the girl was definitely not standard procedure, but Logan figured Barnes knew what he was doing. There would be hell to pay if she went into a seizure, though.

Jay Cee left and returned a moment later with a tablet. Barnes inspected it before feeding it to the girl. She dry-swallowed the pill mechanically, still staring at nothing, a film of sweat on her flushed face. Her mind was far way.

Kinshasa brought in a quart bottle of orange juice. Logan uncapped it, tipped it to her mouth. He poured slowly, careful not to spill. He kept pouring till the bottle was empty.

"Gonna have to piss like a racehorse before long," Jay Cee said.

"That's the idea," Barnes told him. "Cranberry juice would have worked better."

"I hate fucking cranberries. Taste like fucking shit."

"The streetwise gourmet," Barnes muttered.

Logan stared down at the girl. The T-shirt rose and fell with her fast, shallow breathing.

"Think she'll be all right?" he asked Barnes.

"Yeah. She just needs to stay calm till she eliminates the drug as waste. The Valium will help. And we should keep our voices low, provide minimal sensory stimulation."

Logan frowned. "I've had enough sensory stimulation as it is."

They both watched her for a long moment, both knowing what an outsider would say: that it was callous to leave her here, in this narrow slice of hell, with Jay Cee and his endless stash of hog and horse.

There was no good alternative, though. Yes, they could take her to the hospital and have her tested, but the odds were that the results would be negative. Designer-drug labs were constantly modifying their products, altering the standard formulas of popular drugs by one or two molecules to beat the serologists and the law.

Even if the girl did test positive, Jay Cee would not be criminally liable. No one had seen him give her the drug. He would deny all knowledge and responsibility.

And she appeared to be over eighteen. She couldn't be forced to leave him, and there was little doubt she would refuse to go voluntarily. By now she had come to need Justice Christian Emory, or think she did.

"Nothing else we can do for her," Barnes said softly. "Not a damn thing."

Logan nodded and turned to Jay Cee. "So this is Billie?" He talked softly, not to disturb the girl.

"How'd you be knowing her name? Yeah, that's her. She been sort of fucked up since that mo'fucker played with her head."

"Which is why you keep her flying on Peter Pan," Barnes observed.

Jay Cee displayed his missing tooth in an ingratiating smile. "Telling you for the last time, I ain't sprinkled her with no magic dust."

"Shut the fuck up."

The pimp looked away abruptly, as if afraid he might catch a chill from Barnes's stare.

Logan didn't want to say it, but the issue was there, in the room with them, an unacknowledged presence, and it had to be raised.

"She thought she saw the Rag Doll Man," he said. "And she was looking at us."

Jay Cee tossed off a shrug. His narrow shoulder looked as angular as a chicken wing through the thin fabric of his shirt. "Well, you ain't him, is you?"

Logan didn't answer that. "Did you ever get a look at this guy?"

"Never seen him. Far as I know, he only messed with Billie. Ain't heard nothing from no other fluff about him."

"Did Billie give you a description?"

"No, she was bugged out, couldn't talk straight."

"But apparently he resembles one of us."

Jay Cee laughed. "Aw, shit, man, she acts this way 'round every white dude. I told you, she goes psycho sometimes."

"You mean whenever she sees a white male, she things he's the Rag Doll Man?"

"Yeah. When she's on her medicine, I mean."

Logan relaxed a little. "I see."

"Phrencyclidine is a hallucinogenic," Barnes said thoughtfully. "That might account for it."

"Might," Logan agreed. He could have let it go, but the habit of pressing for details spurred him on. "The attack took place a month ago. Why is she still so scared?"

"Well . . ." Jay Cee hesitated. "A couple of weeks ago there was this dude asking about her—like, where she hangs, you know? And then one time Kinshasa sees a guy tailing us on the street at night. He runs like a rabbit when Mr. K. goes after him."

"You think this guy tracked her down?" Barnes asked. "Knows where she lives?"

"Could be the same bad-news dude, yeah. That's

why poor Billie's so nervous, needs her medicine.
She thinks he's found the guts to finish the job."

"Could be she's right . . . if he's been stalking her."

Jay Cee laughed. "Hell; she be safe with us. Old
Kinshasa here ain't a-scared of no Raggedy Ann
Man, is you, Mr. K.?"

The bodyguard rumbled like a mountain. "No
fucking way."

Logan didn't pursue that angle. "Does she always
get this excited? So excited she passes out?"

"No, usually she ain't this wild. Only other time
she fainted was when your bro Sinclair stopped by.
Wasting my time with some Micky Mouse bullshit
as usual."

"Does Sinclair look like either of us?"

"Thought he was your good buddy. You never
even seen him?"

"Does he look like us?" Logan repeated, not sure
why he was pushing so hard for this answer.

"No. Other than he's white like you—and a cop,
like you." Jay Cee's eyes were cool. "Maybe it's cops
that set her off big-time. Maybe she don't like that
smell, you know. That *pork* smell."

Kinshasa grunted a laugh, and the pimp smirked,
his hips bobbing as he shifted his weight from leg to
leg in a loose-limbed dance.

Logan averted his face from them. His circling gaze
surveyed the living room. The decor looked more
funhouse-grotesque than before. Every stick of furni-
ture, every rug and ashtray, had been bought with
some girl's life. Some girl like Billie . . . or Wanda.

He shut his eyes briefly, tired of ugliness, of mean-
ness, of Cinderella and Sugar and Kinshasa and Jay
Cee, needing some respite, needing some air.

He looked at Billie again, rigid on the couch, then
turned away. "Let's get the hell out of here." His
voice sounded hollow to him, weak and drained.

Barnes nodded. "Not a moment too soon."

"You gentlemen come up and visit any ol' time," Jay Cee said with unconvincing affability as Kinshasa showed them the door.

22

Donna was replacing the last of the personnel files when she heard heels clacking toward the office door.

It was two o'clock by her watch. Lunch hour was over. She had cut it too fine.

She stuffed the folders into the file cabinet and pushed the metal drawer shut. It got away from her and slammed, the sound perhaps audible in the hall.

Then the door was swinging open and Lynn was walking in, her mouth full of Snickers, the candy wrapper sticky in her hand. She saw Donna standing by the cabinet—the wrong cabinet, not the one to which she'd been granted access.

"Hello, Detective Wildman," Lynn said. Her pretty face pinched. "Is ... is there anything I can help you with?"

"No, thank you. I was just finishing up." Donna was uncomfortably conscious of the file cabinet at her back, a violated safe.

The girl looked her over. "I thought you were going through the rejected-applicant files."

"That's right."

"Then why ... ?"

"I was just ... checking to make sure there weren't any additional folders in this cabinet." It sounded very lame.

"Those are all employee files."

"Yes. Yes, I see that." Donna managed a shrug. "So I guess I've seen everything."

"I guess so," Lynn said quietly, her tone nicely balanced between politeness and irony.

Donna gathered her notes and left. She wasn't happy. The girl would talk.

Damn, I should have been out of there ten minutes ago. Lost track of time, and now everybody will know I've been in the personnel files. Stupid, Wildman. Stupid as hell.

Well, maybe Lynn wouldn't gossip after all. Maybe she would put the incident right out of her mind—

Donna stopped in mid-stride.

"Got a new girlfriend," she remembered Joe Kurtz saying. "Lynn's great . . ."

The same Lynn? Could be. Could easily be.

If so, it was a safe bet that at least one cop would know what she'd been up to. Lynn was sure to tell Joe.

And he would grasp the significance of a criminal profiler searching the files. He was sharp, and he'd passed the detective exam, though he'd chosen to remain on the patrol side of the force.

If Brody's secretary was the same Lynn. Maybe she wasn't.

But Donna felt uncomfortably sure that she was.

She found Mueller in his hot little office with his jacket off and his tie loosened. Afternoon sun blazed on the lacquered surface of his desk. His chrome ashtray was a puddle of blinding light.

"Here's someone you should check out," Donna said as she gave him the file of the rejected applicant who'd interested her.

"Only one man?"

"That's all I found."

She could not share her suspicion about actual employees—not so soon, when she had nothing to go on but spikes on an MMPI graph. Mueller would never believe one of his own men capable of homicide without stronger evidence than that.

"I'll send someone over to pay this gentleman a visit," Mueller said, tapping the file against the desk.

She nodded. "Right." Her unvoiced suspicions made her feel guilty, and she was in a hurry to leave. She was moving toward the door when his voice stopped her.

"Donna."

She turned. Mueller was looking down at his desk.

"I know you resent me for bringing you in on this case. I know how difficult it is for you—for all of us."

"It's hardest on Mark," she said quietly.

"He can handle it."

"I hope so. But I'm not sure. He's been hurt so much already." She shut her eyes. "I contributed to that."

"It was losing Sharon that left the deep scars," Mueller said gently. He stood up and came around his desk, shirt-sleeves flaring as he passed through a mote-dusted fan of light, and touched her arm in a fatherly way. "I was at the accident scene. Arrived right after the RA unit. The beat cops should have called a morgue wagon instead. There was never any hope she could be revived. Her . . . or the baby."

Donna nodded, imagining how it must have been—the woman folded in the wreck, nested inside layers of crumbled metal like a crushed insect in a napkin. She had visited enough crime scenes to know the brutal ugliness of such tableaux, the stomach-twisting stink of blood, the red spatter patterns like some hellish abstract art.

"Mark was there already," Mueller went on slowly. "He'd been working a case when the watch commander beeped him. The first officers didn't even recognize Sharon, though they knew her. All the cops

did. Used to go over to the Logans' bungalow on
South Street for weekend barbecues." He smiled at
the memory, a tight, painful smile that squeezed a
gleam of dampness from the corner of his eye.
"Funny to think of Mark throwing a barbecue, isn't
it?"

"I wish I'd known him then."

"He was a different man. That day—it's like a di-
viding line in his life. Like a boundary on a map,
and when you cross it, you're in another country."

A gloomy country, Donna knew. A landscape
fogged and dark.

"Sharon was awful to see," Mueller went on softly.
"As bad as the most terrible thing you've seen in
any morgue. But worse than that ... much worse ...
was the baby."

Donna had seen a stillborn child once, when she
was working patrol in Newton Division. The mother
had been asleep in bed when a stray 9mm Parabel-
lum round from a gang fight punched through the
wall into her side. The trauma had brought on a
spontaneous abortion. She remembered the woman
screaming as the paramedics strapped her onto a
stretcher, screaming not in pain but in loss, still
struggling to reach the dead fetus and hold it to
her breast.

"That wasn't the hardest part of it, though,"
Mueller said. "Death you can look at. What was
tough was seeing how Mark reacted. More accu-
rately, how he didn't react. He was weak in the
knees, looked a little dizzy, but in his face there was
no expression. No anger. No grief. Nothing."

"You're not saying he *felt* nothing?"

"I don't know what he felt, then or after. I recom-
mended psychological counseling; he said it was unnecessary. I couldn't argue. There'd been no change
in his work. If anything, he was more intense, more

driven. Some of his friends advised me to force him to take a long vacation, but I thought it was healthy for him to stay on the job. It kept him active. And he was working to help victims of other crimes.''

Donna nodded. ''Helping surrogates of Sharon and the child, in effect. Saving them or avenging them vicariously.''

''That was my thinking, yes.''

''You'd have made a good psychologist, Chief. Or a good profiler.''

He didn't answer, merely retreated behind his desk and hunted for a cigarette.

The compliment had made him uncomfortable. Was that because she'd glimpsed his insight into people and, with it, his facility for manipulation?

She wondered if his decision to bring her in had been meant as another round of therapy for Mark. Shock therapy, perhaps. That worked sometimes.

Other times it pushed the patient irrevocably over the edge.

23

The bartender at Midnight Blue didn't know Jay Cee. "But that don't mean nothing," he explained to Logan and Barnes. "I only work days. It's the night man you want. Eddie Brago is his name."

Logan got Brago's number and called him at home from a pay phone in the back of the bar.

"Jay Cee? He's a regular. Shows up every night. Doesn't tip worth a damn, the nigger motherfucker."

"Was he there two nights ago?"

"Yeah, sure. Like I said, the little shine's always hanging at the Blue. He sticks to the place like stink on shit. With freaking Mighty Joe Young right next to him, growling at you if you get too close."

"Is there anybody else who might have seen them?"

"Everybody saw them. Everybody in the fucking joint."

"Anybody with a name?"

"Wait a minute. Two nights ago? There was a couple of cops come in that night. Asking if I'd seen some ex-con they was after. Two Vice cops. The guy was Barker, Baxter, something like that. I don't know about the other one. Fuck, they're *your* guys; *you* find 'em. Why the fuck are you wasting my time?"

"Thank you very much, Mr. Brago," Logan said with cutting courtesy. "You've been extremely helpful."

He called Hollywood Division. Only one Vice officer had a name remotely similar to Barker or Baxter, he was told. He got Vince Bartlett's home number.

"Sure, me and my partner checked out Midnight Blue, along with a bunch of other places. Looking for a paroled sex-crime offender who used to spend time in pimp bars. CCAP coughed up his name on an MO run in connection with a two-sixty-one."

A small child was shrieking playfully in the background of the call. Intermittent splashes could be heard. Logan pictured a backyard, a wading pool, a boy in swim trunks. He could have had all that in his life—if Sharon hadn't been lost to him.

For an irrational moment his envy of Vince Bartlett was intense enough to take the form of hate.

"Anyway," Bartlett concluded, "our suspect wasn't there. But Jay Cee was."

"What time was this?"

"Eleven o'clock to maybe midnight."

"He's alibied, then." The bartender's word was not worth much, but a cop's was.

"Jay Cee's not homicidal. His pal Kinshasa is a different story. That's one scary dude. But he was there too."

"They're always together, right? Kinshasa is Jay Cee's hired muscle."

"His love muscle too." Bartlett chuckled. "That's the rumor anyway. If you catch my drift."

In the distance, a thin, eager voice: "Daddy, Daddy, watch me swim, watch me *swim!*"

"I'll let you go," Logan said past the tightness in his throat. "Thanks, Vince."

The child was till crying for his daddy, calling out from the void, as Logan cradled the phone.

"So Jay Cee is a dead end," Logan said as he steered the motor-pool sedan onto the southbound 101.

Barnes made an affirmative noise. Logan could still feel the older man's hostility, hot and focused like the glare of a lamp.

"Hey, Ed. I'm sorry about what I said on the way up here." Apologies were difficult for him, and the words came hard. "It was stupid. I'm turning paranoid."

"You got that right."

"It's just that I'm sure it was somebody in the department."

"You should drop it. Let it go. You don't want to churn out ulcer acid your whole life."

"Why not?" Logan tried a small joke. "It's gotten me this far."

Barnes smiled, a warm smile that spoke of remembered friendship, and Logan decided things were all right again.

The rest of the drive back to Corona Beach was companionably quiet. They listened to police chatter on the radio, the crackles and squawks soothing like distant thunder.

As Logan pulled off the freeway, Barnes said suddenly, "You shouldn't have slapped her."

It took Logan a moment to supply a context for the remark. "She was getting to me."

"We were out of jurisdiction. There were witnesses. Not everybody in that place was a street louse. If one of those yuppie cokeheads had flashed an ACLU card, we could've had a situation."

"You're right," Logan conceded. "She asked for it, though." It sounded stupid when he said it, a child's belligerent self-justification.

Oddly, Barnes seemed satisfied with his answer. "Yeah," he said slowly. "She did. She was being provocative, and you lost your cool. I know how that is."

The car waited at a stoplight. A kid shot past on

a racketing skateboard, an oversized T-shirt ballooning at his back.

"Sometimes," Barnes went on, half to himself, "you just want to beat the hell out of them. Just whale on them, knock heads." He nodded, said again, "I know how that is."

Logan looked at Barnes and saw his hands, idle in his lap, close slowly into fists.

24

In midafternoon Donna sat down to finally do the job she'd been brought in to perform in the first place: writing the profile.

Before getting to work, she reviewed the case file one last time. Crime-scene log . . . autopsy protocol . . . death investigation report . . . press release form . . .

The crime-scene photos were in the pocket of the folder's back cover. Donna spread them on her borrowed desk in the detective squad room, empty save for her.

Wanda lay before her in a montage of angles, her slender legs twisted, miniskirt hitched up in an accidental cheesecake pose. Her brown eyes were wide open as if shocked, staring in astonishment at death.

Donna studied the girl's battered face and thought of the emotional battering she had received in her mother's home, the daily shuttle between normality and craziness. She wondered if Jo Ann had tried to kill herself in Wanda's presence, if Wanda had called 9-1-1 to save her, if later Jo Ann had cursed her for it.

After that hell, life on the street might have seemed an improvement. And yet there would have been times when Wanda recalled Jo Ann's better moments. Perhaps the stuffed penguin had come out of the suitcase then, its softness comforting like a mother's breast.

Donna touched a close-up of Wanda's face, running her fingertip over the tangled mop of the girl's dark hair. Had Jo Ann stroked that hair, caressed it, singing nonsense songs or humming lullabies?

Her hair . . .

Something was caught in her hair.

Donna raised the eight-by-ten to the light. Behind Wanda's left ear, there was a pale smudge, yellow-orange, very small.

It might only be a dust speck on the negative or a bubble of back-scattered glare from the flash.

She removed a magnifying glass from her purse. A grainy blur swam in the lens like an unfocused specimen on a microscope slide. She could distinguish no detail, but the blot of color appeared to be the image of a real object.

It should have been bagged and tagged. She scanned the property report.

Wanda's clothes. Her one shoe. A few small rocks picked up near the body on the chance that they had been transferred from the murder site.

That was all. Nothing from her hair.

Donna flapped the photo gently to fan herself and considered the problem.

Barnes and Logan had examined the body after Anderson shot the photos. Had one of them surreptitiously pocketed the item while kneeling by the body? Or, in the confusion and darkness, had someone else at the crime scene removed it before they set to work?

In either case she was dealing with the deliberate concealment of evidence. And she could think of no motive for that other than the obvious one.

The crime-scene log, filled out by Joe Kurtz, included the names and badge numbers of every cop present at Third and Bay that night. Donna checked the names against those taken from the files. Three matches: Lieutenant Walters, who had brought some lighting equipment at Barnes's request; Barnes himself; and Kurtz, the first officer at the scene.

Of course, she hadn't put Logan on the list.

Any of the four could be a suspect. Any of them could have removed the item.

She realized she was chewing her thumbnail and quit it.

All right, what to do? Take this to Mueller? No, too soon; she had only a smudge to show him.

Tim Anderson, then. His enlarger ought to be able to tease additional detail from the negative.

Could she trust Tim?

He had been at the scene. He'd had the opportunity to walk off with the object, assuming he'd noticed it after shooting the roll.

But in that case, he would have destroyed any photo that recorded the item's existence.

He was safe, then. She could show him what she'd found—him, but no one else present at the crime scene.

Christ, this job is starting to feel dangerous.

For a moment she considered just writing the damn profile and getting back to her regular duties at LAPD. But she didn't think Wanda would let her go now. That brown gaze, so like her own, would burn unblinking in her dreams.

Anderson was alone in the lab, bending over an ancient reel-to-reel tape recorder, when Donna entered. "Ed around?" she asked casually.

"He and Detective Logan just got back from Hollywood. They're briefing Mueller on what went down."

"Well, you're the one I wanted to see, anyhow." She decided to ease into her request by way of small talk. "What's wrong with this dinosaur?" she asked with a nod at the machine.

"Wow and flutter. The pinch rollers are worn, need to be replaced."

"What do you use it for?"

"Recording suspect interrogations and witness interviews."

"So you're more than just a photography expert."

His deft fingers removed the two rubber rollers and discarded them. "Photography is what I love. This other stuff is just chores." He smiled at her. "You didn't visit me to ask about this."

"No. About this." She showed him the photo. "See that blotch there? It might be some small item that got overlooked at the scene. Or do you think it's dirt on the emulsion or what?"

Anderson took the photo. "A flaw in the emulsion would print black. A pale spot like this could indicate a scratch on the top side of the negative, or maybe dust on the enlarger's diffuser lens or in the negative carrier. I don't think so, though. Looks like something authentic to me."

"I was thinking a blowup might show more detail."

"Could. I can crop it really tight, give you an eight-by-ten of just that spot."

"You can achieve that much magnification?"

"Yeah, if I turn the enlarger head horizontal and project the negative onto the darkroom wall. I can pin the printing paper to the wall and focus the image on that. It'll be bleary and grainy, but big."

"Sounds good."

"I'd better put a higher-wattage bulb in the lamphouse to cut down on the exposure time," he said, getting interested in the project. He looked at the real-to-reel with distaste. "Just let me finish this up."

She watched as he attached two new pinch rollers

to their shafts and cleaned them with an alcohol-soaked swab.

"Actually," she said, "I'm a little hesitant about asking you to do this. It's not really my job to commandeer lab resources. I may be stepping on some toes."

He swabbed the capstan and heads. "Just turn it over to Ed, let him authorize it. That solves any political problems."

"Ed and I aren't exactly on friendly terms. If I bring this up with him, he may take it the wrong way. I mean, let's say there *was* something on the body, and he missed it. . . ."

Tim saw her point. "I guess that wouldn't look good. Ed wouldn't take it well, either. He's already worried that he's getting old." He threaded a tape through the tapeguides onto the take-up reel.

"That's why I'm thinking it might be a good idea to keep this between us right now. If there's nothing in the photo, nobody has to know about it and no egos get ruffled."

"You want me to do the blowup but not tell Ed?"

"That's how I'd rather handle it, yes."

He switched on the machine, and the reels turned. A monotone hummed from the speaker. He listened till he was satisfied there was no variation in the frequency.

"All right," he said finally. "It may be tricky, though. I'll have to wait till Ed leaves for dinner before I use the darkroom. Thing is, I've got sort of a hot date tonight, and I have to be out of here by six-thirty. It's a narrow window. I'll give it my best shot."

"Thanks, Tim. Look, if you're able to get it done tonight, can you leave the photo someplace where I can pick it up?"

"In my locker. That one there." He fished a key

out of his pocket. "The lab is locked at night. Here's a spare key."

"You're terrific. Really."

She saw him blush and realized he was shy. She supposed he had been one of those camera-club nerds in school, the ones who always operate the slide projector; and school, for him, had not been long ago. Well, he had a date tonight, anyway. That was more than she had.

The thought made her feel lonely and just a bit old.

25

Donna finished the profile at six. She was feeding pages into the copier in the detective squad room when Logan walked in. Fear brushed her heart as she thought of Wanda, perhaps dying at his hands. She steadied herself.

"Any news?" she asked, keeping her voice casual.

"Some. None good." He picked up the coffeepot and poured a steaming arc into a mug. "LAPD found the ex-con whose name came up in the MO run. He's been in the hospital—recovering from a tonsillectomy, believe it or not—for the past three days."

"Terrific."

"None of the tips on the hotline has panned out so far. Mueller took one of your suggestions; he assigned a patrol unit to make the rounds of service stations and car-stereo shops. They're asking about vehicles equipped with a CB radio or a police scanner. I think they've gotten a few names."

"The names won't help unless they can be cross-referenced with a list of gun owners or detective-magazine subscribers, something to narrow down the list."

"Mueller ought to realize that, but you'd better remind him. He may have forgotten it already."

"He hasn't slowed down as much as you think."

"He didn't need to slow down. He was never any good to begin with."

She saw how much it hurt him to have lost the chief's respect. Mueller had been almost a fatherly presence in his life. The contempt Mark projected was only a flimsy cover for disappointment and shame.

"Anything else?" she asked gently, feeling less afraid of him now she had glimpsed his vulnerability.

Logan sipped his coffee. "The desk clerk at the hotel. Reynolds and Hill met with him. He's alibied."

"Solid?"

"Very. There was a disturbance in one of the rooms—drunken guest making a racket. The clerk went up there several times during the night to quiet him down. Other people on that floor confirm the story."

"You knew he wasn't the one, anyway."

"And you knew I knew it. So I guess you were right: seven months together *must* count for something."

"Not for much," she said lightly, throwing his own words back at him.

"I shouldn't have said that." His eyes were on her, dark and thoughtful. "There's a lot of things I regret saying. A lot of mistakes I've made."

"Both of us," she said, giving him that much.

He moved closer. Green light spilled out from under the lid of the copier, and the machine whirred. "That the profile?"

"Uh-huh. Stick around, one of these sets is for you."

"I'd like to review it with you."

"It's fairly self-explanatory."

"Like my notes, right? But I want to hear your *impressions*."

She had said that to him on the pier. It was funny how they were reciting each other's lines, like actors reading the wrong cue cards. Some kind of ritual was being played out between them, stylized and formal as a dance.

"There's probably not much I can add to what we've already discussed," she said, stapling the collated pages, not looking at him.

"Let's try."

"Right now?"

"Over dinner."

The words were unexpected and rattler-quick. She very nearly stapled her forefinger before recovering.

"Do you think that's a good idea?" she asked, stalling.

He shrugged. "You're done with the profile. You'll be off the case after today. This might be our last opportunity to get together for a while. And I think we've got some unfinished business to deal with."

That was plausible, she supposed. He might be trying to find the graceful end to their relationship that had eluded them before.

Or he might secretly hope to renew their affair. Working together had been undeniably a turn-on. There had been a few moments in the past twenty-four hours when their minds had locked onto a common target; she had found it pleasurable, almost sensual, like the movie cliché of lovers sharing a smoke.

Of course there was another possible motive on his part. If he were the killer, he would want to know the contents of the profile ahead of anyone else. And the contents of her mind, as well.

She realized he was waiting for an answer. Easy enough to turn him down; but suppose he was sincere in wanting to be gracious at last. Besides, she needed to resolve the question of his guilt. And—hell, admit it—there was a certain thrill in dating him again. Memories of last summer were part of it; danger was another.

"All right, Mark," she said as her heart kicked into

a steady pounding rhythm. "Got a restaurant in mind?"

"Angelo's."

"I knew it would be that one."

"Where else?"

"First the carousel, now this. We're revisiting the scenes of our former happiness."

"Think of it as a flashback. The non-traumatic kind."

He was smiling and everything seemed fine, but she remembered the click of the handcuff locking behind her back. Suddenly, she wasn't sure dinner was a good idea.

You've got to trust him, that's all, she told herself severely.

Wanda must have trusted the man who placed her under arrest. Donna thought about that as she let Mark lead her to his car.

26

Logan hadn't planned to ask Donna out. The invitation had been spontaneous, surprising even to him. As he watched her across the checkered tablecloth and the blur of candle flame, he wondered what had moved him to do this, what he'd hoped to gain.

He looked around at the restaurant, busy with the tinkle of silverware and the mutterings of strangers' voices. In the romantic dimness, candles burned like spot fires, casting their pale wavering glow on ocher-tinted faces. He thought of portraits on museum walls, yellowed faces standing out against the background gloom, faces of people long dead. For a disoriented moment he was dining with ghosts.

He studied his menu, and Donna did the same. A waiter took their orders. They passed the time in careful conversation. She spoke of her duties at Headquarters Bureau; he sketched in some unusual cases he'd handled during the past few months. Gradually their wariness ebbed and the discussion moved toward more personal matters.

"Still living at the old place?" he asked.

"Sure. Building some equity. The American dream. How's your new apartment?"

Lonely, he almost said, but stopped himself in time. "Okay."

She seemed to sense his unspoken answer. "Ever have company over?"

"Not often." Never, was the truth. "My social life hasn't been too exhilarating recently. How about you?"

"Work keeps me busy."

"You seeing anyone?"

She hesitated. "No."

"No one—since we broke up?"

"I guess I haven't been ready to get back out there. You know."

"Sure." He was mildly astonished at how pleased he felt at knowing that she had, in some sense, remained faithful to him.

Donna changed the subject. "When was the last time we were here?" she asked, sipping her Scotch and soda.

He lifted his own glass, filled with white wine. He meant to keep his drinking light this evening. "December, I think."

"Oh, sure. Just before Christmas."

"Christmas—yes."

He remembered the red and green place settings and, outside, fig trees garlanded in tinsel along Corona Beach Boulevard. He and Donna had gone for a walk after dinner in the early winter dark. The air had been cool and so had the silence between them. Only a week earlier he had discovered her affair, and though he hadn't yet told her that he knew, she'd seemed to sense it somehow.

Her thoughts reached the same destination. "Things were already going bad by then," she said. "We had fun at the start, though, didn't we?"

He smiled ruefully. "That seminar wasn't fun. You worked us hard. Not that I'm complaining. You were a good teacher."

"And you were my best pupil."

He rotated his wineglass by the stem. "Is that why you went out with me?"

"That, and because of something I saw in you. Strength. And ... hurt." Her voice was gentle. "I saw the hurt right away—even before I found out about Sharon."

"You were the first woman I'd been with since I lost her. Did you know that?"

"I suspected it."

"Didn't think I could ever put all that behind me. But when I met you ... I knew I had to try."

Her smile was sad. "It felt so right. For both of us."

"It *was* right ... at first."

"Yes. At first."

But not for long. They had been living together only two months when the Slasher's first victim was found.

Dinner arrived, two steaming plates, his heaped with linguine and clams, hers a fastidiously spare arrangement of veal cutlets and baby carrots. The smells of sautéed meat and garlic butter blended like intertwined motifs of a musical composition.

"I've always been curious about something," Donna said slowly, cutting the veal. "As long as we're sort of on the subject, I mean. How did you find out?"

He wound a string of pasta around his fork. "Came home early one afternoon in December. It was one of your days off, and you were in the shower, singing; you didn't hear me come in. The song was 'How High the Moon'—funny I remember that.

"Went in the bedroom to get changed. The bed was unmade, a mess, and in the wastebasket I found a used rubber, pushed down under the crumpled-up Kleenex and the *Time* blow-in cards.

"He must have left just before I arrived. I barely missed running into him—or catching the two of you together. Don't know what I would have done then.

"I went out while you were still in the shower,

came back later. Didn't bring up the subject that day, or for several weeks afterward. Had to wait till I was calm about it, could think clearly. I never did tell you how I knew; you might have thought I'd been spying, and I didn't want that." He shrugged, exhausted by the story. "That's all."

A frown pinched the corners of Donna's mouth. "Hell, Mark . . . I'm sorry you learned it that way."

"At least when I finally did bring it up—when I asked you to answer yes or no—you didn't lie."

"I never intended to lie. I never thought it would be necessary. I thought the whole thing would be just temporary, and then you and I would go on. Maybe we would have . . ."

"If I hadn't found out? Do you believe that?"

She looked away. "No." Melting ice played soft musical notes in her glass. "You know, what happened—it was hard on us both. But it doesn't have to ruin our lives."

"Oh, sure, we'll survive. I know *you* will."

Her gaze ticked toward him. She set down her fork. "What does that mean?"

"It means you're a survivor. You're tough."

He said it lightly, but she took the statement like a slap. The muscles in her cheeks twitched.

"Oh," she said. "I get it."

"What?"

"That's how you've always thought of me. Tough." Bitterness flavored the words. "Too tough to be hurt. Too tough to cry."

"I didn't mean it that way."

She ignored him. "What exactly is it that makes me so goddamn tough, anyway? The gun under my jacket? The bad Jersey accent that comes out when I'm pissed?"

"For Christ's sake—"

"If I were half as tough as you think, the Slasher

wouldn't have . . . fucked me up the way it did. I tried to talk to you about that. You didn't even hear."

She was putting him on the defensive and he didn't like that. "I don't want to discuss this."

"Of course you don't. You were never willing to *discuss* anything. That was what drove me crazy— you were never really *there*."

He raised his hand in a signal to stop. "Donna—"

"See? You *still* don't want to hear. You said we had unfinished business; now you don't want to deal with it. Because you're afraid. When we met, I thought I saw strength in you. But it wasn't strength; it was remoteness, distance, holding back, pushing away. Weakness. Weakness and fear."

Abruptly she stopped speaking, as if startled by her own outburst. Logan stared at her, hands flat on the table, fingertips squeezed white. Anger had him now. The cold, still anger he recognized as most dangerous.

He waited a long moment, unspeaking, until his heartbeat returned to nearly normal. Then he reached for his copy of the profile. "Let's get to work."

"Mark . . ."

A shake of his head silenced her.

He read slowly, flipping back and forth through the three single-spaced pages, as if the profile were another menu to study.

Finally he put it down. His mind was working fast, his thoughts icicle-sharp. He saw a way to repay hurt with hurt, sweat her as he'd done in the carousel house. A reckless hand, but he would play it.

"Interesting analysis," he said slowly. "You push the would-be cop angle pretty hard."

"I still think it's our best shot."

"Maybe. But why not a real cop?"

A carrot was speared on her fork, shiny with butter. It hovered untouched near her mouth. "I hadn't thought of that."

"Come on, Donna." He leaned forward. "It had to occur to you that a Corona Beach cop, a member of the force, fits this profile better than any wanna-be."

"That's a good thought, Mark. I'll bring it up with Mueller—"

"Stop acting like this is some kind of revelation. On the pier you said you would check the files of rejected applicants. Do that today?"

"Yes."

"And you checked the files of current employees, as well. Sworn officers."

"I didn't say that."

"You don't have to say it. So you're looking for a cop with a failed relationship in his recent past, a reason to hate women. I can think of a few."

He read confusion in her darting eyes. Logan had been in a few fights, and he remembered them now— the blur of his fists as he threw unexpected jabs, first low, then high, in a varied rhythm and sequence, keeping his opponent unsteady. This was like that.

"Such as?" she asked.

"Joe Kurtz, for one. He got divorced not long ago. Ed Barnes—he lost Marjorie. And then there's me."

"You know I couldn't suspect you."

"No?" He was smiling, his grin tight and painful like a wince. "Like the purloined letter, I'm too obvious?"

"Too obvious—and too close."

"We're not that close anymore."

"How sure are you of that?"

He was the one who didn't reply this time. She had landed a blow of her own, and he felt himself draw back, remembering that the woman across the table was a good fighter too.

"Of course," she added in a whisper, "I might be wrong not to see you as a suspect."

"You might."

"Am I?"

"You're the profiler. What do you think?"

She shut her eyes. Breath left her in a sigh. "I think . . . I'm afraid, Mark. All of a sudden . . . afraid."

27

Donna felt like she'd been kicked in the stomach. She kept trying to suck air, but her lungs wouldn't work. If Mark had been out to hurt her, scare her, in retaliation for the cruelty she'd inflicted, he had accomplished his purpose.

Wrong of her to have called him weak, anyway. Insensitive and unfair. He wasn't weak. He had absorbed too many shocks, and something inside him had given way. Everybody had a limit to endurance, and he had reached his. She ought to know about that. She had reached her limit also, and that was when she had taken another man into her bed, a man who had listened and comforted and seemed to understand.

Dinner was concluded in silence. Logan put it on his credit card. Donna didn't argue; she was not in the mood to haggle over splitting the tab.

Then they were outside in the late summertime twilight. Horsetails swished in the salmon sky. A breeze from the ocean slipped through the branches of Indian laurel figs and excited the leaves into brief ecstasies of shivering.

She let Mark drive her back to the station. Being in the car with him was bad, and she had to keep reminding herself that people had seen them dine together, so he couldn't *do* anything.

Even so, she got out fast once he pulled into the lot behind the civic center.

"Aren't you going to thank me for the wonderful evening?" he asked through the open window.

She couldn't think of anything to say except *fuck you*, and she was tired of telling him that. As she walked away, low laughter drifted after her.

The police station felt safe and friendly after the tension in the car. Most of the offices and squad rooms were deserted. She left copies of the profile on the desks of all relevant personnel. She was left with two sets, one for her and one for Barnes.

The crime lab's glass door framed darkness. Donna inserted her borrowed key in the keyhole before realizing the door was unlocked.

Tim had said he had a hot date. Must have left in such a hurry he'd forgotten to lock up. She hoped he'd had time to make the enlargement.

Her hand frisked the wall and found the light switch. Banks of fluorescents snapped on.

Barnes was there, seated at a table in the middle of the large windowless room. Slowly he turned in his chair.

"Hello, Donna."

"Ed." Bad to show she was flustered, hard not to. "What are you doing here?"

An eight-by-ten rested under his hand. Near it was a manila envelope, her name printed on it in block letters. The door of Anderson's locker stood open.

"I spend most of my time in this place." His voice was flat, devoid of affect—a killer's voice. The thought buzzed her like a fly; she brushed it away.

"I meant, why were you sitting in the dark?"

"Resting my eyes. Trying to clear my head." He pushed the photo around on the table. "You're wondering about this."

"Well . . . yes."

"I came back a little while ago, after dinner. No reason to go home, nothing for me there. Tim was gone. Ordinarily I wouldn't look in his locker, but I needed some of his lens tissue for these." He tapped his bifocals.

"That envelope was left expressly for me."

He regarded her over the steel-rimmed frames. "I assumed that anything pertaining to the investigation was for all of us to share."

She couldn't answer, not without explaining her reason for secrecy.

"Tim left a note for you," he went on. "Said there's definitely some minute object in her hair, but even with this much magnification, he can't tell what it is. Goddamned if I can, either."

Donna approached the table, conscious of the open door behind her, the night-watch cops on duty down the hall, within range of a scream.

Tim had enlarged only the key portion of the frame. The grain was coarse and sandpapery. There was nothing solid or distinct in the photograph, only shades of tone and color, soft edges blending in a mist. Donna thought it resembled abstract art, the kind she hated, soupy and vague.

"Any ideas?" Barnes asked.

"No."

"Guesses?"

"Scrap of tissue or cloth."

"Could be. Whatever it was . . . I missed it."

She wondered if that was really why he'd been communing with the dark. Overlooking evidence, failing at his job, had depressed him. She remembered Tim saying, "He's already worried that he's getting old."

Ed did look old with his potbelly and fallen chest, his slumped shoulders and thinning hair, his bifocals cupping the pouches under his eyes. He was only fifty-five, but he'd aged two decades since Marjorie's death.

Of course there was another reason he might be disturbed by what she'd found. The obvious reason.

"Maybe you didn't miss it," she said slowly, watching him. "Maybe it walked."

He blinked, as if considering the idea for the first time. "Possibly. But then, whoever took it . . ."

They looked at each other. Donna tried to read his eyes, but the glasses hid them behind sheets of glare.

She finished his thought: "Whoever took it was present at the crime scene."

"Is that why you had Timmy do this job on the sly?"

"That wasn't the reason I gave."

He nodded. "But it *was* the reason."

"I was being cautious."

"Appropriately so. You were right to withhold this from me. And I was wrong to look at it."

"It probably doesn't matter."

"Probably not. Unless the evidence did walk, and I'm the one who gave it legs."

"Are you?" She tried to keep the question light.

"No. But I can't prove it, and a simple denial is hardly persuasive."

"I'll just have to trust you, then."

"I guess you will." He gave her the photo. "Take this home, study it, see if you can puzzle it out."

"I'll do that. Here's some bedtime reading for you." She handed over his copy of the profile. "Don't let it give you nightmares."

"Oh, it's too late for that."

He took off his glasses and twirled them by the stem. The frames threw sparks of steely light. His face was sad, and his eyes, underscored by puffiness and edged with fractured crinkles, held some of the melancholy wisdom she had seen in portraits of Einstein.

"After I found Marjorie in the tub," Barnes said softly, "nothing could ever shock me again."

"Not even Wanda, what was done to her?"

His mouth formed an unhappy smile, thin and bloodless as a paper cut. "Not even that."

Donna didn't like his smile. It seemed to hold within it all the world's bleakness. She thought of the endless stretches of the Mojave between L.A. and Vegas, flat land bristling with scrub, raked by dusty winds that blew out of nowhere. She wondered if Ed's soul was equally barren now that Marjorie was gone—or if it had been so lovelorn and empty even while she lived.

"I never understood how she could have . . . done what she did," Donna said slowly.

"Neither did I." Ed gazed off into some unseen distance. "At first."

"You understand now?"

"I think I do." He was speaking more to himself than to her. "It's a surmise, nothing more. She never told me. The only note she left was the one about that cat."

His lips tightened as he spoke the last word. She read hatred in the shape of his mouth. Hatred for the pet that had meant more to Marge than her husband had.

"What was the reason?" she asked gently.

He blinked, and when he looked at her again, he seemed to be surfacing from the deep waters of a trance.

"No, Donna." His voice was very quiet. "You're not going to know that."

"I have a right."

"Why?"

"She was my friend."

Barnes turned away, shoulders hunched. "Then you should have saved her."

28

Donna was feeling tired and jumpy as she drove back to Parker Center, LAPD headquarters in downtown L.A. She dropped off her motor-pool Caprice and picked up her personal car, a Toyota Celica GT notchback, fun to drive even in city traffic.

It was 9:45 when she shot onto the westbound Santa Monica Freeway, heading for West L.A. In Culver City she stopped at a supermarket for tomorrow's breakfast, picked a cereal box off the shelf, stood in the express lane while the cashier scanned price codes and the P.A. system played a Muzak version of "Strawberry Fields Forever."

The customer ahead of her was buying a house plant. Donna thought of Garden Gifts in Joliet, of Jo Ann Gardner alone now in the dark, perhaps fingering the veins of her wrist.

A shudder danced over her. Christ, this case really had her rattled.

She hadn't gotten this emotionally involved in her work since the Slasher investigation. She had been alone then too—not literally alone, not with Mark lying beside her at night—but alone in every way that mattered.

Yet for a few weeks between Stanton's arrest and his disposition in Superior Court, she had found someone to share the heavy load that threatened to crush her under its killing pressure.

She remembered the windy November day when she'd come to the Corona Beach station, planning to meet Mark for lunch. He had been delayed in the field, and she'd been forced to wait.

Loitering in the hall, thinking of nothing but the nightmares that continued to chew at her sleep, she had gradually become conscious of a man watching her.

An awkward moment passed as their gazes locked, then drifted apart, then locked again.

He smiled. "You're Donna Wildman, aren't you? Mark Logan's girlfriend? Great job on the Slasher case."

A hundred people, a thousand, had expressed similar sentiments in the week since Wayne Allen Stanton's arrest. In each instance she had accepted the compliment politely.

But this time what came out of her mouth was: "It hasn't been so great for me."

He moved closer. "Why do you say that?"

"Because I can't get the damn case out of my head. And it's been worse since we caught Stanton." Her voice slipped into a whisper. "It's getting worse every day."

This wasn't like her. She was not the type to reveal the intimacies of her emotional life to a stranger. She told herself to shut up, stop acting like a fool.

But the man looking down at her didn't seem to think she was a fool. "Worse—how?"

She studied him before answering. Though he wore civilian clothes, he was obviously a cop. Probably patrol; she knew most of the detectives. Morning watch had ended three hours earlier, but some cops worked overtime or exercised in the station-house gym. Now, having changed out of his uniform, he must be on his way home. His face was blunt but intelligent, his eyes warm and searching. She thought of Mark's eyes, cool gray eyes that would not focus on her pain, eyes that stared past it in willful blindness.

This man was looking right at her. He was not afraid to see.

And suddenly she knew she couldn't hold it in any longer. She had to get it out, get it all out now, or she would go insane.

And so she told him. Everything. The nightmares, the panic attacks, the loss of control. Mark's indifference to it all. Her loneliness and fear.

They were sitting in the interrogation room when she finished, though she hadn't been quite aware that he had taken her there, just as she was not quite aware that he was holding her hands in his.

"I know about loneliness," Joe Kurtz said gently. "My wife and I broke up a couple months ago. I'm glad I work nights. I don't like being in the apartment . . . in the dark . . . without her."

"Being with Mark right now is like being alone."

"You shouldn't have to handle this all by yourself."

"I'm not even sure I can."

"Well, maybe you won't have to."

She pursued it no further that day. But a week later she returned to the station at eleven and waited for Kurtz in the parking lot. The damp autumn air swirled around her; she dug her hands into her jacket pockets and tried to control her thumping heart.

When he emerged, she waved to him. "I thought maybe we could . . ." *Have lunch*, she meant to say, but the words seemed so absurdly pointless she couldn't force them out.

"I was hoping you'd come back," he said, and he took her behind a parked van and cupped her face in both hands and kissed her, tentatively at first, then desperately, and she responded, not knowing what she had gotten into and, in that moment, not giving a damn.

"Five sixty-three."

Donna blinked at the cashier and remembered she was making a purchase.

Her car was low on gas; she stopped at a Shell station, choosing the self-serve island. She watched the changing numbers on the fuel pump, gallons running a race with dollars and falling ever farther behind.

She knew how it felt to run as fast as you could and still lose ground. Throughout the Slasher case, she had felt that way as she worked frantically to get inside the killer's mind before another kid came home from school to find his mom ripped open like a paper bag. Even afterward, the feelings had persisted, irrationally, maddeningly.

But finally, in Joe Kurtz's arms, she had been able to forget.

Their affair lasted only a month; they were together no more than a dozen times, always at her place, during the day, when Mark was on duty in Corona Beach.

Joe was a good lover, and he took pleasure in trying new things, but it was the intimacy after sex that meant most to her, when they lay together in bed and she was free to talk out her problems with a man who listened and cared.

Guilt dogged her only toward the end, when she began to worry about what might happen if Mark found out. And then, of course, he did.

She ended the affair the next day. Again, she surprised Joe in the parking lot; but this time as he reached out to her, she drew back.

"I'm sorry," she whispered. "Mark knows."

Kurtz frowned. "I saw him today. He didn't say anything."

"He knows I've been seeing somebody, but not who. And I won't tell him. I swear I'll never tell."

"You're going to end it, aren't you?"

"I have to."

"You could kiss him off. I'm better for you."

"No, I . . . I couldn't do that."

"I won't give you up."

"Joe—I'm sorry—you've got no choice."

She fled in a haze of tears. He didn't follow. But shortly afterward, he began calling her at work, first reasoning with her, then pleading. Once Mark had moved out, Joe visited her condo late one night, begging her to reconsider. Finally he left her alone.

She hadn't meant to hurt him—to hurt anyone. She had simply needed to get through a difficult time in her life. The affair had rescued her from a psychological hell, and she couldn't regret it. But the cost had been high, and somehow all three of them went on paying it, even now.

As she pulled into the garage of her condominium building at ten-thirty, Donna had the Beretta unholstered, the decocking lever up. Both Mark and Ed knew more than they should about her work on the case. And there was Brody's secretary, Lynn, who might have gossiped to some of the cops—even to Joe Kurtz, if he really was her boyfriend.

Wanda's murderer could be getting nervous enough to try something. She would not be caught with her guard down.

The garage was empty. She entered the ground-floor hallway, carrying the sack of groceries in one hand and the gun in the other, hoping she wouldn't run into any neighbors.

The building had some security features, but a cop would know how to get in. Would know how to pick

the worthless locks on her apartment door too. Could
have done so already. Could be in there now.

She set down the groceries outside her door and
wondered if she was being paranoid.

Probably. But her place would be dark; the lamps
were not on timers. Silhouetted in the doorway by
the lights in the hall, she would be an easy target.
And she'd already entered one dark room tonight, to
be startled by a man waiting there.

All right. Go in fast, the way they trained you.

She unlocked the door as quietly as possible, let a
silent moment pass, then bolted inside and hugged
the wall. She waited till she was certain the only
breathing in the dark was her own.

Then she flicked on the lights. No one else in the
room.

She remained alert as she explored the rest of the
apartment: kitchen, bathroom, bedroom. She left
lights on everywhere.

Finally she came to the most likely point of entry,
the patio at the rear. It was a small patio, screened
off from the back alley by four-foot brick walls, easy
to scale. The sliding door was glass; there were two
locks, one at chest height and the other at floor level.
A patient intruder could defeat them both.

Donna switched on the patio lights and, ducking
low, went outside. The patio was her garden; she
grew rosebushes in redwood planters, potted cacti,
and Italian honeysuckle woven into a trellis. The
honeysuckle's nectar had risen in the flower tubes at
dusk to lure night-flying moths. It perfumed the air
with heavy, cloying sweetness.

Carefully she peered over the wall and scanned
the alley, then nodded, satisfied. Nobody there.

She stepped inside again, shutting the door and
securing both locks. The soft double click was faintly

audible to the man crouching behind the Dumpster several yards away.

He watched the patio and the curtained windows through eyeholes in a ski mask. To blend with night, he was camouflaged in black corduroy pants, a black windbreaker, and black leather gloves that would leave no fingerprints on Donna's body.

Knowing she would come home wary of an ambush, he had chosen to wait and watch. Once she was asleep, he would slip into the condo and finish her with one blow of the club in his hands.

Brown blood streaked the weapon. Whore's blood.

In the holster strapped to his waist was an Iver Johnson .22, purchased at a gun show several years ago, untraceable. It was fitted with a homemade silencer cut from a TV-antenna mast, an accessory that would muffle, but not entirely eliminate, the sound of a report.

The .22 was his backup weapon, to be used only if something went wrong. It would make for a less satisfying kill, and he would not be able to linger with her body as he wished to do. But if necessary he could forgo that pleasure.

All that really mattered was that Donna must die.

It would be so good, killing her. He wondered how her face would look after he finished pounding. Like the dead thing he'd left at Third and Bay? Worse, maybe. Yes. Worse.

Inside the gloves, his fingers tingled. His lips tightened in a bloodless smile.

29

In the bedroom Donna kicked off her shoes and put on slippers, hung up her jacket but left her armpit holster on. She liked the feel of the Beretta snug against her ribs, near her heart, its gentle pressure reassuring like the touch of a lover's hand.

She returned to the living room, propped up the photo on the mantel, and studied it from a distance.

The thing in Wanda's hair was a truncated crescent, greenish at bottom, yellow on top, with a blob of orange within the yellow part. A suggestion of shadows and creases gave it a folded or crumpled appearance. Donna estimated its length at one inch.

An insect? It might have alighted on the body momentarily, drawn by the camera flash. If so, her theory about concealment of evidence would be a bust. She wouldn't mind being proved wrong.

Alternatively, it could be a dead bug picked up at the murder site.

Or an earring—but it didn't seem to be attached to the earlobe.

Perhaps a pebble or a chip of seashell. Evidence that Wanda had been murdered on the beach? Her clothes had been streaked with dirt, not sand.

How about a flake of paint from the murder weapon?

Problem was, it could be any damn thing.

She walked back and forth in front of the mantel,

considering the picture from different angles like a visitor to an art gallery.

The thing did not really resemble a paint chip or a shell or a rock, she decided. It looked soft, tissuey. Like cloth or felt or paper.

Folded paper? A note? Some sort of tag?

It was multicolored, remember. Thin as paper, folded or crushed, in yellowish-green and yellow and orange.

She recalled a display of origami at a Brentwood art fair. Colored paper creased into sculptures of birds and butterflies and flowers.

Flowers . . .

She stopped pacing. She felt the kiss of a thought, light and teasing, and her blushing response, sudden heat on her face.

What she was looking at could be a flower. A real flower, not paper, not art. A flower with an unusual trumpetlike shape.

She grew honeysuckle on the patio.

Crushed, flattened, a honeysuckle flower would have much the same shape as the blur in the photo.

Honeysuckle grew wild everywhere. It could easily have been present at the murder site. Could have been transferred to Wanda's body like the mud on her skirt, the clumps of soil on the spiked heel of her shoe.

The colors were wrong for Italian honeysuckle, the kind she grew, and too orange for Japanese honeysuckle this early in the season. Perhaps it was another member of the *Lonicera* family, or an unrelated flower with a similar appearance.

There were gardening books in the bedroom bookcase. One of them might contain an illustration to help her identify the species.

She was close, very close, to something important. The nearness of it speared her with a thrill of brutal pleasure, the controlled frenzy of a cat stalking a bird.

Heart working hard, blood thrumming in her ears, she hurried down the hall. It seemed to take a long time to pick the book she wanted from the confusion of titles on her shelves.

The volume opened to the color section. She flipped through pages of illustrations. Several *Lonicera* species were possible candidates, though none seemed exactly right.

She went on turning pages, examining other plants, till her mind was numb and she wasn't seeing anything anymore.

There were too many flowers to choose from. She needed a botanist's help. She would contact one tomorrow.

Last night you were sure you'd be done with this case by now. Must have been crazy, Donna.

The thought brought her down from her adrenaline high and left her more fatigued than before. Long day, and she would need to be fresh in the morning.

It was eleven o'clock by now, and felt much later. Her feet were dragging as she double-checked all the locks and switched off the lights. The Beretta went under her bed. In satin pajamas that Mark had bought for her, she slipped under the covers. With the windows closed, the room was stuffy and hot, and when the bedside lamp clicked off, she felt a weight of darkness and stale air press down on her.

She reached down and touched the gun to reassure herself that she could find it in the dark. Then she rolled on her side, nuzzled her pillow, and courted sleep.

At first the residue of the day's excitement kept her awake. Gradually she felt the onset of sleep in ripples of drowsiness. They washed over her, faster,

faster, beating in a soothing tidal rhythm that became the steady susurrus of a single wave forever breaking, frozen in the instant of its shattering crash.

In the endless static hiss she slept, her muscles relaxing, breaths becoming deep and regular.

After some blank and peaceful stretch of time, dream images popped like flashcubes in her darkness. Wanda's face in the crime-scene photos. Bruises and brown eyes. Split lips and swollen tongue. Flowers in her hair, growing with the crazy rapidity of a time-lapse study. Her hair was a garden, rich with honeysuckle, glittering with the zigzag courses of bees.

Donna sniffed the flowers. A heady fragrance, nectar-sweet, bloomed in her world. The smell of childhood summers, strong in her nostrils, impossibly strong, stronger than the ghost smells that scent the air of dreams. Because this smell was no dream—it was real—it was the perfume of the Italian honeysuckle out back, wafting into her apartment from the patio, through the open door. . . .

The clicking of her eyelashes in the dark told her she was awake.

She had not bolted upright out of sleep. She lay rigid on her side, hugging herself, strait-jacketed by fear.

The air was sweet with flowers.

The patio door had been opened.

Someone was in the apartment.

Wanda's killer. Had to be.

Coming for her. Perhaps already in this room.

Her eyes ticked, searching the darkness. She listened for a footstep, a rustle of clothes.

There.

A sigh of movement. Swish of a trouser leg, creak of a rubber sole planting itself gently, gently, on the short-nap carpet.

In the bedroom. No more than a yard away. Close.

Her gun was within reach, but she would have to move fast to get it, gamble on a lunge of her arm and a blind trigger pull. If he was armed, he would fire when he saw her move.

Jesus, I don't like this. Don't like this at all.

A whisper of fabric as he took another step, closing in.

Do it. Now.

She grabbed for the gun, touched bare carpet—*shit, where is it, where the hell is it?*—her fingers groping for an endless fraction of a second, then finding the familiar shape of the pistol.

As her hand closed over the plastic grips, she sensed something coming at her, swooping down out of the dark.

She jerked sideways, snap-rolled off the bed with the Beretta in her hand, and the thing flickered past her, raising a breeze that stirred the down on her cheek. A hard, solid thump as it struck the pillow.

With a grunt of pain she slammed into the floor, landing on her side, her legs snarled in the sheets that had come with her.

She kicked free and twisted into a half crouch, heart hammering like a bastard, adrenaline surging.

Her Beretta came up fast. She fired off two rounds, not aiming, just point-and-shoot.

Twin cracks of sound, shockingly loud.

Instinctively she knew both shots had missed. She flung herself sideways just as the killer's gun spat twice, the reports muffled. Soft thuds of bullet impacts in the wall. But no muzzle flashes—must be using a silencer.

Rolling on the floor, she squeezed off four more rounds, laying down a field of fire, hoping for a lucky hit.

A second later she bumped up against the open

closet door and scrambled for cover inside, then waited in a crouch. Scanned the grainy dark, alert for movement, any movement.

Nothing.

Over the ringing in her ears, she heard a rapid drumroll—a tattoo of fast footsteps pounding down the hall, diminishing with distance, and finally fading out.

He had fled.

She'd wounded him, she hoped. But maybe not. Maybe she'd simply scared him off.

Donna stood up slowly, thigh muscles fluttering, a sour taste at the back of her mouth.

Voices murmured through the wall she shared with the apartment next door—her neighbors, panicked by the fusillade, probably already dialing 9-1-1. Good move, but it would take too long for help to arrive. She couldn't wait.

Her first impulse was to follow the intruder at a run, but she knew better. He might be setting a trap.

She took a breath and did it right—pivoting into the doorway in the Weaver stance, scoping the hall, then moving to the next door and repeating the procedure.

The sliding door to the patio was open, two perfectly round holes cut in the glass near the locks. Glass cutter and suction cup—that was how he'd gotten in without making noise.

The smell of honeysuckle was close and cloying as she sidestepped toward the patio, hugging the wall. She flipped the switches that turned on the outside lights and dared a look through the doorway.

The patio was empty. She crept outside into the warm night, bent double, head lower than the walls.

He might be kneeling just beyond the patio, waiting for her head to rise into view so he could waste her like a pop-up target in a shooting gallery.

But she doubted he would stick around to try, not with the whole neighborhood alarmed and people probably peeping out of every window. Anyway, she had to chance it, had to see.

She looked over the wall and scanned the alley in the weak starlight. Empty.

Of course he might not have left via the patio. He might still be in the apartment.

It took her another two minutes of wary searching, the Beretta shaking in her two hands, before she was satisfied that he was gone.

Only then did emotion hit her. She doubled over, swaying. The room wheeled; she thought of riding the carousel with Mark.

"Jesus, that was close," she whispered, her voice unexpectedly hoarse, as though she had been shouting. "Jesus, that was close. Jesus, close. Jesus."

Keep it together.

She had never been nearly killed before. Well, there was that time in the alley downtown when an angel-dusted punk had come at her with a knife. Panic had made her fingers spastic, and she'd had trouble popping the snap on her holster. She'd managed, though, and put the asshole in the hospital with a bullet in the knee.

Yes, that had been close too. But it hadn't felt so . . . personal.

The man who'd tried to kill her tonight could have been Mark. Or Ed Barnes, who once had been among her closest friends. Or Joe Kurtz, so recently her lover.

Maybe it was none of them. Maybe it was some other cop, any cop who'd been present at the crime scene.

Yet the details of the attack suggested an assailant who knew her. He seemed aware that she kept the gun under the bed; when she reached for it, he struck. He was familiar with the layout of the apartment, could find her bedroom in the dark, could retrace his steps and escape even when dazzled by muzzle flashes. It seemed likely he had been here before.

Mark had shared the condo with her. Ed and Marjorie had visited often. Joe had spent a dozen afternoons in her bed.

No, she thought with a reflexive shake of her head. *Not them. I don't want it to be Joe, or Ed, or Mark— anybody I know.*

Christ, this is too much. Too damn much.

A convulsive shiver trembled through her body. Chills hurried up and down her arms. She knew what was about to happen, and she made it to the bathroom just in time.

Afterward, she flushed the toilet repeatedly, her hand jerking the lever with a robot's mechanical obsessiveness until she realized what she was doing and made herself stop.

She looked in the mirror. For an eye-blink of time, Wanda's face looked back. The hallucination almost cost her whatever was left in her digestive tract, but she got hold of herself.

"You're all right," she said, nodding her head in confirmation and encouragement. "Not a scratch on you, Wildman, you're a survivor. Damn straight."

Her knees were not too shaky as she returned to the bedroom and switched on the overhead light. Brass shell casings winked at her from the floor. There was no blood spatter or trail. The slugs she'd fired had drilled holes in the door frame, bureau, and walls, missing the intruder. His two shots had punched into the wall near her bed.

Bisecting the pillow where her head had rested, crushing the foam rubber as it would have crushed her skull, was the first weapon he had used, the one meant to kill her silently while she slept.

It was a cop's side-handle baton, labeled *Corona Beach P.D.*

30

The phone woke Mueller at midnight. His first thought came with a flash of fear: *Another body.*

They had worried that the killer was a repeater. As he lifted the phone, interrupting its third ring, he was sure a second girl had been found beaten to death.

"Mueller."

"Chief. Donna Wildman."

"What's happened?"

"Just had sort of a near-death experience. Somebody broke into my apartment and tried to bash my brains in. When that failed, he used a gun. I popped a few caps, scared him off. Didn't nick him, though."

Her voice was unsteady and frightened, though she was working hard to sound calm.

"Christ, Donna. Are you okay?"

"Shaken up, that's all."

"Call LAPD?"

"I think everybody in the neighborhood called. We don't get much gunfire around here. There are two patrol units at my place now, and the West L.A. watch commander is sending over two D-ones and some SID people."

"Did you get a look at the guy?"

"No. It was dark."

"Any impressions of him at all? Tall, short, fat, thin?"

"I didn't have time for impressions. It was over in a hurry. But he did leave something behind."

"What?"

"You're not going to like this, Chief."

"Tell me, for Christ's sake."

"A PR twenty-four—with a CBPD label."

Mueller let his head fall back slowly on the drift of pillows piled against the headboard.

"Chief? You there?"

"Yes, Donna. I'm here." He shut his eyes. "So he's one of our own. Not a phony cop. A real one."

"It looks that way."

"Hell. Goddamn it to hell." He got hold of himself. "Tell me about the baton."

"It's your standard twenty-four-inch side-handle model. There's an inventory-control number at the end of the handle: fourteen."

Mueller forced his mind into gear. Twenty-four-inch batons were issued to uniformed cops, eighteen-inch models to plainclothes officers. The killer wore a uniform, then.

"We can track him through the serial number," he said.

"I doubt it. The baton is caked with dried blood. He must have used it to kill Wanda, and if he hasn't cleaned it since then, he can't have been carrying it on duty."

"Which means it was never issued to him in the first place. He stole it, probably right out of the kit room, and its absence hasn't been noted."

"That's my assumption too."

"Then anybody could have taken it—uniform, plainclothes, even a civilian employee. Anybody who has free run of the station."

"At least we know he works there."

"Yeah." Mueller tried to keep the ugly bitterness out of his voice. "Yeah, he works there."

"I've got a few ideas as to who it might be."

"Do you?"

"When I was working in Brody's office, I, well, I took the opportunity to look through the employee files."

"Without authorization."

"Correct."

Mueller sighed. "All right, Donna. What did you find?"

"A couple of men scored unusually high on relevant categories of the MMPI."

"Which men?"

"Lieutenant Walters, for one. He showed indications of paranoia."

"You'd be paranoid too if you thought God was looking over your shoulder every damn minute of the day. Who else?"

"Sergeant Kurtz."

"Joe Kurtz is one of my best officers."

"He's also the man who found the body."

"Came across it while riding patrol."

"So he says."

"Anybody else on your list?"

She hesitated. "Ed Barnes."

"You've got to be joking."

"Ed never took the MMPI. But he had a complaint history at LAPD. Though the file doesn't specify the nature of the complaints, I have to wonder if they didn't have something to do with his being transferred off patrol."

"You're reaching."

"Maybe. But there's more. Ed might have had a specific reason to shut me up. If he was worried about . . . Oh, *shit*."

"What is it?"

"You'd better phone Tim Anderson."

"Christ, is *he* a suspect too?"

"No, it's not that. I just realized he might have been a target also. He'd learned some ... sensitive information."

"Too sensitive to share with me?"

"I don't have time to go into it now. Just call him, please, and make sure he's all right."

"I will. But first, isn't there somebody you've overlooked?"

"Like who?"

"Come on, Donna. It seems to me you're working pretty hard to avoid the obvious. If the man we're after is a cop with emotional problems, there's a much more likely candidate than any of the three you mentioned."

"You think it's Mark. Is that what you're saying?"

"He had motive," Mueller said simply. "Given his personal history, it's not unthinkable that he would go after you."

"I ... I don't believe Mark is capable of violence." The words came haltingly, her voice empty of conviction.

"Why not? He's got enough anger in him. Enough hate."

"Yes." A whisper, barely audible. "Yes, he does."

"You admit he could have done it?"

"It's possible."

From the way she answered, Mueller knew she believed it to be more than merely possible.

"How long have you suspected him?" he asked gently.

"Consciously? Only since I saw his file. But ..."

"But even before that, you were worried."

"Yes. Worried and ... scared." She cleared her throat. "Look, Chief, I've got to get going. LAPD is going to need a statement from me. When I'm through with that, I'd like to go down to Corona Beach for interrogation."

"Reynolds and Hill can handle it."

"No." She drew a shaky breath. "Logan and Barnes."

"You want to be interrogated by two of your prime suspects? Why?"

"To see their eyes. And to see if one of them lets something slip."

"Okay. I'll arrange it."

"I'll get down there as soon as I can. By two-thirty, I hope."

Mueller wanted to say something personal, express relief that she was unhurt and regret at having involved her in all this, but he'd never been good at such things. Perhaps if he had been, he wouldn't have remained unmarried his whole life.

All he said was "Two-thirty. Right."

He hung up, then switched on the lamp and hunted in his bedside Rolodex for Logan's home number.

Never should have brought Wildman into this investigation. His intention had been good—he'd hoped to jolt Logan out of his decline. It hadn't occurred to him that her proximity to Logan would place her at risk. Deadly risk.

Kill or cure, he remembered thinking at the time.

The words taunted him now.

31

The TV was on, but Logan wasn't watching.

Naked, hot, exhausted, he lay on his living-room sofa with a bottle for a friend. His muscles ached from tension.

The picture tube threw flickering light on the ceiling. He watched the colors change and thought of some distant Christmas, himself as a small boy prone on the floor, mesmerized by the tree's blinking lights.

Wonderful to be a child again. To escape all this.

Wanda had escaped. She was better off. No more pain.

He thought of how she'd chafed her wrists, tugging at the handcuffs. Funny she had fought so fiercely to live, when her life was so clearly not worth saving.

But they all fought like that, life's victims. Crippled and in pain, they struggled on. Human nature, he supposed. He didn't know if it was noble or absurd. Pointless, though. Pointless either way.

Everyone dies eventually. Why suffer and struggle for a mere postponement, a stay of execution, an extra portion of pain?

He wondered what Donna would say to that.

She wouldn't agree, of course. She was a fighter.

Maybe it was her skill at fighting, her vigorous adeptness at survival, that made him hate her so much. If he did hate her. Part of him wanted to put hostility and hurt aside, to reach out as he'd failed to do during their relationship. Part of him wanted to live, wanted to be happy, wanted her back.

Another part of him, the ugly part he knew too well, wanted her dead.

Dead like Wanda, dead in the street—dead because she'd betrayed him, humiliated him, soiled their bed . . .

Anger stirred in his dark interior, stirred and twitched and scrabbled at his insides like a bottled scorpion. He screwed the lid on tight to contain it.

On the end table beside the couch, the phone shrilled.

Lifting his head, Logan looked at it. He felt no astonishment despite the late hour. He let seven rings cry out unanswered before picking it up.

"Logan."

"This is Mueller."

He tipped the bottle to his mouth, not caring if Mueller heard. "Calling kind of late, aren't you, Chief?"

"You don't sound as if I woke you."

"Couldn't sleep. Figured I'd watch some bad TV." The sound track of the late-night movie would be audible on Mueller's end. "What's up?"

"Someone just tried to kill Donna."

Logan put the bottle down. Rose slowly to a sitting position. Licked his lips and looked for the right words to say.

"Mark?"

"Yeah. I'm here. I heard you." The words came finally. "She all right?"

"He didn't hurt her. Gunshots chased him off."

"Wound him?"

"No."

"Did she see his face?"

"No."

"Where is she now?"

"Still at her place, giving LAPD a guided tour. She'll come down here after she's done. I thought you and Barnes should take her statement."

He didn't want to say it, couldn't help himself. "You thought? *She* thought."

"What's that supposed to mean?" Mueller was not a good actor, even over the phone.

"She thinks a cop did it. Maybe me. She wants to see what kind of questions I ask, whether I give myself away." He smiled at the mouthpiece, a smile of gritted teeth. "You suspect me too, don't you, Chief?"

"The thought crossed my mind. Are you drinking?"

"Beer." It was bourbon.

"Can you establish your whereabouts earlier tonight?"

He remembered when he was the one who asked suspects for alibis. Starting tonight, he would be the suspect, the pariah, the object of everyone's distrust. Well, who was to blame for that?

"I've been home all night," he said, sudden weariness dragging him down. "Since I dropped off Donna at the station. We had dinner together. She can tell you about it."

"What's there to tell?"

"I may have led her to believe I was responsible for Wanda Gardner's murder."

"Why would you do that?"

"Stupidity. I was angry."

"You're angry all the time, Mark."

"You noticed?"

Mueller grunted. Logan heard the click of a cigarette lighter, then a sharp intake of breath as the chief took a good long drag.

"The assailant left a department nightstick at the

scene," Mueller said. "It may have been stolen from the storeroom. Probably it's the same blunt instrument that killed Wanda. LAPD will check for prints."

"There won't be any."

"How would you know?"

"I told you, Chief—this man is smart."

"As smart as you," Mueller said softly, not asking a question.

"I think so."

"And as angry."

Logan shut his eyes. "Yes."

"Be at the station at zero two hundred hours. You and Barnes will interview Donna. Then I want to talk to you."

"I'll look forward to it." Empty bravado, embarrassing to hear.

"Sober up before you come in."

"I'm sober now."

"Sober up," Mueller repeated, as if he hadn't heard. "That's the last friendly advice you'll get from me."

Click and buzz, the connection broken.

Logan stared blankly at the humming phone. A recorded voice came on, scolding him to hang up. He ignored it.

So here he was, the chief's prime suspect, the obvious choice, with a motive and no alibi and a reckless impulse toward self-incrimination he couldn't seem to control.

It was as if he wanted to be charged and convicted in order to satisfy some chortling death wish.

Maybe that was true. Maybe he was looking for a way out of the hell of his life, and this was it.

He had not consciously set out to destroy himself. Even now the prospect of jail, of hard time in that friendless place, made his stomach clench.

Of course they had nothing on him. Nothing solid.

Nothing they could take before a jury. But Mueller was desperate to clear this case and salvage his job. He might find something that looked bad. Hell, might even plant it—easy enough to do. Just put some damning item in Logan's desk or locker and conveniently discover it.

He could go down on this one. All the way down.

Perhaps jail was the best place for him. Stone walls and iron bars. He could rage like a bear in a trap, hammer with his fists and roar. It would be the final surrender to the pain that hounded him.

Scary to think of that as the shape of the rest of his life. Was it too late for renewal, redemption? Was the hate buried too deep to be excised? Was he lost?

He knew he was. That awful certainty clanged inside him like the slam of a cell door.

He dropped the phone, clutched his head, felt the angry pounding of the veins in his temples. Hands fisted, he beat his knuckles slowly against his forehead, gripped by the blind urge to attack something or somebody, even if only himself.

The recorded voice was replaced by an insistent beeping, then a high-pitched whine that went on and on.

Logan leaned forward on the couch, head down, clumps of hair knotted in his fingers, his body shaking.

He made no sound. The phone spoke for him with its endless scream.

32

It was 2:35 A.M. when Donna got to the Corona Beach civic center. She was worn out from reliving the attack in response to questions from the DHD non-hits shooting team. Her neck hurt, and her face felt numb. She badly wanted a shower, but she'd have to settle for some black coffee before she sat down with Logan and Barnes. To confront them she needed to be sharp.

She sure as hell didn't look sharp. Her hair was an uncombed horror, her eyes filmy and red-rimmed. Before leaving her apartment, she had thrown on yesterday's suit jacket, slightly rumpled, and a mismatched pair of long pants that concealed her J-frame Smith .38 in its ankle holster.

Her Beretta and the partially emptied clip had been briefly examined by the DHD team, then returned to her; they would have been confiscated only if the shooting had resulted in a hit. The gun rode in her underarm holster packing a fresh clip.

Her purse carried two extra clips for the Beretta, a speedloader for the Smith, and a can of pepper spray. Under her jacket she wore a Kevlar Second Chance vest. It was heavy and uncomfortable, but she wasn't complaining.

Whoever had tried to kill her was doubtless frustrated at having failed, angrier than before. He might try something desperate. She would be ready.

Donna parked near the rear of the station and scanned the lot before getting out. Her heels clicked on asphalt, bouncing echoes off rows of motor-pool cars.

Approaching the stairway to the back door, she heard another set of clicks and echoes superimposed over her own. She turned, sinking into a half crouch to make herself a smaller target, the Beretta in her hand.

"Donna. It's only me."

His voice identified him even before he stepped out of shadows into the mist of glareless yellow light from the sodium-vapor lamps. Joe Kurtz, standing before her in his creased blue uniform. His hands hung loosely at his sides, unthreatening.

Slowly, Donna rose to a standing position and holstered the gun. "Jesus Christ," she hissed in a ragged voice. "You scared the shit out of me."

"Sorry. Shouldn't have sneaked up on you like that. Tonight, especially. I know you've got plenty of reason to be on edge."

She tried to make her heart slow down. Joe could be the killer, but even if he was, she doubted he would try anything here, only a few paces from the station house.

"You heard about my little situation?" she asked.

"I heard. Got here just before midnight." Not early enough to provide him with an alibi, Donna noted. "Soon as I checked in, Lieutenant Alvarez let me know what had gone down."

"Did he tell you I'd be coming in to give a statement?"

"Yes."

"So you waited here for me, in the dark." *Lying in ambush. Like a predator at a watering place.* "Why?"

"For a chance to talk to you, alone, and make sure you're all right."

"I survived."

"I already knew that. I want to know how you're handling it."

"So far I've been staying busy, trying not to feel very much."

"That'll only work short-term."

"The short term is all I'm focused on right now. I've got to figure this thing out and try to keep myself alive. Later I'll deal with the rest of it."

Kurtz studied her. "You've gotten stuck in another nightmare, haven't you?"

"It's not like last time."

"No—it's worse. This time the Slasher's coming after *you*."

"I'm not intimidated."

"I know you aren't. But maybe you should be."

Donna wondered if that was a warning or a threat.

"Too late for me to do anything about it now, anyway," she answered with a shrug. "I'm in this thing for the duration. Couldn't get out if I wanted to."

"That's what I mean. You're stuck. Just like before."

She thought she saw what he was getting at, and she didn't like it.

"Maybe I am," she said quietly. "But this time I don't need a shoulder to cry on."

"Everybody needs a good shoulder now and then."

She met his eyes. "It's over, Joe. Please accept that. It's over."

His face registered no reaction except the slight flaring of his nostrils and the pulse of a vein in his temple.

"Sure," he said, straining for a casual tone. "I already knew that. Besides, you don't need me anyway. You've got your lawyer now."

She blinked. Lawyer? Then she remembered having told him about the new man in her life.

"Yeah"—she flashed a smile—"I'm doing all right."

But her reply had come a beat too late, and Kurtz had noticed.

"There is no lawyer," he said slowly, "is there, Donna?"

She couldn't answer, couldn't find the words to shape the lie.

"I knew it. You haven't found anyone. You're alone."

She took a step away from him. "I'm expected inside."

"You don't have to be alone."

"Maybe I want to be."

"Nobody wants to be."

"Good night, Joe."

"It wasn't so bad between us."

She was walking away. Wouldn't listen. Didn't want to hear.

"Give me another try, and I'll show you how good we can be together."

Up the stairs. The rear door was locked—a security precaution. Mueller had given her a spare key. She used it, not looking back.

"We can make it work." His voice was plaintive, childlike, awful to hear. "It can be better than before. If you give me a chance—"

The door swung shut behind her, and he was gone.

Donna leaned against the wall, breathing hard, eyes closed. Obsession. Frightening. Particularly tonight.

Joe loved her. She had no doubt of that. But the line between love and hate was so fine, so easily blurred, so easily crossed.

Had he crossed it earlier tonight? Had he visited her condo in the dark? Driven by a blind need to have her, to possess her again in some form, any form, whether alive or dead?

A shiver moved through her, raising a stubble of gooseflesh on her arms. She walked away from the door, striding swiftly down the hall.

33

Eyes studied Donna Wildman as she marched through the Corona Beach station, past open doorways and intersecting corridors. The eyes of uniformed officers, night clerks, plainclothes cops.

She felt more than curiosity in their silent gaze. She felt resentment.

It was irrational, of course, but in some absurd way she had become a threat to the department. She had nearly been killed, and her assailant had left the calling card of the CBPD on her pillow. Through her involvement in the case, the department itself had become the prime suspect.

She felt like shouting: *Wait a minute, I'm the victim here!*

But victim or not, she was also the outsider who had redirected the investigation down a new and ominous path.

Maybe they think I shouldn't have reported the assault, she thought angrily. *Maybe I should have just thrown the baton away, kept my mouth shut, for the good of morale. Or maybe I should have been cooperative enough to get myself iced.*

There were some, perhaps, who really did believe as much. The others were moved by a blind feeling of solidarity against an interloper from the LAPD, the stupid tribal loyalty that was the dark side of camaraderie.

Whatever their thinking, one thing was clear: she was not welcome here.

Well, hell. She'd been plenty of places where she wasn't wanted. Ought to be used to it by now.

When she entered Mueller's office, she found the chief at his desk, his face cobwebbed by wispy strands of smoke. He had a phone in one hand, a cigarette in the other.

"Nothing else you can try? All right, I understand. Thanks." He hung up. "That was the SID officer in charge. Markham."

"He was at my apartment."

"Says they dusted the baton and lasered it. The only prints are smooth gloves."

"Did you expect any different?"

"No." Jets of smoke streamed from his nostrils. "Would have made my job too goddamn easy. On the positive side, you can stop worrying about Tim Anderson. I phoned him and woke him up. Woke a female friend of his, also—she was bitching in the background about cops and late-night calls."

A current of relief trembled through her. "Tim told me he had a hot date. I'm glad he's okay."

"More than okay. That kid's the only one of us who's getting any fun out of life. Have a seat."

Her body ached as she sank into a chair. She experienced a momentary heart palpitation, one of many in the past three hours.

Mueller looked her over. "You're worn out."

"Very."

"Want some coffee?"

"I'd better not. My nerves are raw enough as it is."

"I've got decaf." Mueller smiled. "Nicotine is my vice, not caffeine."

"Decaf sounds great." She made a move to rise. "I can get it."

"You stay put."

She watched his cigarette smolder in the ashtray till he returned with a steaming mug. "Thanks, Chief."

"My pleasure, Detective. I mean that." He resumed his seat and his businesslike manner. "Better bring you up to speed. I called Logan right after I talked to you. He was home—awake and drinking—sounded bad."

"Bad, how?"

"Moody and giddy at the same time. He said he took you to dinner and hinted at being Wanda's murderer."

"He was having fun with me."

"What kind of fun?"

"Telling me how well he fit the profile."

"Was he right?"

"A lot of people could fit it."

Mueller didn't pursue the matter. "I tried calling Barnes also. Couldn't reach him by phone, finally had to call his beeper. He called back five minutes later from a pay phone."

"Where was he?"

"On PCH." Pacific Coast Highway.

"At midnight?"

"Said he started feeling claustrophobic at home. Too many memories. Said when that happens, sometimes he takes a drive along the coast." Skepticism colored his voice.

"You don't believe him."

"I haven't said that." Mueller brushed away a clinging coil of smoke. "When I talked to Tim, I asked why you might be worried about his safety. He told me about the photo. I take it that's what you meant when you said Barnes might have a reason to silence you."

"The three of us are the only ones who saw the

blowup or knew it existed. If Ed had wanted to keep it quiet ..."

"I hear you. Did you determine what the hell it was a picture of?"

"A flower, I think. Maybe honeysuckle. I want a botanist to look at it tomorrow." She showed him a bleary smile and ran a hand through the stiff hills of her hair. "Later today, I mean."

"Okay, good idea. Incidentally, I checked the kit room. Baton number fourteen has been missing for an unknown period of time. Nobody noticed it was gone." He shook his head grouchily. "Sloppy record keeping, slipshod inventory control."

"If he hadn't had the PR-twenty-four, he would have used a baseball bat or a lead pipe. It doesn't matter."

"When department equipment is used in a homicide, it matters." Mueller fretted over it a moment longer, then let it pass. "Logan and Barnes are waiting for you in the interrogation room. I'm going to talk to Logan once you're done. You're welcome to sit in if you'd like."

"Not sure I want to, but I will."

"After that, you should get some rest."

Donna managed another wan smile. "I don't know it I *can* rest—until this guy is caught."

The two men turned to look at her as she stepped into the interrogation room. Behind her, the door hissed shut, cutting off the faint noises of activity from down the hall and filling the room with silence.

There was an uncomfortable moment when they all stared at one another in the ugly fluorescent light. Logan was seated and looked more tired than she had ever seen him. Barnes, standing, seemed restless and edgy. The pale aquamarine walls lent both their faces an unhealthy green hue.

Then Barnes reached out and clasped her hand. "Jesus, Donna, I'm glad you're okay."

She watched his eyes, probing for insincerity. "Thanks, Ed."

Logan stood. His arm went around her shoulder as he hugged her tight. "You may not believe it," he murmured in her ear, "but so am I."

He seemed drained of defiance, bewildered, even scared. His vulnerability was unexpected and appealing, more human than the angry isolation that had been his leitmotif.

"I believe it," she answered.

"You want to. You're not sure you can."

That was true, but she was surprised he knew it.

"You seem to have come through your brush with death unscathed," Barnes observed as they took their seats.

"Oh, it's not really so bad, almost getting killed," she said lightly. "Afterward you feel real lucky, like you won the lottery."

Logan's finger was poised over the controls of a tape recorder, the reel-to-reel model Anderson had fixed. "Mind if we record this interview?"

"Go ahead."

The reels turned languidly, tape sliding over the head.

Having been through this procedure in L.A., Donna could have narrated the entire incident in a few minutes. Instead she spoke slowly and elliptically, forcing her interrogators to ask questions and make comments. Her strategy was to lure one of them into volunteering some detail that only her assailant would know. Twice it almost seemed to work.

"Amazing the guy wasn't hit," Barnes remarked after she mentioned firing blind at the intruder. "He's got the luck of the devil if he can dodge six rounds at close range."

She looked at him sharply. "I haven't said how many shots I fired."

Barnes held her gaze as a slow smile widened on his face. "The LAPD ballistics tech, Phillips, used to work under me when I was running the lab at Parker Center. I remember watching him test-fire Saturday night specials into the tank. Had a little plastic squid floating in there, name of Millie. He called me a half hour ago to say he'd dug six nine-millimeter Parabellums out of your bedroom walls, door frame, and bureau. Not to mention two twenty-two Long Rifle slugs fired by your assailant."

"I see."

He looked at her over the tops of his glasses, chilly merriment in his stare. "Thought you had me, didn't you, Donna?"

"I don't want it to be you, Ed." Her eyes cut toward Logan. "Either of you."

She finished her story and went through it again, filling in details overlooked the first time. Barnes asked what had awakened her.

"I'm not sure," she answered carefully. "A noise, maybe. Or the night air . . ."

"The smell of honeysuckle," Logan said.

She stared at him but didn't speak. Barnes asked the obvious question. "What makes you say that?"

"Donna grows Italian honeysuckle on the patio. It's particularly fragrant at night. I remember how the scent would fill the whole apartment when the sliding door was open."

"Yes," she said. "That must have been it."

"Of course"—Logan's tired eyes studied her—"had I been the intruder, I would have known that. I could have cut the flowers and thrown them in the alley before breaking in."

"Unless you got careless," Donna whispered. "Most repeat killers do."

"Not this one," Logan said.

She answered the rest of their questions. Then Logan switched off the tape recorder and they considered what avenues to pursue.

"Do you have any evidence to suggest that he was familiar with your place?" Barnes asked.

"He apparently knew I had no alarm system, no dog or other pet to worry about, no roommate or live-in boyfriend. He may have known the floor plan; he found his way to and from my bedroom in total darkness. And he knew where I live. My address is unlisted."

"So either he was acquainted with you in some way," Barnes said, "or he followed you home."

"I wasn't aware of being followed, and as keyed up as I was, I would have noticed."

Logan shrugged. "It's conceivable he tailed you the night before. Could have cased the building from the alley."

"If so, he might have watched for hours," Barnes said. "LAPD can run a check on overnight parking violations in that neighborhood."

"Did SID comb the alley and street for items he might have dropped when he ran off?" Logan asked.

"They were starting a modified grid search when I left for the station. There was a crowd of gawkers outside, and some plainclothes cops were asking if anyone had caught a glimpse of the guy. At first light they'll start ringing doorbells—every apartment within a two-block radius."

"You said he broke in using a glass cutter," Barnes said. "Must have used a suction cup to avoid letting the glass fall and shatter. Sometimes those things need some spit to get a good grip; there might be saliva on the glass pieces left behind."

"We already have a saliva sample from the body," Donna pointed out.

"Yes, but I'd like to match it with a sample from your place to confirm that this is the same man. Same with the blood on the baton; I want to be sure it's Wanda's. Another thing—there are two locks on your patio door, you said."

"Right."

"It might be possible to tell which one he defeated first. If he stacked the glass pieces, the one on the bottom was the first one he cut."

"And if he attacked the lock at floor level before the more obvious one at chest height," Donna said, "then he may have had prior knowledge of how the door was secured."

"In other words," Logan put in, "he'd been there before." He leaned forward. "Let's consider the attack itself. The blow he struck—it was meant to kill?"

"Definitely."

"Wanda wasn't killed instantly. She was cuffed and beaten. This time there was no apparent intention to torture. Why?"

"Because he knows I'm a cop," Donna said. "I was likely to be armed, and I'd sure as hell fight back."

"Then why didn't he just shoot you to begin with? He wouldn't have needed to get so close."

Donna knew the answer. "He was hoping for a soundless kill."

"You said the gun was silenced," Barnes objected.

"Even a silenced pistol makes *some* noise. Enough to alert the neighbors, call attention to himself."

"Still, he could have gotten away before anyone knew what was happening."

"Could have. But that's not the way he wanted to play it. He didn't want to just shoot and run." The next part was hard for her to say. "He intended to spend time with . . . the body. So he could abuse it."

The word *it* came easier than *me*.

"The way he abused Wanda," Logan said quietly.

"Yes. Right." She crossed her legs, hugged herself. "Another Wanda—that's what he wanted. And what he almost got."

This time the silence lasted. There was nothing more to say.

34

The interview over, Barnes left for home, and Logan headed for Mueller's office. Donna was about to join him when it occurred to her that Jim Walters, the morning-watch commander, must be on duty.

Walters and Joe Kurtz were good friends. They had often gone camping together. Joe had relied on Walters for emotional support during and after his divorce.

She took a detour into the watch commander's office, just down the hall.

"Lieutenant?"

Walters was seated at his computer terminal, reading MDT messages from patrol units as they appeared on the screen like ghostly handwriting. He looked up at her and rose from his chair.

"Good to see you, Detective. It appears you had a very close call."

"My luck was holding."

"Not luck. Einstein said God doesn't play dice with the universe. Whatever happens is for a reason."

Tell it to Wanda Gardner, she thought. "I'd like to believe that."

"I heard about the nightstick. Everybody's heard about it by now." Walters shook his head. "It's absolutely incredible to think that someone here—someone in the department—"

"There are bad cops everywhere."

"Not this bad. Not . . . killers."

"Lieutenant, do you mind if I ask you a question?"

"Of course not. Sit down."

She settled in a chair before his desk and studied him. He was a stern, stolid man of medium height, totally bald, his face as hard and chiseled as a block of stone.

"What can I help you with?" Walters asked.

She decided to be as truthful as possible. "Even before tonight, it had occurred to me that a CBPD officer might be implicated in Wanda Gardner's murder. I had done a little informal checking on my own."

"What sort of checking?"

"An examination of some personnel files."

"I see. Mine included?"

"Well . . . yes."

"Am I a suspect, then?"

She didn't know how to answer that. "Everybody's a suspect," she said guardedly.

"In that case, you'll want to know if I have any alibi for tonight. The answer is yes. I was participating in a Bible study group from six to eleven. Fifteen people can vouch for that."

Donna nodded, unsurprised. In her mind, Walters was not a prime suspect anyway. After tonight's attack, she was reasonably sure the killer knew her personally and had visited her condo. Walters had never been there.

Still, if the meeting had ended at eleven, it would have been possible for him to get to her apartment by eleven-thirty. His alibi was not as airtight as he seemed to think.

"Five hours," she said slowly. "What did your group discuss for all that time?"

"Deuteronomy. Are you familiar with it?"

"I'm not really up on my scriptural studies."

"You should read Deuteronomy sometime. In many ways, it's the most important book of the Old Testament. Sets down the laws that form the basis of all western societies. Laws we would do well to live by today." He leaned forward. "Now what was it you wanted to ask?"

"I have reason to believe that Lieutenant Brody's assistant, Lynn, found out what I was up to. I'm afraid she may start to spread the information around."

"You'll have to ask Lynn about that."

"Well, yes, but what mainly worries me is this rumor I've heard. Supposedly, Lynn is going out with Sergeant Kurtz. If they're an item, I have to assume that anything she knows, he knows."

"And Joe is also a suspect?"

She was getting tired of his defensiveness. "As I said, Lieutenant, *everybody* is a suspect now."

Walters snorted. "Joe is totally incapable of hurting anybody. He's the type who'll go out of his way to help people. A genuine Good Samaritan." He fixed his shrewd gaze on her. "As you ought to know."

She stiffened. "What are you implying?"

"Joe Kurtz is more than a colleague, Detective. He's a good friend. He tells me a lot."

"Including . . . ?"

He nodded.

"Jesus. Uh . . . sorry."

Donna remembered wondering if Joe had told Walters about the affair, but she hadn't really believed he could have done it. Still couldn't quite believe it now.

"I know it was a violation of your privacy," Walters said. "But don't blame Joe. I don't think he could help talking it out with someone." A tactful pause, then: "He was in love with you, you know."

Donna lowered her head. "I think he still is."

"You may be right. He still mentions you at times—not as often as before, but occasionally. It's a wound that hasn't healed. Maybe it won't heal, ever."

"I never wanted to hurt him."

Walters looked down at his hands. "I'm sure that's true. But some situations make hurt inevitable. I know this is going to sound stuffy and moralistic to you, but ... we all pay for our sins."

She lifted her head sharply. "Joe and I are sinners?"

"We're all sinners."

"But us, especially?"

"You cheated on Mark. Joe encouraged you, and you went along."

"Doesn't the New Testament talk about forgiveness of sins?"

"If you repent. Have you?"

"There's nothing to repent."

"Then there's no forgiveness."

She frowned. "Is this the kind of thing you've been saying to Joe? When he comes to you for help?"

"I tell him only the truth. That's what he needs to hear."

"Christ." This time she did not apologize. "No wonder he's so fucked up."

Walters flinched. "Don't take out your guilty conscience on me."

She wasn't listening. She was thinking of Joe Kurtz, sad and lost after his divorce, angry and bewildered at the end of their affair, sitting with this man for hours, in a tent under a ceiling of leafy branches somewhere in the high San Gabriels, listening to the hard moral law Jim Walters expounded, hearing a hundred variations on the theme of guilt and punishment.

A man could take only so much self-condemnation and self-loathing. Then he projected his hatred outward. When his feelings grew too large to be contained, they would spill over, destroying whatever was convenient, whatever was close.

"You haven't been helping Joe," she said quietly. "You've been warping him."

"You're the one who warped him, if anyone did. You led him on, then threw him aside. The same way you treated Logan."

"Shut up."

"Two lives destroyed. Joe, trapped in unrequited love. Mark, drinking himself to death."

"Shut up."

She stood. For a long moment they stared at each other, Walters calm, displaying the eerie serenity of unquestioned conviction, Donna hot and flustered and outraged.

"You still haven't answered my question," she said finally.

He drummed his fingers on the desk. "He's dating Lynn. She's been good for him. She's helping him get over it."

"No thanks to you."

She turned to leave. His voice, gentler than it had been, stopped her at the door. "Donna."

It was the first time he had addressed her by name. Reluctantly she looked at him.

"It wasn't luck tonight," Walters said softly. "Whatever else you believe, accept that. Somebody is watching over you. Somebody more powerful than either of us. Somebody who knows every move you make."

She nodded, her face grim. "That's what I'm afraid of."

35

Mueller wasn't smoking, but the odor of smoke permeated his office as a permanent presence, like the smell of disinfectant in a hospital. Logan breathed it in, tasting it at the back of his throat, exhaling slowly.

"Why don't we get started?" he asked the chief, seated stiffly at his desk.

"I'm expecting Donna to join us."

"Great. Just like old times. One big happy family."

Logan looked around the office. The tape recorder from the interrogation room, he noted, had not been brought in. Mueller wasn't treating this as a formal interrogation, hadn't advised him of his rights or suggested he call a lawyer. This was just a chat.

Sure it was. Logan felt the twitch of a smile at the side of his mouth and suppressed it. Only a madman smiles before the firing squad.

The door opened, and Donna entered. "Sorry to hold you up. Had to use the rest room. My insides are still a little queasy."

Logan waited as she took a seat across from him. Then Mueller rested his forearms on the desk and stared at him as if trying to see into his soul.

"Let's begin with your activities earlier tonight. You had dinner with Donna, then let her off at the station. Correct?"

"Yes."

"What time did you say good night?"

"About eight-thirty."

Mueller glanced at Donna for confirmation. She nodded.

"Then what did you do?"

"Drove home."

"No stops along the way?"

"I went directly home."

"And?"

"Lay on the couch. Did a little reading."

"What did you read?"

"*Newsweek.*"

"Which articles?"

God damn you, Chief. "I don't remember. I wasn't paying attention. It was just something for my eyes to look at."

"You didn't lie there all night staring at a magazine."

"No, I tried to get some sleep. Kicked the covers around for a long time. Then I got up and drank some beer and turned on the TV."

"What time was this?"

"Half past eleven."

"Which is approximately when the attack on Donna took place. What were you watching?"

"Some World War Two movie."

"What was the title?"

"Christ, I don't know."

"You weren't paying attention to the TV either, is that it?"

"That's it."

"During all this time, there were no phone calls, no neighbors dropping by, no noises you made that would have been audible in adjacent apartments?"

"Nothing like that."

"Not even the sound of the TV?"

"It wasn't on that loud."

"So the bottom line is, you have no way of proving your whereabouts?"

"No."

Donna broke in. "What about your car? If it was parked in an assigned space all night, some other tenant might have seen it."

Logan shook his head. She had never been to his new place. "There's no garage. I park on the street. Tonight I had to park more than a block away."

"All right," Mueller said. "Let's talk about the night Wanda was killed."

Logan shifted in his seat. "I suppose you want to know what I was doing then."

Mueller waited. Donna watched him, her features drawn tight by tension.

"I was home by myself," Logan said slowly. "Home drinking. When I'm really drunk, I think of Sharon. And the baby. Sometime late, well past dark, I decided to see their graves. I wasn't hysterical or irrational about it; it was just something I felt I had to do. I took a bottle and a flashlight. And went to the cemetery."

"The gate is locked at night," Mueller said.

"I wasn't going to let that stop me. I climbed a tree and swung over the fence. Landed hard. That's when I noticed I still had on my suit from work. Jacket and pants were a grass-stained mess."

"Has that suit been cleaned?"

"No. Still in my closet."

"We'll need to see it."

"So Barnes can compare the soil stains with the ones on Wanda's clothes? Yeah. Okay."

"What happened next?" Donna asked, impatient at Mueller's interruptions.

"The flashlight showed me the way to the grave markers. Two of them; you probably remember we buried Mark, Jr., in a little casket, though he'd never really been born. I read the inscriptions, finished the bottle. Lay on my belly, kissed Sharon's plaque. Sang a lullaby to little Mark . . ."

In the brief silence that followed, Logan felt Donna's pity for him and hated it. He had never wanted to be a figure of pathos to her, or to anyone.

"You just lay there all night," Mueller said, his voice flat, "communing with the dead. Is that it?"

The words, the tone, pricked Logan, made him mean.

"No," he breathed, "that's not it." His own voice surprised him: it was a small growling animal, furred and scratchy in his throat. "I couldn't be quietly philosophical about it. I had too much liquor in me, and . . . too much hate."

They waited.

He pulled in a breath, expelled it in a ragged stream of speech.

"I'm down on my knees, very drunk, staring at those two plaques, running my hands over them—and suddenly they're not grave markers anymore. They're doors. Bronze doors in the ground, closed doors, slammed shut in my face, with everything I love on the other side. And I feel—I just want to—I don't know—shout or cry or something—I'm prying at them, trying to pull them loose, but they won't yield and I'm screaming now, screaming and pounding at the ground with my fists, and then I remember the flashlight—big steel flash, department-issue—I pull it out and hammer at Sharon's plaque, wham, wham, *wham*, every jolt going up my arm into my elbow, till the flash is dented and crushed like a beer can, bits of the busted lens flying around me, and I don't care. I keep pounding and pounding and pounding, screaming into the night, and it feels good. Feels like . . . liberation."

His voice dropped on the last word. He let a long

moment slide past. When he spoke again, he was drained and empty.

"Finally the anger was gone, or the craziness or whatever it was. I was just tired and my head hurt. My whole body hurt. I went home and fell asleep ... and Walters's phone call woke me at one forty-five."

He stopped speaking and looked first at Mueller, then at Donna.

"No one saw you, heard you?" Mueller asked finally.

"Not that I know of. The cemetery is isolated. You can make noise in there and not be heard."

"What did you do with the flashlight?"

"Threw it in a trash can near the gate. I'm sure the can has been emptied by now."

"Did you requisition a new one?"

"Haven't had time to get around to it."

Donna had been listening, eyes shut. Now she looked at him. "When you started beating at the ground, screaming—what exactly were you angry at?"

Logan hesitated before answering. "I don't know. Death, maybe. For taking my future away. Or the world in general. The unfairness of things."

"Nobody gets angry at abstractions, generalities."

"Then what do you think it was?"

"Somebody who hurt you. Who wasn't there for you. Who left you alone with all that pain."

He said nothing.

"That's right, isn't it, Mark?" Donna watched him. "Isn't it?"

He should not admit anything more. But he couldn't deny her this truth.

"Yes," he whispered.

"It was me you were really attacking. Hammering. Pounding. It was me you wanted to kill that night."

He met her eyes. Nodded slowly. "It was you."

She sat unmoving for a long, thoughtful stretch of time. "And Wanda looked something like me."

"I didn't kill her."

"But you could have."

"I didn't."

"You hated me enough. Maybe . . . you still do."

Logan rubbed his face. "I'm sorry, Donna."

Her voice was very low: "Me too, Mark. I'm sorry too."

36

Donna didn't go home after leaving the station. Another ambush was possible, and she was taking no chances.

She drove to a motel in Redondo Beach, checking frequently to make sure no one was following. The desk clerk was asleep. She rang the bell to rouse him. He was blearily amazed that she wanted a room at 4 A.M., even more astonished that her only luggage was the manila envelope tucked under her arm. She'd left the photo blowup in the glove compartment of her Toyota while inside the Corona Beach police station, but she preferred to have it with her for the rest of the night.

The room was clean, though faintly depressing in the manner of all way stations. She kicked off her shoes and climbed into bed without undressing and without turning down the covers. Her Beretta lay beside the pillow, an inch from her hand.

Her last waking act was to set the alarm on her digital wristwatch for eight. All the energy left her then, and she fell instantly down a deep well of sleep. She had been afraid of nightmares but there were none. For four hours she slept without dreams.

A phone call from the motel room established that a professor of botany, Howard Morrow, was teaching summer classes at UCLA; his office hours were from noon to 2 P.M. The switchboard operator confirmed Donna's police credentials, then gave her Morrow's home number. She called and arranged to meet him at twelve.

"I've never been involved in a police investigation," Morrow said. "Sounds exciting and rather glamorous."

"The glamour wears off real fast," she assured him.

He had a slightly high-pitched voice and a breathless way of talking. She pictured him as a Hollywood-movie professor, the Cecil Kellaway type, elfin and portly, blinking distractedly, adrift in a sea of books.

Her condo still might not be safe, but she would have to return sometime, and she was desperate for clean clothes. She drove home and entered cautiously, the gun leading her. No one was there.

The patio door was shut and locked, the holes in the glass covered by squares of cardboard secured by electrician's tape. Fingerprint powder smudged door frames and end tables, things the intruder might have touched. The ID techs had done a thorough job, dusting the apartment even though the baton showed only glove prints. Comparisons with the print card in her file would undoubtedly show most of the prints to be hers.

Ragged holes scored her bedroom walls, marking the places where bullets had been dug out. Eight rounds in all: the killer's two .22-caliber slugs, and the six 9mm Parabellums she'd fired.

She fixed breakfast and changed, being careful to include the bulletproof vest as part of her ensemble, concealed under a clean suit jacket. Her backup gun, the little Smith, was again holstered to her left calf under her trouser leg.

By then it was ten. She had time to get to Parker Center and back before noon.

Captain John Turner, commanding officer of Personnel Division, was in his office when she got there. Turner had been her CO when she worked Burglary at Harbor Division years ago, and they'd kept in touch after his transfer to Personnel. His letter of recommendation had helped her secure a place in the NCAVC program. She hoped he could help her again now.

"Donna." Pleasure flashed in his eyes as he rose to greet her. "Hell, let me shake your hand. I heard what went down last night."

She'd already known that the news was all over the department. During her trip from the underground garage to Personnel Division's offices, half a dozen people had congratulated her on being alive and pressed her for details of the attack. She was surprised at how quickly the routine became tiresome, but she went through it again with Turner, her impatience concealed behind a wan smile.

"What can I do for you, Donna?" he asked finally.

She drew courage with a breath. "I'd like access to the file of a retired officer. Lieutenant Edward Barnes."

A paper clip flashed in the captain's hands as he bent it into a series of odd shapes. "You'd need a very good reason."

"I've got one."

She summarized the situation in Corona Beach. "Barnes's file at CBPD includes Form 1.6, which makes reference to three sustained complaints during his time as a patrol officer. But there's no 1.6.2. attached."

"You want to see if the nature of the misconduct makes him a more likely suspect?"

"Right."

Turner flicked the crippled paper clip into the wastebasket. "Okay. I'll give you the authorization.

But Ed's a good man. I think you're wrong about him."

"I hope so."

In five minutes she found Barnes's file. Stapled to his Personal and Work History Summary was Form 1.6.2., the Complaint History. She read it, then read it again.

From an unoccupied office she called Mueller.

"All three complaints were allegations of excessive force against female suspects," she told him, excitement straining against the short leash of her self-control. "Two of the females were prostitutes."

"What was the disposition?" The chief sounded weary. She wondered if he'd gotten any sleep.

"The complaints were sustained. Disciplinary action was taken by his CO. Voluntary relinquishment of days off in the first two instances, a ten-day suspension in the third. Immediately afterward, Barnes was pulled from patrol duty and transferred to the lab. He has a B.A. in biochemistry, so he was a logical choice for criminalistics, but you have to wonder if his superiors decided he was too unstable for the street."

"All right, Donna, I hear you. Here's the latest from this end. Reynolds and Hill interviewed all department personnel present at Third and Bay when the body was found. Most of them are alibied for last night, and the alibis are checking out. Jim Walters was at a Bible study group till eleven; he might have been able to make it to your neighborhood by eleven-thirty, but the time frame is tight. The only ones with no alibis at all are Logan and Barnes—and neither of them can verify their whereabouts for the night of Wanda's murder either."

"How about Sergeant Kurtz? Can we eliminate him as a suspect?"

"Kurtz has no alibi for the night of Wanda's murder. But he's covered for last night, during the time period in which the assault took place. He was with his girlfriend, at his place, until 11:45, when he left for work. He arrived a few minutes before midnight."

Donna thought for a moment. "It was just the two of them—Kurtz and his girlfriend?"

"That's right. Why?"

She let it go—for now. "Nothing. Any other news?"

"Got a FedEx package from the outside lab Barnes uses. He's conferring with SID in downtown L.A.—must be at Parker Center, where you are—so I took the liberty of opening his mail. It's an analysis of the soil on Wanda's body."

"What does it say?"

"Damned if I know. Chemistry's not my field. I called the lab to have the results translated into English, but so far they haven't gotten back to me."

"I'm going over to UCLA to have a botanist identify that flower. Maybe I can find a chemist who'll decipher the lab report too."

"Let me give you the data." Mueller read off a list of trace elements and compounds detected in the soil, quantified in micrograms per cubic millimeter, while Donna scribbled in her pad.

"Greek to me," she said when he was finished. "Of course I could just pay a visit to SID on the fifth floor and ask Barnes to explain it himself."

"You could." Mueller hesitated. "But I had another reason for opening his mail. I'm not sure how deeply he should involve himself in the investigation from this point on, or how far I can even trust the analysis he's already done. Until this case is cleared, I'll have to rely on outside experts."

"You didn't buy his story about cruising PCH last night."

"Let's just say it was awfully convenient. And now there's his complaint history. . . . I don't know."

Donna sighed. "I don't know either, Chief. I'm not sure of anything anymore."

37

In the station-house locker room, toweling off after a weight-room workout and a shower, Sergeant Joe Kurtz and four patrolmen were having a talk.

"I don't see what all the bullshit is about," a P-2 named Jackson complained. "Everybody knows who did it."

His partner, Kendall, grunted agreement. "The chief knows, that's for damn sure."

"So why doesn't he do something about it?" asked a third cop, Gilbran.

Kendall knew the answer. "Can't arrest a man without evidence. Right, Sarge?"

Kurtz nodded in a distracted way. "Right."

In the workout room next door, the steady, monotonous thumping of gloves on canvas began—somebody letting off steam on a punching bag. The sharp thuds of blows beat in the air like the pumping of an overtaxed heart.

Kurtz wondered if it was an echo of his own heart, throbbing in his ears. He was still worked up about what he'd said to Lynn in his phone call from the station last night.

"Aw, shit." Jackson tugged on his boxer shorts. His muscled torso, oiled with sweat, shone in the fluorescent light. "You look in his apartment, you'll find all the goddamn evidence you need. Fucking fruitcake probably has that whore's pussy on ice in his fucking freezer."

"Eskimo pie," quipped the fourth cop, Edwards. Everybody laughed.

Everybody but Kurtz. His mind had traveled backward from the phone conversation with Lynn to his meeting with Donna in the parking lot half an hour earlier.

The way she'd rebuffed him—her obvious discomfort, even fear—had made it clear that he was a suspect. She thought he'd left the PR24 on her pillow. Thought he'd killed Wanda Gardner. Or at least, she thought he might have.

"Now, wait just a minute here." Kendall stood on a bench in his underwear, striking a declamatory pose. "Let us not be unfair to Detective Logan. Just because a man is a drunk . . . and a wacko . . . and a total personal fuck-up"—laughter from his audience—"doesn't mean he's a sex killer." He paused for effect. "It only means he *probably* is."

The punching bag had fallen silent, but Kurtz still heard the pounding of his heart.

"Did I explain the legal situation correctly, Sergeant?" Kendall shouted over the boisterous reaction to his testimonial.

"No." Kurtz stood up, bare-chested, swinging his thick arms. "No, you didn't."

The gravity of his tone, the imperfectly suppressed fury, stopped the laughter like a bullet stopping breath.

"You said probably. Probably he's guilty. Probably." With sudden violence Kurtz cracked his fist against the meat of his palm. "*Fuck* probably! We know he did it. He had to. He's the only cop sick enough. Twisted enough. The only suspect. The only possible one."

Edwards shrugged, unnerved by his sergeant's

outburst. "Well, he's sure as shit giving the department a bad name."

"That's nothing new," Jackson said, showing a faint edgy smile. "He was doing that even before our little working girl got cooled."

"He sure as hell was. Jackson's right about that. Damn right." Kurtz wished his heart would slow down, wished he could contain the desperate insistence jumping in his voice. "A drunken cop. A bum with a badge. Christ, that—that fucking makes me sick."

"He should've resigned by now," Kendall said.

"Or blown his frigging brains out." Jackson turned away and pulled on a T-shirt. "That's what I'd do if I was . . ."

His voice trailed off as he stared at the doorway to the workout room.

Gilbran didn't notice. He was chuckling and nodding in witless concurrence. "Blow his head off, yeah. Man, he'd be doing the world a favor."

From the doorway, a cool, even voice. "Maybe I don't owe the world any favors."

The room chilled.

Logan stood in the entry, naked except for baggy sweat pants, his rib cage expanding and contracting with shallow, rapid breaths. A pair of boxing gloves hung from his fist by their strings. He'd been the one slapping the canvas; he must have heard everything.

The four patrolmen looked at him, then shifted their glances, discovering new points of interest in the dusty floor and scuffed baseboards.

Only Kurtz did not look away. His gaze was fixed on the loose muscles of Logan's abdomen, the sagging pecs, the slumped shoulders.

The man had not been through a real workout in months. Too busy nursing bottles and his own stale grief. Weak.

Yet this inferior specimen, this physical wreck, had enjoyed more nights with Donna than Joe Kurtz ever had.

The thought pricked the angry, ugly part of him.

"Very dramatic entrance, Detective," he said slowly, pressing his palms together in an isometric exercise that made the corded muscles of his forearms bulge. "Now I guess we're supposed to apologize, act repentant, explain how all of us are under strain."

Logan approached his locker, opened it. He hung up the gloves, then climbed out of the sweat pants, taking a long time with his answer.

"I haven't asked for any apologies," he said finally.

"That's good, Detective. Because you aren't getting any. Not from me."

Logan looked at him. A slow, thoughtful look. "All right," he said finally.

"All right?" Joe echoed, mocking his reply. "Oh, that's all right?" He was riding a stallion, rampant and untamed, and he couldn't dismount now if he'd wanted to. "Well, I'm real glad it's all right with you, Mr. Detective, sir. Now how about if I say you're a miserable alcoholic sack of shit? A fucking disgrace to your badge? Is *that* all right?"

Logan pulled on his trousers. "You sound judgmental, Joe. You've been spending too much time with Jim Walters."

Gilbran released a little cough of laughter. Kendall silenced him.

Kurtz stepped closer. "He's a better man than you," he said, his blood roaring, his voice very soft.

Logan showed a rueful smile. "That wouldn't take much."

"You got that right."

"Lay off, Sarge," Edwards said quietly.

Kurtz ignored him. Took another step. "Why don't

you just admit it? Why don't you come right out and say you killed that whore?"

Calmly, Logan buttoned his shirt. "Because I didn't."

"Yeah. And you didn't try to whack Wildman in her bedroom."

"I spent the night in my apartment. Alone."

"With a bottle."

"Maybe."

"Until you got so wasted you couldn't think straight. Then you went over to Wildman's place, broke in—"

"Wrong."

"You must've been real disappointed when you couldn't finish her off. Bet you were looking forward to having her the same way you had the Gardner girl."

Something flickered in Logan's eyes. "What way would that be?"

"Humping her corpse. That's your only chance with her now." He drove the words home like spikes. "If you want another piece of that high-quality cunt, it'll have to be over Donna's dead body—"

Logan's fist came at him so fast he didn't even see it.

Kurtz felt the electric sting of contact, his head snapping sideways as his left cheek caught fire.

Fury seized him. He lashed out wildly, connected once, and then Logan was in close, jabbing furiously at his midsection—a blur of fists hammering his ribs, abdomen, breastbone—pummeling the breath out of him, turning his stomach inside out, driving him back, relentlessly back, till he collided with a bench—another sickening blow—he lost his balance, the room cartwheeling crazily as the floor spun up and struck him in the face.

Kurtz rolled onto his side and lay there gasping. He stared up at Logan, standing hipshot over him, the other cops holding back.

Beaten. *Christ.*

The pain in his head and gut was nothing compared to the intensity of his humiliation. His strength was his pride, and now he'd been decked like an amateur in front of his own men.

By a washout. A drunk.

"Keep quiet about things that don't concern you," Logan whispered. A thread of blood leaked from the corner of his mouth. He had no other injuries.

"Who ..." Kurtz struggled for air. "Who says it doesn't concern me?"

"Why would it?"

He had an answer for that, the one answer that would nullify every blow Logan had landed.

Because I fucked her too. Fucked her in the same bed you used.

Yes. Tell him that. Tell him that Joe Kurtz had known how to satisfy beautiful Donna when Mark Logan had not.

But if he said so, he would be implicated even more closely as a suspect in the assault. He would have publicly admitted to a personal motive equivalent to Logan's own.

"Well?" Logan demanded. "Why would it concern you?"

Kurtz swallowed. "It ... doesn't."

In his sinking voice he heard cowardice, and hated it.

Bang—the locker-room door swinging open—Jim Walters striding in, already shedding his uniform jacket, a melody whistling from his lips. He stopped a yard inside the doorway, the tune dying like a shot bird.

"Hey. *Hey!* What's going on here?"

Logan stepped away from Kurtz. "Little difference of opinion between the sergeant and myself."

Walters was outraged. He approached with a tramp of boots and a jangle of handcuffs and the empurpled visage of an Old Testament prophet. "This is totally—*totally*—unprofessional conduct."

"I'm off duty," Kurtz said mildly, and a couple of the men laughed.

"That's not an excuse." Walters stared hard at the cops till no trace of mirth remained on their faces. "Who started it?"

"The detective threw the first punch," Jackson said, staying loyal to the patrol side.

Logan strapped on his shoulder holster, then donned his suit jacket. "I was provoked."

"By what?" Walters seethed.

"Uncharitable comments about . . . a former friend of mine."

Kurtz lurched to his feet. "Former friend, my ass." He had seen the change in Logan's face when his relationship with Donna was introduced into the dispute. "You're still in love with her."

"I thought you said I tried to kill her."

"You did. You're sick. Crazy. If you can't have her, no one can." He threw the words at Logan, desperate to see him flinch. "You want her dead. Or you want her alive. It doesn't matter. You *want* her, that's all. *You want her.*"

Logan shut the locker. His face was stone, his eyes ice. "That's another thing you got wrong, Sergeant."

He left the room, silence presiding over his departure. The door clicked shut behind him.

Walters turned slowly to Kurtz. "I'm surprised at you, Joe." His stern gaze crept over the other cops. "At all of you. This is no way to settle things."

Kurtz touched his injured cheek and felt the aching tenderness of a bruise.

"Logan's a sinner," he said carefully, hoping to turn the lieutenant's philosophy to his own advantage. "I decided he was due for some punishment."

The tactic failed. "It's not your job to dispense punishment," Walters said coolly.

Kurtz bristled. "Leave him to heaven. Is that it?"

"The Lord will balance the scales."

"When? On Judgment Day?"

"I believe so."

"What are we supposed to do in the meantime?"

Walter fixed his stare on him. His bald head gleamed like a bullet. His mouth was a bloodless line.

"You're supposed to have faith." The intensity of his gaze deepened. "And bear in mind your own sins."

Kurtz's belly tightened up as if under the impact of another blow.

"Before I go casting any stones, huh?" he said in a chastened voice.

"That's right."

"I . . . I never claimed to be a saint."

"I'm not asking you to be a saint, Joe." Walters gentled his tone. "Only a man."

Kurtz had nothing to say to that.

38

Professor Howard Morrow took Donna by surprise. He was not a Hollywood cliché after all. He was young and vigorous, his tanned skin tight as a drumhead. In his sport shirt and jeans, he exhibited the fighting trim of the best cops she knew.

She introduced herself, pleased by his strong handshake. "Sorry to interrupt your session." He had been talking to a student when she arrived, fifteen minutes late. The young man was now exiled to the hall.

"No problem. We weren't discussing anything as urgent as a homicide case. Louis just needs a little help understanding the distinction between racemose and spicate inflorescences."

"I've had that problem myself," Donna deadpanned.

She told him what she needed and tamped the photo out of the envelope. He studied it, lips pursed in a frown. "Not a very clear image," he said finally.

"That's an understatement. It took me twenty minutes just to see that it was a flower. I'll understand if you can't narrow down the identification."

"I didn't say that. The image is bleary as hell, but not indecipherable—at least not when you've been looking at plants as long as I have." He glanced at her with a playful smile. "Tell me, Detective. What's *your* best guess?"

She felt like a student facing a pop quiz. "I thought it might be a honeysuckle flower. I grow honeysuckle on my patio, and this seems to suggest the same general shape."

He nodded. "A reasonable supposition. But wrong. The corolla of a *Lonicera* is typically gibbous at the base. This corolla appears to be ventrally spurred."

"Then you know what it is?"

"I think so. But I'll need a little expert help to be sure."

He got up and removed a thick book from a crowded shelf.

"Gray's *Manual of Botany*," he said, flipping to the index. "Standard work in the field. First published by Asa Gray in 1848. Revised many times since, naturally."

His fingertip raced down a column of indexed listings and stopped. He turned to the middle of the book and found the page he needed, scanned it, then looked up another listing. After a moment he raised his head.

"All right. What we have here, as best I can judge, is a gamopetalous bilabiate corolla." He smiled. "In simpler language, it looks to me as if the petals are joined so as to form distinct upper and lower labia, or lips. That's a feature found in both the Snapdragon and Mint families."

"So it could be either?" She was taking notes.

"No. According to Gray, a mint's labia would have only four lobes, and these appear to have five—two on the upper lip and three on the lower." He angled the photo so Donna could see it too. "Here . . . and here. See them?"

"Yes." The series of rounded projections was what had given the object a crumpled appearance. "It's part of the Snapdragon family, then?"

He nodded. "Technically the *Scrophulariaceae*. Still,

of course, a fairly broad classification. To narrow it down, we need to look at other details."

She thought he must be a good teacher. He knew his subject, and he was patient.

"Note this orange patch, for instance. That's the palate—part of the lower lip, raised to close the throat of the corolla. You see that feature in the genus *Linaria*, colloquially Toadflax. And note the long, pointed spur of the corolla." He traced the curved end of the truncated crescent in the photo.

"What does that tell us?"

"The shape of the spur is one of several means by which we can distinguish one species of *Linaria* from another. Gray tells us that *Linaria maroccona* has a conical spur, while the spur of *L. canadensis* is filiform. We can rule those out. *L. repens* has a short spur—too short. On the other hand, *L. vulgaris* has a long subulate spur, exactly what we see here.

"Now let's consider another feature of this specimen: color. *Vulgaris* has a yellow corolla and an orange palate. Exactly what the photo shows. The other species have corollas of blue, white, or violet—all except *L. dalmatica*, which has a yellow corolla but not an orange palate.

"Finally, size. Were you able to estimate the length?"

"An inch."

"Two and a half centimeters. Exactly the length Gray gives for *Linaria vulgaris*. Detective, I think we've identified your flower."

Morrow pulled an illustrated encyclopedia of wildflowers out of the bookcase.

"Here's a picture of it, growing wild. Colloquially it's known as butter-and-eggs. The plant grows from one foot to three feet tall and is found on roadsides and in dry fields."

"May I Xerox that artwork?"

"Certainly. There's a machine down the hall."

When she returned the book to Morrow in his office, he had resumed his consultation with Louis.

"Would this plant grow in sandy soil?" she asked.

"More likely on drier ground."

"But possibly somewhere in Corona Beach?"

"*Vulgaris* is Latin for 'common.' You'll find it almost everywhere. It's in bloom from May through October, and it spreads prolifically."

"Like a weed?"

" 'Weed' is a four-letter word around here, Detective. For the botanist, all plants are equal."

The UCLA Chemistry Department offices were deserted. In the chem lab Donna found a young woman in a white apron and goggles, working alone. She seemed too young to be a professor, and she was.

"I'm a graduate student," she explained, one gloved hand shaking a stoppered flask filled with hot liquid. "Karen Bernstein."

"I see. Will any of the professors be back soon?"

Karen straightened her spine. She was petite and soft-spoken, barely more than a child by Donna's reckoning, all smooth skin and sun freckles, but when she stood stiffly upright she projected a wiry, tensile strength. Behind the plastic safety lenses, her green eyes flashed.

"I'm as good as a professor myself. I'll be teaching undergraduate courses in September. What do you think I'm doing *this* for?" she added with an irritated nod at the scatter of equipment around her.

"Frankly, I have no idea what it is you're doing."

"Isolation of the ortho isomer of nitrophenol. I guess I'll go ahead and separate out the para isomer too. It's an experiment I'll have to teach, so I'm reviewing it for practice." She shrugged. "Simple procedure."

"Doesn't sound simple to me."

"Anyway, my point is that I can help you, if anybody can."

Donna smiled, impressed. "I don't doubt it."

She showed her badge and presented the relevant facts. She did not mention that the case was a homicide or that the victim was a woman younger than Karen herself.

"So what are the trace substances they found?" Karen asked. She had assembled a complicated apparatus made of flasks, stoppers, and a funnel, mounted over a Bunsen burner, while Donna spoke.

Donna handed over her notepad. Karen studied the list.

"The first few items are called nitrosamines," she said, giving the liquid-filled flask another brisk series of shakes. "Nitrous oxides—auto exhaust, primarily—combine with water to make nitrous acid, which then combines with organic compounds in the dirt. *Voilà.* Nitrosamines." Her nose wrinkled. "Highly carcinogenic. They're all around us. In the air and water, too."

"Great."

Karen poured the fluid from the flask, cool now, into a large distended funnel sealed with a stopcock at the narrow end.

"Then you've got some trace metals. Chromium, mercury, lead, cadmium, barium—pretty nasty stuff to have lying around. You could account for some of these things as vapor discharged from burning fossil fuels. Not all of them, though. For a range of metals this wide, I'd say incinerated waste is a more likely source."

"Waste? You mean sewage?"

"No." She stoppered the large end of the funnel, then shook it vigorously. "A sewage incinerator would spew out cadmium and barium, but it wouldn't explain the rest. Solid waste is a better bet. Everything goes into those incinerators, everything that gets tossed in the trash."

Donna blinked. There was a solid-waste incinerator at the north end of Corona Beach, a huge complex surrounded by a wild, brush-choked field. The sort of field where *Linaria vulgaris* was likely to grow.

"How about the next item on the list?" she asked, controlling her excitement.

"Ammonia. Decay of fecal matter in the soil could account for that, but then again, it can come out of an incinerator's smokestack too. People bag their pet droppings and chuck 'em in the garbage. The stuff vaporizes—the shit hits the fan, you might say—and ammonia is released."

The fluid in the funnel had separated into two layers. Karen drained the oily layer into the three-neck flask, added water, and lit the burner.

"And hydrogen chloride?" Donna asked. It was the last substance the lab had reported. "Is that consistent with incineration also?"

"You bet. In fact, it's the clincher. You know PVC plastic? Polyvinyl chloride plastic is the technical term. It's in everything—plumbing pipe, garden hose, floor tiles, you name it. Burn PVC and you get hydrogen chloride. Once it's in the air, it precipitates out as drops of hydrochloric acid. Tell Fred Astaire to try singing in *that* rain."

It was Gene Kelly, but Donna didn't correct her. "I'm not clear on one point. Doesn't an incinerator have filters, scrubbers? How would all this stuff escape?"

"Unfortunately, you can't catch everything. An electrostatic precipitator will separate out most of the big particulates, but the smaller particles escape. They disperse with distance, of course. To find significant concentrations, you'd have to look right near the incinerator. Maybe right on the grounds."

"On the grounds," Donna repeated thoughtfully.

The oily mixture was boiling now; in a long flask attached to one of the three necks of the larger bottle, a dry particulate substance was beginning to accumulate. The ortho polymer of nitrophenol, Donna assumed, although she had no idea what the hell that meant.

"Guess I'd better leave you to your work," she said, picking up her notebook. "Thanks very much for your help."

Karen smiled. "No problem. Told you I could handle it. I'm going to do big things in chemistry. You just wait and see."

The cheerful cheekiness, the faintly defensive braggadocio, reminded Donna of herself in the police academy many years ago.

"I don't have to wait," she answered quietly. "I believe it already."

39

The Phaethon Waste Disposal Facility was a long, squat concrete building sprawled like a lizard, its belly in the earth, thin towers of irregular heights erupting from its back like ragged spines. It lay sunning itself in the middle of a large blowing expanse of weeds under the sky's white dimensionless glare.

Donna stood by her car, parked on the dirt shoulder of a two-lane road bordering the field, shading her eyes as she studied first the building, then the land.

Phaethon. She remembered enough of a long-ago college literature class to place a story with the name. Phaethon was the arrogant mortal who tried to steer the sun's fiery chariot, only to crash in flames.

She wondered if Wanda's murderer, having dared too much, was about to be brought down. She hoped so.

The unfenced field covered at least twenty acres. Too large an area to be quartered by one person. Even a search party would find it difficult to comb this much brush and weed with no clear idea of what to look for.

But the search could be narrowed. If the killer had brought Wanda to this place, he must have led or dragged her out of the car, through the scraggly foliage along the road. And *Linaria vulgaris*, Morrow had said, often grew on roadsides.

Find the flower, and she might find the path to the murder site.

Donna walked slowly along the shoulder, inspecting each thicket of wildflowers, stooping occasionally to compare a particular plant with her photocopy of Morrow's artwork.

Traffic swept past, tires hissing on the smooth road. The incinerator throbbed like a heart. White smoke rose into the sky from the concrete towers, dispersing as it climbed, fanning into a mist and vanishing. It was pretty, and Donna almost didn't mind the particulates and metal vapors it carried.

She reached the end of the lot. Beyond it was bare land, sere and dusty. Wanda hadn't been killed there. She had died among flowers and black earth.

Donna turned back, retraced her steps to the car, and continued past it, exploring the other end of the field.

Strange how calm she was, how quietly certain of herself. She would find the flowers. She would stand on the spot where Wanda had been beaten to death. Patience and attentiveness were the only skills required.

What is this? she wondered. *Some kind of mystical experience you're having?*

She smiled at the idea, so unlike her typical hard pragmatism. Then the smile faded as she realized there was no mysticism involved, simply the unexpected intimacy of an emotional connection with a girl she'd never met. The Kevlar vest under her jacket might stop a bullet, but it had not prevented this case from penetrating to her heart.

Wanda had gotten to her, Wanda with her wide brown eyes so much like Donna's own, with her depressive mother and her romance paperback and her stuffed penguin shiny with wear.

The girl had been almost young enough to be Donna's daughter. She had been a runaway and a whore, but Donna didn't see her that way. She saw Wanda as a lost child, innocent despite the cruel lessons of the street, sensitive and smart—as smart as Karen Bernstein, maybe, though without her education and opportunities. She had known enough to escape from a hell of abuse, but not enough to survive on her own once she was free.

Donna's sense of closeness to the girl was real to her, irrationally real, and so was her insistent feeling that Wanda had been here, had ended her life here.

Shut your eyes, she thought, *and you can hear her sobs . . . her screams.*

Donna did not shut her eyes.

She was staring at something by the side of the road, something that fascinated her, though she needed a moment to grasp why.

Yellow-orange blossoms on spicate stalks. *Linaria vulgaris,* butter-and-eggs—a grove of it, tangled and dense.

Her surreal calm was broken by the sudden pounding of her heart. This was it. She knew, she knew, she *knew* this was it.

With reflexive professionalism she mastered her excitement, slowed her heartbeat, cleared her mind. First things first. She had to be sure.

Meticulously she checked the flowers against the illustration, ticking off points of comparison, till she was certain her identification was correct.

Okay, it's confirmed. But that proves nothing. This is a common weed, grows everywhere. I need more than that.

She waded into the brush, separating thick bunches of manzanita and purple chia, looking for some item she could link with the crime.

Brambles bit her palms. The buzz of insects encircled her. The sun, unshielded by cloud, beat down with a hard, steady intensity that lifted ripples of

light-headedness from the base of her neck. The vest
grew heavier; her back ached.

*Must be something here. Come on, Wanda, help me.
Help me to help you.*

Crazy, talking to a ghost, but she couldn't stop
herself. The girl's presence was strong, overpower-
ing. Donna could almost share her terror as, handcuffed, she was pulled out of the car on the lonely
road, under the uncaring stars.

A few yards from the first *Linaria* patch, she came
to another one—and directly alongside it, a strip of
flattened brush, the dry stalks splintered, green
shoots tenaciously weaving through the debris.

Something had passed this way, crushing foliage
as it went.

Donna looked back and saw that the path began—
or perhaps ended—at the roadside.

Wanda had been dragged along this route, either
alive and struggling as she was borne into the killing
field, or dead, her body hauled back to the car to be
taken to the dump site at Third and Bay.

Donna didn't want to walk on the path. Too great
a risk of inadvertently destroying evidence. Instead
she scanned its length. It zigzagged through the
brush and abruptly dipped out of sight, into a gully
or ditch.

He must have killed her there, in that private
place, unseen from the road, out of range even of the
headlights of passing cars.

Scattered along the trail were bits of white fuzz.
She bent and picked up the nearest one. A scrap of
polyester fiber—similar in appearance to cotton, but
rougher in texture—the kind of material that would
come out of a ripped pillow or a child's fluffy toy.
It fluttered in her fingers like a captured butterfly.

She put it carefully in her pocket. She didn't know
what it meant.

Lowering her head, she studied the brush edging the path. The red fruits of a young Christmas-berry shrub, only two feet tall, caught her attention. They gleamed prettily, bright against the dull browns and greens around them, shining like cast-off marbles.

Donna moved closer to the shrub. In its interior, amid the webbed shadows of the delicate branches, hid a small dark shape, a firmer blackness.

She crouched down and reached for it, her fingers passing over dead leaves and fallen berries to touch something hard and tapered and, at one end, sharp.

Carefully she removed the object, holding it with two fingers.

It was a long, spiked heel, attached to a black shoe.

Wanda's shoe.

The twin of the one she was wearing when she was dumped in the street.

Had to be. No possible doubt. The brand name and shoe size matched details she remembered from the evidence inventory.

Donna knelt there, head down, the shoe swinging slowly as it dangled from her hand. There was heat in her eyes, and wetness. She felt as if she were kneeling at a grave, as in a sense she was.

"So this really is where it ended for you," she whispered to the girl in the crime-scene photos, the girl with a crushed flower in her hair. "Wanda, I'm so sorry. So sorry for what happened, how unfair it was. All I can do is get him for you, and I will. I'll get him—no matter who he is."

40

Mueller was on the phone when Donna burst into the office.

"I found the murder site."

"Call you back," the chief said into the mouthpiece, and hung up without explanation. "Where?"

"Phaethon incinerator." She was out of breath after sprinting in from the parking lot. Her stomach rolled, and it occurred to her that she'd had very little breakfast and no lunch.

"Are you sure?"

She held up the high-heeled shoe in a plastic evidence bag. "Hers."

"Collect anything else?"

"There were polyester-fiber scraps on the ground. I picked up one. Didn't look any farther. I was afraid of disturbing the site."

"Good move. Excellent work all around, Donna." Mueller stood up, circled his chair, sat down again, his movements agitated and uncertain as he considered his next step. "We need an evidence-collection team to go over the scene. But we can't have Barnes supervise."

Donna had already thought of that. "Get LAPD to loan you some SID people. It's unorthodox, but what the hell; they're looking for Wanda's killer in connection with the assault on me last night."

"Right." Mueller nodded once, then went on nodding, as if he couldn't stop. "I'll do that."

"What will you tell Barnes?"

"The truth. He won't like me for it, but I didn't take this job to be liked."

"You can let him observe SID as they bag and tag, at least."

"From a distance. We don't want any other items walking off. Same with Logan."

"Is he here?"

"Showed up a little while ago. Doesn't look like he got any sleep. Let him know what's up, then go back to Phaethon and watch the site till SID arrives. I'll have a patrol unit take you there and stay with you. Just in case."

"Thanks. I don't mind the protection."

"Still wearing your vest?"

"Hell, yes. I'm getting to like it. Gives me a nice secure feeling."

She found Mark alone in the detective squad room, seated at the typewriter, his two fingers tapping out a report or a letter of some kind. His tie was loosened, shirt collar unbuttoned in violation of department regulations. A Band-Aid was stuck near the left corner of his mouth, blood visible through the translucent plastic.

"What happened to you?" she asked.

He turned in his chair, resting his arm carelessly on the typewriter. "Cut myself shaving."

"You haven't shaved." Stubble crusted his cheeks and chin.

"All right. There was a minor altercation between me and Joe Kurtz."

"Sergeant Kurtz?" She struggled to keep her face clean of expression. "What about?"

"The likelihood that I murdered Wanda Gardner and tried to murder you. Among other things."

"I see." She wondered how much Joe had revealed.

"He seems to have some strong personal feelings about you," Mark said slowly.

"I hardly know him." Nice note of indifference there.

"Maybe he just feels threatened by your involvement in the case."

"Everybody else seems to."

He nodded, studying her face. "Get any sleep last night?"

"Four hours. You?"

"Four minutes, maybe. So are you feeling better—or does it keep coming back?"

"Haven't had time to think about it. I've been busy."

"Doing what?"

"Finding the murder site."

She watched his reaction. She saw the slight widening of his eyes, the purse of his lips, the flare of his nostrils with a short intake of breath. Surprise? Or concern? She would have given a lot to read his thoughts at that moment.

"How'd you manage that?" he asked after a tick of silence.

"Identification of the flower in Wanda's hair and lab analysis of the soil on her clothes both pointed to the same place: the field around the Phaethon waste-disposal plant."

"Waste disposal. Christ. I wonder if that's how the killer sees his function."

Donna frowned. "Hadn't thought of that. It's possible. There was a guy we learned about at Quantico—left his victim's body near a NO DUMPING sign. His idea of irony."

"I wasn't thinking in terms of irony. More like a sense of appropriateness. Phaethon—it's a big roaring funeral pyre of waste. Everything unwanted and unneeded ends up there. Maybe that's all Wanda was to him: garbage to be disposed of.''

She recoiled from viewing the girl's death so coldly. A highly unprofessional reaction; it was necessary to get inside the killer's head, and Mark's supposition was a plausible one. Maybe too plausible.

"I found her other shoe there," she said, changing the subject slightly. "She must have kicked it loose while struggling. And there's a kind of path through the brush, as if he dragged her."

"That would explain the streaks of dirt on her clothes. Anything else?"

"No. Well, yes, but I don't know what it means. There were bits of polyester fiber on the path."

"You mean carpet threads?"

"No, not like that." She showed him the scrap of white fiber.

As he examined it, Donna noticed that he remained awkwardly turned in his chair, his arm still on the typewriter, blocking the page in the rollers from view. She wondered if the pose he'd struck was as careless as it was meant to appear, or if he had been writing something he preferred her not to see.

"Friend of mine uses this material for making quilts and potholders," she explained. "It's sold under brand names like Fiberfill and Mountain Mist. Generally you find it used as stuffing for pillows, teddy bears, dolls—anything soft and fluffy."

Logan nodded slowly. "Dolls."

"Right."

"But the doll would have to be torn up—ripped to pieces—in order for the stuffing to spill out."

Donna didn't see his point. "Well, I guess if the guy is crazy enough to kill a girl, he's not going to flinch from mutilating a doll."

"No," Logan said, half to himself. "I'm sure he's not."

She frowned. The expression on his face was strange. "Mark . . . is there something you're not telling me?"

"There's a great deal I'm not telling you."

"Maybe you should start."

He looked away, toward the wall, and far beyond it, toward something she couldn't see. His voice was very soft: "Not yet."

41

The patrol car assigned to take Donna to the Phaethon plant was waiting for her outside the station.

"Thanks for the ride," she told the two uniformed officers as she climbed into the backseat, "and the protection."

The driver nodded. "Our pleasure."

The car was pulling away from the curb when she saw Brody's assistant, Lynn, strolling down the sidewalk, returning from her lunch break.

"Hold it. I have to talk to her."

She got out of the car and hailed the girl with a wave. "Lynn."

Lynn stopped near the station's front door. There was a chocolate bar in her hand, partially consumed. Snickers yesterday, Baby Ruth today.

"Oh. Hello, Detective." She swallowed a hasty bite of the candy. "Jeez, I hope you're all right—"

Donna didn't want to hear any more good wishes. "Just fine. Need to double-check something with you, though. As I understand it, you were with Sergeant Kurtz continuously from the time you got off work till he left for the station, correct?"

"That's right."

"At his place?"

"Yes."

"But when I was in the administrative office yesterday, I heard you arranging to meet your mom at eight, to see a movie."

"Yeah, well . . . she canceled." Her eyes were darting, and Donna knew she'd caught the girl in a lie.

"How did you and Joe spend the evening?" she asked gently.

"We went grocery shopping. Then I fixed dinner at his apartment."

"Did you talk to him about your day at work?"

"Sure."

"Including how you found me near the personnel files?"

She saw the heavy swallowing motion of the girl's throat. "Yes."

So Joe could have a motive to attack her. He'd known she was investigating CBPD employees.

"Did you tell anyone else?" she asked Lynn. "Anyone at all?"

"No. Why does that matter?"

"It probably doesn't," Donna answered vaguely. "So what happened after dinner?"

"Well, we . . . you know . . . *did* it."

Momentarily Donna felt Joe's muscled back arch over her. "After that?"

"Just hung out together."

"In bed?"

"Uh, yeah." She took another bite of the Baby Ruth. A quick, nervous bite.

"Did you make love again?"

"Christ, it's none of your business."

"It *is* my business. And you know it."

Lynn finished the candy bar, then balled up the wrapper, compressing it into a crumpled wad.

"We only did it that one time last night," she said, her voice low.

"So what *did* you do afterward?"

"I don't know. Listened to music. On the radio."

"You lay there listening to the radio till 11:45?"

Melted chocolate from the wrapper dirtied her hands. She wiped them on a tissue, not looking at Donna. "That's right."

"Lynn, did Joe tell you to lie?"

"I'm *not* lying." She went on wiping, wiping, though her hands were clean.

"After he found out about the attack on me"—Donna bored in remorselessly—"did he call you up and tell you what to say?"

"Of course not—"

"Because he knew he would be a suspect if he had no alibi?"

"He never called me. You're making all this up. You're *crazy*." She flung the tissue and candy wrapper to the ground with a petulant swipe of her hand.

"Did he tell you to say you'd stayed with him the whole time, so there could no question of his whereabouts?"

Lynn was struggling against tears. "Just shut up."

"You went to the movies after dinner, didn't you? And Joe didn't come along. You don't know where he was at eleven-thirty."

"I didn't say that."

"But it's true, isn't it?"

"You're a goddamn bitch. No wonder Logan broke up with you."

"Isn't it true, what I said?"

"No wonder," Lynn said again, spitefully, as she pivoted on her heel and hurried away, blindly seeking the interior of the station as if it were a sanctuary.

Donna stared after her, thinking hard. Joe Kurtz had asked Lynn to cover for him, lie for him. Was that enough to establish his guilt?

Not necessarily. Nobody wanted to be the target of a homicide investigation. Joe might have panicked when he learned that a CBPD baton had been used in the assault; he would know that Donna, at least, would see him as a possible suspect because of their personal history, his jealousy, his obsessiveness. Frightened, not thinking clearly, he might have phoned Lynn from the station last night and convinced her to lie on his behalf.

A fairly plausible scenario. But no more plausible than the alternative: that Joe, having failed to kill her, had persuaded Lynn to supply him with an alibi in a desperate attempt to deflect suspicion from himself.

Donna sighed. She would have to consider Joe still a suspect, but only one of three.

There was Logan with his incipient alcoholism and his hate. Barnes with his history of violence against women. Kurtz with his obsessiveness, his phony alibi.

Ed had been her friend, Mark and Joe—her lovers. All three were men who mattered to her.

Yet none of them meant as much as Wanda Gardner, whom she had never met.

42

Logan sat for a long time looking at the typewriter under his hands. Its dull electric hum was oddly soothing, like a kitten's purr. He found himself idly stroking the keys.

Abruptly he switched off the machine and got up. He removed the paper from the rollers, tore it into strips, and dropped the shredded pieces in the trash.

There was a peculiar distance to the world around him, as though he were not fully part of it. An unreal sense of invulnerability armored him. He recalled a dream he sometimes had, in which he moved through layers of dissolving reality, untouched by his environment. This was like that.

Brody's secretary was just settling in at her desk after her lunch break when Logan entered the administrative office. "Hi, Lynn."

"Hello, Detective." She was biting her nails and looked upset. Logan didn't know why, didn't care. Her problems were as remote from him as the travails of a fly in a web.

"Have to borrow something," he said lightly, crossing behind her desk. "Hope you don't mind."

He lifted a photo off the wall. The snapshot of the softball team fielded by the department in last year's charity game.

Lynn turned awkwardly in her seat and stared up at him. "What ... what do you need that for?"

"Call it a keepsake. I've always enjoyed the memory of that day." He smiled at her. "I hit a triple, and Donna cheered. Detective Wildman, I mean."

"I've met her." Her voice was oddly flat.

"I remember hearing her whoop and holler from the stands when I rounded the bases." His smile softened, melting like wax under the warmth of his remembrance. "A good day," he said fondly. There had not been many good days since.

Lynn fidgeted, uncertain what to do. "That's Lieutenant Brody's picture. I really don't think you should—"

"It'll be all right. Trust me." He was already moving out the door. "So long, Lynn."

Whatever else she said he didn't hear, and it didn't matter anyway.

He walked down the hall, through the familiar station, past the rows of offices and the tacked-up bulletin boards, seeing it all as if for the first time, or for the last.

In the parking lot he unlocked his personal car, the Buick Skylark, then slid behind the wheel and put the photo on the passenger seat. He favored it with another look. A line of smiling men and women, happy even in defeat. Yes, a damn good day.

Not like this one, he thought as the engine started with a growl. *This one may not be so good at all.*

He pulled out of the lot and headed north, toward Hollywood. Traffic should be light in early afternoon.

He could be at Jay Cee's apartment in half an hour. Maybe sooner.

43

Lynn waited till Logan was gone before calling Joe Kurtz at home. Her heart was banging like crazy, and she heard the high-pitched chiming in her ears that she got whenever she was nervous.

The phone rang nine times. Finally he answered. "Kurtz."

"Joe? Sorry to wake you." He normally slept in the middle of the day.

"It's okay." He didn't sound too groggy. "What's up?"

"That L.A. detective, Wildman?"

"I know her."

"She cornered me on the street and started asking a lot of questions. About last night. You know."

"What did you tell her?"

Lynn lowered her voice, fearful of being overheard from the hall. She wouldn't put it past that Wildman bitch to be eavesdropping outside the door. "I stuck to the story. Said we were together at your place the whole time."

"But?"

"She heard me on the phone with my mother. I said our movie date got canceled, but Wildman didn't buy it. I guess maybe I'm not such a good liar." The last words came out choppy with frightened trembling.

"Christ," Joe hissed, "it should have been simple enough—"

"It *wasn't* simple." Lynn was upset and scared, but she wasn't going to take any shit, either. "Not with her staring at me like she could read my mind. I don't see why I couldn't just tell the truth in the first place, like I wanted to."

"Because I would have had no alibi for last night. And none for the night of the prostitute's murder either."

"So what? You didn't kill her, did you?"

"That's not the point. They've got to pin it on someone. Goddamn it, you don't know how these things work. There's all kinds of pressure from the community, the city council, even that fucking rag, the *Guardian*. If Mueller wants to save his fat ass, he's got to clear this case fast—especially when people find out that the killer is a cop."

"But why you?"

"Why not? I'm not too high in rank. I can be sacrificed."

"The chief wouldn't do that."

"Bullshit he wouldn't." Panic thinned and stretched his voice. "That cocksucker would nail Jesus to the cross to save his fucking job."

She shifted the receiver away from her ear, not to catch the venom he was spitting. "Joe—I've never heard you talk like this. It . . . it's scary."

A beat of silence on the line. When he spoke again, he sounded calmer, back in control.

"You're right. I'm sorry. It's just that I'm so worked up about this. I mean . . . for *her* to suspect me. It's incredible."

"It's not just you. She's checking out everybody."

"She ought to know better, in my case."

"What for?"

Another pause. "Nothing. Forget it. I just mean

there's a hell of a lot more obvious suspect. Her god-damn alcoholic ex-boyfriend."

"Hey, that's another thing." Lynn was grateful for the opportunity to switch the subject. "Logan's acting really weird."

"Weird, how?"

"Came into the office a couple minutes ago and took that photo of the softball team. I told him he shouldn't, but he didn't listen. What would he want that for?"

"Hell if I know. Look, Lynn, I'd better get some rest."

"Sure."

"I shouldn't have told you to lie. But it's too late now. You've got to stick to that story no matter what. Even if Wildman comes after you again."

"I'll try. It's hard, though. She . . . she kind of rattled me."

Kurtz let out a brief, cryptic chuckle. "I know the feeling." Then his voice turned serious. "Thanks for telling me, Lynn. And don't worry about it. Everything will be all right."

"Of course it will."

"I love you, honey. I love you."

A dial tone pressed against her ear. Lynn put down the phone slowly.

It was the first time Joe had ever said those words to her. She wondered why he'd chosen this moment to tell her what she had so desperately wanted to hear.

44

Al Klein, editor-in-chief of the Corona Beach *Guardian*, arrived at the murder site only ten minutes after Donna got there.

She'd never met Klein, but she recognized his face, which was prominently featured in the *Guardian*'s "Goings On About Town" section. Mark used to bring the paper home when they were living together.

Klein was a lively, pudgy little man, the kind of person she ordinarily would have been glad to see, but not now. "What are you doing here?" she asked as he climbed out of his wood-paneled station wagon.

"Hey, this is a big story. I missed out on it the night the body was dumped. Not this time."

He made a move toward the field, scanning it as if for signs of blood. Donna stopped him. "You can't go in there."

"Who says?"

"I say." She flipped open her badge wallet. "Donna Wildman, LAPD."

The two patrol officers got out of their car and stood beside her in a silent statement of authority.

"Okay, okay. No problem." Klein cocked a thumb at Donna. "You're the FBI expert."

"Right."

"You caught the Slasher."

"I helped."

"And you nearly got iced last night?"

"Nearly."

"Hey, Jerry, get a photo of Detective Wildman here."

Cadaverous, slow-moving Jerry, Yin to Klein's Yang, was just getting out of Klein's car on the passenger side, a camera dangling from his neck.

Donna wasn't in the mood to pose for pictures. She turned away from Jerry as he unscrewed his Minolta's lens cap. "I still don't understand how you found out about this," she said to Klein.

"Oh, hell, that was nothing. I monitor the police band all day long."

"What did you hear that tipped you off?"

"Patrol unit called in a 10–23 at this location. Said they were standing by, awaiting the arrival of an LAPD crime-scene squad. Now, why would Corona Beach call in LAPD experts for help? I figure it's got to have something to do with what happened to you last night. Presumably it was the Gardner girl's killer who attacked you—and the girl was killed outdoors. So I put two and two together, and I figure this must be the scene of the murder. Correct?"

Donna didn't answer. She looked at the patrol cops. "Should have used your MDT to transmit that message."

"Aw, come on," Klein groaned. "Have a little compassion for a hard-working newshound. What difference does it make, anyway?"

Donna didn't answer. She was thinking of the killer she had profiled—the killer who was a cop. If on duty, he would be monitoring the police band as part of his normal responsibilities. Even off duty, he might be listening to a scanner at home. Either way, he would now know that the murder site had been found.

Unless, of course, the killer was Mark. He had known already, because she'd told him. A mistake? Possibly—

A rapid succession of snaps and whirs interrupted her thoughts. Jerry's camera, clicking off exposures, taking her portrait a dozen times.

She turned away, irritated, distracted by worry, yet still vain enough to wish her hair wasn't such a goddamn mess.

Fifteen minutes later Mueller arrived at the site in a mist of cigarette smoke and a flurry of rasping coughs. He pushed past Klein without comment and had the two patrol officers hold the man at a distance so he could confer with Donna in privacy.

"Talked to the Phaethon management. They're totally cooperative. We've got permission to search the field and take anything we find. Not that obtaining a warrant would have been any problem, but it's neater this way."

"How about SID?"

"On the way. Should be here any minute. Oh, another thing. Phaethon's supplying a list of their night-shift workers so we can make some phone calls, find out if anybody saw or heard anything."

"I'll bet they didn't. This field must be pitch-dark at night, and the incinerator makes enough noise to drown out any cries for help."

"Probably true, but it won't hurt to ask." He jerked his head at Klein. "What's he doing here?"

"Monitored the radio chatter and heard what was up."

"Hell. Where's Barnes, anyway? He ought to have shown up by now."

"You spoke with him?"

"Yeah." Mueller took a long, contemplative drag

on his Marlboro. "He wasn't happy about letting LAPD do his job for him, but he said he understood."

Another suspect had been informed of the break in the case. Donna wondered if the news should have been guarded more carefully. She hadn't had time to think it through before. If the man panicked—tried to run—

Mueller was speaking again. "Where's Logan, by the way?"

"Back at the station, I guess."

"His car wasn't in the lot when I left. I thought he'd come over here."

"Maybe he's still en route."

"I stopped off at Phaethon for fifteen minutes. No chance I could have made better time than he did."

Dona frowned, her body stiffening with the shivery beginnings of fear. "You'd better check with the station and see if he's returned."

"If not, I'll have them call his apartment."

Mueller gave the orders in a low voice. A moment later one of the patrol cops was tapping the inquiry into the squad car's computer terminal.

Donna turned back to the field, gazing past the patches of *Linaria vulgaris* to the faint path tracked through the brush, the path that ended where Wanda's life must have ended, in a ditch invisible from the road. She stared at the rustling weeds for a long time.

Then the chief was back at her side. "No one's seen him at the station. His car's still gone. No answer at his apartment. The watch commander called his beeper; so far, no reply."

"Not sure I like that," Donna whispered as something chilly clutched her stomach, squeezing tight.

"Me neither," Mueller said. "I don't like it at all. That's why I put out an alert. All units are to keep an eye out for Detective Logan or his car. He took his own vehicle, the Skylark."

"CBPD units only?"

"For now. I'm trying not to blow this thing out of proportion. We don't *know* anything yet. Hell, he may just be running down a lead on his own."

"You don't really believe that."

Mueller exhaled a feathery plume of smoke. "No."

Donna shut her eyes. "I don't know if I can believe it, either."

45

He parked outside the Hollywood Regal and sat in the car, listening to the clockwork ticks of the cooling engine, finding the place inside himself where he kept his fund of courage and tapping it dry.

He didn't want to enter the Regal, didn't want to be here at all, but he had no choice. The murder site had been found. What he had left there—what he had stupidly, unforgivably left, because he'd assumed the scene of the killing was his permanent secret—would soon be discovered. Then the connection with the attack on the little whore Billie would be made.

She had seen his face in the motel room. She could identify him in a lineup.

But only if she was still alive.

He had meant to kill the bitch when he picked her up on Hollywood Boulevard last month. He hadn't pretended to arrest her, as he'd done later with the girl named Wanda. His CBPD badge was useful only in Corona Beach, and he'd known he couldn't operate there; the handful of whores on the south side knew all the local cops by name and would never fall for any setup he could devise. So he had to go outside of town and use some other tactic.

He'd approached Billie as a customer, shy and a little nervous. The nervousness was real; he'd never killed before, wasn't certain he could go through with it.

For fifty bucks, paid in advance, she agreed to everything he said he wanted. His true desires remained unspoken at first.

She took him to the motel she used, a warren of cramped rooms with thin walls and rodent droppings ground indelibly into the worn carpet. The doll came with him, concealed at the bottom of a shopping bag under a folded blanket.

With his belt he tied her to the headboard, the first step in the S and M game he'd described to her. The belt was part of his plan, and before leaving for Hollywood that night, he had scrubbed it thoroughly to remove any fingerprints. It was imperative to leave no prints at a crime scene; as was the case with any cop, his ten digits were on file and would come up in any blind computer run.

For the same reason, he had put on gloves. He remembered flexing them slowly, watching the black leather crinkle and shine.

Only once she was immobilized did he show her the doll. "I'm going to do you the same way I do this little raggedy bitch," he whispered, watching bewilderment shift to panic in her face as he started to twist, to rend. Her fear tasted good; he lapped it up and wanted more.

But something stopped him as he moved in for the kill. Some remnant of conscience, possibly, or the simple fear of being caught. Or perhaps there was no meaningful distinction between the two.

He couldn't make himself hurt her, though his hands ached with the need to batter her pale face to blood.

And so he fled the motel, hating himself for his failure of nerve, leaving her untouched.

But he did not forget her. She was the unplucked flower, the untasted fruit, tantalizing, maddening.

He returned to the boulevard several times, lured back by an obsessive need to see her again, ambush her, finish what he'd started. In their first encounter he had flinched from recognition of the deepest part of himself. Now he was ashamed.

She no longer worked the street where he'd met her, and it took patience and money to hunt her down. Finally he learned that she was hiding out with her pimp, Jay Cee, and his bodyguard Kinshasa, in apartment 819 of the Hollywood Regal.

For three nights he watched the place. Twice he saw her leave with the two men, no doubt to be taken to some private club or party where there was a market for her services.

On the third night, the bodyguard spotted him spying from across the street and came after him. He lost the man in a maze of shadowed alleys.

He had not stalked her since. It seemed impossible to get near her without first dispatching the other two, and he hadn't wanted to take the risk. Instead he had found another girl, a girl with no pimp to protect her, a girl conveniently available in Corona Beach, new in town, unfamiliar with the local police, exquisitely vulnerable to the ruse of a phony arrest.

After the exhilaration of killing Wanda, he'd lost all concern over Billie. But the press of events had renewed his interest and sharpened it, till it gleamed like a stropped razor, hungry for blood.

The same black leather gloves were now in his jacket pockets. He pulled them on and admired his hands, black and glossy and sleek as panthers, and as deadly.

He removed the Iver Johnson .22 from the glove compartment, where he'd stashed it this morning, knowing it might be needed. Checked the newly loaded clip: seven rounds. Two spare magazines went in his pockets.

Onto the barrel he fitted a new silencer cut from television-antenna mast. With the silencer attached, the handgun was long and bulky, and it printed badly against his jacket when he slipped it into his vest pocket.

What the hell. He didn't intend to be seen by anybody. He would leave no witnesses and no fingerprints, and the gun could not be traced.

He emerged from the car and took a moment to contemplate the Art Deco pile of the Hollywood Regal. It rose before him like a monument to yesterday's glamour and today's decadence. He thought it would make a good headstone for L.A. when riots and earthquakes and craziness finished the city off.

A motorcycle roared by; he turned away to conceal his face. When it was gone, he crossed the street, pushed open the lobby doors, and left daylight behind.

Nobody in the lobby. Good. He didn't want to start killing yet.

He hesitated between the elevator and the stairwell, then decided the stairwell would be safer: less chance of being seen.

His footsteps racketed off the steel treads as he ascended, breathing hard, fighting fear.

What he was about to do was the most dangerous hand he had yet played. He would need good reflexes and steady nerves—and maybe luck—to come out of it alive.

Well, he'd been trained in the use of deadly force. And he'd been in a few street fights. He could handle it.

"Sure you can," he whispered, mounting the last flight of stairs. "No problem."

But the clammy sweat under his arms gave the lie to any effort at bravado.

He reached the eighth floor and stepped warily into the hall. Empty. His good fortune was holding; he might have been the last man in Hollywood, the last man on earth. He could enter and leave this neighborhood unseen, ineffable as a ghost, silent as a death angel.

The carpet swallowed his footsteps as he approached apartment 819. From behind the closed door, a hard raucous beat throbbed like a migraine.

The pistol came out. He held the gun away from his body, his finger exerting light pressure on the trigger, his hand almost steady.

All right. Make it happen. Now.

He lashed out with a kick, planting his shoe on the door latch, his full weight behind it. The lock held, but the cheap hollow door splintered, and a second well-placed kick blew it open, and then he was charging into the apartment, the gun leading him, and he swiveled to pan the living room while a fury of rap music howled from pulsing speakers.

No one here.

Kitchen? Empty.

One of the bedrooms, then.

Fear had left him. He was a machine, programmed to kill, intent only on performing that function. His senses—heightened, sharpened—tracked every detail of his environment. Time slowed as his perceptions accelerated. He was filled with a sense of boundless power, ultimate control.

He ran down the short hallway that snaked into the rear of the apartment, unconcerned about stealth, knowing the stereo would hungrily devour any sound he made.

The volume of the music remained constant as he left the living room behind. Speakers must be wired together throughout the place, carrying the noise into every room. He was grateful for the cover the music provided; it must have drowned out even the thuds of his two kicks and the crackle of breaking wood, just as it would cover the pops of his silenced handgun when he used it.

He reached the first room off the hall, looked in, and there they were, Jay Cee and Kinshasa, both naked in bed, the pimp on his knees and the bodyguard mounting him like a rutting dog, Jay Cee's mouth twisting in a soundless moan and Kinshasa flexing his huge muscles as he forced himself in deeper.

Frenzied as animals in heat. Oblivious of everything but need.

In the doorway he gripped the pistol in both hands, planted his feet in the Weaver stance, drew a bead on the bodyguard.

At the last second Jay Cee saw him, and the unvoiced moan became a shouted warning. Kinshasa was turning his head when the silenced gun fired.

One shot, and Kinshasa's throat was torn open in a gout of blood as he was blasted backward, off the bed, onto the floor in a snarl of mauve sheets.

A second shot, and Jay Cee was winged as he tried to hurl himself at the nightstand, where undoubtedly there was a gun.

A third shot, and the pimp's belly opened up, spewing blood, and he was whipsawing wildly on the bed, long bony limbs flailing spastically.

A fourth shot found his forehead like a wafted kiss, and he was gone.

By then Kinshasa was dead also, his massive body contorted at the foot of the bed, head cocked at a sickening angle on the ruptured stalk of his neck.

Done. It was done.

He'd killed them both.

A long-held breath shuddered out of him, leaving him flaccid and weak. Abruptly he was a machine no longer, human again, and with humanity came fear, the dizzying recognition of the risk he'd taken. He had danced on the lip of the abyss.

Inside the gloves, his hands were wet and hot. Tremors of nervous excitement hurried through him, loosening his knees. The room wheeled slowly, the floor canting, and for a bad moment he thought he would pass out.

No. Keep it together. More work to do.

With effort he squeezed panic out of his body and mind, till he was safely emotionless, a robot once more.

The four shots had been muffled by the silencer, their faint noise eradicated by the stereo still pounding out its furious wall of sound. If Billie was elsewhere in this apartment, she hadn't heard a thing.

Four of the seven rounds in the clip had been expended. He removed and pocketed it, heeled in a fresh clip, then left the bedroom and proceeded down the hall. The music pursued him, squalling like a storm.

The next doorway framed a small, cluttered bathroom—empty.

At the end of the corridor was the guest bedroom, the door half open. He peered in, inhaling the strong scent of ether, and saw Billie stretched out supine in bed, her slender legs protruding from under a loose T-shirt. She gazed fascinated at the ceiling as if at the face of God. In her mouth was a hand-rolled cigarette, a pinroll joint.

Angel dust. She was flying.

She would be soaring with the real angels soon.

He eased the door open and stepped in.

"Billie? Oh, Billie . . ."

She blinked, losing sight of the private vision that

had held her transfixed. She rolled her head to look at him. The cigarette dangled from her lip, then dropped onto the mattress, tied to a string of spit.

"Rag Doll Man," she whispered.

Fear jumped in her voice but found no other expression. Shock paralyzed her facial muscles. She might have been staring at a TV set or a hypnotist's watch.

His smile was a hungry thing. In that instant he knew he still wanted her, had never stopped wanting her.

"That's right, Billie. It's me. I've come back for you. Back to make you mine."

Abruptly her face twisted into a fright-mask caricature, all wild pop-eyes and gaping mouth. Great whoops of breath exploded from her lungs. She was screaming.

"Rag Doll Man! *Rag Doll Man!*"

He shot her twice, in the left thigh and right hip. Her screams broke up into grunting sounds, good to hear. Wounded-animal noises, glottal vocalizations of witless terror. Currents of twitches and spasms rippled through her body. She thrashed in bed, beating at the covers, gargling froth.

He approached her. Tore off a strip of bed sheet and lashed her wrists to the headboard. Her eyes were rolling up white in the sockets, and he feared she might be losing consciousness. No fair; he wanted her awake, wanted her to know what was happening, to feel every twinge and bite of pain.

A slap roused her. Her eyes refocused on his face. "Rag Doll Man," she whispered again, her voice fluttery and soft. Those must be the only words her mind still held.

He stepped back to look at her. Her stomach heaved with desperate gasps. Blood soaked through the thin fabric of the T-shirt where the bullets had struck. Arterial bleeding would kill her soon enough, but a gentle death, a loss of vitality by slow degrees, was not what he had in mind.

She would die as Wanda had died, hammered into oblivion. All he needed was a club, a blunt instrument. His gaze swept the room and settled on a telephone on the night table.

He tore the phone out of the wall. The plastic handset made a solid weapon, hefty in his hand.

No hesitation now. No second thoughts. No nip of conscience.

The anger, the hate, the savage, blind rage that lurched and thrashed within him—it had been his companion for a long time, for years, and yet he had not yielded to its urgings. For as long as possible, he had resisted the impulse to kill, held in check by fear, by shame.

With Wanda he had learned that resistance was futile and stupid and unnecessary. He had learned to be who and what he was, and to revel in it.

The phone came down, smashing Billie's face, crushing bone, and he was laughing.

46

There was sun, and there was heat, dry heat moistened by tendrils of ocean breeze gusting inland. A jet powered into the hazy sky from LAX, engines screaming; the world shook briefly in the grip of its roar. It threw a sliding shadow across the Phaethon field and curved west, toward the sea.

Donna watched it go. She wished she were on that plane, traveling somewhere faraway, escaping from Corona Beach and its secrets. Secrets she almost did not want to learn.

She turned back to the field and stared out at the distant figures of the SID evidence collectors, hunched over as they searched, only the tops of their heads visible above the lip of the gully. They looked like stoop laborers at their grim work, bending and rising, bending and rising.

Al Klein and his cadaverous associate, Jerry, had positioned themselves on the roof of Klein's station wagon; Jerry was clicking off telephoto shots of the search. The intermittent snap of the shutter release and buzz of the automatic film-advance cut through the stillness like the song of some peculiar hybrid of cricket and cicada.

Donna put her hands in her jacket pockets and paced the roadside. Under the Kevlar vest, her blouse was sticky with sweat. Waiting was hard. She felt as though she were suspended in a kind of purgatory,

the fate of her soul undecided. If something in that
field tied the crime to Mark—or Joe, or Ed—a small
part of her would die.

Or maybe not such a small part. Not if it's Mark.

She had thought she'd lost all feeling for him. Now
she wasn't sure. Certainly she'd tried hard enough
not to implicate him in the homicide, *not* to see him
as the obvious suspect. Was it only nostalgia for their
failed love affair that had blinded her, or was it
something more? Could she still be in love with him,
even now?

A tramp of heavy footsteps, and Mueller was at
her side, his eyelids drooping wearily over red-
rimmed eyes.

"A little bit of news for you," he said in an undertone too low for Klein to hear. "Fifteen minutes ago I
sent a blue-and-white over to Logan's place. Thought
maybe he was there, but just wasn't answering his
phone for some reason."

Donna grimaced. "Because he was drunk, you
mean. Passed out."

"It's possible."

"So was he home?"

"The cops banged on the door and got no response. His car isn't in the neighborhood. Neighbors
haven't seen him."

"Maybe your guys should watch the place anyway."

"That's just what they're doing. The other patrol
units are continuing to cruise the town, checking out
some of his favorite haunts—the pier, the cemetery,
some stores he frequents."

"Shit." The idea of Mark on the run, pursued by
the law, a hunted criminal—it was a hot knife twisting in her heart. She turned away, an acid bath of
tears stinging her eyes. "Shouldn't have told him I'd
found the murder site. It might have caused him to

panic. He could be heading for the border right now."

"If that's his plan, he won't succeed," Mueller said with chilly resolve. "There's plenty of time to contact the border guards—if it comes to that."

She looked at him. "How do you feel about all this, Chief?"

"Me?" The question surprised him. He allowed a thoughtful moment to pass before answering. "Betrayed."

"Because he's one of your men?"

"Because he was my friend." Mueller lowered his head. He kicked one shoe against the other in a way that made him seem shy and awkward, almost boyish; and in that instant Donna glimpsed the very young man he once had been. "Not only a friend. I've got no kids; never married. Mark was . . . something like a son to me."

"I know you two were close, once."

"Until Sharon died. After that, he retreated into himself. He was still a solid professional, a good cop—best in the department, other than Barnes—but not someone you could connect with on a personal level anymore. When he met you, I thought he'd found a way out of all the hurt and the guilt. But maybe"—he sighed, a slow, deep sigh of mourning—"maybe even then it was too late."

Dust clouded the air. Tires crunched gravel. Donna looked up and saw Barnes park his unmarked Chevy on the shoulder of the road. He got out, looking fatigued and more rumpled than usual.

Mueller readjusted his mood to his usual curt authoritarianism. "Ed. What the hell took you so long?"

Barnes approached, pushing his bifocals higher on his nose. Sunlight glinted on the steel rims as if on a honed knife's edge. "I was tied up with a little investigation of my own."

He stopped before Donna, his gaze fixed on her. Dark bruises, like stripes of lampblack, underscored his eyes.

"Just came from Parker Center," he went on slowly. "Your appearance made news, Donna; you're something of a celebrity today. I wondered what you were doing there, so I made a few discreet inquiries. Found out you met with Turner at Personnel—and he gave you access to the files."

She nodded, holding his stare. "Yes."

"I'm the only current Corona Beach cop who ever worked for LAPD. It was my file you were looking at."

"Yes."

"I think I can guess why." He looked away, shaking his head. "Christ, that was thirty years ago."

"I still had to check it out."

"I never hurt those girls in any serious way. Just pushed them around a little to get their attention, show I meant business. Sometimes you have to do that."

"The complaints were upheld. You were disciplined."

"It was *nothing*."

"Your CO didn't think so. Neither did the top brass, apparently. Or have I misread the reason for your sudden transfer to the crime lab?"

All the fight went out of him then, and he was just tired. "No," he said in a lifeless voice. "You haven't misread it."

An insect's drone filled the silence between them, the noise diffuse and sourceless, like the hum of vibrating molecules in the air itself.

"This whole issue may be beside the point," Mueller said finally, a practiced note of diplomacy in his voice. "Logan is missing."

Barnes grunted. "I heard the alert on the radio. Did

he disappear immediately after learning that Donna
found the murder site?"

"Apparently so."

"Hell. It *can't* be him. He's not that crazy. Crazy
enough to drink himself to death, sure. But not to
kill someone."

Donna wanted to agree, but couldn't. She no
longer knew what Mark Logan was capable of.

Brush rustled like crackling newspaper. One of the
SID investigators trudged out of the field, toting a
small plastic bag. Donna had worked with him at
many L.A. crime scenes; his name was Lorentz. A
small, neat man with a tidy mustache that was
mostly fuzz.

He saw Barnes and sketched a wave. "Afternoon,
Lieutenant."

The greeting was friendly but awkward. Everyone
was aware that the LAPD was conducting the search
only because Barnes was a suspect in the case.

Barnes acknowledged the wave with a sullen nod.
"How's it going, Pete?"

"Pretty well. There's no question this is the murder
site. That declivity over there, I mean."

He cocked a thumb at the ditch where his colleagues were still working. From the roof of the station wagon, Jerry fired off another series of
Kodachrome exposures.

"Find anything significant?" Barnes asked.

"Bits of torn clothing. Dried blood on some leaves.
There's even an impression of her body in the dirt.
Everything fits the scenario of a brutal homicide on
that spot. Problem is, we've got a bunch of crap
there, illegally dumped trash bags, some of which
have split open. It complicates the evidence collection. Hard to distinguish what the killer left from the
junk that spilled out." He held up the bag. "We did
find an interesting item, though."

Inside the bag was what looked like a heap of torn cloth, multicolored, ragged with sprung threads.

"What is it?" Donna asked.

"The source of those polyester-fiber scraps you noticed." Lorentz shook the bag lightly, shifting its contents. A small smiling face flopped into view. "See?"

She blinked, startled.

Grinning at her through the plastic was the savaged remnant of a Raggedy Ann doll—red-yarn curls, black-button eyes, spangled lashes, sewn triangular nose.

Lying shapeless in the bag, deflated and mangled, it seemed somehow grotesque, a fetus in a jar.

"Our preliminary feeling is that the killer tore up the doll and got bits of stuffing on his clothes. Some of them fell off as he carried the girl's body up the path to his car. We—"

"Jesus . . ."

The word was a gasp, hissing out of Barnes. His face had paled; he stood staring at the bag as if at some supernatural manifestation, inexplicable and malign.

"The Rag Doll Man," he whispered. "Oh, sweet Jesus. The Rag Doll Man."

Donna glanced at Mueller, then at Lorentz. The words meant nothing to any of them.

"Care to explain yourself?" Mueller inquired in the tone of a command.

Barnes glanced at him, his eyes clearing. He wore the dazed, slightly silly expression of a man surfacing from the depths of a trance.

"It's something we heard about in Hollywood," he said slowly. "Logan and I. When we interviewed those hookers who bought Wanda her clothes. They told us about another prostitute, name of Billie, who'd been tied up and threatened by a john. A john who ripped apart a Raggedy Ann . . ."

"Christ, the same MO," Lorentz breathed.

"There's more. After that, we went over to see a pimp named Jay Cee, and while we're talking to him, this same girl, this Billie, shows up and sees us and she . . . she starts screaming. Screaming about the Rag Doll Man."

"Why didn't you report it?" Mueller asked sharply.

"Didn't think too much of the incident at the time. Billie was obviously dusted. Phrencyclidine is a hallucinogenic. And her pimp said she freaked out whenever she saw a strange man while she was high. It seemed straightforward enough." Barnes ran a shaky hand over his face "Now I don't know. . . ."

Donna heard a female voice speak up and realized it was her own.

"Assuming the girl did recognize Mark, she can do it again. We can put him in a lineup." She hated saying this; every word was a small, separate pain. But she had made a vow to Wanda, here in this field, and she would keep it. "If Billie fingers him as the Rag Doll Man, then we've got him for both crimes."

"Unless . . ." Barnes glanced at Mueller. "How long has Logan been unaccounted for?"

"Nearly an hour."

"Enough time to get to Hollywood. He knows where she lives."

A rush of fear stopped Donna's breath. "LAPD better take a run over there." She jerked her radio handset out of her pocket, punched the transmit button. "Right now."

47

Out of the apartment. Moving fast down the hall. Discordant music blaring like a banshee at his back.

Logan glanced down at his clothes as he ran, checking for bloodstains. None. He'd been lucky. If his suit had been soiled, he wouldn't have been able to change at home; by this time, Mueller surely must have put a blue-and-white or an unmarked car on watch outside his building.

All right—what now?

Simple enough. He had to get back to Corona Beach, establish his whereabouts, explain his disappearance somehow.

The alert, which had crackled over his portable radio half an hour ago, had caught him by surprise. He hadn't expected his absence to be noted so quickly. Still, it was impossible to prove he'd been here. He had left no prints, been seen by no one.

You'll be all right, don't worry about it, everything will be all right.

Sure it would. Sure.

He approached the elevator. Taking it would be faster than descending via the stairs, but he didn't dare; too much risk of someone getting on while he was aboard. Then his face would be seen and perhaps remembered. The stairwell had been empty on his way up; he prayed his luck would hold.

He was moving toward the stairwell door when

he heard the clatter of the ascending elevator in the shaft. Close. Too close.

He froze, a yard from the elevator, ten feet from the stairwell, exposed and terribly vulnerable, as the doors began to rattle open.

No place to run. All he could do was brazen it out and hope whoever got off paid him no attention.

In the widening gap between the steel doors, a shock of blue.

Uniforms. LAPD.

Christ.

Terror ballooned in him, and he nearly lost it, nearly ran blindly for the stairwell.

No, that's suicide. Keep it together. Bluff your way through.

Two patrol cops emerged from the elevator, their eyes moving over him with trained wariness. The nearer cop was ten years older than his partner. Training officer and probationer, P3 and P1; Logan knew the routine. He'd been a CBPD probationer— a "boot," as they were known—many years ago.

He smiled at them. Not a nervous smile, he hoped, and not too friendly, either.

"Officers," he said with a nod. A polite greeting. Fine.

The older cop acknowledged the hello with an expressionless nod. The younger one was already looking down the hall, toward the music.

Logan brushed past them. He felt the T.O.'s cool, level stare on his profile, on the back of his head.

The man was suspicious of him, smelled his fear.

But the alert had gone out only to Corona Beach units, not to the LAPD. These two wouldn't have his description, wouldn't be looking for him.

When he turned, the cops were moving away. He stabbed the lobby button. The doors struggled shut, and the elevator car groaned into motion, gliding downward.

He let out a shuddery breath. At least he'd gotten past them, avoided immediate arrest.

But it wouldn't take them long to push open the shattered door of Jay Cee's apartment and find the reeking carnage inside. Then they would remember the nervous man who'd boarded the elevator as they got off.

There was only a single elevator. To intercept him before he exited the building, they would have to take the stairs. Even then, it was doubtful they could catch up.

He should be all right. If only the elevator wasn't so goddamn slow. He willed it to accelerate, trying to urge it on with sheer concentration.

The numbers above the doors changed with dreamlike languor. Sixth floor ... fifth ... fourth ...

A hiss, a shuddering, a creak of cable. The elevator slowing to a halt. Stopping on the fourth floor.

Fear disoriented him, made him simple. He didn't understand what was going on. How could it stop halfway down? The lobby button was the only one he'd pressed.

The voice in his mind was a small child's whine, petulant and frightened: No fair, *no fair!*

The doors parted. An elderly man in a cardigan sweater, too warm for June, shuffled into the elevator, coughing with quiet insistence.

Damn.

The doors moaned shut.

Less margin for error now. The cops must be already pounding down the stairs. He could almost hear the clangor of their shoes on the steel treads as they took the steps two at a time.

"Nice day," the old man observed.

Logan didn't answer.

The old man blinked several times in bemusement, then turned away, his mouth working soundlessly.

Third floor . . . second . . .

Logan's hands were fisted at his sides. His heart beat hard enough to shake his body with small, controlled convulsions.

They reached the lobby. There was a chance—a small chance—that the cops were there already, standing outside the elevator, guns drawn.

The tension stiffening his muscles was becoming physical pain. He waited like a man before a firing squad as the doors separated.

Nothing.

The lobby was empty.

He could still make it.

He elbowed the old man out of his way, eliciting a whine of feeble protest, and then he was charging through the lobby, impelled by terror and by the escalating drumbeat of footsteps in the stairwell.

Jesus, they were *close.*

He shoved open the lobby doors. Emerged into sun and air.

Down the steps. Across the street. *Come on, come on!*

He'd left the car door unlocked, thank Christ. Opened it, flung himself behind the wheel.

As the engine caught, sunlight flashed on the lobby doors, swinging open. Two blue uniforms crowded out.

He spun the wheel. Tore away from the curb. Floored the gas pedal.

From behind him, a shouted order, ignored.

He cornered the car onto Cherokee Avenue, made another turn at Lexington, and proceeded to Cahuenga Boulevard, where he hooked north.

Checked the rearview. No LAPD black-and-white in pursuit.

He let out a long, grateful exhalation of relief.

They would have no idea which way he was going. Wouldn't find him right away. For the moment he had eluded capture. That was something, at least. As long as he remained free, he had a chance.

But they had seen his face and his vehicle. The description already would have gone out over the radio.

He couldn't return to Corona Beach. Couldn't explain his temporary absence with any facile lies. Not now.

He was a wanted man. Wanted for four homicides. A grand slam.

Hell, this was bad. Everything had gone wrong, totally wrong.

He would have to ditch his car, steal one to replace it. Then figure out what to do next. There had to be some plan of action, some strategy he could develop. It couldn't end like this.

His throat was dry with more than thirst. He needed a drink. Needed one badly.

No.

No more alcohol. He had to stay sharp, keep his mind clear. He'd made enough mistakes as it was. He could afford no more.

A traffic signal snared him. As he idled at the intersection, it occurred to him that Donna would hear this news very soon. He wondered what she would think.

Stupid question. Irrelevant, pointless. But he couldn't shake free of it. The answer mattered to him, mattered with an urgency that startled him.

"Guess Kurtz wasn't wrong about that, after all," he whispered as the light changed and he steered the Buick onto Sunset Boulevard. "I do still care about her." His voice thickened and slowed, dropping to an almost inaudible undertone, faint as the murmur of thought. "Still . . . love her."

The words and the truth behind them—the truth long denied and finally accepted, now, when it was too late—set his eyes burning.

Logan gripped the wheel and drove on through a blur of tears.

48

Past the shock, stirrings of pain. Faint now, only a distant ache, but not for long.

Donna was grateful for the numbness that froze her mind. It protected her like an anesthetic, dulled her reactions, held grief and horror at bay.

She hadn't expected to take it so hard. She'd believed she was prepared for anything. But the thought that it had been Mark in her bedroom last night, wielding the baton that narrowly missed her skull, firing blind shots at her in the dark—it was too much.

You can't be certain yet, she reminded herself. *Not a hundred percent. There's still room for doubt. For . . . hope.*

Not much room, though. Not anymore.

It had been more than an hour since two Hollywood Division cops had entered Jay Cee's apartment and stumbled over a tableau of slaughter.

Their description of the man in the elevator matched Logan pretty closely; the vehicle observed racing from the scene was a late-model Buick Skylark, Logan's personal car.

Still, eyewitness accounts—even from cops—could be unreliable. And they'd gotten only a momentary look at the man and the car.

There was a chance that their identification was

mistaken. A small chance. She clung to it with ferocious need.

Standing on the gallery outside Mark's second-floor apartment, Donna watched through the doorway as the SID crew from the Phaethon field performed a brisk, thorough search. A warrant had been obtained by telephone only minutes ago; the landlord had opened up the place.

Mueller and Barnes loitered at the bottom of the staircase, conversing in low tones. There was probably no good reason not to let Ed personally search the apartment; he was no longer under suspicion. But to avoid any possible question of planted or doctored evidence, he'd been excluded when the LAPD officers went inside.

She thought about how hard she'd worked to shift the focus of her suspicion away from Mark—to Ed, with his complaint history; to Joe, with his obsessive love for her. All her effort had been wasted. Worse than wasted. Maybe if she hadn't blinded herself to the obvious answer, three people in Hollywood would not be dead now.

The pimp and his hired thug were probably no loss. Petty criminals, exploiters of confused and vulnerable young girls. But poor Billie, hiding out from the Rag Doll Man, only to be shot and beaten by him, beaten to death ... She was too much like Wanda, another lost innocent.

Donna wondered if SID would find a Raggedy Ann in Logan's apartment, or even a closet full of them. She couldn't guess what significance the doll might hold, what it represented in his mind. A baby, perhaps? The stillborn child he'd lost?

"Detective."

She looked up as Lorentz approached.

"We're just about through inside," he said. "You can take a look, if you'd like to."

"Found anything?"

"Nothing of interest so far. We're still checking out the bedroom."

She didn't want to go in, but curiosity impelled her. Curiosity—and a sense of professional obligation. Having lived with Mark, she might notice something in his home that even a trained evidence collector would miss.

This apartment was new to her. He had rented it after they split up, and she had never visited him here. It felt strange to cross the threshold into the narrow living room.

SID had opened the curtains and turned on all the lights. The glare was unflattering to the apartment, a harsh spotlight on an aging face.

It was obvious Mark did not hire a housekeeper. Old newspapers were stacked near a bulging trash bag. Dust dulled the leaves of a shriveled plant. Heaped in the kitchen sink, under a ceiling light with a dead bulb, were dishes crusted with food. There were too many bottles in the cabinets, too many six-packs in the refrigerator.

On an end table by the couch, she found a copy of *Newsweek*, the pages creased and smudged. Mark had claimed he'd read this week's issue last night; that was all the alibi he'd offered. Of course finding the magazine proved nothing.

Testimony to loneliness and boredom was given by the well-used copy of *TV Guide* tented on the coffee table, by half-finished paperbacks scattered around the living room, by the solitary chess game in progress on the dining table. The black king was in check and would have to sacrifice his queen to escape.

She went into the bedroom, where one crime-scene investigator was still at work. She knew him only slightly. Grady was his name. Overweight, harried, sloppy in his grooming but meticulous on the job, as all SID personnel had to be.

In the closet hung a rumpled suit smeared with grass stains. That fit the story Mark had told about his visit to the cemetery, but it would fit the circumstances of Wanda's murder equally well. Barnes would have to check the soil stains and see if they matched samples from Wanda's clothes. It was a safe bet they would.

Among a litter of mailings on the bureau was a dating-service questionnaire, partially filled out. Mark must have been drunk when he penciled in his answers. Under "religious preference" he'd scrawled "Moose Worship." She smiled at that, a furtive, hurtful smile.

The bureau drawers were open. In the top drawer she was surprised to find a cache of sentimental items commemorating their relationship. Christmas and birthday cards from her to him; photos of their vacation in Colorado, each one carefully labeled on the back to record the date and locale; a bogus edition of the L.A. *Times* with a huge front-page headline announcing the commencement of their cohabitation, printed by his friends as a joke.

She would have expected him to throw out all that stuff. Instead he'd kept it close to him, but hidden. The small, sad collection looked like the visible form of heartbreak.

She felt a twinge of pain and realized she was biting her lip.

"What the hell . . . ?"

The voice was Grady's. She turned in his direction. He was crouching by the nightstand, a small spiral notebook in his white-gloved hands.

He felt Donna's stare and looked up at her. "Does he write poetry?"

"Poetry?" She was baffled. "Not as far as I know."

"Take a look at this."

He showed her the notebook. She looked without touching. The pages were filled with careful handwriting. The big looping letters looked feminine, childish.

"That's not Mark's writing," she said.

She read a few lines. The spare, heartfelt verses, dense with misspellings, spoke of love for "a mother whose not there, who did her best to care, ecsept when kissed by black dispair."

Black despair. Depression.

Wanda's mother.

Wanda had written this.

The notebook was hers, and Mark had taken it.

Stolen it from her hotel room—or from the girl herself.

"Hell," she whispered. "Oh, hell and goddamn it."

A souvenir. That was what this was.

It was a known tendency of the organized nonsocial killer to take mementos of his victims as keepsakes and, often, as masturbatory aids.

There could be no doubt any longer, no denial, no self-delusion. Mark had done it, done all of it. Killed Wanda and Billie and the two Hollywood scum.

And tried to kill me, too. Tried to cave in my skull while I slept.

"Goddamn it," she said again, the sudden huskiness of her voice startling, like the rasp of a stranger.

"You know what it means?" Grady asked gently.

"It's the girl's. Wanda Gardner's, I mean." She cleared her throat, fighting to speak normally. "The first victim."

He was tactful enough to avoid meeting her gaze. "Guess that's all we need, then."

She ran the back of her hand across her eyes; it came away damp.

"Yes," she whispered. "I guess it is."

49

At three Logan steered his Skylark into the parking lot of a downtown L.A. eatery called Philippe's. Being there called back good memories: hot lamb sandwiches, sawdust on the floor, trading stories and smiles with Donna over lunch. They had eaten at Philippe's several times during the early days of their affair, before everything had gone wrong.

Would she think of those lunches with him when she learned where the car had been found? Would the memory make her almost smile? He hoped so.

He parked the car, then crossed the street and hurried south to Union Station, the city's central railroad terminal. Entering, he plunged into a swirl of passengers and their relatives, beggars and crazies, echoing voices, strange smells. Vagrants slept curled up on the marble floor. Babies squalled, their hiccuping cries reverberating off the vaulted ceiling, competing with the garbled squawks of the P.A. system.

It was risky to be in this place. By now his description would have been circulated to the terminal's security personnel. Plainclothes LAPD cops might be eyeing the crowds. But he was gambling that most of the scrutiny would be focused on passengers actually boarding trains.

At the Amtrak office, he perused a brochure of timetables, then purchased one coach ticket on train 580, scheduled to depart for San Diego at 4:45.

"Too bad you didn't get here fifteen minutes sooner," the ticket clerk said, accepting his cash. "The five-seventy-eight just left. You wouldn't have had to wait."

Logan flashed a twitchy, nervous smile, not too obvious, but odd enough to be noticed. It was important that the clerk remember him later. "Looks like it's not my lucky day."

He took the ticket and left the station. His breathing became easier once he was outside. The ticket, torn into strips, disappeared inside a trash can a block away.

Now he needed a car. He walked west along Sunset Boulevard to North Broadway and began searching for a likely vehicle to steal.

In a municipal parking garage on Hill Street he made his selection: a blue Mazda 323, the make and model ubiquitous in this city, easily lost in traffic. The car was unprotected by an alarm system or steering-wheel lock.

He scanned the dark interior of the garage—empty—then cracked the driver's-side window with the butt of his service pistol. Two more hard blows, and the window dissolved in a soft, tinkling rain. He rolled down the window to conceal the crumbs of gummed shatterproof glass still clinging to the frame.

Hot-wiring the engine was no problem. Years of investigating auto thefts had given him a working knowledge of the specialized skills required.

He guided the car out of the garage, drove for a mile, and parked on a deserted side street behind another Mazda 323. Using a pocketknife, he unscrewed both vehicles' plates and switched them. The owner of the second Mazda probably wouldn't notice the change right away, and Logan was less likely to be pulled over now that his plates wouldn't raise a red flag in a DMV check.

In West Hollywood, he purchased scissors and sunglasses at a pharmacy, then parked in an alley. Five minutes later he'd given himself a quick trim, losing thick clumps of hair to the scissors' greedy snips.

With short hair and mirrored shades, he looked sufficiently different from Mark Logan to avoid immediate recognition by any cop in a cruising patrol car.

His precautions wouldn't keep him safe indefinitely, but they would buy him time. And time was what he needed. Time to get to Donna.

No more games. No sly innuendo. He intended to let her see who and what he really was. And he would.

Tonight.

50

The sky hanging in the windows had dimmed to a sheet of black silk, punctured by the rare winking pinpoints of stars. Cars motored past on Corona Beach Boulevard, headlight beams fanning wide in the misty air. Behind the breath-frosted windshields were pale blurred faces, the faces of strangers living other lives, intimate with other sorrows, other varieties of pain.

Donna watched the cars and their occupants sweep by, each anonymous driver or passenger sharing her world momentarily, then moving on. She wondered what heartbreak those people had faced in their time, and whether it was anything like what she was facing now.

"It will stop hurting, you know. Eventually."

The words pulled her out of her melancholy reflections. She smiled at Ed Barnes, seated across the table in the half-empty coffee shop. "Wish I could believe that."

She and Ed had spent the evening together, sharing stories about Mark. Donna was desperate to understand the path he'd taken, desperate to convince herself that there was nothing she could have done to save him, even had she known. And Barnes had been willing to nurse her grief and soothe her fear, kindly, as if neither animosity nor suspicion had ever come between them.

Of course there was another reason he had stayed with her, an unstated reason. As long as Logan remained at large, she was in danger. She needed protection. The Kevlar vest she wore and the two guns she carried, one in her ankle holster, the other near her ribs, were not enough.

"Everything heals in time," Ed said quietly. "Believe me, I know about that. When I lost Marjorie, I thought I'd never recover. And I guess I haven't, fully. I've aged—"

"No," she lied.

He brushed off her politeness. "I look in mirrors. I can see. Losing her made me an old man." He took off his bifocals and polished them with the corner of a napkin. His eyes, sunk deep in shadowed hollows, gleamed bright and hard with hard-bought wisdom. "But it didn't kill me. And this won't kill you either. You'll learn to live with it. You'll adjust."

"Sure. The same way I'd adjust to losing a limb. Or an eye." The bitterness in her voice shamed her, but she couldn't help it. Ed meant well, and she was pleased to have his company, but she would not be jollied out of her grief so soon.

If he was wounded by her tone, he didn't show it. "That's how it does feel," he acknowledged with a thoughtful nod. "Like you've given up part of yourself. And you have." He slipped his glasses back on, caging his eyes in the steel-rimmed frames. "But face it, Donna—you gave him up before this. He wasn't part of your life anymore."

"I know."

"It's not as if the two of you were still together."

"No."

"So why are you taking it this hard?"

"Maybe because . . ."

Because I still love him, she wanted to say. *Even*

though it's insane. Even though I didn't even know it until now.

"Because I feel guilty," she offered instead. "I can't help wondering if the way we broke up precipitated all this."

"That's nonsense."

"Outbreaks of violence among organized nonsocials are typically triggered by stress factors, by traumas in their personal lives. It's what pushes them over the brink—"

"Don't talk like a profiler."

"That's what I am," she returned, more harshly than she'd intended. "Anyway, you're the one who said I'd kicked Mark. Kicked him like a beaten dog."

He stared out the window. Headlights glided like comets across the bifocals' smooth lenses. "That was thoughtless of me," he said softly. "Thoughtless and wrong. I'd heard only his side of the story. I was being loyal."

She heard the regret in his words and gentled her voice. "And now?"

"Now I see . . . the other side. What he was capable of. Living with him couldn't have been easy."

"He never abused me."

"Not physically. But emotionally . . . ?"

Donna smiled. "Now *you're* talking like a shrink." The smile died. "He didn't mean to hurt me. At least I don't think he did." Guilt stabbed her as she thought of her unfaithfulness, her betrayal. "Hell, I'm the one who hurt him."

"So it's all your fault?"

"I don't want to think so." She shook her head. "I don't know."

A sudden shrill piping knifed through the stillness. Barnes plucked his beeper from his pocket and checked the phone number displayed on the liquid-crystal readout. "Watch commander."

She caught her breath. "Do you think they . . . got him?"

Gently he touched her arm. "Let's find out."

There was a pay phone in the back of the coffee shop, near the rest rooms. Barnes made the call to the station. Donna listened tensely to his end of the conversation, but heard only a series of grunted affirmatives and acknowledgments. "Right . . . I see . . . Yeah . . . Okay."

He hung up and turned to her.

"He's still at large. But they think they know where he is. LAPD patrol unit spotted his Skylark. It was ditched in a parking lot in downtown L.A. At that sandwich shop, Philippe's."

Her mouth found a compromise between a wince and a smile. "We used to go there . . . together."

"The restaurant is only a short distance from Union Station," Barnes went on briskly. "Plainclothes cops found an Amtrak ticket agent who remembered him. He booked a coach seat to San Diego. Train left at 4:45, arrived at its destination at 7:35." He checked his watch. "Two hours ago. There's connecting bus service from San Diego station to the Mexican border."

"Has the train crew been contacted?"

"Yeah. They're doing the return run to L.A. right now. The conductor can't remember any passenger matching Mark's description, but that doesn't mean much; the train was crowded."

"Christ, wasn't anybody deployed at Union Station to eyeball departing passengers?"

"LAPD says yes. Plainclothes personnel in all boarding areas. Nobody saw him get on any train. Of course he might have altered his appearance after purchasing the ticket. He bought it over an hour in advance; he would have had time to buy new clothes or some other disguise."

"Why didn't he just drive to the border?"

"After we put out the APB? There's a lot of road between here and Tijuana."

"In a stolen car he could have made it."

Barnes heaved a gloomy sigh. "Looks like he made it anyway."

"If . . ."

"If what?"

Donna chewed a knuckle, thinking hard. "If he was ever on that train."

"What does that mean?"

"This whole thing seems a little too clumsy, too obvious. It could be a ruse. Suppose he bought the ticket just to throw us off his trail."

Barnes studied the idea. "In that case, where would he go?"

"Back here, maybe. Back to Corona Beach." She swallowed. "Looking for me."

"Unlikely. He has nothing to gain by going after you now."

"It's not a question of gain. This type of killer is motivated by obsession. He doesn't give up."

She was thinking of Franklin Rood, who had not given up till he was dead. Horrible to think of Mark as equally twisted; but he was. He was.

"You may be right," Barnes said slowly.

"Of course I am, and you know it. You haven't been sticking by me all night just to hear me cry in my beer. You're my unofficial bodyguard—and I'm grateful for it, Ed."

He ran a hand through the sparse strands of his hair. "It's nothing," he mumbled. "But since you bring up the issue of your, uh, personal security . . . have you considered staying in a hotel tonight?"

"Sounds like a highly reasonable precaution. But first I need to pick up some things from home."

"Okay, tell you what. I'll go in with you to check

out the place, make sure you've got no uninvited guests."

Uninvited guests. Nice phrase. She remembered last night, the scent of honeysuckle in the dark. A shiver tickled the base of her spine like a cold finger.

"Good idea," she said, straining for a casual note. "I hate it when company drops by unexpectedly."

Barnes paid the tab and led her outside into the cool summer night. The mist blowing in from the beach had thickened and spread; coils of cottony fog curled around lampposts and smeared traffic signals to pastel streaks.

Her Celica was a blurred shape at the curb, Ed's unmarked Caprice directly behind it. Donna strapped herself into the driver's seat and started the engine. She pulled away, cutting a wake through a rippling sea of mist, and Barnes followed, his headlights reassuring in her rearview mirror, like bright watchful eyes.

Across the street from the coffee shop, a gray Ford Tempo eased away from the curb, executed an illegal U-turn, and followed the other two cars. Screened by mist, headlights dark, it was invisible behind them.

The glow of passing street lamps washed over the man at the wheel, his hands gripping the hard contoured plastic, his mouth set in a grim, bloodless line.

So Barnes was going with her. Back to her place, probably. Her protector, looking out for her.

Well, that was fine.

Barnes would have to leave eventually. Sooner or later Donna would be alone.

He only had to be patient.

Joe Kurtz licked dry lips and drove on through a deep, winding tunnel of fog.

51

Donna's condo was dark when they entered. Barnes went first, gun drawn, flicking on lights as he stepped into each room. Donna followed, the Beretta held steady in both hands.

The apartment was empty. There was no sign of a break-in.

Donna opened the patio door. She and Barnes scanned the alley. Nothing.

"Looks okay," Barnes said as they went back inside. He slipped his gun into his armpit holster.

Donna leaned against a wall, shoulders slumping. "Thanks a lot, Ed. For everything. I can take it from here."

"Why don't I tail you to the motel and make sure you get there in one piece?"

"That's hardly necessary."

"He could be watching from the street. Could follow you when you leave."

"You're being paranoid."

"Humor me. I don't mind a little night driving. I do it all the time—up and down the coast highway for hours."

"Like you did last night."

"Yes."

"And I didn't believe you. Or at least I wasn't sure. I'm sorry for that."

"It's your job to be suspicious."

"There was a much more obvious suspect. One I didn't want to see."

"None of us wanted to see it, Donna. Now pack your things. I'll wait in the living room."

She returned to the bedroom. Ragged holes in the plaster walls, where bullets had been dug out, stared sightlessly at her like the empty eye sockets of a skull. The narrow depression made by the police baton was still visible in her pillow, though the baton itself had been removed as evidence.

Nearly died in here last night, she thought, and shuddered.

No use dwelling on that. Briskly she dragged a small suitcase out of the closet, then filled it with essentials. She was packing a folded blouse when the phone on her nightstand chirped at her.

She stared at it for a long moment. A weird premonition of the caller's identity held her frozen, breathless.

A second chirp. A third.

Her fingers closed over the handset. She lifted the mouthpiece to her lips.

"Wildman."

"Hello, Donna."

A cold fist squeezed her heart.

"Mark . . . ?"

Movement in the bedroom doorway. Barnes stepped in and stood silently, listening.

"By now, they're looking for me in Tijuana, I guess," Mark said. Traffic hummed in the background. A pay phone, outdoors somewhere. Not a long-distance call; she was pretty sure of that. "It's a diversion. I'll bet you figured that out, didn't you?"

"Mark, you have to give yourself up."

"I didn't do it, Donna."

She closed her eyes. "Don't tell me that."

"I'm innocent."

"We searched your apartment. We found Wanda's notebook."

"Did you?"

"I suppose you'll say you have no idea how it got there." Easy to trap him in that lie; ninhydrin had already lifted his prints from most of the spiral-bound pages.

"I know exactly how it got there," he said calmly. "I took it from Wanda's hotel room. Hid it in the vest pocket of my jacket."

"But you're not guilty of anything." Sarcasm froze her voice.

"Of concealing evidence—yes. Not murder."

She sat on the bed, to rest her shaking knees. "Why would you conceal it, if you had nothing to hide?"

"I looked through the notebook at the hotel. Read some of the poems. It was obvious there was nothing of evidential value in what she'd written. Nothing that would help us identify her or track down her next of kin."

"That still doesn't explain—"

"I'd already read the letter from her mother. I asked myself if I wanted to see Wanda's poems locked in the property room with the rest of the evidence, for no good reason, only to follow procedure—or sent home to her mother, where they belonged. The answer wasn't hard."

"We didn't even know who her mother was."

"There were clues in the letter. I knew you'd find a way to locate her. And you did."

"So you were planning to send Mrs. Gardner the notebook? Is that it?"

"That's it."

"Come on, Mark."

"After Sharon died, I found a journal she kept. Never knew about it before that. I read the entries, night after night. It helped . . . cut the pain. At least a little bit. It allowed me to keep her alive—and accept her death. I thought this might help the girl's mother in the same way."

Donna had to harden herself against whatever emotional ploy he was using. "But you never sent the notebook, did you?"

"I was typing the cover letter in the squad room today when you came in. You told me about finding the murder site. After that, there was no time. I had to hurry."

"Hurry to that pimp's apartment. So you could kill them all."

"I didn't."

"Goddamn it, Mark"—she tightened her grip on the phone—"you were *seen* leaving the building."

For a heartbeat of time she heard only the buzz and rattle of background traffic. She was afraid she'd lost him, afraid he would hang up.

Then he said softly, "I was there. But I didn't kill anyone. When I showed up, they were already dead. Somebody else did the job and left, probably only a few minutes before I arrived."

She wondered how suggestible he thought she was, how stupidly gullible. "So what was your purpose in going there at all?"

"When you told me about the polyester fiber, I made the connection with the Rag Doll Man. I knew Billie could identify the killer. And I knew the killer, whoever he is, would realize it too. I had to get there first." A shaky breath, drawn through pursed lips. "But I was too late."

"You were trying to protect her, you mean?"

"Yes. And hoping she would show me who the killer was. That's why I took the photo from the administrative office. Brody's secretary must have told you about that."

She glanced at Barnes, still standing just inside the

doorway, interpreting the conversation from her half of the dialogue only. He looked tense and pale.

"Lynn reported it, yes," Donna said. "Told us that you removed a picture from the wall."

"The team photo from the softball game. It's as good as a lineup or a photo six-pack. You were there that day; you remember the team we fielded. Half the men in the department were on it, including everyone present at Third and Bay on the night Wanda's body was found. Me, Barnes, Kurtz—all your suspects or potential suspects standing in a row. If Billie had looked at that picture, she could have fingered the Rag Doll Man."

"Why didn't you explain all this to me and Mueller in the station? We could have called Hollywood Division—"

"Because I wasn't sure. All you'd found was some polyester stuffing. It was a stretch to connect it with the assault in Hollywood. Anyway, explaining would have taken too long. I got there too late as it was."

Anguish or desperation spiked his voice. If he was lying, it was a hell of a performance.

But of course he was lying. Crazy to think otherwise.

She had blinded herself to his guilt throughout the investigation. She would not shut her eyes to it again.

"You can't expect me to believe any of this," she said coldly.

"Maybe I can't. But it's true. Billie and the others were dead when I got there. I knew I couldn't be found at the homicide scene. LAPD would never accept my story, not when I was already a suspect in the case. So I ran. When those patrol cops saw me, I knew I had to hide out, ditch the car, throw off pursuit. And contact you."

"Why me?"

"You're the only one I can trust."

"Trusting me didn't work out so well the last time you tried it. Why would you do it now?"

"Because I have no choice. And because I don't think you'll let me down."

"And in return, I'm supposed to trust you?"

"Yes."

"And do what?"

"Meet me in Corona Beach. Let me explain the whole thing in detail. Hear me out. Then if you believe me, help me nail the real killer. If you don't . . . I'll surrender myself to the CBPD."

"How do I know I'm not walking into a trap?"

"Because you know I'm not a murderer."

"I used to know that. I don't, anymore."

"I think you still do. And if you don't . . . if you really don't . . ."

"Yes?"

"At eleven I'll be on the beach, waiting under the pier. Either meet me yourself . . . or call Mueller and have him send an army of cops to arrest me. One way or the other, I'll be there—and I'll learn your answer."

Click, and a dial tone buzzed in her ear.

Slowly she cradled the phone and turned to Barnes. She was trembling.

"He's not in Tijuana," she whispered. "He's in Corona Beach. And he wants me to meet him there."

"He set up a rendezvous point?"

"Under the pier. At eleven." She checked the bedside clock. "Forty minutes from now."

Barnes moved away from the door, toward the nightstand. "I'll call the watch commander. We can have the area surrounded—"

"No." She stopped him as he was reaching for the phone.

"Why not?" Barnes narrowed his eyes. "I know he

was trying to convince you he's innocent, but you don't seriously think that's possible. Do you?"

She hesitated, her certainty wavering slightly, then steeled herself against the tug of emotion. "No."

"Then . . . ?"

"If he's surrounded, cornered—he may fight. Or just kill himself, rather than be taken. I don't want that. I want to talk him into surrendering."

"If you go there, you'll end up being killed yourself."

"Possibly."

"He's setting you up. Isn't that fairly obvious?"

"It's too obvious. If he was trying to lure me into an ambush, he wouldn't be this clumsy about it."

"You're assuming he's rational. He isn't."

"He sounded rational enough on the phone."

Barnes suppressed a swear. "You're determined to do this?"

She hadn't been sure until that moment. "Yes."

"Then I'll go with you."

"There's no need to risk—"

"Shut up. Two of us have a better chance than one. To meet him alone is suicide. Besides . . . he was my friend once. I owe him something."

She thought about arguing, saw that there was no point. Rising from bed, she clasped his hand. A warm, leathery hand, the hand of a father.

"Thanks, Ed."

They left her condo and went rapidly down the hall, speaking in the low voices of conspirators.

"We'll both take my Toyota," she said. "If he sees your unmarked car, he may run."

"In this fog he wouldn't see it anyway."

"We can't count on that."

She opened the door at the end of the hallway and entered the garage, Barnes close behind.

"When he sees me with you," Barnes said, "he may bolt. He wanted you to meet him alone."

"You'll have to reassure him about that." The garage was dimly lit and empty. Their shoes clacked briskly on the concrete floor. "Call his name, tell him you're there as his friend."

Barnes grunted. "Hope he believes me. We'll be awfully damned exposed on that beach."

She reached her Celica, parked in its assigned space near the security gate, and bent to unlock the driver's-side door. "Maybe we should stop at the station and get you a vest." The key turned, and the door lock released. She reached for the handle. "Problem is, I don't know how we'd explain—"

Brightness bloomed in her field of vision like a burst of lightning and with it came a tingling rush of electricity, surging through her body in a numbing wave.

An instant later, pain walloped her, a delayed report of pain from the back of her skull.

Donna swayed, one word blinking in her mind like an idiot light.

Hurts. Hurts.

She knew there was more to think about than that, more to say, but nothing would come. The world was pain and dizziness, a murmur of voices growing louder, a buzzing clamor in her ears.

Hurts . . .

Her knees buckled, the car door sliding past her as she slumped down, and cold concrete kissed her mouth like death.

52

Her name was Wanda Gardner and she had a mom in Joliet, Illinois, a good mom but crazy sometimes, too crazy to live with, so she'd run away. But the craziness of L.A. had proved worse than anything she'd faced at home, and now she was handcuffed in the backseat of a stranger's car, being driven who-knew-where, for a purpose she was afraid to think about.

If she got out of this, she would go home, she swore she would; but it sure didn't look like she was going to get out.

It looked like she was going to die....

No.

That wasn't right. Wasn't her.

I'm Donna, she told herself, the thought startling like a slap. *Wanda is dead. I'm not dead.*

Am I?

Blinking. Blurred patterns flickering in and out of focus. A distant awareness of pain.

She gritted her teeth, opened her eyes, and willed herself to full alertness.

Reality wavered, then locked in. She held it steady, fixing her concentration on one significant detail at a time.

Engine hum. A car engine. She was in a car.

Hiss of tires on a smooth road surface. A freeway.

She lay on her side in a cramped, narrow space.

The trunk? No; her cheek pressed against cloth upholstery.

The backseat of her Toyota. That was where she was. Bent in a fetal pose, hands behind her.

Her wrists twisted. The tender skin met steel.

Handcuffs.

She was cuffed like Wanda. Taking a ride like Wanda. A long silent ride through a corridor of darkness, death waiting at the end.

A low moan warbled out of her throat.

From the driver's seat, a grunt of acknowledgment. "You awake?"

She lifted her head and saw his eyes in the rearview mirror, gazing at her in cold appraisal. The steel rims of his bifocals flashed in the dashboard's glow.

"Yes, Ed," she breathed. "Wide awake . . . now."

Barnes turned the wheel. The Celica eased into the right-hand lane, cutting speed.

"I hadn't planned to do this tonight," he said in a quiet conversational tone. "Wouldn't have done it at all, if Logan was in custody."

"Do what, exactly?"

"Kill you both. Close the case. Tie up all the loose ends."

Rattle and bump as the car shot down an exit ramp.

Donna tried to raise herself to a sitting position, found she couldn't. He'd strapped her down with two seat belts. Her manacled hands had no way to reach the buckles.

"I'll shoot the two of you under the pier," he went on with a sociopath's chilling casualness. "Someone will find your bodies sooner or later. I'll be called in to figure it out. My conclusion will be simple enough: murder-suicide. Logan lured you to the beach, shot you, then turned the gun on himself."

She became aware of a pulsing ache at the back of

her head. He must have struck her hard, probably with the butt of his gun. At least she could remember her last moments before blacking out: walking to the car, unlocking the door, bending to open it. No amnesia meant no concussion. That was something anyway.

"Hard to make murder look like suicide," she said, holding her mind in sharp focus despite the pain. "You know that. It's a scam that almost never works."

"But how many scam artists are personally running the investigation? I can finesse any details that don't quite add up."

"Like you finessed the flower in Wanda's hair?"

"That was sloppy of me. I should have checked the body more carefully before I dumped it. I only noticed the flower when Logan and I were examining her at Third and Bay."

She squirmed, moving her shoulders, trying to judge if she was still wearing her Kevlar vest and armpit holster. She was, but the holster felt empty.

"And when I saw it in the photo," she said, "you decided to kill me."

"There was no alternative." A street sign was briefly visible in the window as it blurred past: Corona Beach Boulevard. They were in town, then. Not far from the pier. "You were getting too close. I had to put you out of the way, then convince Tim that the object in the photo was something insignificant. Would have been easy enough to talk him into it; he's just a kid, looks up to me."

She pressed her left leg into the seat cushion and felt her ankle holster flatten against her calf. He'd removed that gun too. Damn.

"Didn't you know that the soil analysis would lead the investigation to the Phaethon site anyway?" she asked.

"But it wouldn't have. You see, I'd thought it through in detail. I had to send out a soil sample for analysis. That's standard procedure; failure to follow it would have raised unnecessary suspicion. But I always expected to interpret the lab results myself. I could have claimed that the particulates found in the soil were consistent with a landfill or a cemetery or the dark side of the moon. Anything but the truth. It's a small department; I'm the only biochemist. No one would have questioned my expertise."

"But then you became a suspect in the case."

"That was the one thing I hadn't counted on. I never anticipated that Mueller would call you in. If not for you, I wouldn't have come under suspicion. My reputation and seniority would have protected me."

He spun the wheel again, and the car veered west, onto Pier Avenue. Only a couple of blocks from their destination.

She clamped down tight on the fear in her chest. "Why did you kill Billie?"

"Had no choice about that. Mueller called me at Parker Center and told me you'd found the murder site. Said he was bringing in SID to conduct the search. I knew it would be only an hour or so till the rag doll was found. Then Logan would remember the Rag Doll Man."

"I'm surprised you didn't go after Mark directly, instead of Billie."

"Wouldn't have done any good. The assault on Billie was reported; it's in LAPD files. Any MO run that specified the mutilation of a rag doll would cough up the Hollywood incident instantly. Billie was certain to be contacted, probably by the end of the day."

"So you killed her, along with the other two."

He nodded. "Logan must have shown up immediately after I left. I'd heard the APB go out on him while I was driving into Hollywood, and I knew that if he couldn't account for his whereabouts, he would become the only logical suspect."

"What made you start doing it in the first place, Ed? Marge's suicide? Was that it?"

Barnes guided the Toyota into the empty parking lot adjacent to Pier Beach and shut off the engines. "Sorry, Donna. No more talk. We've got business to attend to."

He eased out of the car, and a moment later the front seat swung forward. Donna lay rigid, staring at him as he loomed in the doorway, a hunched silhouette, backlit by white fog, an image from a nightmare.

Then the fog behind him was blotted out as he reached inside, filling the doorway, his gloved hands fumbling with the seat belt strapped around her waist.

Breathing was difficult with him so close. A scream of blind panic welled in her throat; her jaws locked; with effort she swallowed it down.

Now he was unbuckling the other belt, the one that had secured her legs. This might be her single opportunity to fight. With her legs free, she could kick. A solid blow to the throat could crush his larynx, block his windpipe, shut off his oxygen.

She waited, her body tensed to strike.

The seat belt came loose, and he drew back slightly, preparing to pull her from the car.

Now.

She lashed out. A driving kick, scorpion-quick, to the side of the face—her jerked his head away, swearing. She kicked again, caught him sharply in the shoulder, and then he had hold of both legs and was hauling her out of the car, repeating one word with obsessive insistence.

"Bitch. Bitch. *Bitch*."

She groped for the doorframe, fighting pointlessly to hang on to the car. No use. Her fingers slid over the smooth steel, and then she dropped down hard onto the asphalt on her side, groaning.

Barnes dragged her a yard clear of the Toyota, then slammed the door.

"Get up," he ordered.

She raised her head to stare up at him. Hectic craziness inflamed his face like fever. She knew how Wanda must have seen him in her last moments, a frenzied predator, quivering with blood lust, hungry for a kill.

"No," she said simply.

"I'll shoot you right here."

"Go ahead."

She knew he wouldn't. He needed her alive, as bait for Mark.

Reluctantly he reached the same conclusion. He circled around her, avoiding her legs. She rolled away from him, but not fast enough, and suddenly he was crouching at her shoulder, his right hand fisted in her hair.

He yanked her head back. She bit her lip to suppress a shout of pain.

"That other little whore kicked me too," Barnes whispered, his mouth close to her ear. He tightened his grip on her hair and tugged harder, punching needles of pain through her scalp. "Kicked me in the gut. I was sore for hours. Logan saw me wince, but I told him I had indigestion. He believed me. I'm a good liar, aren't I, Donna?"

He gave her hair another jerk. She hissed pain through clenched teeth.

"Yeah, good liar," he said with a snarl of laughter. "You never doubted the fatherly concern I showed tonight, did you? I was just trying to stay close to you. Figured Logan would contact you eventually, and I wanted to know about it when he did."

He wrenched his hand sideways, twisting the clump of hair in his fist into an agonizing knot.

"Now are you going to get up, or do I have to start ripping it out by the roots?"

"I'll stand," she gasped.

He released her hair and backed away. Slowly she struggled to her knees, then rose upright.

She stood facing him in a haze of mist bleached pure white by the blurry oval of the moon. Around them stretched empty acres of asphalt, like the floor of some immense spotlighted arena.

Barnes reached into his jacket and brought out a polished blue Iver Johnson, the barrel unnaturally extended by a homemade silencer. A .22—the gun that had killed Billie, her pimp, and his bodyguard in Hollywood, and had nearly killed her last night.

"Turn around."

She didn't move.

"Do it, Donna." He pointed the gun at her hips. "Or I'll put a bullet in the base of your spine and drag you to the fucking pier. Nothing will be gained that way except some extra effort for me and a great deal of unnecessary pain for you."

She studied his eyes. He was serious.

Wordlessly she turned her back to him.

He stepped up behind her. The silencer nuzzled the nape of her neck, an inch above her jacket collar and the Kevlar vest.

"Now walk."

"Did you lead Wanda at gunpoint when you took her into the field?"

"I dragged her. Like a sack of garbage."

"Is that what she was to you? Is that why you killed her on the grounds of the Phaethon—"

"*Walk.*"

She obeyed. The gun planted chilly kisses on her neck with every step.

He marched her out of the parking lot through clots of mist like dancing ghosts. Three concrete stairs descended to the beach. Shells crackled like twigs under their feet. There was no other sound but the sibilance of the surf and, somewhere far away, the brief caterwauling of a car radio, booming through the night and fading out.

Ahead lay the gray hulk of the pier, dark and empty, closed for the night. Rising over the flat expanse of sand, extending backward into the limitless white fog, it looked like the carcass of some great beached whale, flesh eaten away, the black posts of its ribs exposed.

Donna paused just outside the pilings, hesitant to pass between them into the cavelike darkness they enclosed. Barnes shoved her roughly forward. She stumbled, nearly losing her balance, but recovered, and then she was underneath the pier, inhaling the smells of fish and seaweed and wet, aged wood.

The odors of organic decay only reinforced her impression of a rotting carcass, some great mound of death vomited up by the sea. She shivered, not with cold.

Barnes stopped her a few yards within. A gloved hand clapped over her mouth. The gun found the hollow where her neck met the base of her skull, and nosed in deeply like a snuffling dog.

"Quiet now," he whispered. "I'll do the talking." Then, louder: "Mark. It's Ed. I'm here with Donna. She invited me along. Come on out and show yourself. I know you're here."

The low tide sloshed lazily against the more distant pilings.

"Mark? Don't you want to see us, talk to us? We're waiting for you. We want to help. We—"

Donna jerked her head sideways, pulling free of his grasp, and screamed. *"Don't listen, he killed Wanda, he—"*

Barnes silenced her. The pressure of his hand on her mouth forced her head back, all the way back; she stared up at slivers of moonlight filtering like icicles through cracks in the planks of the pier. Hot on her cheek was Barnes's breath, great bursts of air, hoarse and ragged. She knew he was wrestling with the impulse to pull the trigger and kill her now, right *now*.

After a long moment he seemed to master himself, temporarily, at least. "Fuck you, Donna," he whispered. "I'll get him anyway."

He raised his voice to a shout.

"She's right, Mark. I killed two bitches already. And I'll kill Donna too, and make it bad for her, as bad as it was for the others—unless you show yourself. You don't want to just sit there and watch her die, do you? *Do you?"*

An endless pause, the pier creaking gently in the surf's caress.

Out of the meshwork of shadows ten feet away stepped the figure of a man. He moved into a trickle of moonlight and stood facing them, a blue-black Beretta in his hand.

"Hello, Ed," Logan said.

Barnes clucked his tongue, a wet, hungry sound. "I knew you wouldn't stay hidden. Not when you understood the situation."

"Let me talk to Donna."

"Drop the gun."

"First let us talk."

"I said, *drop the gun."*

Logan hesitated, then slowly spread his fingers and let the Beretta fall softly to the sand.

Barnes removed his hand from Donna's mouth.

"Mark ..." Her voice was a plaintive whisper. "You shouldn't have come out. Shouldn't have given up the gun. It's ... it's suicide."

"I had no choice. He's holding all the cards."

"Not all of them," Barnes said. "Only the Queen of Hearts."

Logan smiled, looking at Donna, locking on her gaze. "That one is enough."

53

Joe Kurtz, flat on his belly, snaking through the sand.

Not far ahead, low voices barely audible over the slaps of gentle waves on the pilings. Voices he recognized.

Donna ... Barnes ... Logan.

Logan.

What in the name of Christ is going on?

Kurtz had never wanted to be here, on his stomach amid the bottle tops and crushed oyster shells. He had only wanted to talk with Donna, to explain why he'd asked Lynn to lie, and to plead that she not report his deception to Mueller. Falsifying an alibi would get him bounced off the force if the chief found out.

All evening he'd been watching her—first at the coffee shop, then outside her condominium building in West L.A. Waiting patiently for Barnes to leave, so he could speak to Donna alone and maybe save his job.

At ten-thirty her Toyota had pulled out of the garage, a smear of headlights in a gauze of mist. He'd followed, expecting her to go to the Corona Beach police station or to a motel or a friend's home. Instead the car had ended up in the deserted parking lot next to the pier. By the time he crept close enough to even see the car in the fog, Donna and Barnes were already down on the beach.

He had no idea what he'd gotten into. Some kind of secret rendezvous with Logan, apparently.

Whatever it was, it wasn't good. And it could get dangerous in a hurry.

Leaning on an elbow in the sand, Kurtz unzipped the leather pouch at his waist and withdrew a six-shot revolver, his off-duty weapon, a sleek, nickel-plated K-frame Smith .38 Model 10. Like most cops, he never went anywhere unarmed.

Before this was over, he might have to kill Logan.

He touched his throbbing cheek, remembered the humiliation in the locker room.

He could do it if he had to. Yes. He could put a bullet in Mark Logan's head.

Gun in hand, he crawled slowly forward, toward the voices in the dark.

Donna's heart was pounding, and not from fear alone. She had discovered something tonight—that she and Mark had only misplaced their love, not lost it. Each of them was willing to die for the other.

It was a sweet revelation, but a hard lesson to learn now, when they faced the final seconds of their lives.

"Why did you do it, Ed?" Mark asked, and Donna was mildly amazed to hear that his voice was clean of anger, empty of hate, conveying only sorrow and an honest desire to understand.

"Because I wanted to," Barnes answered. "It was my own choice. I've never bought into any of that criminal-as-victim routine."

"I'm not saying you couldn't help it. But something must have set you off."

Behind her, Barnes breathed in, out—a long, slow breath deep with thought.

"Set me off," he said finally. "Like a bomb, you mean? Well, if that's what I am, then I started ticking a long time ago—back when I was riding patrol. I pounded sense into a few bitches in those days. Liked it too. Liked it so much the brass put me in the crime lab, where I wouldn't face any further temptation. Their strategy was successful, I guess. For twenty-five years I was able to hold myself in check."

"You went all that time without acting on your impulses?" Donna asked. It seemed impossible to suppress an urge so intense for so long.

"I had ... other outlets."

"Such as?"

She felt Barnes stiffen. "You don't need to know that." His voice roughened and turned cold. "You don't need to know any of this. I'm the one asking the questions now. And I've got one for you, Mark, old buddy. Which of you do I shoot first?"

"Ed, please," Donna whispered. "Please don't do this. Please think—"

His hand on her mouth again, sealing her lips.

"I'm waiting, Mark. Give me your answer."

"You already know it," Mark said softly. "Me. Kill me first."

Barnes tightened his grip, choking off Donna's scream of protest.

"Very noble," Barnes said. "And exactly what I expected." The gun snaked past her head, the silencer-extended barrel gleaming like a water moccasin in the chancy light. "Watch him die, Donna. But don't pity him too much. You'll be next."

She struggled fiercely in his grasp, twisting her manacled arms, straining to break free.

Barnes steadied his aim.

Mark stood defenseless, unmoving.

A single gunshot, echoing like a cannonade of thunder in the dark.

Donna expected to see Mark go down in a bloody tangle, but instead it was Barnes who rocked under a stunning impact, reeling sideways, releasing his hold on her. She had time to realize that he'd been shot somehow, how and by whom she couldn't guess, and then instinct took over and she twisted to her knees and snap-rolled clear of him as a second gunshot exploded from the shadows at her back.

Barnes flung himself behind a post and returned fire, the silenced .22 popping like a string of firecrackers, an insanely cheerful sound.

Kurtz had been trying for a fatal shot, but Donna's squirming had jostled Barnes at the last second, shifting his position, and the bullet must have caught him only in the left arm or shoulder. Now Barnes was firing back, and Kurtz, prostrate in a hollow in the sand, was caught in a gun battle, the first of his career.

He saw Logan retrieve his gun and take cover behind a row of pilings. Shots rang out from that location, pinning Barnes down.

Kurtz had grasped what was going on as he crept closer to the three figures and picked up snatches of their conversation. Barnes, not Logan, was the real killer. And Barnes would have to die if Donna and Logan were to survive.

He had never shot a man before, and perhaps it had been the shaking of his hand as he took aim, even more than Donna's struggling, that had misdirected the shot by a few critical inches.

A geyser of sand flew up in his face. Barnes's latest shot had struck only a yard short of its target.

The shallow declivity offered no real protection. He had to retreat, find better cover.

He squeezed off another round, then dug his palms into the sand and shoved himself backward, toward what he hoped was safety, and suddenly a bolt of red pain streaked through his shoulder, his chest, his ribs, pain that buzzed like a thousand alarm clocks shocking him out of sleep.

Jesus, I'm hit.

Kurtz tried to crawl backward another yard, but the effort defeated him, every contraction of his muscles a twist of the knife.

Exhausted, crippled by agony, he lay down his head, seeking only rest.

He'd seen gunshot victims. Knew what a bullet could do. A tumbling metal-jacketed round could drill a wound channel through multiple internal organs, splinter ribs and vertebrae, puncture and deflate lungs, sever arteries and veins, and drown the viscera in a bath of blood.

Images came to him. Images of bodies bundled into plastic sheets and wheeled away on gurneys. He would be riding one of those carts soon, riding it to a refrigerated cabinet in the morgue.

He closed his eyes and thought of Lynn. Lynn, who loved him enough to lie for him.

"Sweet girl," he muttered, "sweet," as his thoughts tunneled down into the dark.

54

Logan waited in the sudden stillness.

He had heard a shot from Barnes, an answering groan from the shadows. After that, nothing.

Deafened by gunfire, he had no idea if Barnes was still in his position or if he'd fled.

A slow minute inched past.

Still nothing.

The ringing in his ears subsided. He scanned the patchy darkness under the pier, the whorls of drifted sand, the colonnades of pilings that stood like the decaying pillars of some abandoned temple.

Barnes was gone.

Cautiously he emerged from his hiding place. "Donna?" he whispered. His voice was unexpectedly hoarse, as though he'd been shouting.

"Over here."

He moved toward her, his gaze ticking restlessly, alert for any flicker of motion. She lay sprawled on her side, her dark hair speckled with clinging crumbs of sand.

"You all right?" he breathed, crouching beside her.

"I'm okay. Can you unlock these damn cuffs?"

"Hold on."

All handcuff keys are interchangeable. Logan found the one he carried and inserted it into each keyhole in turn. Two clicks, and the handcuffs were open, easily lifted free.

Donna rubbed her sore wrists. "Whoever was firing from behind me was hit. I heard him go down."

Logan took her hand and helped her up. "Come on."

They passed between rows of pilings and reached the prone figure of a man. Donna took out her pocket flashlight and beamed it on his face, in profile against the blood-darkened sand.

"Joe," she whispered.

Logan learned everything he needed to know from the way she spoke his name. He held her flash as, kneeling, she felt his carotid artery.

"There's a pulse."

Logan pulled out his portable radio and handed it to her. "I'm still a fugitive. You call it in. We use the ten code. Ten-ninety-nine will get their attention."

She pressed the transmit button. "Ten-ninety-nine. Repeat, 10–99. Officer down. Backup units and R.A. requested. Location is under the Corona Beach Pier. That's *under* the pier."

The RTO's voice crackled over the speaker. "What unit is reporting the 10–99? Identify."

"This is Detective Donna Wildman, LAPD, on special assignment with Corona Beach P.D. Send a rescue ambulance *now*."

"Detective, I'd better patch you through on a Tac frequency to the watch commander—"

Logan held up his hand. "Listen."

Donna shut off the radio.

From the far recesses of the pier, a soft splashing.

"Barnes," she breathed. "He's gone into the water."

"Why?"

"Maybe to swim to another point on the shore, try to escape that way."

"Think he can make it?"

"He might."

"I'd better go after him, then."

"Both of us will."

"You're not armed."

She picked up Kurtz's revolver, then dug extra shells out of his pouch and snapped them into the cylinder in the pale circle of her flashlight's beam. "I am now."

Together they advanced toward the smell of brine and the lapping of the sea's wet tongue on sand and wood. The pilings became glossy with seaweed, crusted with barnacles. The stink of dead fish poisoned the air.

"Switch off your flashlight," Logan said. The beam gave away their position, made them easy targets.

Ahead, the splashing had stopped. Perhaps Barnes sensed their approach.

Wet sand sucked greedily at their feet. A ripple of current glided over their shoes, then retreated with a hiss and bubble. A second wave did not retreat. They had passed the low-tide mark.

Water rose to their ankles, then their calves, their knees. It swirled around them, thick as jelly, littered with slimy ribbons of kelp. Logan's pants were plastered to his skin; his socks, soaked through, felt heavy as lead.

"He's close," Donna whispered.

"You see him?"

She shook her head. "*Feel* him."

Logan frowned.

He felt Barnes too.

Very close . . . and moving in for the kill.

55

Barnes had never planned to swim any distance. The bullet in his shoulder had left him no strength for that. He only wanted to finish what he'd started.

His clumsy splashing had drawn their attention, as he'd hoped. Now Logan and Donna were wading deeper into the surf, searching for him. But he would not be found.

The long silencer from his .22, detached, made a perfect breathing tube. He drifted along, submerged in four feet of water, one end of the steel cylinder in his mouth, the other extending inches above the surface.

Slowly he maneuvered around his pursuers, unseen and unsuspected. They would not realize he was behind them until too late.

Waist-high in the water, the chill numbing her legs, Donna turned in tight circles, scanning the tenebrous dark. Barnes was here—not far away—she was sure of it.

Beside her, Mark stood motionless, listening.

She wondered how he could hear any noise at all if his heart was pumping as fast and loud as her own. . . .

There.

A slow ripple of movement ten feet away, like a current of breath fogging the surface of a mirror.

She narrowed her eyes. Saw a glimmer of steely light that cut a thin wake of foam.

A gun barrel? The silencer?

"*Mark*," she breathed.

An eruption out of the water.

Barnes breaking the surface like a missile, exploding into the open, a dripping, seaweed-festooned mass, the .22 in his gloved hand, a roar of triumph bellowing from his mouth—

Mark was still turning, turning, as if in slow motion.

Donna raised the revolver, and suddenly she was not standing in the frigid surf under a deserted fishing pier; she was on the shooting range, feet planted in the Weaver stance, earmuffs bracketing her head, a silhouette target illuminated at a distance of three yards, an easy shot, and as she squeezed the trigger she was not thinking of Franklin Rood or even of Wayne Allen Stanton; she was thinking of Ed Barnes.

For Wanda, she thought.

The gun bucked in her hand.

In the same instant, a whip-crack of sound, thud of impact in her chest, and she staggered backward, gasping.

Something hard slammed into her spine—one of the pilings—and drove the air out of her lungs. She went limp, as limp as one of Ed's rag dolls, her legs and arms unresponsive to mental commands, and then she was sinking down, drawn under the surface by the weight of the Kevlar vest beneath her jacket, straining for a last breath and failing to get it as black water closed over her head.

56

Logan turned just in time to see Donna and Barnes fire simultaneously at each other.

Donna—*oh, Jesus!*—she was hit in the chest.

Barnes's howling battle cry leaped up an octave into a ululant scream. It took Logan a split second to perceive that Donna's shot had hit home also, scoring a direct hit on Barnes's .22, blasting the gun out of his hand.

Logan fired twice, but Barnes had already submerged, and there was no time to hunt him down, not with Donna gravely wounded, surely dying, maybe already dead.

His gaze swept the dark. He didn't see her.

Must have gone under. Unconscious, her lungs already filling with water.

Logan sucked in a desperate breath and dived into the surf.

Barnes was in agony. Every bone in his right hand was broken. Tissuey strands of blood leaked from beneath his glove.

But he could still shoot left-handed. If he could find the pistol.

It had cartwheeled into the water with a splash. He had only a general idea of where it had gone.

Like some outsized bottom-feeding fish, he dragged himself along the sand, groping among layers of crustacean shells and fragments of glass and crushed beer cans. The cans reminded him of the stimulation he'd required to get up his nerve the night he killed Wanda, to go through with it that time, all the way through.

He had no regrets. Even now—no regrets.

The tidal current teased the sparse strands of his hair across his face. He brushed them away, lifted his head to steal a quick breath, then went on searching.

He wasn't sure if he'd killed Donna. The Kevlar vest might have saved her. He'd meant to try for a head shot, but he hadn't expected her to be looking right at him when he surfaced. Losing the element of surprise had cost him the fraction of a second he'd needed to place the bullet where it had to go.

Well, he would have another chance. He would take her out, her and Logan, if only he could find the gun. The goddamn gun . . .

Yes.

His hand closed over satin chrome, walnut grips, the sleek, familiar shape of death.

Donna rolled on the silty bottom, drowning in four feet of water. Stunned, winded, she could not find the strength to propel herself to the surface.

Hope I got him for you, Wanda, she thought as her consciousness wavered on the brink of a blackout. *Hope I made him pay.*

She was closing her eyes when gentle hands took hold of her and lifted her up.

The ceiling of water shattered, and she tasted air. Her lungs worked fitfully, pulling in shallow gulps of oxygen, reviving her starved muscles, bringing her back to life.

Logan was already reaching under her jacket, probing for the bullet wound, discovering the vest.

"Thank Christ," he hissed as his fingers found a

shallow crater in the Kevlar and, inside it, the bullet flattened like a coin. It had pierced only the armor's outer layers. "You're okay, Donna. You're going to be okay."

She struggled for the breath to voice a question. "Barnes?"

"You hit him. I don't know how bad, but it doesn't matter much. He can't go far now, not bleeding from two wounds."

"I don't need to go far, Mark."

The harsh, unsteady voice came from behind them. Slowly Donna turned her head.

Barnes stood there, his right arm curled around a mossy piling for support, his left hand holding the .22.

He'd been present the whole time. Silent. Watching. His glasses must have been lost during the gun battle; his hair was matted to his forehead in a skein of black threads; his suit, wringing wet, clung to him in wrinkled patches. Stooped and bent-kneed, grotesquely bedraggled, he had been transformed into a horribly unfunny parody of his usual rumpled disarray.

Logan started to raise his Beretta.

"*Don't,*" Barnes said sharply.

Logan met his eyes, then slowly lowered his gun hand to his side.

In the distance, sirens. The rescue ambulance and backup units. Useless now.

Barnes aimed the gun at Donna in a hand that did not shake.

There was nothing in his eyes but hate, the blind pointless hate that had eaten away at him, an ulcer, a tumor, for so many years, until no better part of him remained.

Donna thought that all her study of the psychology

of killers had not taught her as much as this one last look into Ed Barnes's soul.

"Good-bye," he whispered. "Bitch."

He pulled the trigger.

And there was pain.

Pain and the clamor of chimes in his ears and somewhere a terrible high-pitched screaming *and there was pain* and he was plunging his head and hands into the water as it clouded over with swirls of blood and the screaming turned to choked sobs and mewling whimpers and *there was pain, there was pain, there was pain. . . .*

A thunderclap, a rush of heat, an orange bloom of flame, and for a breathless instant Donna was sure she was dead.

Then she understood.

Barnes's gun had fired. But the barrel, damaged when she'd shot the .22 out of his hand, bent perhaps or crushed at the muzzle, had not permitted the bullet to escape.

The trapped cartridge had blown the pistol to pieces, spraying Barnes with a hail of shrapnel that had torn apart his hands and savaged his face.

And now he was screaming, screaming as he pawed wildly at the air with the mangled stumps of his fingers. . . .

Abruptly he thrust his head under the water, seeking to numb the pain with cold. The echo of his scream faded in the sudden stillness like the wail of a vanishing ghost.

"Oh, Jesus," Donna whispered. "Sweet Jesus Christ."

Logan said nothing, only stood at her side, motionless, watching.

Slowly Barnes raised his head out of the water.

His face was a twisted ruin, loose flaps of skin exposing patches of raw skull, one eye socket a bloody crater, the other eye milky and staring.

He opened his mouth, a red, lipless cavity like a fresh wound. His lacerated tongue struggled to form speech. Two words rose above the escalating din of sirens.

"Kill me."

He waited, his mutilated hands held palms out in a mute gesture of pleading.

Mark turned to her.

Slowly she nodded.

He returned his gaze to Barnes. Raised his gun.

Donna looked away.

One shot.

The splash of something large and heavy meeting the water.

Ed Barnes sinking facedown into a mist of blood.

Logan watched the body go under, his face stricken.

"We were friends once," he whispered.

Donna clasped his hand. "And you acted as his friend. Released him from his pain—all his pain—and all the pain he caused."

57

Joe Kurtz was asleep when Donna and Logan entered his hospital room in midmorning. Lynn sat at his bedside, holding his hand.

The bullet had torn up his right shoulder, shattered his clavicle, and punctured one lung. But remarkably it had done no irreparable damage. He would recover, though it would be a while before he was lifting weights again.

Lynn rose when they entered. "I'm glad you came," she told Donna, speaking quietly so as not to disturb Joe's rest. "It was wrong of me to say what I said yesterday. I was upset."

"Of course. I understand."

"Joe was scared. That's why he asked me to lie. And I went along with it because, well, I *knew* he wasn't guilty."

"How could you be sure?" Logan asked.

"I just knew. I guess . . . because I love him."

Joe's eyes fluttered open; the heart monitor registered a slight increase in his pulse. "I heard that," he said weakly, with a faltering effort at a smile.

"You shouldn't talk." Lynn clasped his hand again. "Go back to sleep."

His grip on her fingers tightened. "Love you," he whispered. "Never knew it till you lied for me . . . till I saw how much you were willing to risk."

"It was no risk," Lynn breathed.

Kurtz shut his eyes, and for a moment it appeared he had drifted off to sleep again. Then softly he murmured, "Life is complicated, isn't it?"

Lynn stroked his hand. "What do you mean?"

"Sometimes we do things that are supposed to be wrong. Like lying. Or ... other things. Only, they're not wrong. But we feel guilty anyway. Guilty and dirty, for no good reason." His eyes opened; his gaze moved first to Donna, then to Logan. "It's a waste. Most pointless kind of waste."

"No," Logan said, holding his stare. "There's one kind that's worse. Being angry. Angry all the time. Giving your life over to rage."

Kurtz nodded. "Ed Barnes knew about that."

Logan smiled, a slow, sad smile of hidden meanings. "He's not the only one."

At noon, Mueller called Logan into his office. The chief sat behind his desk, rolling an unlit cigarette between thumb and forefinger.

"Looks like an apology is in order," he said gruffly.

Logan thought the strong daylight streaming through the window made Mueller look old. Or perhaps this case had aged him.

"You can't be blamed for suspecting me," he said gently. "Anybody would have, under the circumstances."

"I'm not talking just about that. I mean an apology for underestimating you as a cop—and as a man."

Logan smiled. "I'd say I owe you the same apology."

Mueller let a moment pass in quiet appreciation of that statement. Then: "You're not going to start drinking again, are you?"

"No."

"Because if you do—"

"I won't."

Squinting, Mueller looked into his eyes. Slowly he nodded. "I believe it."

The search of Barnes's house began in early afternoon. Logan supervised. Tim Anderson, pale and shell-shocked, still half disbelieving the news about his mentor, listlessly snapped photos.

Donna looked over each significant item after the Corona Beach detectives were through with it. Ed had answered most of her questions; what he'd left behind told her the rest.

In the bedroom was a scrapbook of news clippings. Donna had seen many similar scrapbooks. Franklin Rood had kept one, and so had other multiple murderers of the organized nonsocial type.

Ed's hobby had been collecting reports on brutal killings of women. The *Guardian*'s story on Wanda's murder was the last article. He must have been proud to add the work of his own hands to his inventory of horrors.

The photo album in his study was more personal, and more revealing. The contents covered three decades and took many forms, from recent Kodachromes to black-and-white Polaroids spotted with chemical-developer stains. No vacation pictures, no portraits of friends and relatives, only crude snapshots taken in a flashcube's harsh glare, showing Marjorie Barnes in a variety of poses and costumes.

In many she was handcuffed; in some, bound; in a few, restrained by more cumbersome methods. She wore lace underwear or swimsuits or miniskirts or, often, nothing at all.

The nude shots were worst. In them, you could see the bruises and scars that clothing would conceal.

Roughly a third of the photos had been shot with a timer mechanism that permitted Barnes to get into the picture with his wife. It was the contrast between his face and hers that made Donna tremble and finally cry.

Ed's was the face she'd seen in the parking lot, the face of a hungry beast, feverish with malign needs. Marjorie's delicate features reflected fear and discomfort and a terrible, viscerally real embarrassment.

As time passed, Ed had taken fewer pictures. The ones he had shot showed Marjorie in increasingly youthful outfits and increasingly unflattering positions. In those last years, the expression on her face was the visual equivalent of a whimper of pain.

She had hated the game, but she had been willing to play. It was Ed who had grown tired of her, who had sought a younger woman better suited to his fantasies.

Donna recalled his playful flirtation with her at Arrowhead last Christmas, only a couple of months before Marjorie's death. His jocular smooching and caressing, and his wife's plaintive protests, had been amusing then. Not now.

Marjorie had ended her life not because her husband treated her as a masturbatory toy, but because he had stopped.

"Marge," Donna whispered, shaking her head slowly, "I wish you'd told me. Told somebody."

Perhaps the attraction he'd felt toward Donna had driven him to select girls who vaguely resembled her when he began to stalk and kill. His frustrated desires would explain his hostility toward her, his brooding bitterness over her affair.

She was lucky he hadn't gone after her first, when she was unprepared for an attack. Caution had stopped him, she supposed. It was too much to believe that he had been held back by any remnant of genuine affection.

And then there were the cartons of dolls in the garage. Raggedy Anns, all of them.

Weary of Marjorie, but not yet ready to stalk other women, Ed had turned to the dolls for relief of his special needs. He'd bought dozens; and in the privacy of the garage, he had indulged his fantasies and rehearsed the crimes to come.

One doll had been soaked in what appeared to be blood. Another's arms and legs had been amputated, the ripped fabric neatly stitched up at the shoulders and hips. Jammed inside the skirts of others were bottle shards, knives, wooden dildos. And there were still more Raggedy Anns, their sewn eyes and mouths sealed with tape, hands bound, necks looped with rope and nylon clothesline, stomachs stuffed with excrement, faces charred with flame.

Barnes had suppressed his most violent urges for more than twenty years, but only by finding these "other outlets," as he'd called them. Outlets that had proved inadequate after Marjorie's suicide.

The search team finished work inside the house and moved outside. Worried that Barnes might have killed other women before Wanda and buried them in the yard, Mueller had borrowed a methane probe from the LAPD. It turned up nothing human, only the decayed remains of Marjorie's cat, planted near a weed-choked flower garden.

Her suicide note had consisted of three words: "Feed the cat." Ed had killed it instead, perhaps out of resentment or spite, or perhaps because the need to kill had grown too strong to resist. The exact reason would never be known, and hardly mattered now.

The cat had been beaten to death, like Wanda, then bundled in a plastic garbage bag. Garbage. That was all the animal had been to him, and all Wanda had been, and Billie, and Donna herself.

She remembered the bleakness she had glimpsed in his eyes. She understood it now. His soul had been a bottomless emptiness; like a black hole in space, it had drawn in the light and energy around it and mashed that radiance into something unrecognizable, incomprehensible, something that had no place in the universe she knew.

The sea ran red with the blood of the dying sun. Scattered sand blew in stinging gusts across the beach.

Logan walked with Donna along the water's edge. The crash and sizzle of the surf, the drone of a jetliner flashing silver in the sky—for a long time these were the only sounds in their world.

Finally he spoke. "You made a good choice, Donna."

Though they had left Joe Kurtz's hospital room many hours earlier, he knew she would understand.

Donna swept a net of windblown hair from her face. "I made two good choices."

The sun descended, thickening as it met the horizon's resistance. Creaming curls of foam rolled toward the shore and broke apart into white shards of spray. The eastern sky dimmed as the west turned more deeply crimson.

"So what happens now?" Logan asked.

Her reply didn't come for a long moment. "I suppose I'll return to my normal duties—and my normal life. Unless . . ."

"Yes?"

"Unless you've got some better idea."

He looked ahead, toward the pier far down the beach, the Ferris wheel shining in the sun's last light. Slowly he smiled. "How about a carousel ride?"

The breeze kicked up another swirl of sand. Donna turned her head away. She kept her face averted even after the air was still. "Are you sure you want to take that ride again?"

"Yes, Donna. I want to."

"Then so do I, Mark. So do I."

He held her, the two of them swaying slowly, slowly, in the gathering dark.

"I'd lost all faith in you," she whispered. "I'm sorry."

"That's all right. I'd nearly lost faith in myself."

"Good thing for second chances."

"For both of us."

They were silent then, thinking of someone who'd had no second chance, whose first ride had been her last.

High overhead, gulls wheeled, keening for the expiring day, their thin, shrill cries like distant screams—a child's screams, or a woman's—screams caught by the wind and carried out to sea, and dying there, unheard.

SUSPICION OF INNOCENCE

by Barbara Parker